30 SECONDS

30 SECONDS

Cover design by: Sarah Scutt
www.sarahleescutt.com

Author photo by: Poppy & Olive Photography
www.poppyandolivephotography.com

For Wendy Zimmerman.

30 SECONDS

A Novel

Noelle LM Powers

PROLOGUE

KALEY

30 seconds doesn't seem like a lot of time. In actuality, you can do a lot in 30 seconds. You can text a friend, toast a pop-tart, change your Facebook profile picture. Your body can make 72 million red blood cells in just 30 Seconds. In my case, I went from being married to the love of my life to becoming a widow. My entire life changed in just half a minute.

My husband Nathan had been a cop. I met him on my twenty-first birthday at a bar. It's not what most people assume. I wasn't doing the whole coming-of-age twenty-first birthday bar tour. I was working at my grandpa's tavern in Northern Wisconsin, Henry's Irish Pub. It was early December. I had a terrible head cold, and I was freezing my ass off. I just wanted to be home cozied up with a good book.

Grandpa Henry had been short-staffed, so I agreed to help cover the afternoon shift, which led to the evening rush; and as luck would have it, the last call. I'd been waiting tables since one in the afternoon and was dead on my feet.

There was a group of obnoxious, frat-type guys that came in around ten and spent the night hitting on me. Their behavior wasn't anything unusual. I was used to that kind of attention. Many years spent around the nighttime bar crowd had toughened me up, maybe even calloused me. Ordinarily, I'd blow off the behavior. Sometimes I'd choose to flirt back because happy customers were simply good for business.

That night, however, I'd had it. Ted, the burly old bartender, was having trouble getting the guys to leave. In an effort to preserve Grandpa's sterling reputation, I stepped in to help. I'd wrongly assumed my softer, sweeter approach would be better than whatever Ted had up his sleeve. Judging from Ted's expression, a fist was the only thing up his sleeve.

I gently squeezed the shoulder of the biggest guy in the group. "Come on, boys, time to call it a night."

Unexpectedly, the big guy took the gesture as an invitation to grab my backside. In response, I seized his hand and bent his finger so far back that it made a cracking sound.

"You little blonde bitch!" he hollered.

"Asshole," I muttered under my breath. Perhaps it was better Ted handle them after all.

I started to walk away, but his cohorts rose from the table to block my path. I tried to squeeze past, but one of them grabbed me by the arm and tried to force me back toward the table.

I looked over his shoulder toward the bar. Ted had ducked back into the kitchen, and most of the customers had cleared out.

I pulled back from the big man and felt his buddy press up behind me. I was gearing up for a fight when this good-looking man suddenly appeared out of nowhere.

He barked something at the guys, but I wasn't really paying attention. I was slightly dizzy from either my head cold, fear, or both. Although I had no idea what he said, I could tell you how he looked. At that very moment, Ted had returned and flipped on the overhead lights. The dining area was bathed in a glow of fluorescence. I was definitely feeling the effects of my illness because, to me, it was as though a ray of sunshine had miraculously broken through the bar ceiling from the dark fall sky. Like a cheesy rom-com, a spotlight shone on my dark-haired guardian angel.

The big guy let go of my arm. There was an exchange, which I didn't follow due to the buzzing in my ears and the surge of adrenaline still coursing through my body. The handsome newcomer led the crew to the rear of the establishment, leaving me to sink into a nearby chair, trying to sort through the incident.

Ted was back at the bar, towel-drying mugs. He caught my eye and gave me a curt nod as if to ask, 'You good?' I nodded back and ran my hands down my face, noting I felt both feverish yet cold and clammy. Probably the reason I felt so out of it.

The frat guys came shuffling back dejectedly. Before I had the chance to move, they gathered their stuff and threw a wad of cash on the table while muttering apologies. Not one of them dared look back as they fled the tavern.

"Thank you," I smiled at the stranger. "I had the situation under control, though,"

My guardian angel returned the smile with one of his own, revealing flawless pearly whites. "You totally had that," he agreed. "But... I was afraid you were going to hurt those jerkoffs. I decided to step in before you did something you might regret."

I laughed aloud, which turned into a coughing spasm. I used my arm to conceal my mouth and collapsed back into the chair.

Mr. Blue Eyes strode off and returned a moment later with a glass of water. I gratefully accepted the offering, and after a few sips, I was able to catch my breath. "Thank you, I'm sick," I explained, taking another large gulp of water.

He arched an eyebrow, "Interesting name... I'm Nathan."

Rather than spit my drink back in the cup, I managed to maintain some self-control and swallowed the water instead. "Sorry, apparently, I wasn't clear. I'm Kaley, and I'm not feeling well at the moment."

He smiled again, and I noticed a tiny dimple on his right cheek. Could this guy be more perfect?

"I'd offer to shake your hand and say I'm pleased to meet you, Kaley, but no offense—I really don't want whatever you have."

I waved away the comment. "None taken. I wouldn't want to give this to you, especially after the way you stepped in. What did you say to those guys, anyway?"

Nathan shrugged and pulled a wallet from his back pocket. He folded open the black leather to reveal a silver, shiny badge. "I asked them to accompany me to my office to chat. Sadly, they declined. I guess they had better plans."

"Ahhh—so you're a cop?"

"Guilty," he said, shoving the wallet back into the rear of his jeans pocket and rocking back on his heels.

"Kaley! Let's get moving," Ted bellowed from behind the bar.

Nathan raised an eyebrow, "Boyfriend?"

I laughed again but managed to keep my coughing to a minimum. "Ted! He's like thirty years older than me!"

"Nothing wrong with that," he teased.

I rolled my eyes and pushed myself upright. "Well, Officer Nathan, I guess my boyfriend is waiting."

"Stone," he replied.

"Excuse me?"

"It's Officer Stone; Nathan's my first name."

"Ahhh—right. Officer Stone, then. Can I walk you out?"

"Walk me out?" His forehead creased in confusion.

"Yes—out of the bar. I gotta kick you out. It's time to lock up."

"Oh, you're in charge?"

"Gawd no!"

"Your boyfriend, then?"

I laughed despite myself. He was trying a little too hard; but with the muscles, eyes, and now the badge—I'd let it slide. "It's my grandpa's place. I help out when he's short-staffed. And the bartender is Ted; I've known him my entire life. He's not my boyfriend."

"So, the job's open?"

Again—he was trying too hard. "Goodnight," I said, shooing him toward the exit.

I opened the door; the wind was harsh, the cold cut through my t-shirt and jeans. I shivered involuntarily.

Nathan was just about to leave when he stopped and gently touched my wrist where I held tightly to the door handle. "I like your tat," he commented.

I looked down. He was referring to the three black-inked daisies I had tattooed across my wrist. "Thanks," I responded.

The design was in memory of my mom. Her name was Daisy. She passed away from cancer when I was ten; but I didn't feel like sharing that with this stranger, no matter how attractive.

Nathan eyed me curiously, "You don't strike me as the tattoo type, though."

"Oh yeah," I replied defensively. "How do I strike you?"

He didn't respond right away. I could tell he was putting some thought into his words. It paid off. "You strike me as the type who doesn't give a crap what a guy like me thinks."

I couldn't help but smile. "Nice save."

He winked and proceeded to zip up his black leather jacket. "Well, then, Kaley—goodnight."

"Goodnight, Nathan." I started to nudge the door closed.

"Hey, Kaley—If things don't work out with the old guy—give me a call." He passed his card through the narrowing crack.

"I'll let you know," I said, taking the card before fully easing the door shut for the night.

I didn't call Nathan; I was holed up at home with the flu for the next few days. On day number three of the virus, he appeared at my apartment with homemade soup, a fresh loaf of bakery bread, and ginger ale. Had I known it was him, I never would have answered the door. My short blonde hair was tied into an untidy ponytail, I had dark circles under my eyes, and was wearing a pair of my grandpa's old sweatpants with a Col. Sanders t-shirt.

He, on the other hand, was in uniform and looked just as spectacular as the night at the bar. Nathan took one look at me and chuckled, "I thought it might be me, but clearly, it was you."

"Excuse me?"

"The reason you haven't called. Your grandfather said you weren't feeling well, but I thought maybe you were blowing me off. Now, I see that's not the case."

I put my hands on my hips, "What exactly are you saying here, Officer Stone?"

"I'm saying you are the most beautiful sick person I've ever met. I can't imagine what you must look like well."

"Ha! Nice save!"

"Here," he handed me a white lunch bag. "I took a chance that your grandfather was actually telling the truth and brought you something."

After he handed me the goodies, he left. That was the moment I knew I'd marry Nathan Stone. One year later, I did precisely that.

We spent thirteen fabulous years together. Not every day was perfect; but it was, for the most part, a pretty great life. Nathan was not only my husband but my best friend.

I've always loved art and creating. When I told Nathan I dreamed of opening an art gallery, he not only supported me but surprised me by renting space in one of the old buildings downtown. At first, it was a money pit, but Nathan never complained. He just picked up extra shifts to supplement our income.

Eventually, through trial and error, I learned how to actually add to our income instead of drain it. I started teaching drawing and painting classes for the community, and we rented the space out for small gatherings. Word got around, and I invited other artists to rent space. My grandfather was a huge help too. He was a smart and savvy businessman. Henry knew a few tricks of the trade after having owned and operated a hugely successful business for over thirty years. He did all the marketing and took over the financial end of things. I didn't want to use all my creative time to navigate tax laws and learn the latest business accounting systems. Nathan was just too busy. We were grateful for Henry's assistance. Everything in my home and business life felt perfect. Until it wasn't.

The year our daughter turned four, Nathan made detective; and that was the year my dreams came crashing down around me. Nathan was called out in the middle of the night. He kissed me goodbye and promised to be home for breakfast. It was the one promise he couldn't keep. At four o'clock in the morning, the doorbell rang. I opened the door to find his partner Shane Gavin and the police chief standing on our front stoop. Just like the moment I had known I would marry Nathan, at that moment, I knew I would never see him again.

MATT

30 seconds doesn't seem like a lot of time. Believe it or not, a lot can be accomplished in 30 seconds. You can order a pizza or add a few songs to your Spotify playlist. Hell, you can get in a mini workout, a couple of burpees, push-ups, crunches... you get the idea.

I've made two huge decisions in my life that took only 30 seconds. One of those decisions destroyed the life of a great man. The other decision put me in the position to do that. Before there was death, there was life; and I'm so grateful I was able to save the two most important people in my life.

I had hoped the move from Alabama to Wisconsin would be a fresh start. I'd grown up in a culture of drugs, violence, and abuse. When I met Aionya Green, I knew things had to change. Aionya was twenty-three, about five years younger than me. She was a single mom; and I knew from the start, I wanted to give her and her daughter, Layla, everything I'd never had. People flowed in and out of my life, and I knew better than to become attached. Aiyona was a whole new ballgame. I knew, without a shadow of a doubt, I wanted Aiyona and Layla to stick around for the long haul.

Aionya rarely mentioned Layla's father. However, I knew enough to understand the guy was bad news.

He had no idea his daughter even existed. Since he was, and still is, a resident of the Alabama corrections system, it was easy to minimize contact. Contact with the rest of our family and friends was not so easy and was also likely destructive. My mom and my little brother Bobby were okay, but even they turned on me when they discovered the love of my life and her daughter were black. So, I added another label to my loser bloodline: racist. We needed a fresh start. I asked Aiyona to marry me, and she said yes. I packed up my new crew and did the only thing that made sense. We got the hell outta Dodge, which is how we ended up in Round Rock, Wisconsin.

I was so close to a clean life I could taste it. Aiyona got a job at the Piggly Wiggly, and I found work as a framer with a building crew. Things were going okay until I got laid off. Then Aiyona's hours were cut at the supermarket; before I knew it, we were in a downward spiral. With little to no income, we were scrambling for the basics. So, I did what I knew. I got involved with drugs again, nothing hardcore like before. I was clean and planned to stay that way. No more using, just selling. That was easier said than done. Sometimes old habits die harder than you think. I made connections through my cousin, who was in the Twin Cities area. He had some contacts just over the Minnesota border selling prescription drugs; and bing, bam, boom, I was in business. I justified my actions because I had to take care of my family. The plan was to get in and out fast, just long enough to get ahead. Had I really thought the idea through, I would have realized how stupid it was. As often happens in life—I got more than I bargained for.

Once I had a supplier the rest was easy, economically speaking. My clientele was primarily high school kids from upper-class families. It's surprising how many high school kids have way too much time and way too much money. They were easy targets. That worked just fine for me until talk started up about bigger scores. There was mention of transporting teenage girls to various locations and booking hotels for a hefty chunk of change. I knew I needed out. No way in hell was I getting involved with that shit. Aiyona, I knew, was suspicious of our sudden influx in income. She was smart and knew better than to ask questions to which she didn't want to know the answers.

Eventually, our luck started to turn. Aiyona got an administrative assistant position in a vet clinic just outside Round Rock. The commute was longer, but they were able to offer her full-time hours with benefits. More importantly, they valued her and her work ethic. Soon after, I landed a new job working at the local hardware store. The pay wasn't great, but it was better than nothing, and it was honest. I started cutting ties with my newfound entrepreneurial friends. That, too, was easier said than done. Prescription drugs were one thing, but the game had changed. They were moving some hard-core shit. Even though I didn't know the details, I knew enough to understand I couldn't just walk away.

This led me to the other decision; I'd work for the right side of the law for a change. I'd narc out my connections and hope I didn't get burned in the process. Not the best idea, I know. However, I was working with what I had. Armed with information, I placed a call to the Round Rock police department. That's how I met Detective Stone.

Stone was probably the only stand-up cop I've ever known. We met at a small coffee shop a couple of blocks from the station. For some reason, maybe desperation, maybe the fact that I had virtually no friends, or perhaps it was stress, but whatever it was—I spilled my guts. Not only did I tell Detective Stone about the drugs and girls, I told him my whole sordid story. I shared my fear of making ends meet and providing for my family. I told him about my past and why we got out of Alabama.

He could have easily arrested me with the information I provided about my activities in Round Rock, but he didn't. Instead, he excused himself and asked me to wait. A few minutes later he returned with a wad of cash. Stone made it clear he wasn't payin' for information. I got to keep the money no matter what. Detective Stone empathized with my situation and said he understood what it's like to fall on rough times. The money, he explained, was his contribution to helping me stay on the straight and narrow. Stone promised to help me if I promised to stay on my current path. It was a no-brainer. I gave him names and numbers, everything I had on anyone.

It took some time, but Stone managed to put away most of my associates. I knew none of them were upper management, but at least I'd given him a starting point. To his credit, he managed to keep me out of all of it.

That wasn't the end of our partnership, though. Stone would check on me from time to time. He'd ask if I was staying clean and if I needed anything. I got the impression the guy really cared. More than two years have passed since I met Detective Stone. Not a day goes by that I don't think of that man. He's the reason I managed to keep my family together, and I feared that I might be the reason his was torn apart.

Chapter 1
NATHAN

The buzzing of his cell phone woke him from a deep sleep. Detective Nathan Stone rubbed his eyes and squinted at the bright glow emanating from the screen. He sighed and reluctantly pressed the green button instead of red.

"This is Stone," he answered, his voice gravelly with sleep.

"Hey man, sorry to call so late... I uh," the familiar male voice stammered.

"It's fine. What can I do for you?" He did his best to keep his voice low so as not to wake his wife, sleeping soundly beside him.

"Something is going down tonight. The north trail by the bluff."

"What kind of something?"

There was a brief pause and then: "Never mind... I shouldn't drag you into this."

"Into what?"

"I don't know exactly..." The caller sounded shaky, unsure of himself, which was not what Nathan had come to expect from this individual.

"Well, you called, so there must be a reason." The detective stretched and dropped his feet to the chilly laminate floor. "Now, tell me more. What part of the trail?"

"Look, Stone... I think it was a mistake to call you. Go back to sleep. We'll talk in the morning."

"Screw that! I'm already out of bed," he muttered heatedly into the phone. Nathan's proclamation was met with silence. The asshole had hung up. He'd woken him for what exactly?

Nathan tossed the phone, bouncing it across the bed. The action caused his wife to stir, "What's going on?" she asked, her voice heavy with sleep.

"Sorry, I didn't mean to disturb you," he whispered.

"It's fine," she yawned and pushed herself up against the excessive number of pillows that lined the headboard. Pale moonlight shone through the sheer curtains above their bed, her skin seemed to glow in the luminescence of light, her blonde hair tousled and damp from the shower she'd taken before bedtime.

He leaned across the bed and brushed his lips against hers. "I have to go to work. I'll be back for breakfast."

"Promise?"

"I promise."

Nathan stealthily made his way across the room and to his side of the walk-in closet. He threw on the first thing he came across, jeans and a hoodie, then grabbed a pair of tactical boots. He hoped this midnight venture was not for nothing. Nathan glanced back at his wife, who seemed to have easily retreated into a sound sleep. Venturing out of the warmth of their bedroom and into the cold fall night was the last thing he wanted to do.

With that thought in mind, he crept down the hallway past his young daughter's bedroom. He debated whether or not to open the door to peek in on her but decided against it. If he accidentally woke the toddler, his wife would be stuck trying to pacify the child for a good portion of the night.

Using only the light from the streetlamp outside, Nathan made his way to the home office off the kitchen, where he collected his heavy-duty coat, gloves, and the keys to his truck. Then, he swiftly clicked the code into the steel safe occupying the back corner of the room. He slid his Sig into the well-worn conceal holster at the small of his back. The weight of the weapon gave him comfort, and with that, he was ready to roll. As quietly as possible the detective moved through the kitchen to the back door, where he slipped out into the cold dark night.

Chapter 2
KALEY

October twenty-fifth. It was the two-year anniversary of Nathan's death. It's why dragging myself from bed went from difficult to impossible. I called Summer in sick from school. I'd planned to spend a quality day with my daughter. Instead, she sat at the end of my bed watching cartoons while I tried to muster the energy to move. My phone chirped from across the room, where I'd deposited it the night before after a few too many servings of rum and coke. The sound eventually stopped but started up again a few minutes later. I snuck a peek at the ugly rustic bookshelf I'd plucked off the curb a few years earlier. It was intended to be a funky DIY project, but that was... before... Anyway, the bookshelf was just another visible representation of everything I'd no longer accomplish.

The damn phone started up again! I couldn't help but groan as I realized whoever wanted to reach me wasn't going to stop. However, answering was going to require effort. My daughter, Summer, sensed my reluctance to meet the day, so she hopped off the bed, and grabbed it for me.

"Hello," her voice sweet, innocent, and so far untouched from the cruelties of the world. The greeting was followed by a giggle. "No, this is Summer, not Kaley... No—mommy's sleeping... hang on."

I felt the bed sink slightly under her weight as she climbed back into bed, her sharp little knees jabbed into my shoulder. "Mommy, are you awake?" she whispered into my ear.

"No," I replied, throwing the pillow over my head.

"She says she's not awake," Summer relayed to whoever was on the other end of the call.

She was quiet for a moment then I felt the tug of the pillow and the warmth of her breath in my ear again. "Mommy, Uncle Shane says to get your butt out of bed."

"Uggggg!" I tossed the pillow and held my hand out to Summer for the phone. She cheerfully dropped the device into my palm and turned her attention back to the small flat screen on the edge of the dresser.

"What do you want, Shane?" I asked groggily.

Shane had been Nathan's partner. They worked well together and did the occasional social activity, but other than that weren't particularly close. It wasn't until after Nathan's death that Shane became like an extended member of the family. At first, I'd protested his kind gestures, his watchful eye, and his annoying constant presence. As time passed, however, I realized Nathan would probably have done the same for Shane's family had the situation been reversed. I also believed Nathan would be grateful his family was cared for and protected, so I allowed it to continue. At some point, it became natural to have Shane around, constantly nagging, like an annoying older sibling.

"Kay—I feel like you're not even listening!" Shane reprimanded.

I sat up and rubbed my eyes, "Because I'm not."

"Get up. I'm coming over. I'm taking you and Summer to lunch."

"No. It's okay—we're going to have a special mother-daughter day."

"Hell with that! You're still in bed, and it's after ten. Summer is probably eating junk food and watching TV."

"Not even close," I snapped. Summer was eating a granola bar, so he was totally off base with the accusation.

"Right. I'll see you in forty-five minutes."

"Shane—I really don't want to go out today," I whined.

"Forty-five minutes," he repeated, and then he was gone.

I sighed and threw my fluffy comforter aside. "Hey cutie, can you go get dressed?" I asked Summer. "Uncle Shane is taking us out to eat."

"Yaay!" Summer cheered as she catapulted off the bed, discarding her granola bar wrapper on the floor. Her little feet slapped against the hardwood as she sprinted across the hall to her bedroom.

"Yay," I mumbled. If only I could muster a sliver of her enthusiasm.

I decided to forgo a shower or makeup. I ran my fingers through my chin-length bob, which was starting to look pretty shaggy. I desperately needed to make a hair appointment. My dark roots were more than noticeable against my golden blonde tresses. I managed to find clean jeans and paired them with a baggy sweatshirt. The ensemble was completed with Nathan's old Brewer's cap pulled tightly over my head. I padded across the hall to the bathroom, thinking I should at least brush my teeth.

Summer took a little more time to get ready; but when all was said and done, the Stone girls were ready to roll in under fifteen minutes. I chose to take Summer down the street to the park to kill time while we waited for Shane.

∞∞∞∞∞∞

We sat across from Shane at Tabby's, a retro family-owned diner. It was a popular hot spot in our little city, and it was usually difficult to find seating. Shane didn't have any trouble getting us a table, though. He was well-know and liked by the community at large.

We slid into a red vinyl booth, and Summer announced she was having mini corn dogs and a chocolate shake. Ordinarily, I'd encourage the kid to eat a little healthier; but it was an anything goes kinda day. Shane smacked his menu down on the Formica tabletop and declared he was having the exact same thing, which made Summer giggle.

"How about you, Kay? Going for the corn dogs and milkshake?" he teased.

"I am not," I declared. "I will live dangerously with the cobb salad, but you two enjoy."

"Boring!" Shane hissed, and Summer happily joined in.

I slammed my menu down on top of the other two, punctuating my irritation. When Shane realized I was not amused by the taunting, he quickly changed the subject.

"So, what do you think?" he asked, rubbing his hand across his scruffy chin. "I'm thinking about growing a beard for winter."

I noticed his sandy blonde hair was starting to show a few grays and believed the same would be true for his facial hair as well, but I kept that to myself. Shane was a good-looking guy, and he knew it. He also fished for compliments a lot—so I always did my best not to bite. There was no need to feed his already inflated ego. Therefore, instead of telling him it looked good—because it really did—I went the safe route. "What does Josie think of it?" Josie and Shane had been married for nearly five years. She was pretty, wealthy, and boring as hell.

"She loves it. Can't keep her hands off me," he replied, puffing out his chest a bit.

I rolled my eyes and was relieved to see the waitress as she approached our table. I was trying hard to be upbeat for Summer's sake, but it was exhausting. All I wanted was to crawl back under the covers and wallow in misery.

The waitress scribbled our order on a notepad, and Shane winked at her. The pretty young woman blushed before she scurried back to the kitchen to fulfill our request. I wondered, and not for the first time, if he'd ever cheated on Josie. We were close but not close enough for him to share those kinds of details with me. I was probably the only woman in Shane's life he didn't flirt with. I believed it was out of respect for Nathan and appreciated that.

"What should we do after this?" Shane asked.

"Go buy a puppy?" Summer offered.

I sighed. My daughter had been pushing for a dog for over a year. I loved animals and would get her a dog someday. However, between my little girl, the art studio, and my grandfather with his bar—I just couldn't imagine trying to care for one more thing.

"Summer, we talked about this," I said gently. "We're not getting a dog right now. If we choose to do that SOMEDAY..." I strongly emphasized the someday. "We will adopt from a rescue or a shelter."

"I think a rescue dog is a great idea!" Shane piped up enthusiastically.

I narrowed my eyes at him, but either Shane didn't notice or he didn't care. Either way, I was irritated.

"What kind are you thinking? A Collie, Cairn Terrier, St Bernard?"

"All of them!" Summer yelled, enjoying the support from another adult.

"Well, if Uncle Shane is so excited about a dog, maybe you two can go to the shelter after lunch and pick one out for **his** house."

"Yaay!" Summer cheered.

Not willing to be beaten at his own game, Shane offered me a smug smile. "Maybe we will."

"Fine by me," I shrugged.

Needless to say, we had a new family member by the end of the day. Sargent Snuggles Stone, a name I had absolutely nothing to do with, was a shaggy, middle-aged mutt that weighed in at around fifty pounds. He had a long, thick black coat, the sweetest brown eyes, and the toothiest grin I'd ever seen on a dog. I had no idea what mated with what to create the creature, but Summer was in love. Shane promised a joint custody agreement, that I prayed Josie would adhere to, so what was done was done.

I tucked Summer into bed while Shane pieced together the dog crate and carried in an enormous bag of dog food. After reading Summer a few chapters of the *Magic Tree House*, I was ready for bed too. I padded across the house to the living room. That's where I found Shane slouched on my tan imitation leather couch with his feet propped on the matching ottoman. Sargent Snuggles was curled up beside him as he surveyed his handy work.

"Not bad, right?" he asked, gesturing toward the large wire dog crate in the middle of the floor.

"Where are we going to put that thing?" I asked. "It's huge! And if you haven't noticed—our little ranch home is already tight."

"Looks fine right where it is."

"In the middle of my living room?"

"Sure, why not?"

Before I could protest further, my phone vibrated in the palm of my hand. I'd forgotten I'd been carrying the device and the action caused me to fumble but not quite drop the stupid thing.

Shane chuckled at my acrobatics. I ignored him and watched as my Grandpa Henry's name flashed across the screen. I groaned and flashed the display in Shane's direction.

He smiled sympathetically.

"Hi Grandpa," I answered as pleasantly as possible.

"Hi, honey," came the gruff reply. "Any chance you could help me out tonight? One of my waitresses called in sick. Macy has a family emergency. That leaves just Ted and me; but he's too busy tending the bar. We're hopping tonight too."

"Kind of last minute... and I just put Summer to bed..."

Shane mouthed that he would stay, which I appreciated; but that left me no excuse.

"I know—" Grandpa continued. "I'm sorry. I wouldn't ask if I wasn't desperate. Kaley—I haven't forgotten what day it is... I'm so sorry."

I ignored the last part, afraid of opening the emotional floodgates, and instead just said, "Okay, I'll be there soon."

"Thanks, honey. I owe you one."

I clicked off without saying goodbye and turned to Shane. "Are you sure?"

"Yeah—go. I got this. It will be good for you to get out."

"I was out all day!" I exclaimed.

"No—you were in bed for half the day," he corrected. "And Kay—don't take this the wrong way—but you should probably clean yourself up. That is, if you have any hopes of making tips tonight."

"I don't care about tips," I replied nonchalantly. "I do, however, think hygiene is important, so I'll at least take a shower."

"Atta' girl," Shane encouraged.

I flipped him the bird and headed down the hallway to get ready.

Chapter 3
MATT

My co-worker, Dwayne, poked his head around the corner of the aisle, where I was busy stocking space heaters. Dwayne is one of those guys who defies age. I mean, like seriously, I had no idea how old the guy was. If I had to guess, I'd say somewhere between thirty-five and fifty.

He cleared his throat and pushed his thick, silver-rimmed glasses up as he stepped over the discarded packaging in his path. "Your girlfriend is on line one for you, Matt. She's hoping you can pick Layla up from school."

I looked around at the mess I'd created. It wasn't intentional; but once my boss, Ollie, gave me permission to use the whole aisle for heaters along with complete creative control for displaying said heaters, things got out of hand fast.

"I can help you, Matt, don't let this factor into your decision," he said, gesturing to the boxes, plastic, foam, and products littering the floor.

I nodded at Dwayne in appreciation, "Thanks, man, if you don't mind clearing a path, I'll finish the rest when I get back."

"Absolutely, it will be fun!" Dwayne remarked as he ran a hand through his wispy blonde hair.

If those same words were uttered by anyone else, I'd have assumed it was sarcasm. Not with him, though; the guy genuinely enjoyed helping people. He tucked his red Hardings Hardware polo into his khaki pants and got to work while I jogged to the service desk to take Aiyona's call.

I didn't have a cell phone because we could only afford one. Lucky for me, Ollie was fine with me receiving personal calls at work. He was a big supporter of family first. While working in a hardware store was not the most exciting job, it paid decent; and Ollie's flexibility allowed me to be available to Aiyona and Layla.

"Hey baby," Aionya's silky voice filled me with warmth. "Any way you can pick up Layla? I'm running late."

"Sure. Will you be home soon, or should I bring her to work with me?" Another thing my boss was cool with was allowing kids at work, that is if they weren't disruptive or anything. Which Layla never was. All she needed was a pack of crayons and blank paper, and the kid could draw for hours.

"I should be home before you get there. I just can't make it to school before three. The last thing I want is for Layla to worry."

"Got it. I'll see you at home."

Home was a tiny nine-hundred-square-foot rental house. We all slept in one room, which was fine when we first moved to Round Rock; but with Layla turning six it was gettin' real tight.

I grabbed my jacket from the staff lounge area on my way out. With such a short trip I would normally forgo the outerwear, it wasn't like it was snowing yet. However, I always wore a jacket or long sleeves to Layla's school. I felt it best to cover my tattoos. While I personally appreciated the artistry of my sleeves, I realized it gave people a certain impression. Layla was already a minority in a conservative white community. I wasn't going to do anything to add unwarranted attention.

"I'll be right back!" I called out to Dwayne as I made my way out through the automated glass doors.

"Take your time, Matt!"

I turned back to see Dwayne smiling and waving as the doors slid shut behind me. I found myself shaking my head as I ambled across the lot to my old Chevy Impala. Dwayne was definitely a departure from the people I was used to, and that was a good thing.

∞∞∞∞∞∞∞∞

There was a line of cars half a block away from the school. Although it wasn't unexpected, I still found it annoying. Apparently, kids didn't walk or ride the bus anymore. We were too close to the school for busing to be an option but too far for Layla to walk without getting lost. That could not be the case for the hundred other parents waiting to pick up their pampered prodigies.

I found a spot a quarter mile from the brown brick building and took off at a sprint so I'd be within spotting distance when Layla was released. I knew I was attracting attention from the other parents as I ran past the hordes of minivans and SUVs in the queue. It was painfully obvious that even with the effort of covering my arms I didn't fit in. With my bald head, muscled-up physique, and the scars of a past best forgotten I was not a typical Round Rock parent. The suburban parents eyed me warily as though I might be driving a child enticement van and handing out candy to lure their kids with devious intent.

I made it to the sidewalk just as the bell sounded. The doors to the building opened releasing a hyper mob of tiny people. Layla was easy to spot. My little girl had chosen a lime green frilly dress that she'd paired with hot pink leggings and cowboy boots. I could only imagine the discussion I'd missed before school that morning. Aiyona was constantly trying to get her daughter to tone it down. I, on the other hand, fully supported her preference to stand out. As soon as she spotted me, she took off at a run, leaving the other girls in the dust.

"Matt!" She shrieked.

I've always been amazed at Layla's endless amount of energy and overly enthusiastic zest for life. The kid's reaction was over-the-top, like she hadn't seen me in ages. In actuality, it'd only been since breakfast.

I scooped her up in my arms, "Hey baby girl. Where's your coat?"

"In my backpack!" Layla had a tendency to shout rather than speak at a socially acceptable volume.

"How was school?" I asked.

"Boring. My new friend wasn't there."

"Bummer. Was she sick or something?"

Layla just shrugged her tiny shoulders.

"Well, I hope she's back soon."

"Me too!" Again, with the shouting, "Then maybe we can invite her over to play after school?"

"You got it," I replied as we made our way hand in hand down the sidewalk and back toward my Impala.

∞∞∞∞∞∞∞∞

When we arrived home, Aiyona was waiting for us in the kitchen. My girl made her blue work polo look like a fashion trend. She was taller than me; if she wasn't six feet, she was darn close, and could easily put a runway model to shame. I told her that too. Aiyona didn't respond well to compliments. She'd wave them away and accuse me of trying to butter her up for something.

"Mama!" Layla exclaimed, rushing forward with the same exuberance she'd shown me at the end of the school day. "I have a new friend, and Matt says she can come play."

"Wow!" Aiyona said, her eyes widening, as she attempted to mirror her daughter's excitement.

Layla nodded, her curls bouncing up and down. "Isn't that great?"

"So, when's the big day?" Aiyona asked Layla, but her eyes were on me. No doubt she assumed I'd already made arrangements.

"That, baby, is up to you," I replied smoothly.

Aiyona was extremely cautious about who her daughter associated with. Which was completely understandable. When I met her, she was a single mom with a toddler living in a rough neighborhood. They had little to no support system and even fewer resources. It's not like I was any better off, but I didn't have nearly as many obstacles to overcome.

I knew who Layla's biological father was, and I knew he'd landed his ass in the Alabama state penitentiary system. Tyrone Braxton was a shitbag. I had no idea how Aiyona even got involved with him. She didn't talk about it, and I didn't ask. With at least fifteen more years on his sentence, for being part of some murder conspiracy against his cousin's parole officer, he was a non-issue. At least for me. However, even though he was behind bars, Aiyona was terrified of the man. Thankfully, he seemed to have kids all over the place and had little to no interest in Layla.

Freakin' Tyrone was the whole reason we ended up in Round Rock, Wisconsin. I knew we needed out of Alabama but Wisconsin... that wasn't my idea.

Aiyona's head had been so messed up with anxiety I'd have done anything to alleviate her stress. She asked me if I'd move. I said of course. She asked me if I'd move to Wisconsin. I said okay. I'd never been to Wisconsin. I assumed it had something significant to offer if Aiyona had chosen it over anywhere else in the country. Turns out it had cows. I pointed out that Alabama had plenty of cows too. Aiyona's counterargument revolved around the fact that Wisconsin was called the Dairy State, whereas Alabama was the Yellowhammer State. There was no way I could argue with that. So, we packed up my Impala with everything we owned and drove over sixteen hours because Aiyona loved cows. Her anxiety markedly improved with the move, so who was I to question?

"Matt, did you hear me?" Aiyona asked.

I hadn't heard her. I'd totally zoned out.

"I asked why you didn't set something up?" She was rummaging through Layla's backpack while the child was doing acrobatics to climb onto the kitchen countertop. The object of Layla's focus was a large glass canister filled to the brim with Aiyona's homemade chocolate chip cookies. I looked the other way, not willing to acknowledge the act that most certainly would not meet with Aiyona's approval.

"Layla! You know better!" Aiyona snapped.

I stepped forward as though I'd just noticed the whole situation and gently lifted Layla to the ground but not before she had her hands full of treats.

"To answer your question—" I redirected, taking the heat off Layla's bad choice. "Her friend was sick today, so we didn't schedule anything. And—I wouldn't do that without talkin' to you first."

Aiyona smiled appreciatively.

"I hope she's back tomorrow!" Layla exclaimed through a mouthful of cookies.

"It's the weekend, Lay, but I'll bet she's back Monday," I said, ruffling her hair. "Well, I need to go back to work."

"See you in a couple hours?" Aiyona asked.

"Yep, it won't be a late one tonight." I gave her a quick peck on the cheek.

"Perfect," Aiyona called after me. "You remember what tonight is, right?"

I lowered my head before turning the knob.

"Matt?"

"Yes, I know what night it is," I replied, before stomping down the driveway and silently wishing my boss would ask me to stay late.

Chapter 4
KALEY

I pulled open the heavy wooden door that served as the main entrance to Henry's Irish Pub. As I stepped onto the rough, overly abused hardwood, I was nearly knocked over by one of the waitresses. Macy was a tall, middle-aged, brunette with big hair and an even bigger attitude. She'd worked for my grandfather for nearly five years and was considered his number two, right behind Ted the ancient bartender.

"This night is crazy!" She had to shout to be heard over the throng of music combined with chatter from the rowdy bar crowd. "I know Henry called, but I can stay if you want."

"No—it's okay. Go do what you need to do!" I hollered back.

She chewed her lower lip, "That's the thing... I don't have anything I need to do... Henry's still paying me for my shift—plus extra for tips. I shouldn't say anything—"

"Macy... what's Henry up to?"

Her eyes darted around; she ushered me down the hallway to the back of the bar, where it was less chaotic.

"He's worried about you," she said. You know... because of the date. He asked me to take off so he could call you in. Henry wants to keep an eye on you. Don't be mad."

I sighed, "I'm not mad. I'm just irritated."

"Please don't tell him I told you. He means well," Macy offered.

"That he does. And don't worry—I won't mention our conversation."

"Thanks. Do you want me to stay?"

"No, it's fine. I already showered and dug my black Henry's Irish Pub shirt from the back of the closet. I wouldn't want all that effort to go to waste."

She smiled sympathetically, "You're a really good granddaughter."

I nodded in agreement, "Now, get out of here. Enjoy your night."

"I will, but first I want to say, I'm really sorry. I know what this date means and how much you miss Nathan. He was a good one, Kaley."

I looked away, willing myself not to tear up. I had just applied mascara for crying out loud. Then, Macy pulled me into a surprisingly strong embrace. Not being a hugger myself, I wasn't sure what to do with this sudden onslaught of affection. I patted her back awkwardly and waited for the moment to pass.

"Now I'm going to cry," she announced apologetically.

Not sure what to do, I pulled free and shrugged, "Yeah— well, death..." I knew it came across as caviler sounding, but inside I was anything but. Inside, I was a sticky mess of emotions, and all I wanted to do was shed my skin to be free of all feelings.

Macy stepped away and nodded understandingly, blinking back tears. She was kind of overdoing the whole sympathetic thing. Thankfully, a crashing sound came from the kitchen. Macy rushed off to help, which put an end to the uncomfortable exchange.

The bar was absolutely packed. Apparently, the high school football team had won a championship or something. What I knew about sports, especially local sports, you could count on one hand. Nathan, on the other hand, had loved sports. He'd watch, play, even listen to anything sports-related. Without him around I was completely clueless unless it was in my face—like the bar crowd.

"Hey, waitress!" One of the middle-aged guys toward the back of the bar whistled. "Another round back here." I gave him a thumbs up and was off and running.

The whole night became an exercise in patience and maneuverability. I bobbed and weaved my way through the crowd to deliver order after order, carefully balancing my tray like a seasoned pro.

I was feeling particularly proud of my performance as I made my way back toward the kitchen and straight into a man headed in the opposite direction. The collision caused me to lose my perfect balance and end up on my backside in the middle of the floor.

"Oh crap!" the man exclaimed. Then, immediately extended his hand to assist me. Nobody else seemed to notice. Not even the table where I lay sprawled at their feet.

"I am so sorry," he said, as we came face to face or, rather, face to chest. The guy was tall, I'd guess just over six-feet.

"It's fine," I said, dusting myself off. "It's just crazy in here tonight. I guess the high school football team won a championship game."

The guy offered me an amused smile and took a swig of his beer. "I think it was a playoff game."

"Well, whatever. Who knew this many people actually cared about high school football?"

He looked around, taking in the crowd. "Who knew?" he said, repeating my observation.

"Well, thanks for the assist. I'll get your drinks back to you in a few." I nodded toward the table in the back, where his friends were all looking in our direction. I noticed they were sporting ball caps with the Tigers logo. Hopefully, I hadn't insulted the man with my opinions on Round Rock's football enthusiasts. They appeared to have come straight from the game.

"No rush," he said and ducked away through the crowd.

I reached the bar, and Ted handed me a tray of drinks, "For the coach's table!" He raised his voice to be heard over the commotion.

"What table is that?" I yelled back. "We have table numbers for a reason, Ted!"

He ignored my snarky comment and scratched at his white burley beard. "The big one in back. The one with all the guys in ball caps and tiger orange, otherwise known as table ten."

It was the table where the tall, clumsy stranger had been sitting. Apparently, he was friends with the coach himself. I groaned, "Great, I think I just insulted someone from that table."

Ted just shrugged and went back to his duties.

I made my way toward the table and hastily set down the drinks.

The man I had collided with was coming out of the restroom. I purposely placed myself in his path to apologize.

He looked startled, "Second time tonight; at least you stayed on your feet this time." He smiled, a nice smile, I thought. It reached all the way to his eyes. He had to be somewhere in his late forties or early fifties. He looked about ten years older than Nathan and I..., or than Nathan would have been, I thought sadly.

"Did you need something?" he asked, leaning down slightly to be heard above the noise.

"Oh—no, sorry," I said, shaking my head, suddenly feeling embarrassed. "I was just going to apologize. I didn't really mean what I said about high school football."

He shrugged, "What? That nobody cares?"

I laughed, "That's not quite what I said… Anyway, I didn't know you were sitting at the coaches' table so my apologies."

"No apology necessary. I'm John, John Kyler," he said, offering his hand.

"Kaley Stone." I noticed he had a nice firm grip. The handshake of a man with confidence.

"I like that."

"Ummm, thanks," I replied. "I can't take credit, though, my mom named me."

"No—your tattoo," he remarked, nodding toward the daises on my wrist. "You don't strike me as a tattoo kind of woman, though."

I felt a bit weak in the knees. It was almost the exact thing Nathan had said the night we met. My gaze was involuntarily drawn to the front entrance—the place we'd stood when Nathan had made the remark about the daisies etched on my wrist in memory of my mom, Daisy. At the time, the comment had seemed odd maybe even unique, until now…

"Hey, are you okay?" he asked, gently gripping my shoulder.

His hand felt strong and familiar; again, it reminded me of Nathan. I took an unsteady step back, feeling strangely comforted yet completely overwhelmed. I looked up. His eyes met mine; they were hazel, not at all like Nathan's, but with the same kindness and strength behind them.

"Hey, Kaley—are you alright?" he asked again.

"I'm sorry," I said, apologizing for the second time that night.

"It's okay. I hope I didn't offend you? I don't actually know why I said that," he said, running a hand through his brown, wavy, unkempt hair.

I waved the comment away. "Not at all. I'm just tired. I apologize."

"Hey, Coach Kyler! Are you coming or not?" one of the guys from John's table called out.

"Be there in a sec!" he called back.

"You've got to be kidding me!" I exclaimed.

John winked and gave a slight bow. "Kaley—it's been a pleasure," he said, as he backed away with a boyish smirk.

I laughed uncomfortably and turned, what I could only assume, was several different shades of red. After that, I quickly spun on my heel and tromped off toward the back of the pub, where my grandfather's office was located.

I sank into Grandpa Henry's old, oversized desk chair and spun around a couple of times as I contemplated the odd exchange. When I started to get dizzy, I stopped and looked around the room. It hadn't changed much over the years. The bar and restaurant area had been remodeled and now had a trendy pine north woods vibe. Back here, though, the space was untouched. The walls consisted of wood paneling from the seventies with rusty file cabinets taking up a good chunk of the back corner. The décor consisted of old movie posters: *Casablanca*, *Road House*, *Cocktail*, and *Trees Lounge*. How could it be that I'd never noticed the posters were all themed around bar movies?

"Hey darlin'," Grandpa Henry limped into the room supported by his cane. He stopped short of the desk.

Nathan would use the word 'dapper' to describe the old man; it fit. His short-cropped, white hair was neatly parted to the side with not a strand out of place. Tonight, he was dressed in a white wool sweater and Dockers. Henry never wore jeans, at least on any occasion I could recall.

"Hi, Grandpa," I greeted him warmly. "I just needed a moment. I'll be back out there in a few."

Henry stepped back a few feet and seated himself on the arm of the tattered sofa in the middle of the office. He leaned forward, grasping the tip of his cane with both hands, "Anything I can do?"

"Nope. I'm good."

He nodded, appearing relieved. I'd inherited my grandfather's gift for suppressing emotions. "I saw you talking to Coach Kyler."

"Yep," I confirmed, hoping to steer clear of yet another awkward topic.

"I suppose you were congratulating him on his big win?"

I arched an eyebrow, "Really?"

"Well, ya never know. Weirder things have happened."

"Hate to disappoint you, but I didn't suddenly develop a newfound love for sports."

"He's single ya know," Henry blurted out.

"Excuse me?" I said, completely taken aback by my grandfather's proclamation.

"John Kyler, he's single."

"So?"

"So—he's a nice man. His wife was a piece of work, though. She left him for the postal guy a few years ago. He's been hit on by pretty much every single gal in this city—married ones too. I don't think he's dated since Tia left him high and dry..." Henry stroked his chin contemplatively.

"Well, sucks for him. Not sure how any of that is my concern."

"I'm just trying to tell you about John. And maybe a little bit about yourself as well."

"Me?"

"Maybe you should consider taking that ring off and opening yourself up to someone... to life."

I stood and pushed the chair back under the old oak desk. "I have no interest in dating or taking off my ring. Nathan is still my husband, even if he can't physically be here. Nothing is ever going to change that."

My grandfather stood as well, "Kaley—I didn't mean to upset you. But Nathan would want you to be happy.

He would want you to keep living. Find love or at least companionship."

"I am happy. I have friends and Summer. I'm completely fulfilled."

He looked doubtful. "Sweetheart, your only friend is Shane Gavin; and he is a cocky son of a bitch, not to mention married. Summer needs a good male role model, someone to look up to."

"First off—Shane is great with Summer. Also, his wife and I are good friends too." Maybe I was embellishing a tad bit. "Secondly—Summer has the best male role model a kid could have, her Grandpa Henry. Everyone else would pale in comparison."

He blushed slightly, "Thank you; it's not true, but thank you anyway. I just think maybe you and Shane's relationship might be a little unhealthy that's all. You have a strange co-dependent thing happening. I think you might be holding each other back. His wife can't be too happy with all the time he spends with you, either... despite your tight friendship."

He had thrown that last part in just to goad me. You can't bullshit a bullshitter, to use one of his phrases.

My grandfather took a breath and continued, "Kaley, I do my best ya know. When your mom was sick, she made me promise to take care of you. I've always been able to give you the basics, but I realize I haven't done such a good job at some of the other things. Maybe if I just—"

I cut him off, "Henry—enough." I had discarded the grandpa and gone straight to his first name.

"Okay... okay," he conceded. "I just saw you and John talking and well... it got me to thinking."

"Well, don't. Especially not today."

"Maybe today is the perfect day. Maybe Nathan is trying to send you a message."

I thought about the way John had complimented my tattoo and the way he'd grasped my shoulder. I swallowed hard. What had possessed my grandpa to say such a thing? It wasn't at all something he would normally say, and come to think of it, this whole conversation was very uncharacteristic of the old man. He was overprotective for sure; but never before had he butted into my social life or offered any type of advice about life, much less dating.

"See—you're thinking about that aren't ya?" he asked, with an amused chuckle. "You're thinkin' your old grandad may be onto something."

"No—I'm not," I said, marching across the room to the doorway. "I'm thinking the old man is starting to lose his mind and it may be time to stick him in a home."

He laughed at my insult. "You can pretend all you want, Kaley. But I can tell I touched a nerve. You think I might be right about this and that scares ya just a lil' bit—doesn't it?"

"Hardly," I stated, before rushing out of the office and back into the chaos taking place in the heart of the pub.

The table where John and his friends had been seated was now occupied by a group of young couples. I was surprised to discover I was mildly disappointed by that.

∞∞∞∞∞∞∞

By one in the morning, the crowd had pretty much dispersed. There were still a few diehard regulars hanging on at the bar, but other than that the place was empty. Ted was helping me sweep under tables while my grandpa was wiping down the bar. Both Ted and Henry suggested I call it a night and head home. Ordinarily, I would argue and help until the end, but I was really tired. Shane probably wanted to get home as well, so I tucked the broom and dustpan away in the maintenance closet and grabbed my jacket from the hooks in the kitchen. I made my way back to the main area to say goodnight to the guys. Grandpa was underneath the back table, where John and his friends had been.

"What are you doing?" I asked, leaning down for a closer look.

"Somebody dropped their keys. Now, help me back up, darlin'"

I set my bag on the hardwood table and hoisted my grandfather up under his armpits. Once he was upright again, I reached for his cane, which he'd propped against one of the chairs.

Grandpa dangled the keys in front of my face like a mischievous child. "The coach left his keys."

I crossed my arms and shifted my weight. "How do you know they're his?"

"He has his staff ID attached. He'd probably be in trouble if the school district knew he left the keys to the kingdom on a barroom floor."

"I imagine he would," I replied, not sure where the old man was going with this; but knowing I probably wasn't interested. "Well, goodnight then," I said, handing his cane off to him.

"Kaley—you should take these to him. That would be a nice thing to do."

I laughed, "It's after midnight! I'm not going to just show up at his house. Besides, Shane's babysitting Summer. The nice thing to do would be to go home and relieve the poor guy."

Grandpa shook his head disapprovingly.

"What? This is not my problem. Do what you do with all the other crap you find—throw it in your desk drawer. He'll pick them up tomorrow."

"But his staff ID and keys to the school! We don't open until eleven tomorrow. What if he needs them?"

"So..." I shrugged.

"It's okay," Ted called from behind the bar. "I left him a message with Kaley's address. He'll pick them up from you in the morning."

My jaw dropped, "You what!"

Grandpa smiled smugly. "Well then, it's all settled. You can keep his keys safe, and he'll get them from you tomorrow."

"You two are so transparent," I said, snatching the keys away from the old man.

"Don't you think he'll find it odd I took his keys home?"

They both just shrugged. They were completely clueless.

"Thanks for this!" I said, holding the keys up. "I've already had two awkward interactions with the guy—I was so hoping for a third!"

Walter, one of the longtime regulars, turned on his barstool to add his two cents worth. "You're a cute gal, Kaley. The coach will be flattered you wanted to see him again."

I groaned, "See—that's exactly what he'll think," I said, addressing the two perpetrators. "He'll think this is some kind of ploy."

I tried to hand the keys back to Henry, but he stumbled back as though I were wielding a weapon. "Ted already told him you have the keys, darlin'. You better take them."

"Call him back," I pleaded with Ted. "Tell him Henry has his keys."

"It's after midnight, Kaley! I can't call him again. He's probably sleeping."

I narrowed my eyes at Ted and then turned back to my grandfather. "You two are the worst! You hear me? The worst!"

I tossed the keys into my purse and spun on my heel. I pushed through the front door harder than necessary. The sound of it banging shut echoed down the quiet street behind me. My angry exit left me very little satisfaction. I clicked my key fob, lighting up my black Honda CRV that was parked a few feet away at the curb. I tossed my bag over to the passenger side and slid in behind the steering wheel, slamming the car door hard behind me.

My commute was under ten miles, and during the drive, I hadn't come up with any bright ideas on how to handle the key situation. Maybe Shane would have some advice, I thought, as I pulled into the driveway of my little white ranch. The fall air was biting, reminding me again that I needed to clean out the garage so I could actually park inside.

Shane and Sargent Snuggles were curled up on the couch; an action movie of some sort was blaring in the background. I found the remote on the side table and clicked the TV off.

Neither dog nor human stirred. I quietly removed the lid from the ottoman near the couch and pulled out a crocheted blanket from Nathan's grandmother to cover them. I felt slightly guilty for not trying to wake him, but he and the dog looked so peaceful. Hopefully, Josie would understand. Then, I switched off the lights and started to fret about what awaited me in the light of day.

Chapter 5
MATT

Friday night was grocery shopping night. I really hated grocery night. Aiyona made us go to this huge store that had too many choices and way too many people. It was always packed, even on Friday night, which was crazy to me. The prices were really good, though, so there was that. An entire cart full of food cost the same as two measly plastic bags would cost at our little local joint. The worst part of the trip was always the cheese aisle. It was always shoulder to shoulder with an overwhelming number of options. I didn't even know what some of them were. Wisconsin people tend to be freaky about their cheese. I guess that's where the 'cheese head' thing originated. So, I'd go. I'd hate it, but I loved Aiyona so there ya go.

I maneuvered my beat-up Impala into one of the tight parking spaces and took in my surroundings. Based on the number of cars crammed into the lot, I knew this was not going to be an enjoyable trip. I helped Layla get unbuckled and took her tiny hand in my own. Together, we made our way in the same direction as the masses headed toward the sprawling, brown building straight ahead.

The automatic doors slid open with a whoosh, the fan set in the entryway blew directly in my face. It was meant to dry up all the snow and slush people were tracking through; but judging from the slippery state of the floor, it wasn't working. I pulled the knit cap from the pocket of my tan work coat and tugged it over my bald head. The place smelled of corrugated cardboard and metal. I handed Layla off to Aiyona and pushed my way to the cart corral. The red cart handle felt sticky so I stopped for a sanitizing wipe. I struggled with the plastic container attached to the metal pole but eventually managed to snag half a wipe from its grasp.

It was a struggle to stay in step behind my girls. Aiyona would tear through the market with military precision. She had her handwritten list ordered by aisle, and I admired her organization.

As we made our way through the market, it became increasingly more difficult to suppress my emotions. Shoppers continued to irritate me as their carts unintentionally served as roadblocks. I tried to steer around people as they stopped to converse in front of the soup cans or blocked an entire section as they parked their cart on one side just so they could contemplate the peanut butter options on the other. My favorite had to be the customer that stopped abruptly in front of me and whipped out her cellphone to send a text.

I audibly sighed, hoping the skinny blonde would realize she'd completely disrupted the flow. She didn't, and I nudged her with restrained gentleness. I could see Aiyona and Layla getting further ahead of me as they struggled to hold onto the armloads of canned goods they'd managed to accumulate. They had to be wondering where I'd gotten to.

"Excuse you!" The blonde whipped around with a look of utter disdain on her heavily made-up face.

"Move lady. You're blockin' the whole damn aisle," I uttered through clenched teeth.

She gave me a once-over and shrank back, pulling her cart off to the side. She'd wisely decided I wasn't someone to mess with.

"Come on, Matt!" Layla called out as they rounded the corner to the next aisle.

I involuntarily growled as the sea of carts seemed to part for the angry man in the knit cap. I caught up to the girls as they made their way to the produce section.

Aiyona dumped her armload into the cart and addressed me encouragingly. "I know you hate this, baby, but you're doin' great." She blew me a kiss that melted my grinch-like heart.

"Can you get chicken breasts and sandwich stuff?" she continued. "I'll meet you in the soda section."

I nodded and yanked the cart in the opposite direction, set on completing my task with minimal aggression.

That 'Time of Your Life' song by Green Day was being piped through the store intercom system as I approached the deli section. It was at that point that the realization set in—I was going to lose my shit in that store.

Just ahead, a large man was using one of those little grocery scooters meant for the disabled; but clearly the guy did not qualify. He was fat as hell. His gut was spilling over his sweatpants, and his arms were hanging out of his sleeveless shirt like two underdone flank steaks. I had to wonder what possessed him to wear a sleeveless shirt given the current weather conditions. I wasn't just judging him on his physical appearance, either. He actually heaved himself off the scooter to walk across the aisle and budge in front of an elderly woman, who was reaching for a canned ham. The fire that had been simmering in my belly for the last forty minutes was about to blaze out of control.

"Hey, asshole!" I shouted. Everyone in the nearby vicinity turned to look in my direction. "How about you try waitin' your turn and move your damn scooter. Last time I checked fat isn't a handicap."

There was the sound of a collective gasp as all chatter seemed to come to a halt, making the Green Day tune much more audible. He looked at me in confusion. His ugly mustache floated over his open mouth, which was gaping in astonishment. Nobody moved. I took two huge steps forward and grabbed the scooter by the handles. With greater effort than I care to admit, I heaved the electronic device out of the way so I could push my cart forward.

The momentary stillness that had blanketed the group slowly began to lift.

The elderly woman, who I thought I'd been defending, got in my face. Her bony finger poked me in the chest. "That, young man, is completely uncalled for."

Are you kidding me? I managed to keep my mouth shut and pushed past the fat man and old lady, along with a dozen other onlookers.

I made it halfway down the aisle when I heard someone comment just under their breath, "That's the guy I told you about earlier. He's with the black lady and kid. He's probably trying to cause a distraction so they can steal something."

I turned to see the skinny blonde from before. She was leaning into an athletic-looking guy in jeans and a black high-end ski coat. The guy stepped forward. I wouldn't touch his girlfriend, but he was fair game. Before he could utter a single word, my fist jutted out and connected with his square, chiseled jawline.

Everything after that was kind of a blur. Someone jumped on my back—I think it was his damn girlfriend. Hands grabbed and pulled at me from all directions. I took a blow to the head. I did recall hearing a distinct beeping sound before the fat man plowed into me with his damn motorized scooter. I recall being grateful that Aiyona and Layla were on the other side of the store.

∞∞∞∞∞∞∞

The cops came and issued me a disorderly conduct ticket. I thought Aiyona would be pissed; but fortunately for me, she was not.

"Baby, you know you can't go beatin' on people just because they're ignorant." She gently ran her hand along the abrasion on my cheek.

We were left to wait in the small wood-paneled office that served as store security. After an hour, I wasn't sure why we were still waiting. The police had talked to everyone and issued their citations, yet we had gotten the all-clear.

"Are you listening to me, Matt Pine?" Aiyona asked, her tone sharp.

Layla made her way over from across the office and plopped herself down on my lap. "He's listening, mama, but you're making him feel worse. Isn't she, Matt?" Layla asked, sticking her face uncomfortably close to my own and fixing me with her big brown eyes.

I looked up at my fiancée with what I knew was a perfected impression of a wounded puppy dog. "Very sad," I confirmed.

Aiyona sighed and suppressed a little laugh. Turning my gaze downward, I managed to hold the injured expression—that's when I realized Layla was holding something in her lap.

"What's that, Lay?"

She proudly held up a canned ham with a large dent. "This hit you in the head, Matt!" she exclaimed, "Look how big the dent is! They said I could keep it."

In response, I brought my hand to the back of my head and discovered a large, painful knot. "Well, that explains the headache," I replied dryly.

A young, pasty-looking man in a button-down shirt and navy dress pants entered the room. He'd introduced himself earlier as the store manager. "Well, Mr. Pine, you're free to go." The proclamation was made in a loud, exaggerated voice; as if I'd just won a game show or something.

Unlike a game show contestant, I was less than thrilled by my winnings. Instead of celebrating my newfound freedom, I came to a standing position and narrowed my eyes. I gave the man my full unblinking attention. The look had the desired effect.

The manager bowed his head uncomfortably and hitched up his pants. "However, you are not welcome back in our establishment." He mumbled the last part making a clear effort to avoid eye contact.

Now, though, I could barely contain my excitement. Not welcome back? No more Friday night grocery shopping?

"This does not pertain to the rest of your family," he said, gesturing to Aiyona and Layla, who was still marveling over the can of ham.

Best news ever! Aiyona and Layla could still shop, but I was definitely out for Friday night groceries!

"Oh, we're not ever coming back here!" Aiyona declared. "We'll find another store that appreciates and respects our business, even if we have to drive out of state to do it. Matt, Layla, let's go." She snapped her fingers and hitched her handbag high upon her shoulder.

The manager quickly stepped aside as Aiyona brushed past him with Layla and me in tow.

On the way out, another thought occurred to me, and I held my breath as we exited the superstore for the last time. The anticipation of what was about to come next heightened my anxiety.

Aiyona turned to me with a wicked little smile. "Well, Matt, we just shot our whole night here and still need groceries." She sauntered around to the driver's side and nodded for me to ride shotgun. "You're going to have to figure out what store we're going to next 'cause it's Friday night, and we still don't have food for the week."

Layla and I groaned in unison as Aiyona turned over the engine.

Chapter 6
KALEY

"Psst... Kay, Kaley,... hey, wake up."

I rolled over and rubbed my eyes. Shane peered at me from the half-open doorway to my bedroom. "What are you doing?" I asked groggily.

"There's a guy here... he's looking for his keys?"

"Shit!" I bolted upright and glanced at the clock beside my bed—it was eight-in-the morning. "I'll be there in a second."

"Why do you have his keys?" Shane whispered.

"Long story." I hopped out of bed and threw a long sweatshirt over my t-shirt and shorts. Next, I retrieved my purse from the hook behind the door and dug John's keys from the bottom. Shane had disappeared from the doorway, hopefully he could occupy John for a few minutes. I quickly ran my hands through my hair, hoping I didn't look like too big of a disaster before ducking into the bathroom to run a toothbrush through my mouth.

As I made my way down the hallway to the front entrance, I realized I wasn't at all prepared for what lay ahead. Shane was standing at the front door shirtless, with his jeans slipping at the waist. Clearly, he hadn't taken the time to button or even zip. Of all the things I'd worried about the night before—this, surprisingly, hadn't been on my list of possibilities.

I slipped around Shane and pulled the door open further. John was standing there sporting a black Tiger's football jacket and jeans. His face was clean-shaven, and his wavy brown hair held firmly in place by a ball cap. I was suddenly struck by how attractive John was and then what he must think of me. He'd been forced to show up at my house to get his keys; and upon arrival had been greeted by my weird shirtless friend.

"I'm sorry for just showing up." He made the apology, looking extremely uncomfortable. "As I was telling your husband—"

"Husband?" Shane and I repeated in unison.

John shifted awkwardly, "Sorry, I just assumed..." He cleared his throat and pointed to the wedding ring I still sported on my left hand; and, of course, Shane had his on as well. "Anyway, if I could just get my keys."

"No!" I exclaimed much too loudly. "I mean yes—you can but no, he's not my husband."

"And my wife is at home," Shane offered in way of explanation.

"Okay..." John rocked back on his heels and glanced around nervously.

"You just made this so much worse!" I said, backhanding Shane across the chest.

I turned my attention back to John. Before I thought it through, I took hold of his arm and dragged the poor man into the foyer.

John looked as though he were ready to bolt. "Look, I'm not sure what's going on, but I won't mention this to anyone. I swear. I just need to get into my office. If you could—"

I cut him off, "No. Not until you let me explain. First—nothing is going on here." I waggled my finger between Shane and myself. "This is my... my..." I struggled for the words to explain my relationship with Shane and realized there just weren't any. "This is my

Shane. He is happily married to someone else, not me. He stayed with my daughter last night so I could work, and he slept on the couch. Not with me."

"I slept with the dog," Shane offered.

"Again, that's not helpful," I replied through clenched teeth. "Why don't you see if Summer's up."

Shane shrugged and shuffled off, leaving me to try and reconcile the awkward situation.

"I'm really sorry I bothered you," John offered. "If I could just get my keys..." he drifted off. I followed his gaze to the living room just off the foyer. John was squinting at a collage of canvas family photos that adorned the sidewall of the space.

He quickly looked away from the pictures and turned his attention toward his running shoes instead. "I'm sorry," he apologized again. "Your husband was Detective Stone?"

"You knew Nathan?"

"Not well." His eyes met mine, and for some reason, having his full attention made me feel self-conscious in a way I couldn't quite explain.

"I should have recognized you from the funeral," he continued.

"You were there?"

"Most of the city was there."

I nodded, "Nathan was well respected in this community."

"He was. I'd just moved here after accepting the coaching position and had a situation with some of the kids. It wasn't good..." John furrowed his brow at the memory. "Well, anyway, your husband was very helpful. He was good at his job, and I'm very sorry for what happened."

"Thank you," I responded quietly.

"And if you were his wife... that must mean you're the artist?"

"What?"

"You paint. Your husband was very proud of you. He suggested I stop into your store. I'm sorry to say—I never made it."

The direction of the conversation caused my heart to flutter in my chest. *Nathan had been talking me up to this man? This man he barely knew but by some stroke of fate was now standing in our living room?* "It's not too late," I blurted out. "I'm not open as much as I used to be—single mom and all that, but I'm open three days a week and every other Saturday."

He smiled. The gesture was genuine, deepening the fine lines that branched out from the corner of his hazel eyes. "I will definitely do that."

I nodded, feeling flustered, "Anyway, your keys." I dangled them in front of him. "I also need to tell you… taking your keys was not my idea. The bartender and my grandpa, the owner, were trying to set you up. I am so sorry and so embarrassed."

"Don't apologize, Kaley. It gives me the opportunity to ask you out."

"I'm sorry—what?"

He looked away shyly. "Wow! I misread the situation again. I apologize." John turned so quickly that he ran straight into the edge of the front door. We must have left it half open when I'd hastily pulled him inside.

"Oh my gosh! Are you okay?"

He laughed, nervously rubbing his forehead. "Only thing hurt is my pride."

"John—" I said his name softly. "It's not you. I just don't date."

He offered me a firm nod, "Got it. And I got these," he held up the keys. "So, thank you." When he turned around again, he did so much more carefully.

I was at a loss for words, frozen in place, as I watched John amble out the doorway and then down the sidewalk toward the silver pickup truck parked at the curb.

It was as he reached the truck that some unforeseen force jolted me into action. There was no explanation for what happened next. I pushed through the front door and jogged after him, catching him just as he ducked into the cab. "Wait a minute," I reached for the door preventing him from pulling it closed.

His brow furrowed in confusion, "Do you have something else of mine?"

I shook my head. "No, I don't date." I stupidly repeated what I'd just said in the house.

"So you said."

"Wait. There's more."

"Oh good."

His expression implied that it was anything but good. I'm sure John would have preferred to be anywhere else at that moment and who could blame him?

I refused to let his discomfort deter me; I was on a roll. "John—I don't date, but I think I'd like to go out with you." I couldn't really say which of us was more surprised by my sudden admission.

He recovered quickly, "Well, alright then." He dug in his center console and produced a receipt and a pen which he used to scrawl out his phone number. "No pressure. Call whenever you're ready."

I accepted the scrap of paper and was about to walk away when my mouth started moving without the aide of my brain again. "How about Friday night?" *What was I doing? It was like someone else had taken over my body.*

"Friday? I have this playoff game... For the most part, nobody cares; but there are a few people that are kind of invested, so I should probably be there," he replied, with a twinkle in his eye.

I buried my face in my hands, "Oh my gosh... what am I doing? It's just one embarrassing moment after another with you."

He chuckled, "I, for one, would love to give you the opportunity for more awkward conversation. How about Saturday?"

I gazed back at him, wondering why on earth he wanted anything to do with me. "Okay, Saturday works. I can show you around the gallery. You can fulfill your promise to Nathan." Again, I was startled by my sudden directness.

"I'd like that. Seven work?"

"Perfect."

"Mommy, my tummy's hungry!" I glanced across the yard, Summer was beckoning me from the top of the front stoop.

"Looks like someone needs you," John said, acknowledging my pajama-clad daughter.

"Sure does," I confirmed, backing nervously away as I contemplated the whole odd exchange.

"See ya Saturday." John waved at Summer before he climbed back into the truck and drove away.

I met Summer at the front door and ushered her inside.

Shane was already in the kitchen pouring cereal and had, thankfully, put on a shirt. Summer climbed up on a stool and was waiting patiently at the kitchen island for her breakfast. Shane set the bowl of Cinnamon Life down on the gray granite countertop. I reached around him for the milk to top off the cereal, and then handed it off to my daughter.

"Juice?" Shane asked, holding up a bottle of grape juice for Summer's approval.

"Yes, please." She answered politely.

I digested the scene and thought about the impression we'd given John. Maybe my grandfather was right, a bit pushy, but right. Shane had a wife at home, and here he was playing house with me.

"What was that?" Shane asked, while Summer was busy shoveling food into her mouth.

Had he just read my mind? "What?"

"What do you mean what? The guy at the door."

"Oh, John? Nothing—he needed his keys."

"I got that part, Kay, but why did you have them?"

"He forgot them at the bar last night. My grandfather arranged to have him pick them up. You know—because the bar doesn't open until later... No big deal." I wasn't sure why I'd left out a big chunk of the story, or why I didn't want to share my Saturday plans with Shane. It just didn't feel right. "You should go home. Josie's probably waiting for you."

He eyed me suspiciously, "You're changing the subject."

"No, I'm not." I tried to sound innocent, but my voice was a little higher pitched than normal. Even I heard it.

"Okay... not sure why you're not being straight with me," Shane said, leaning back against the counter. "But I'm sure you have your reasons."

I didn't respond. Instead, I turned my attention toward the refrigerator. For some reason, it felt like the perfect time to clean the fingerprints and smudges from the stainless steel. I grabbed a bottle of vinegar and water and went to town.

"Okay, Kay, whatever... Anyway, the guy looks familiar."

"High school football coach. He knew Nathan." And there it was. Our constant elephant in the room. The only reason Shane was here in my kitchen with my family instead of his.

"Can I have some more, please?" Summer asked, capturing Shane's attention.

"You bet, kiddo." He turned from me and filled Summer's bowl.

The distraction provided a moment for me to contemplate the very active morning.

Chapter 7
MATT

I woke up the next day with one hell of a headache. I knew I'd taken a big blow during the tussle in the supermarket, but damn. It felt like I'd been pummeled with a sock full of rocks. I heaved myself out of bed. The sunlight had pushed through the slats in the blinds, leading me to believe I'd slept through the greater part of the morning. Which was very unusual for me. I forced myself upright and spent some time sitting on the edge of the mattress before venturing into the rest of the house.

After a good long ten minutes, I was ready to greet the day. I shuffled out to the living room in search of my family. Layla was watching something on TV. She jumped up and down when she saw me emerge from the haven that was our bedroom.

"Matt's up!" she yelled to no one in particular.

"Hey, Lay, can we try not to yell this morning..." I patted her little head as I made my way past her toward the kitchen.

"Okay, Matt!" she hollered back.

It was hopeless. "Where's your mama?" I asked, reaching for a mug to mix some instant coffee.

"She went for a walk," Layla responded; this time at a much more appropriate level for my headache.

As I was adding creamer, Aiyona entered through the kitchen door and stomped off her hiking boots.

There was a wooded area in our cul de sac, and Aiyona loved to wander the trails whenever she had the opportunity.

"It's freezing out there this morning!" Her volume was at the same over-the-top level I'd just urged her daughter not to use. "It's still fall. Can you imagine what this winter will feel like!"

I nodded, "Probably just as frigid as the last two."

"Or worse!"

I nodded again and contemplated whether or not to ask her to lower her voice too. She handed me her big, bulky, tan parka. I hung it on the last empty hook as Aiyona leaned against the wall to untie her boots.

"How ya feelin'?" Her voice softened without me having to ask. "You slept past ten. I can't remember the last time you were still in bed after me."

"Well, I feel like I've been hit by a semi-truck, but other than that... great."

She reached out and tenderly stroked my cheek with her frigid fingertips. "I'm sorry, baby. That's what happens when you let a ninety-year-old woman kick your ass," she smirked.

"Funny."

"Go shower up. I'll make some pancakes and bacon."

"Now that sounds like a plan."

"But first take this." She opened the cupboard and produced a massive bottle of generic ibuprofen. After handing me two tablets, she turned and grabbed my coffee off the countertop, and promptly dumped it down the sink.

"Hey... Aiyona..." I nearly choked on the medication. "I just made that! What are you doin'?"

"You're not drinking that crap! I'm going to make you a real cup of coffee. Now, get on and get ready for the day."

"I would—but you just dumped my caffeine source," I grumbled.

"Go on now, whiney Mattey," she teased. "You'll appreciate my effort when you return. Now, off with your stinky self." She shooed me away with a swift kick to the backside.

I knew she was probably right. But she didn't need to know I knew that. I grumbled a bit more before trudging my way back down to the end of the hallway.

Chapter 8
KALEY

The week went by in a flash. My anxiety increased with each passing hour. I almost canceled on John a few times but decided that wouldn't be fair. Truth be told, it was probably more unfair of me not to cancel. I had no business dating. After splurging on a dress for the occasion, I immediately regretted it and returned it. Then, there was the whole question of communication. Should I talk to him beforehand or just leave things until Saturday? It had been a long time since I'd dated, and Nathan had made everything so easy. I never had to think about the details with him. Everything seemed to unfold so naturally. In retrospect, I wondered if that were true or if Nathan just made it feel that way. I still hadn't told Shane about my plans with John, and I wasn't sure I would.

On the eve of my big date, I still wasn't sure if I'd go through with it. Then, a thought occurred to me, maybe I should go to the game? After all, we'd be at the gallery on Saturday night, wasn't it only fair to observe him in his natural habitat too? Just like that—I'd turned my date into some kind of zoological experiment. Nevertheless, I'd made up my mind. The only thing left to do was to get Summer on board before I chickened out.

"Hey Summer," I said, entering my daughter's room, which was always an experience. When you have a kid with a vivid imagination and way too many toys—things happen. At that particular moment, there was a naked Barbie, a stuffed bear, Star Wars figures, and a big dump truck in the center of the floor. It wasn't until I sat down next to her that I noticed the dental floss strung around Barbie. The action figures seemed to be dragging her toward the truck. What kind of holy hell had Summer created in her overly active imagination?

"Whatcha doin?" I asked casually.

"The stormtroopers captured Barbie after she destroyed the animal village. Now she gots to go to the dump and plant trees."

I nodded, "Okay, then…" I wasn't sure how a football game was going to compete with the current action, but I'd give it a shot. "How would you like to go out tonight?"

She jumped up and clapped her hands. "Out to dinner? With Uncle Shane?"

"Ummm, no… we'll eat here and then go out. Just the two of us."

She cocked her head to the side, "What do you mean?"

I wasn't sure which part had her hung up. Was it the concept of home-cooking or doing something without Shane? Either way, it was certainly telling.

I plunged ahead, "I thought we could make grilled cheese and then go watch the football game."

She scrunched up her face as though thinking very hard about my proposal.

"It could be fun…" I added.

"Okay, what the hell," she shrugged.

Well, that certainly wasn't the answer I'd expected. "Summer," I did my best to sound parental, "that's not really an appropriate response. We talked about kind words just yesterday… remember?"

"How come it's fine for you and Uncle Shane to say that but not me?" she pouted.

Because Uncle Shane and I don't have teachers calling home concerned about our vocabulary. To her: "It's not okay for us, either," I said. "We'll all have to try and be better."

"That's all I'm askin'," she replied matter-of-factly.

I nodded, as though I understood what had transpired and internally congratulated myself on a stellar parenting moment.

∞∞∞∞∞∞∞∞

The game was packed. We didn't get there early enough to grab seats, so we were forced to stand along the fence line. The crisp autumn air, the excitement of the crowd, and the glare of the stadium lights brought me right back to my high school days. I had fond memories of drinking under the bleachers with Erin Warren and her older brother Jesse, who always had an ample supply of cheap beer.

Summer found some kids from school and was fully involved in a game of tag by the snack shack a few yards away. I prayed she wouldn't end up like me but more like Nathan, he wouldn't have been drinking under the bleachers. Had we known each other back then, I was pretty sure he'd have narced me out.

Around me, the crowd broke out in a surge of raucous cheering, pulling me from my reverie and back to the present. Apparently, the Tigers had done something impressive on the field. The announcer shouted something about number seventeen, Kyle Sterns. I recognized the name. It was the police chief's son, Shane's boss. I leaned into the fence and peered toward the end zone; a hefty-looking kid was celebrating with what appeared to be a cross between a jig and a bumbling attempt at hip-hop. I smiled to myself, wondering when the chief's son had transformed from an awkward middle schooler to a confident athlete.

That was where my interest in the game began and ended. I was much more focused on the coach than the players. John was pacing up and down the sidelines barking orders. I'd never been into athletes, but I had to admit he looked good in his ball cap and black Tigers windbreaker.

Two women along the fence row near me seemed to think so too. They were the kind of attractive, perfectly put-together moms I admired but knew I'd never be. Both petite with delicate features, one blonde and one brunette with equally lustrous locks. They were dressed in Tiger sweatshirts and knit caps to match.

"I swear, I don't even watch Cody play anymore," the brunette said to the blonde. "I just end up staring at his coach the whole time."

The blonde giggled, "If I wasn't married, I swear I'd— well, never mind."

They both laughed.

I hadn't really believed my grandfather when he'd hinted at John's popularity. I'd written it off as a tactic to pique my interest. However, it seemed the old man had been right. Score another one for Henry; and now, score one for me. The moms were admiring my date for tomorrow night, and secretly I was pleased by that.

My attention was divided between the sidelines and Summer with her friends. As a result, I had no idea what was actually happening in the game. That was until the band rushed the field, and their shiny orange uniforms caught my attention. Under the glare of the stadium lights, they blazed like flames of a bonfire, and they sounded good too. On the sidelines, John was animatedly chatting with his players. Another man nudged him, possibly the assistant coach, and together they hustled the players toward the school. I imagined John was about to deliver an inspiring and motivating locker room pep talk, that's what usually happened on TV or movies anyway. According to the scoreboard, the home team was ahead by seven.

"Mommy," Summer tugged at my coat sleeve. "I'm tired, and my friends are leaving." She rubbed her eyes, a signal that the clock was ticking. There was a small window of time to get her home and into bed before she transformed from my sweet kindergartner into a worn-out little monster.

I gathered her into my arms. "Ready to call it a night?"

Her nod followed by a yawn confirmed it was, indeed, go time. "Alright, let's move."

I set her down and we made our way back to the SUV. Unfortunately, my bad sense of direction led us down the wrong aisle.

"Kaley!"

John rounded a rusted-out, dark Chevy pick-up truck just ahead of us.

"What are you doing?" I asked. "Aren't you supposed to be inside motivating your team?"

He chuckled, "Well, I would be; however, my quarterback here…" he jerked his thumb toward a young man coughing profusely behind him. "Locked his keys and inhaler in his truck."

I peeked around John's shoulder to get a better look. Past the coughing kid, Kyle Sterns was concentrating hard on maneuvering a wire coat hanger through a gap in the window.

The situation appeared grim, "Is he going to be okay?" I asked, my voice heavy with doubt.

John patted the asthmatic on the back. "Oh, sure, but the inhaler would definitely help."

"Mommy can get it," Summer offered. "She locks herself out of the house a lot… and she did once with grandpa's truck. But her car won't lock if her keys are in it. Mommy says it's idiot-proof."

John tossed his head back and laughed.

"Thanks, Summer. Remember our conversation earlier about appropriate words?"

"I can't say idiot either?" she huffed dramatically.

"I'd rather you didn't." I turned back to John. "She's not wrong, though. I'm really good at breaking into my house and the occasional car… when necessary, that is."

John stepped out of the way and gestured for me to step on up. "Sterns—give the lady here a chance."

Kyle eyeballed me, "Hi, Mrs. Stone. You're welcome to give it a shot. We don't have a lot of time, though," he passed me the wire hanger.

"Hi Kyle, don't sound so doubtful. I got this."

He surveyed me with skepticism, "If you say so."

I brushed past him and went to work.

As I struggled to pop the lock, another Tiger joined us, "Coach!" he called out. "We gotta go. Halftime's almost up."

John observed the situation as the wheezing from his quarterback continued to intensify. "Have Coach Timmons take you out. I'll be there as soon as we get TJ breathing again."

The kid nodded and sprinted back toward the school just as I felt the hanger connect with the lock. I tugged the wire upward, fully satisfied by the clicking of the lock as I unsecured the vehicle.

"Nice job!" Kyle congratulated me as I passed him his hanger.

We stepped back so the asthmatic kid could get to his medication.

John eyed me appraisingly, "Impressive."

"You haven't seen anything yet," I responded with a little smirk. *Was I flirting?*

"Is that right? Then I'm really looking forward to tomorrow night."

"Coach has a date!" Kyle exclaimed.

The asthmatic kid laughed as he struggled to hold in the puff of medication.

"Hey!" John snapped, turning toward his players. "There's nothing funny about that!"

John's mock indignation only heightened the kids' amusement. From inside the stadium, a roar of applause and the sound of stomping feet carried through the crisp night air.

"You all better get going," I commented, nodding in the direction of the noise.

"Right," agreed John.

Kyle and the quarterback thanked me and then sprinted off in the direction of the stadium. The quarterback, not surprisingly, falling back a bit.

"You too," I said to John.

"See you tomorrow," he offered me a lopsided grin before jogging off after the kids.

Chapter 9
MATT

"Matt!" Layla pounded on the bathroom door. "Hurry up! I gotta go potty."

I'd gotten a late start. It had been a week since my head injury and ever since the ham to the head, mornings were rough. Aiyona thought I probably had a concussion, and I thought she was probably right. My morning sluggishness was a problem for a household with only one bathroom. I'd botched our family's carefully orchestrated routine almost every day this week. At least it was Saturday. I was the only one who needed to be anywhere.

"Hang on, baby girl." Water dripped onto the shaggy, pink bathmat as I exited the shower stall.

Layla knocked again as I realized that I'd forgotten a towel. The linen closet was in the hall; but, fortunately, Aiyona's fuzzy bathrobe was hanging from the hook on the back of the door and would make a satisfactory substitute.

"Matt!" Layla bellowed again.

"I'm moving as fast as I can, Lay!"

My Harding's Hardware polo stuck to my chest, and I did my best to tug the jeans up over my damp legs.

When I pulled open the door, Layla was doing a little jig on the other side. Steam escaped the bathroom and rolled down the hall as Layla rushed past me to do her thing.

Aiyona was buzzing about the kitchen with heavy metal music streaming from her nearby phone. I never understood how she could listen to that crap so early in the day.

"Cuttin' it close this morning, baby," she scolded in a teasing tone.

"I know—sorry." I settled myself on one of our dilapidated kitchen chairs to pull my socks on.

Aiyona stopped the music and set a bagel in front of me along with a large thermos of coffee to go.

"Have I told you lately how much I love you?" I asked.

"You have," she replied nonchalantly before strolling off to check on Layla.

I scarfed down the bagel and grabbed my work boots from the small mat near the side door. Aiyona did not allow shoes in the house. On the edge of the counter was the old tin lunch bin Aiyona lovingly packed for me on workdays. I grabbed that along with my heavyweight jacket from the hook by the door.

"See ya after work!" I called out as the screen door squeaked in protest.

I paused briefly to listen for the door to clang shut again behind me, which it did. Having not started the car earlier, I was forced to sit frozen like a popsicle while I waited for the defroster to work its magic. Why had I given in and willingly moved to this icebox? We'd arrived in this mid-western city in the spring. I could still recall the green lush fields, the big, beautiful barns basking in the glow of the spring sunshine. I closed my eyes and took a deep breath, longing for the days of warmth and growth. Even after over two years here, the cold still caught me off guard. When I opened my eyes again, the windshield was still iced over. The defroster struggled to free the glass from its winter imprisonment. I struck the steering wheel in frustration and looked for the ice scraper thingy.

"Wisconsin, you deceptive little bitch," I cursed under my breath.

∞∞∞∞∞∞∞∞

The morning moved at a snail's pace. Dwayne and I were the only two working, and given the number of customers, it felt like that was two too many.

The lack of stimulation lent well to daydreaming. I was completely in my head about our tight-living situation as I unloaded a shipment of cold-weather gear. The chatter from the overhead paging system disrupted my concentration; it took me a moment to realize the page was meant for me. Tossing aside a pair of gloves, I jogged toward the front to see what Dwayne needed. Surprisingly, a few shoppers had entered the store during my absence. I spotted a young mother and her toddler, but had a feeling the overhead page had something to do with the other customer.

A large, irate-looking man in tan coveralls stood near the cash registers. Dwayne was cowering behind one of the two checkout counters as the man hurled an onslaught of insults toward him.

"Hey, what's going on?" I snapped, positioning myself between Dwayne and the customer.

"Your boy is trying to rip me off!" Coveralls complained loudly, causing little flecks of spittle to sprinkle me in my face.

I swiped the wetness from my cheek and fixed him with my best cold and intimidating look.

The man took a few tentative steps back. His body language had changed, but his voice was still fueled with anger. He started up again, this time at a much higher volume. "He won't take back this drill he sold me last week! The darn thing don't work for crap!"

I glanced toward Dwayne for guidance.

"He didn't buy it here, Matt," Dwayne responded in a shaky voice. He did his best to avoid the customer's eyes, "we don't carry that brand."

"So, sounds like you're trying to 'rip my boy off,' huh." I purposely parroted his phrase back at him.

The guy took a few more steps back.

"Dwayne, why don't you ring up the other customers while I assist Mr... I'm sorry, I didn't catch your name, sir?"

"Never mind!" The guy flicked his hand in disgust and stomped toward the sliding glass doors. "But don't think you're ever getting my business again!" he hollered over his shoulder.

"Glad to hear it! Have a nice day now!" I yelled back.

Instead of heading back to the stock room, I took a seat on the red vinyl stool at the second cash register across from Dwayne. Just in case the asshole decided to come back.

Dwayne finished ringing up the young woman, who hurried past me with her child; both looking a little unsettled.

After they exited, Dwayne shuffled over and leaned on the counter next to me. "I'm sorry I had to pull you into that, Matt."

I shrugged. "Don't apologize, you did the right thing. The guy was being a blowhard. He just needed us to gang up on him a little bit."

Dwayne looked away sheepishly. "He didn't need us, Matt. I didn't do anything. One look from you, though, and that guy sure changed his tune."

I patted Dwayne on the shoulder. "You stood your ground. Give yourself some credit. He wasn't able to bully you into returning his item."

Dwayne straightened up. The compliment boosting his self-esteem, if only slightly, "Thanks for that."

"Well—it's true."

"I wish I could be more like you, though."

Well, that had to be a first. I didn't think anybody had ever wished to be more like Matt Pine. The thought of being admired by someone, especially someone good and upstanding like Dwayne, made me smile. "Funny, Dwayne, I could say the same about you."

Dwayne let out a loud barking laugh. "Why would you want to be more like me?"

"Cause you're a good guy."

"Well, so are you, Matt. I mean you look hardened and mean but—" he stopped himself. "I'm sorry, that was rude."

"Nah—it's okay," I reassured him. "I get it."

"I mean, I know you have a record; but Ollie thought that you deserved a chance and..." Dwayne smacked himself on the forehead. "I'm sorry. Again, I'm being a jerk. All I'm trying to say is you're a nice guy despite... you know... whatever."

Dwayne's face got just a bit redder with every word he uttered. I decided to cut the guy a break and wrap things up for his sake and mine. Truth be told, I was starting to get concerned about the direction of the conversation. I didn't want to talk about my past.

I rose from the stool and gave Dwayne a hearty pat on the back. "Thank you, Dwayne. I did some stupid things before, but I'm not that guy anymore. Now I just want to walk the straight and narrow, take care of my fiancée and be a good dad to Layla."

It felt odd being this forthcoming with someone other than Aiyona. Ordinarily, I didn't make a habit of sharing personal details with anyone, except for Detective Stone; and look where that got him.

Dwayne appeared to think hard about my confession, then nodded solemnly. "You're a standup guy, Matt. I'd vouch for you any day."

"Right back at ya, buddy."

Thank goodness the doors slid open, bringing in a gust of wind and another customer. Dwayne and I were sitting on the edge of a bromance, and I wasn't keen on further exploring our feelings.

I glanced at the clock. At least an hour had passed since the last time I'd checked. I was grateful Layla had an appointment scheduled. At least I'd get to leave early. I excused myself and headed back into the storage area to finish unloading the new inventory and count the minutes until quitting time.

Chapter 10
KALEY

I made arrangements with Grandpa to watch Summer. After all, he was the reason I was in the situation to begin with. After the game on Friday, I was completely wound, which resulted in a restless night. I had stayed awake talking to Nathan until the wee hours of the morning. My religious beliefs were kind of fuzzy. I considered myself spiritual; and although I did believe in God, it wasn't really the biblical God I grew up on. Grandpa was straight-up Catholic and believed in heaven and hell. He had raised my mother the same way and did his best to do so with me too.

So, even though I talked to Nathan a lot, I was under no illusion that he could hear me. It just felt better to pretend that maybe he could. As a result of my high energy level and late-night conversations, I was completely exhausted before my date with John.

I made macaroni and cheese for Grandpa and Summer. John had offered to pick me up so we could drive to the gallery together; and for some dumb reason, I said yes. I tried on about ten outfits and finally settled on jeans, a black hooded sweater, and knee-high boots. I probably went too heavy on the makeup; but in my defense, I was feeling very out of my element. When I finally came downstairs, Grandpa did nothing to ease my anxiety.

"It took you all evening to do that!" he exclaimed. "Good golly, sweetheart, don't you have a dress or something girly you could put on? I should have taken you shopping."

"Thanks, old man," I said, glaring at him. "You're a real confidence booster."

"I think you look pretty, Mommy," Summer offered. She was working on a large floor puzzle with Sargent Snuggles curled up beside her. "I hope you have fun eating with your new friend."

"Thank you, baby," I said, bending over to give my daughter an affectionate squeeze.

"Well, of course, you look pretty," Grandpa sighed. "You always look pretty, Kaley. After all, you take after me. I just thought you'd dress up a little."

The doorbell rang, causing Sargent Snuggles to bark. "Well, too late now," I called out, making my way to the front door, and doing my best to ignore the butterflies fluttering around in my stomach.

"And remember, don't ask him about the game!" Henry yelled. "That loss was heartbreaking."

"You've mentioned that a million times already," I replied sharply.

After taking a deep breath, I eased open the door. To my relief, John was dressed just as casually in jeans, a plaid button-down shirt, black work boots, and a Carhartt coat.

"Hey, come on in," I said, stepping back to give him space.

Henry called out from the living room, "Get on in here, Kyler. What are your intentions toward my granddaughter!"

As if I couldn't embarrass myself enough on my own, I thought. "You don't have to go in there," I said apologetically.

"Naw—it's alright," John replied. He stepped around the corner to the open living room. "Henry, nice to see you again." He offered his hand, which

Grandpa shook enthusiastically. "And hello to you, Summer. I don't think we officially met last night."

"Hello," Summer greeted him back.

"Your Grandpa talks about you all the time."

Summer smiled and introduced John to Sargent Snuggles. "He's new and I named him," she said proudly.

John bent down and gave the dog a pat, receiving a lick of approval in return. "Well, that's a great name, and it's very nice to meet you both. I'm John."

"I know," Summer said. "Mommy's new friend. Grandpa said she needs some friends because she never does anything with anybody except Shane, and he's a son of a bitch."

"Summer!" I gasped. Grandpa and John found the statement tremendously funny. I did not.

"Is that right?" John replied, over my grandpa's howling laughter.

"Yup." Summer nodded. "So, thanks for hanging out with my mom."

"My pleasure," John replied with a lopsided grin.

I retrieved my black peacoat and a pair of gloves then hustled John the heck out of there before my family could embarrass me further.

∞∞∞∞∞∞∞

I asked John to swing through the bar to pick up dinner on the way to the gallery. Burgers and fries were waiting for us, an order I'd placed earlier. I slid back into the pickup truck with the bag of takeout. The smell filled the cab with a greasy, smoky, delicious aroma.

"I don't know how I feel about not paying my way here," John commented, as he pulled back onto the road.

"Oh, no worries, nobody has to pay. The only perk to being Henry McConnell's granddaughter is free food for life."

"Well, that's a great perk, if you ask me. It smells good!"

"It's just burgers and fries. I have soda and beer in the refrigerator at the gallery. Hope you're not a vegetarian."

He laughed, "Do I strike you as a vegetarian?"

"I don't know... maybe."

He glanced over at me uncertainly, "Really?"

"Yeah... why not?"

"I'm a football coach in Wisconsin!" He exclaimed.

"So?"

He opened his mouth as though to explain but nothing came out. He clamped his lips together and shifted uncomfortably in his seat.

"I try not to put people in a box," I explained. "That never works well. People are who they are, not necessarily who you think they are."

He seemed to think about that for a moment and then nodded, "Fair enough."

ooooooooo

Dinner was much more relaxed than anticipated. I used some yoga blankets to cover the floorboards of the main gallery space and we ate picnic-style. John had some nice and genuine things to say about my work, as well as some of the other artists on display. He talked a little bit about football, which in my opinion, evened the playing field. Football was about as foreign to me as the art world was to him.

Despite our differences, the conversation flowed easily. John talked about the boys he coached and shared some interesting and funny stories about his team. He also told me about his ex-wife leaving him for the mailman, and I pretended it was the first I'd heard of it. I talked a lot about Summer, and of course, Nathan. To my surprise, John seemed genuinely interested in hearing about my life with Nathan.

We compared our families and growing up. Again, a contrast. He and his sister were raised on a farm in Iowa, where his parents still resided. Whereas, I was an only child, whose father ran out on my mother when she was eight months pregnant, never to be heard from again. Then, after my mom passed away I was raised by Henry. Talking to John felt comfortable until he asked about Shane. Frankly, I had no idea how he fit into my family, so it was even harder to explain to someone else.

"So, Nathan was pretty close to Shane?" John asked.

"Not really... they worked really well together and socialized sometimes, but they weren't close."

"Oh?"

"Yeah—Shane and I are much closer than Nathan and he ever were. I guess we both ended up with a pretty big hole in our lives and looked to one another to try and fill it."

John finished his burger and crinkled up the wrapper, tossing it into one of the nearby food bags. He leaned back on his elbows and stretched his long legs out in front of him as he regarded me with curiosity. "So, you and Shane were together?"

"Gawd no!" I refrained from choking on a fry. "He's not my type."

John raised an eyebrow. "Really? He was your husband's partner?"

"Yeah—but he's nothing like Nathan. Shane can be immature and self-absorbed..." I stopped, "that came out wrong. I shouldn't have said that. He's been very good to Summer and me. He's just... he's just not my type. Can we leave it at that?"

"Of course."

Our conversation was interrupted by my phone jingling from somewhere deep inside my handbag. I leaned over to retrieve it from just outside our blanket perimeter. "His ears must have been burning," I said, as I tucked the phone back into my bag.

"Shane?"

"Yep," I replied, choosing to ignore the call. "Tell me—what did you think when Ted left you that message? You know—to pick your keys up from my house."

"Honestly?"

"Yes."

"I thought it was odd."

I laughed and my phone rang again. "Sorry," I said, repeating the action to retrieve the device. I furrowed my brow, "Shane again..."

"Feel free to take it. I don't mind."

The ring cut short as the call was sent to voicemail. "Ordinarily, Shane will just shoot me a text if I don't pick up..."

"Call him back," John encouraged.

"You sure?" My phone rang again robbing me of the opportunity. Three calls in under two minutes was not a good sign. "Shane, everything okay?"

"No—Kay, everything's not okay," the tension in his voice set me on edge. "Henry misplaced Summer."

I jumped to my feet and plugged my other ear, convinced I hadn't heard correctly. "Misplaced Summer? What are you talking about?"

"Henry and Summer took the dog out to go to the bathroom and Sargent Snuggles took off. Summer ran off after him. As you'd expect, Henry couldn't keep up."

I started to pace, "When was that?"

"She's been missing since about eight-thirty."

I checked the time on my watch, "That's almost forty-five minutes!" I exclaimed.

"I know, I know. Look, I thought she'd turn up quickly—I should have called sooner."

John, sensing something was wrong, was already on his feet. He gathered our things and tossed the trash. Moments later, we were dashing down the sidewalk toward his truck.

"Tell me the areas you've covered so I don't waste time," I said to Shane.

"Look—we have the whole department on this. Nobody is going to let anything happen to Nathan Stone's kid."

"Just tell me where to look," I said irritably.

We pulled away from the curb and John raced in the direction of my house. I took the phone from my ear. "Can you drive toward Lake Park?"

He nodded, and took a right, changing course.

I relayed the information to Shane, "I'm going to check Lake Park. It's just a couple of miles from the house. We've walked Sargent Snuggles there. He really likes it. Maybe he ran there because it's familiar?"

"Yeah, that's good," Shane agreed. "I'm going to backtrack toward my house—also familiar territory for the dog."

"Okay... Shane," I added. "I'm really scared."

"We'll find her. I promise." I didn't have a great history with promises, that combined with the anxious quality of his tone did nothing to quell my fears.

John turned up the hilly drive toward the park. We bounced across the uneven pavement toward the lake as I prayed she wasn't near the water. Despite countless hours of swim lessons, the kid was hopeless when it came to learning the skill.

"Maybe we should proceed on foot?" John suggested. "It'll be easier to view the shoreline that way."

"Okay," I agreed. "We can each take a side. Drop me here, and maybe you take the south shore?"

He nodded as he slowed the truck. I hopped out, barely giving him time to stop, and used the flashlight on my phone to guide me. It was dark and the ground rough. I called out frantically for Summer and Sargent Snuggles as I jogged and stumbled along the banks. After what felt like hours of searching, but in actuality was probably only a few minutes, panic started to consume me.

When my phone rang, I fumbled with the buttons and almost dropped it in my haste to answer, "John?"

"I have one very tired little girl and one dirty, smelly mutt. We're coming back around for you."

Relief washed over me, "Oh my gosh! Thank you, thank you, thank you!"

"We'll see you in a minute. You better call Henry and Shane."

"Right," I quickly ended the call and dialed Shane.

He answered on the first ring, "Kay?"

"We got her."

"Thank God!" he exclaimed, sounding just as relieved as I felt.

"Can you let Henry know?"

"Absolutely. I'll see you back at your place?"

"Yep," I confirmed. I slipped the phone back into my jeans pocket as headlights cut across the trees. John slowed to a stop, and I darted toward the truck. With some restraint, I pulled open the door and hurled myself inside.

My daughter sat in the center of the cab wrapped comfortably in John's coat. I gathered her in my arms. "Summer! You had everyone scared to death!"

"Sorry, Mommy, Sargent Snuggles wanted to go on an adventure, I guess." She shrugged, not looking remotely upset by the situation.

"If the dog wants to go on an adventure, he will need to go it alone from now on, you understand? It's dangerous to go running around by yourself, especially at night," I said sternly.

"It wasn't dangerous. I was fine."

I was baffled by her attitude, "Honey, weren't you scared? It's really dark outside."

"I was at first—when I didn't know where I was. But then I knew Sargent Snuggles would keep me safe."

"He's just a dog, Summer. He can't take care of you."

Summer yawned and leaned against me, "Daddy said he would."

I caught John's eye and felt a shiver run down my spine. "What do you mean daddy said?"

She yawned again, "He said—don't be scared, Sargent Snuggles will keep you safe. Just like he told me you were going to meet a new friend, who will keep you safe," she said, closing her eyes.

I glanced over at John, who looked just as surprised as I was. Neither of us said anything as he put the truck in drive and pointed us toward home.

My cell rang as John pulled to the curb in front of the house. I saw it was Logan Sterns, the police chief, and apologized to John, explaining I had to take the call. John nodded and proceeded to carry my sleepy girl inside.

"Hi, Logan," I answered.

"Kaley—" the sound of the smokey voice on the other end wasn't at all a surprise. Like Shane, the entire department had kept an eye on our little family since Nathan's death. "Shane told me you found little Summer. I just wanted to check myself. Are you all okay?"

"We're good, Logan. Thank you. I know you have more important things to do than to chase a little girl and her dog around the city." At this, I turned and narrowed my eyes at Sargent Snuggles in the backseat.

He wagged his tail in response.

"Nonsense! There is nothing more important than Summer's safety," Logan assured me.

"Well, thanks for that. Please pass my appreciation on to everyone else."

"Will do. Don't hesitate to call if you need anything. I know what it's like to be a single parent too. You have my full support."

"Thank you, I appreciate that." The comment about being a single parent stung a bit. I recognized he was trying to be kind, but he chose to end his marriage. It wasn't the same for me.

"Goodnight, Kaley."

After ending the call, I slid from the truck and opened the back door for Sargent Snuggles. I'd hoped he'd be ready to go inside after his little joy ride. He was not. Shane bounded down the front steps with a large tan leash as I struggled with the wiggly beast.

"I'm so sorry. I should have called sooner," he offered apologetically.

"Why didn't you?" I asked tersely.

He lifted the dog gently to the ground before responding, "I never thought they'd stray that far. Henry told me you were on a date, and I didn't want to disturb you."

"I get it, but in the future—Summer is never a disruption."

"I know. I screwed up."

"You didn't screw up. Henry did, though. Thanks for dropping everything to look for her."

"It wasn't just me. Everyone was looking. Like I said, nobody is going to let anything happen to Nathan's kid."

I nodded, "I just got off the phone with Logan. I asked him to thank everyone."

He squeezed my arm, "We will. Hey, not to change the subject or anything but... a date? I'm offended you didn't tell me."

I felt my face flush; I'd been busted. "I wasn't sure I'd go through with it. And then—when I did—I didn't want to upset you."

Shane frowned, "Why would I be upset?"

I shrugged, "I don't know. Part of me feels like I'm being disloyal to Nathan, and I assumed you'd feel that way too."

"Kay, I think it's great, really. Nathan would want you to move forward with your life. I want that for you too."

"You think?"

"One hundred percent. Now, if this guy is actually worthy of you or not remains to be seen."

"Thank you for that."

He slung his arm around my shoulders as we made our way back to the house with Sargent Snuggles in tow. I debated about telling Shane what Summer had said about Nathan but decided against it. The last part was a little unsettling—what she'd said about my new friend, who I could only assume was John. Why did Summer think I needed protection?

We crossed paths with John who was exiting the house as we were headed in. The two men exchanged handshakes and a few pleasantries before Shane took the dog inside.

"I should probably get going," John said. "Leave you to your family," he gestured toward the house.

"Probably," I agreed. "I need to have a conversation with Henry."

"He's pretty shaken up. He almost tackled me when I brought Summer in."

"Thank you. This is not how I envisioned our night."

"I'm just glad your daughter is home safe and sound."

"Thanks to you," I said, nudging him with my elbow.

He smiled, "You would have found her eventually."

"I don't want to consider the alternative," I shivered.

"You don't have to," John said reassuringly. "For what it's worth... I had a really nice time tonight. You know—until the whole missing child part."

I laughed, "Me too."

John didn't attempt to kiss or even hug me, absolutely nothing. I wasn't sure if I was relieved or disappointed by that. He just turned and sauntered back to his truck. Before stepping off the curb, he paused and looked back at me, "I'll see ya in the morning."

"You will?"

"Yeah—I have to get my coat back," he said, shaking his head in wonderment. "You Stone women sure like to hoard my stuff."

I laughed. "It's a way to ensure we can see you again."

"You don't have to take my stuff for that. I can guarantee you'll see me again."

I smiled and waved him off, feeling particularly light as I stepped up the front stoop and pulled open the storm door. The front door had remained open, and I was hit with a rush of warmth when I stepped inside. Henry must have turned the furnace up.

"Kaley, sweetheart—I don't know what to say." Grandpa came hobbling around the corner, his face gaunt with worry. It was obvious what a toll the night had taken on him.

My anger dissipated. Henry would never do anything to harm Summer. The whole thing was an unfortunate accident. One we would definitely work to prevent in the future; but in the meantime, nothing I could say could make the man feel worse.

"It was an accident, Grandpa. She's home safe and sound. That's all that matters."

He nodded, "I can't apologize enough."

"We'll have to put Sargent Snuggles on a leash before we open the door. Especially now that we know he's a runner. Also, you should have called me first, not Shane."

"I know. Again—I'm very sorry."

He looked so defeated I decided to cut him a break. I leaned forward and gently kissed the side of his leathery face. "I know. Good night, Grandpa." I leaned around my grandfather to where Shane was seated at the edge of the couch with Sargent Snuggles, "goodnight, Shane."

"Wait—" Shane hopped up to join Grandpa and me in the foyer. "Aren't you going to tell us about your date?"

"Nope." I walked away toward the bedrooms with both Shane and Henry gawking after me in disbelief. "Lock up when ya leave, boys," I called back.

Before going to my room, I looked in on Summer. The light from the hallway spilled into the room. She was on top of her covers with John's coat still wrapped tightly around her. Ordinarily, I would have made sure to tuck her in properly; but she looked so peaceful I decided not to disturb her.

With a contented sigh, I gently pulled the door shut. For the first time in a long time, I was looking forward to what tomorrow might bring.

Chapter 11
MATT

After Detective Stone died, I immersed myself in learning all I could about Kaley and Summer Stone. I watched for updates on her social media accounts, I searched for online articles where she'd been featured for her art, and sometimes I followed her home from the gallery. There's no way to justify my behavior, it was downright creepy. Watching them couldn't change the past. Once I came to terms with that, I backed off. So, although I knew Nathan's little family, I was a stranger to them.

"Matt, wait!" Layla pleaded. She squeezed my hand and tried with all her might to pull me back toward the school building.

"Baby, I can't. Your mama made an appointment for you to get your hair cut. I promised we wouldn't be late."

In response, Layla stomped her foot, "No. You gotta meet my friend's mama. She's picking her up."

"Lay, I'm sorry. Tomorrow, I promise."

"I can't wait anymore. You said we could play together. Remember?"

I was about to lecture my soon-to-be stepdaughter, but one look into her big, brown puppy dog eyes and I was butter. "Fine," I sighed. "Five minutes then we have to go."

"Yes! Thank you, Matt!" Layla exclaimed, glancing wildly around.

I wasn't sure how she planned to find her little friend in the throng of students and parents pouring out of the dated, brick building. I eased her onto my shoulders to give her a better vantage point.

"Is she in your class?" I asked. It was a stupid question; it's not like having the information would help identify the kid. It was a full-on needle in a haystack situation.

Layla responded anyway. "No, she's in Mr. Randolph's class; but we eat lunch together."

I repositioned, stepping up onto the sidewalk. Seconds later, Layla started shouting and frantically drumming her hands on the top of my head. "Over there! Go that way, Matt! Her mommy's picking her up. Hurry!"

"Okay—okay." I did my best to carefully lower the flailing child, which considering her energy level, was no easy task. Once her cowboy boots hit the asphalt, she was off and running, while I was left rubbing a tweaked muscle at the base of my neck.

Layla approached a blonde woman with a stubby ponytail, wearing a brown bomber jacket with a faux fur hood. As I closed the distance, I was touched by an odd sense of familiarity. When I spotted the woman's mini-me trailing behind, I realized why. Before I could re-direct Layla she walked right up to Stone's wife and little girl.

"Matt!" Layla waved me forward through the hoard of parents and children.

I broke out in a cold sweat but somehow managed to put one foot in front of the other until I reached the trio.

Layla was jumping up and down unable to contain her excitement. "This is my friend Summer!" She shouted introductions at us like a drill sergeant tweaking on meth. "Summer, this is Matt. He's gunna to be my daddy soon, right, Matt?"

I did my best to smile and placed a calming hand on Layla's shoulder. I'd never actually been this close to Stone's daughter before. Summer offered me a shy little wave before turning her attention back to Layla. The girl had a head full of golden ringlets and the same piercing blue eyes as her father. It was kind of chilling.

"Hi, I'm Kaley," Stone's wife offered her hand. Meanwhile, the kids had retreated to their own private universe completely oblivious of the adults.

As I grasped Kaley's hand for a friendly shake, I realized how odd the situation was. She had absolutely no idea who I was. Yet, I'd made it my business to find out as much as possible about her. She had blue eyes too but not nearly as intense as her daughter's.

"It's nice to finally meet Layla," Kaley made an attempt at polite conversation.

I tried to act casual. I put my hands in the pockets of my baggie jeans and rocked back on my heels. "Yeah, Layla has been excited for me to meet her new friend."

"I gathered that," Kaley replied with a twinkle in her eye.

"Ha! Yeah—well, she's got one speed."

"I admire her enthusiasm. Summer would love to have her over for a playdate sometime."

I appreciated the compliment and the invite. "Great—ummm, I'll give you my fiancée's number. You can set somethin' up with her." I started patting my pockets like an idiot looking for something to write with.

Kaley handed me her phone, "Here, just add her, and I'll give her a call."

My hands trembled as I accepted the device, "Great. That'll work."

Either Kaley didn't notice, or she was too polite to draw attention as I entered the digits with shaky thumbs. I guessed it was the latter.

"Aiyona?" Kaley asked, looking at the information I'd entered.

"Yup. Aiyona," I stupidly repeated.

Kaley ignored my awkward behavior and continued, "Okay. Is there a particular day or time that works better for you guys?"

"Nope. We're pretty free. Just give her a call... or whatever."

"Sounds good. Well, it was nice meeting you, Matt, and you too, Layla." She said the last part with a smile.

The girls hugged goodbye, and Stone's wife and daughter faded into the crowd. As soon as they were out of sight, I rolled my neck and shrugged my shoulders in an attempt to release the excess of nervous energy.

"I'm so excited to play at Summer's house!" Layla exclaimed as we made our way to the car. "I'm gunna to tell my mama about it as soon as we get home."

"Sounds good, kiddo," I opened the back door and waited as she scampered into her booster. Once settled, I secured the safety harness around her before shutting the door and ducking into the driver's side.

I couldn't help but wonder... was it fate that Layla and Summer had become friends or just a strange coincidence?

Chapter 12
KALEY

On the way home, Summer and I swung by the bar to check on Henry. We were seated on the tattered sofa in the back office while Henry was at his desk listening intently to his great-granddaughter tell him about the favorite parts of her day. She was just starting to tell him about her friend Layla when my phone started to vibrate. I slipped it from the back pocket of my jeans and was pleased to see John's name flash on the screen.

It had been a week since our date. Since then, we'd met for morning coffee and a lunch date. I was looking forward to seeing him again, which made me happy and extremely nervous. I never pictured being with anyone after Nathan. Contrary to the opinion of my grandfather, I was completely content with that choice. I slipped into the hallway to answer the call, making sure to close the door behind me. I wasn't in the mood to watch Henry gloat about the success of his set-up.

"Hey, John," I found myself smiling as I waited for a response.

"Hey, hope you're having a good day," his husky voice was starting to sound familiar to me.

"I am. What's up?"

"I only have a couple of minutes, but I wanted to nail down our next date."

I laughed, "Nail it down, huh? You are a charmer."

He laughed too, "Thank you, I'll take that as a compliment."

"As you should."

"Anyway, how would you feel about dinner at my place on Saturday? My sister is going to be in town. I'd love for her to meet you. It would be great if you brought Summer too."

He wanted me to meet his sister? After only a week? That seemed quick... Maybe even a little presumptuous. I wasn't sure what to say.

"Kaley...?" He waited a beat before continuing. "Ahhh, jeez, I screwed up, didn't I? It's too soon, right? Never mind—forget I asked."

I forged ahead, not wanting him to feel uncomfortable; but, more importantly, because I realized I did want to meet his sister. Truth be told, I wanted to get to know this guy. He was forthright and genuine. Those were pretty remarkable qualities.

"John, relax. I would love to have dinner with you and your sister."

His sigh was audible, coming through loud and clear. "It was too soon to ask, though, wasn't it?"

I laughed again trying to break the tension, "Maybe a little... but I like that about you. You just put it out there. No games or fuss."

He chuckled, "I'm too old for games, not that I ever played them. I enjoy your company and Summer's too. I got the impression you felt the same but if not—"

I cut him off, "We'll be there!"

"Great! Gotta run. I'll get back to you with the time."

"Perfect!" I replied, perhaps a bit too enthusiastically; but I was happy and there didn't seem to be a need to disguise that.

Henry looked up and caught my eye as I stepped back into the office. Summer was still chattering away, oblivious to my presence; but a knowing smile played across Henry's lips. My grandfather was impossible.

Chapter 13
MATT

I pulled into the driveway of the modest, white ranch home with the one-car detached garage. It appeared tidy from the street; but upon closer inspection, I noted small imperfections signaling a more recent state of neglect, perhaps due to finances. The red trim was peeling around the windows and garage. The lawn hadn't been kept up; the grass was slightly overgrown, and the leaves needed to be raked.

The day Stone had given me money I'd just assumed the guy was loaded. It wasn't until after his death I realized the truth. Which made his gesture even more meaningful. I mean, the guy had been better off than me; but I'm betting his wife and little girl could have used that money too. A lump started to form in my throat. I needed to grab Layla from her playdate and get out quick.

Ringing the doorbell set a dog off from somewhere in the bowels of the house. In response to the barking, I instinctively stepped down from the stoop. The last thing I needed was to be caught in the path if the dog decided to charge.

To my surprise, Kaley didn't answer the door. Instead, it was her husband's partner who pulled open the red interior door. The guy peered down at me through the glass of the exterior door. I knew he was married to a hot redhead. They'd been in the store together on a couple of occasions. Although he seemed to be the type to sneak around, Kaley did not. He was rugged-looking; wearing jeans and a button-down dress shirt.

"Are you Layla's dad?" he asked, squinting down at me from his elevated position. With the glass separating us, his words sounded muffled. The dog was not visible but still audibly protested my presence.

"Ummm, soon-to-be step-dad," I replied.

The guy took a bite of whatever was in his hand, possibly beef jerky... and opened the door for me.

Hesitantly, I stepped forward. "You have a dog?" I asked, glancing around nervously. I liked animals as a rule but had my fair share of run-ins with dogs in the past and had learned to be cautious.

"No worries, dude. Sargent Snuggles is in his crate," the detective assured me, taking another bite of his jerky.

"Sargent Snuggles?" I asked.

"Yep, the kid named him."

"Ahhhh," I climbed the few steps leading to the entrance, reassured after learning of the dog's containment. "I'm Matt, by the way."

"Hey, Matt—I'm Shane," he offered. Shane eased the door open wider, indicating I should step inside. "The girls are in Summer's bedroom. I'll get them."

"So, are you and Kaley together?" I blurted out, my curiosity getting the better of me.

Shane stopped and fixed me with a steely glare.

I stammered a bit. Silently scolding myself for letting my inquiring mind cloud my judgment.

"I mean... I just didn't know Kaley was seeing anyone."

Shane eyed me suspiciously. "Didn't you and Kaley just meet?"

"We did," I replied, trying to sound as casual as possible. "I just—I just know what happened with her husband... ya know... I guess I just didn't expect another man to answer the door. But really—none of my business." I finished stammering and held my hands up in way of surrender.

Shane stepped forward just enough to encroach on my personal space. A classic dick cop move. "I thought you said you were about to become Layla's stepdad?"

"I am," I confirmed.

"Then why are you concerned about whether or not Kaley is single?"

Sweat beaded on my forehead. I swiped it away and did my best to act normal. "I'm not. I just wasn't expecting my daughter to be here with a strange man when I picked her up," I countered, turning the tables on him.

Mr. Macho relaxed slightly but still appeared skeptical. "Kaley was here but had to run to her gallery. She'll be back soon."

I nodded, "No offense."

Shane shrugged and finished the stick of jerky. "None taken. You can never be too careful. And just to set the record straight, Kaley is seeing someone, but it's not me."

"Oh—okay," I said, unsure how I was supposed to react to the information. *When had Kaley started seeing someone? Maybe the same time she got the dog? Or was it the boyfriend's dog?* I felt Shane's eyes on me. I doubted he'd be at all comforted by my inner dialogue. "Is Layla ready?" I asked, hoping to re-direct his attention.

"Wait here," he instructed and then sauntered off down a hallway just left of the foyer.

I inhaled deeply and turned my attention in the opposite direction. An archway separated the foyer where I was standing from the living room. The room was light and airy. The furniture was tan; a couch and two easy chairs made up a matching set. I couldn't recall the last time I'd been in a home where all the furniture matched. There was a large picture window dressed with gauzy white curtains. The view wasn't impressive, a meager front yard and beyond that the quiet residential street. It was the adjacent wall without the window that captured my attention, a collage of canvas family photos. The lump returned as my eyes rested on a smiling, carefree, very much alive version of Detective Stone. He was dressed in a white shirt and blue jeans, his wife and daughter matching in white sundresses. The landscape was rich and green; that, along with the clothing choices, led me to believe the photo was most likely taken in the heart of the summer. I advanced a bit further into the room. The floorboards creaked under my weight as I inspected the pictures closer. Detective Stone was hamming it up for the camera or his daughter… either way, it was smiles all around. Judging by the age of Summer and the season, I concluded the photo session had taken place just months before his death.

"She's coming," Shane called out from behind me.

He'd startled me with his abrupt reappearance, but I tried not to show it. "Ahhh–great. Thanks," I said, stepping back into the foyer. Then, realizing I'd most likely been busted, felt the need to offer an explanation. "The pictures are really great. Kaley must dabble in photography too. I mean—I realize she's a painter, but the photos are very artistic."

"Yeah…" Shane replied, continuing to watch me with the cynicism of a seasoned cop, which I supposed he was.

"Matt!" Layla came barreling down the hall. She made an odd squealing noise as she ran. Her overabundance of enthusiasm on full display. Relieved for the distraction, I scooped her up in my arms.

"Hey kiddo! Did you have fun?" I asked.

"Yes!" She shouted. "Can Summer come over to our house next week?"

Before I could answer, Shane stepped forward, protectively placing both hands on Summer's shoulders. "How about you come back here next week, Layla? I know there's things you girls didn't get a chance to do."

"Can I? Can I, Matt? Please…" Layla pleaded.

"You'll have to ask your mama about that one, kiddo." I lowered her back down to the floor. "Now, where's your backpack and coat?"

"I'll get it," Summer offered, and scampered back down the hallway with Layla hot on her heels.

With the girls gone, it left Shane and me alone again. He took the opportunity to heighten my discomfort by silently staring daggers in my direction during their absence.

I cleared my throat, "Hurry up, Lay." I called in the direction in which the girls had disappeared. "We have to get dinner started for your mama."

Thankfully, Layla reappeared with her coat and backpack ready to go. "Bye Summer," she said, hugging her new friend. "Thank you, Shane," she added politely.

"Anytime, Layla," Shane replied. His demeanor changed when addressing the kids. "Summer would love to have you over again soon. Right, Summer?"

Summer shyly bobbed her head up and down in agreement.

I quickly led Layla away from the house and muttered, "Bye, asshole," just under my breath.

Layla looked up at me with a quizzical expression but thankfully didn't say anything.

We made it to the vehicle just as Kaley's little Honda pulled into the driveway. I fastened Layla's harness and quickly ducked in behind the wheel. I got the hell out of there before subjecting myself to further awkward interactions for the day.

Chapter 14
KALEY

I waited for Layla and her mom's boyfriend to clear the driveway. As I shifted into park, my phone rang from the passenger seat where I'd tossed it. I noticed it was Shane and ignored the call as I'd see him in a minute anyway.

I parked the SUV and made my way to the house. I was looking forward to getting the scoop on Summer's playdate. I slipped in through the side door to the kitchen. Shane was ready and waiting to bombard me.

"Kay—I don't want you alone with that Matt guy."

"Layla's step-dad?"

"Yeah—I got a weird vibe off him."

Actually, it was reassuring to hear Shane say it. I'd also felt unsettled the day I'd met Matt. I thought perhaps I was being paranoid or judging him too harshly by his toughened exterior.

"Did he do something?" I asked, setting my bag and keys down on the kitchen island.

"No—he was perfectly fine with the kids." Shane paced back and forth, his white crew socks sliding across the gray tiled floor. "And Layla seems to really like him. I can't give you an exact reason…"

"What about the girls, though? Summer and Layla are friends, and Layla seems like a really sweet kid."

He stopped pacing, "I know. Maybe have Layla here for playdates or pick the kids up and take them somewhere. I just don't want you or Summer around that guy—understand?"

I nodded. I didn't want to tell him this, but Shane was making me feel very uneasy. He always appeared so relaxed—I'd never really seen him agitated. Maybe it was an aspect of his job. Maybe I was witnessing work Shane rather than the fun Shane that Summer and I were accustomed to.

My face must have betrayed my innermost thoughts because the next thing I knew Shane was apologizing and trying to set my mind at ease. "Ahhh—hell! Sorry—I didn't mean to freak you out or anything. I'm sure I'm just being paranoid, but I'm not taking any chances with Nathan's family."

I reached out and squeezed his hand, "Thank you."

"For what?"

"Being paranoid. Making us feel safe. Keeping Nathan alive."

"He would have done the same for me," Shane stated quietly.

"Yes, he would have."

"Anyway—Kay, I have to get going," he said, dropping my hand. "But before I do—are you going to fill me in on this John guy?"

"Rapid topic change," I stated.

Shane just shrugged.

I sighed, "Not just yet."

"Really? Why?" His tone was a mix of irritation and surprise.

"I don't know... because you were Nathan's partner and... and... it's weird. Because you and I are just..." I was trying to search for an explanation.

"Hey, you can't explain us, so don't even try."

"When you're right you're right," I said with a laugh. "I just need some time to figure out what this is with John. When I decide it's something, I'll let you know."

He raised his eyebrows, "When, not if?"

I chewed my lip trying to look nonchalant and doing my best not to smile.

"I'm happy for you, Kay. You deserve this." He leaned in for a quick hug before reaching for his coat draped over a kitchen chair. "I'm going to say goodbye to the kid, and we'll talk later."

I nodded and felt appreciative for all the wonderful support Summer and I had in our lives.

Chapter 15
MATT

Layla slept on a twin-sized air mattress at the foot of our bed. I knew someday I'd be able to give her a space of her own, a room she could decorate, redecorate, and grow up in. I needed 'someday' to be sooner rather than later.

I peered down at the tiny sleeping figure. She must have crashed sometime before I finished the *Magic Treehouse* book. I couldn't help but wonder where in the story she'd drifted off. Hopefully, I wouldn't have to reread a large portion of the book again the next night. Beside the bed, there was a small file cabinet I used as a nightstand. It's where I set the book without bothering to mark the page.

I stretched and did my best to stifle a yawn. I'd always loved books. Growing up, it had been hard to get my hands on reading material. My little girl would have all the books she ever wanted; I'd make sure of that.

"Matt," Aiyona whispered from the doorway. "Looks like you're done in here," she pointed to the sleeping form. "Can we talk?"

"Yeah. I'll be right out."

I watched as Aiyona's graceful silhouette slipped away into the darkened hallway. My eyes felt grainy and heavy with sleep. I rubbed them and did my best to muster the energy to meet her in the living area. My day usually started at four-thirty in the morning with a workout, so staying up past eight-thirty at night was a challenge.

Aiyona was seated on our blue imitation leather loveseat. She patted the cushion next to her. I moved forward with caution but chose to stay standing. Aiyona rarely summoned me for a conversation, and on the rare occasion that she did—it was never pleasant. Her posture was ramrod straight; I sensed a formality to her movement that did not bode well for me.

"Everything okay?" I hated asking the question. If the question needed to be asked—everything was most definitely not okay. I lived my life waiting for the other shoe to drop—until recently that is. I had become so comfortable in our new life I'd almost forgotten there was a big bad world outside of Round Rock that was just waiting to tear me apart.

Aiyona raised her eyebrows, "I don't know? You tell me?"

I was at a loss. "Tell you what exactly…"

She sank back against the cushion with a deep sigh. "Matt, what have you gotten us into this time?"

Now I was really confused. "Aiyona, I swear to you, I have no idea what you're talking about."

"Really?" her tone was sarcastic as she cocked her head to the side.

"Baby, I swear to you—I have no idea."

"Where did you get the money, Matt?"

"What money? The only money I get is from my paycheck and it's not a lot."

"I'm not talkin' about now. I'm talkin' about a couple of years ago when we were real hard up. You dug us out of a hole, and I want to know how."

"You've got to be kidding!" I responded irritably. "Why are you askin' about this now? You didn't seem to care where it came from when we needed it."

"Damn it, you did do something illegal didn't you? When we moved here, you promised me it was a clean start. No more crap! Remember that?"

I rubbed my hands down my face. "I remember. I've done my best to stick by that. We got in a little trouble financially... do **you** remember that?"

She didn't say anything. She didn't need to. The stink-eye she was giving me was communication enough.

"Look, I screwed up; but I made it right. We are, for sure, one hundred percent honest citizens now."

"You're positive about that?"

"Again—Aiyona, I gotta ask—where is this coming from?"

"I got a phone call at work today. A phone call about you."

"Me? Who called you?"

"I don't know—some guy. The number was blocked. He said, and I quote, 'tell your boyfriend to mind his own business. If he can stay in his lane, we'll stay in ours.' What do you make of that, Matt?"

My mind was racing. A buzzing sound filled my ears. "What the hell? What does that even mean?"

"Don't you think I asked that very question?" Aiyona cried.

"And?"

"And the response was to threaten me with Layla's bio-dad!"

"Tyrone?" I asked.

"Yes, Tyrone!" Aiyona was having difficulty keeping her anxiety or anger or whatever it was contained.

"Wait... what?" I couldn't get a handle on the information she was sharing.

Aiyona lowered her voice slightly so as not to wake our sleeping child and then continued through gritted teeth. "The man said that if we wanted to keep Tyrone out of our lives you needed to keep your head down and stay out of the way."

"He said that?"

"I don't recall his exact words but yeah, that was pretty much it."

I shook my head, "And you think the call has something to do with the money I brought in a few years ago?"

"I don't know, baby," Aiyona cried. "I've been tryin' to figure it out all day. The only hint of you being up to no good was when we were in financial trouble, and you seemed to come up with funds pretty quick. Way too quick, actually. At the time, I knew something wasn't right; but I didn't want to know."

I turned to face her, "Okay—here's what happened. I got involved selling drugs to help us pay bills—"

"Ahhh—Matt!" The disappointment in her voice was evident.

"Just listen—" I urged. "I was only selling prescription crap. Nothing hardcore and as soon as I had enough to get us straight I stepped back. I haven't sold in years. That was the end of it."

"They just let you out? Just like that?" she asked, her voice heavy with disbelief.

"No—It was a little more complicated, but I got out. The bad guys went to jail, and I walked away. That's all that matters. That phone call couldn't have had anything to do with that. Could it?"

She shook her head, "That all sounds really neat and clean, Matt. Things don't really work that way."

I shrugged, "I got lucky."

Aiyona narrowed her eyes at me, "Since it's the only shady thing you can think of... pretty hard to discount the call was linked. Were you using again when you were sellin'? Did you maybe do something you don't remember doing?"

"No, Aiyona, I swear. I was drinking a little but nothing else." I thought back to the night in the bar. The night Stone died. Back to the last drink I'd had in over two years.

"Is there anything else you can think of? Maybe something more recent?" Aiyona asked, interrupting my unfortunate walk down memory lane.

I ran my hands over my bald head. I really had been doing everything straight. The only thing I could think of was the guy in coveralls, and the grocery store incident, but that kind of stuff just happened from time to time. Maybe not to everyone but definitely in my world. None of those people would have any idea who Aiyona was, though, let alone how to contact her.

"What are you thinking?" she asked anxiously.

"I'm thinking... I don't know. Back off what? All I do is go to work, the school, and home—that's it."

Aiyona's lower lip started to tremble. "I can't do this, Matt. I can deal with anything but Layla being at risk—its too much. Her demeanor had switched from anger to fear in less than 30 seconds.

I took a seat next to her and pulled her close. "Don't be scared. I'll figure this out. Nobody is going to hurt our family. I swear."

She buried her face in my sweatshirt, making her voice sound small and muffled. "You swear?"

I kissed the top of her head, "Absolutely."

Even as I said the words, I wondered if it was a promise I could keep. It wasn't the first time my family had been threatened, but it was the first time I had no idea what I was dealing with. My mind was racing. For Aiyona, I put on a brave face; but my gut told me the other shoe had finally dropped.

Chapter 16
KALEY

I was nervous to meet John's sister. My anxiety had nothing to do with her as a person, it was more about the stigma of meeting family. All of a sudden, things seemed to be moving too quickly; and I wondered why I had agreed to the dinner in the first place. I tried on my tenth outfit, black leggings with a hooded swing dress, then quickly discarded that in the growing mound of clothes littering the bedroom floor. Maybe I should just go with jeans again. I fished out a pair of dark denim skinny jeans and paired them with a red gauzy blouse over a tank top. After making several frightful faces at myself in the mirror, I decided it was as good as it was going to get, and went to hurry my daughter along.

As hard as it was for me to settle on an outfit, getting Summer ready proved to be a hundred times more difficult.

"I want to finish my painting first," she whined.

It was like watching a mini version of myself. Which was both frustrating and amazing. How many times had I said that to Nathan? Sometimes inspiration struck during very inopportune times like when my husband was trying to get us out the door for an appointment or a dinner engagement.

"If I can't get this out of my head and onto the canvas right now…" I'd said that phrase to him so many times.

Nathan would just sigh and walk away. Later, I'd find him sitting in the kitchen or the living room, nervously tapping his foot or biting at his nails. At the time, I don't think I fully realized how anxious being late made him feel. In the moment, my behavior felt justified; now, it just felt selfish, especially with Summer pulling the same crap on me. Nathan never once chided me for the behavior. He was a much better person than I could ever hope to be. Confirming that notion, I picked up my squealing daughter and carried her to the bathroom to wash up and get dressed.

"We can't be late," I explained. "John is expecting us at a certain time, and I don't want to disappoint him."

"But it's okay to disappoint me?" she shot back, her lower lip quivering.

She's only six! What would her teenage years be like? If she was using this logic on me in elementary school, what would I do with her in high school? I cringed and did my best to quell my rising anxiety. "No, Summer," I took a calming breath, "it's not okay to disappoint you. However, we made a commitment to John before you started your painting. We need to stand by that."

She crossed her arms and furrowed her brow. "I don't care if he's waiting. You made the commitment. Not me."

What was happening here? My lovely, carefree girl was turning into a sassy, self-absorbed brat right in front of my eyes. I slid down the doorway of the bathroom and sighed. I was never really a kid person. Nathan was the one who pushed for kids, not me. Although Summer was the joy of my life, I didn't always know how to handle her. Nathan knew what to do with the tantrums in the terrible twos. Nathan knew what to do when she was teething or had a fever. Me—sure I was okay when things were going smoothly. I was good at playing and making sure she had everything she needed. I really rocked out the arts and crafts, but with this type of behavior... I was hopeless.

"Okay, Summer, you win," I said, burying my face in my hands. "I'll call John and tell him we can't come, but I know that will make him very sad."

Summer sighed and plopped down next to me on the floor, mimicking my behavior. "I don't want John to be sad."

I shrugged, "Nothing I can do about that. You're the one choosing to be difficult here not me."

She hopped to her feet and then proceeded to step over my legs on her way down the hall toward her bedroom. Did she really not care? Was she honestly going back to her watercolor, or was there a chance the kid was getting ready?

After a few minutes, Summer reappeared in the doorway of the bathroom wearing red leggings and a long black sweater. "Why are you just sitting there, Mommy?" she asked, tilting her head like a confused puppy. "I thought we had to go."

I pushed off the wall and looked at her curiously. "What just happened?" I asked.

Summer sighed as if I were the one that exhausted her. "You told me to get ready and I'm ready. Now, here you are, just sittin' on the floor." She gestured to the ground dramatically. "Are we going or not?"

"You're killing me, kid!" I exclaimed before heading to the hall closet to fetch our coats. Sargent Snuggles was at Shane's house, so at least that was one less thing to worry about.

∞∞∞∞∞∞∞∞

John lived in a two-story modest cape cod. I was pretty sure it had been the home he'd shared with his now ex-wife, but I never broached the subject.

John greeted us warmly at the front door. If he'd gotten the house, the ex had gotten everything inside. The furniture was a mismatch of color and sizes. The walls practically bare, except for one large, generic, beach painting that could only be described as ugly hotel art. It reminded me of an apartment where a young twenty-something might reside. That time in life when your decorating style is simply a reflection of the hodgepodge hand-me-downs your relatives are kind enough to pass down.

John's sister strolled into the living room as he was helping us with our coats. She was tall, like her brother, with the same hazel eyes and wavy brown hair, although hers fell way past her shoulders. She offered her hand and greeted both Summer and me with a friendly handshake.

"Hi, I'm Julia. It's so nice to finally meet you!" she gushed. "Johnny's been going on and on about you two."

Including Summer in her compliment meant everything to me. Julia's mannerisms were similar to her brother's. They were very close in age, and it struck me that the similarities seemed to go beyond normal sibling genetics. "He's said a lot of wonderful things about you too," I replied, trying to remember if he'd said Julia was his older or younger sister. I knew she was his only sibling if that counted for anything.

"He did?" she feigned surprise. "Well, it's nice to know he still speaks highly of his family, even if he hasn't made any effort to see us in the last two years."

John rolled his eyes. "We get together more often than that. Don't be dramatic."

"Only because I make the trek to Wisconsin a couple of times a year!" she said, backhanding him across the chest. "I swear, when is the last time you were back to Iowa?"

"Point taken," he said. "Now, why don't I take Summer into the kitchen and show her some of the arts and crafts I bought today."

Summer clapped her hands together. "You got stuff for me?"

"You bet he did!" Julia chimed in. "My better half just about bought out the entire craft market in preparation for your visit."

I raised an eyebrow, "Your better half?"

John sighed and shook his head, "I've explained to her that's not what that term means."

Julia scoffed at her brother as he led Summer off to check out her entertainment for the evening.

Julia turned back toward me. "I assume Johnny told you we're twins…"

Ahhhh, that explained a lot: "Nope—he seems to have left out that detail," I commented.

"Oh, nice! Do I embarrass you, Johnny?" Julia raised her voice in an attempt to get a rise out of her brother. It didn't work. She waved it away and took a seat on his tattered brown sofa and patted the cushion next to her. "Come sit a bit. I would love to hear what on earth you see in that sad sack of a man," Julia teased.

I laughed and sank onto the sofa next to her. "Actually, your brother has many admirers in this town."

John peeked around the corner, "Kaley, do not tell her that! Actually, don't tell her anything." His head swiveled back and forth between the two of us.

Julia grinned, "I guess that shouldn't surprise me. He's always had a handful of followers. But he's old now—I thought some of that attention would die down."

"We're the same age!" he called out from the kitchen.

It was amusing, watching them banter back and forth. I'd never had a sibling, but I'd always pictured it this way.

"Some of us age better than others," she shot back.

∞∞∞∞∞∞

The evening was much more enjoyable than I could have imagined. John and Julia continued to rib each other. Summer had created enough art to decorate John's entire house, which she did; and I found out the guy was surprisingly accomplished in the kitchen. He served a mouthwatering parmesan chicken dish that Julia swore he did all on his own.

I learned that Julia was a nurse back in Iowa; and she was married to her high school sweetheart, who was an attorney of some kind. They had two boys, ages twelve and fourteen. Nathan also made his way into our conversation, as he always did. I appreciated the fact that John never appeared intimidated or annoyed when I brought up Nathan. He seemed to genuinely enjoy hearing both Summer and me talk about him.

By the end of the night, Summer had crashed on the sofa; and John went outside to warm my car. Julia and I were just finishing with kitchen clean-up, which gave her the opportunity to have a few words with me in private.

"I can see why Johnny likes you," she stated, wiping down his beige marble countertops. "You're really easy to talk to, and I can tell by the way you're raising Summer you're a good person."

"Thank you. I could say the same about him. I'm glad I had the opportunity to meet his 'better half'," I said, using her phrase from earlier in the evening.

"He really is you know." Julia had stopped cleaning and leaned up against the counter. "A good person, I mean."

"I know," I confirmed, unsure where she was going with the statement.

"It's just that—well... he hasn't shown interest in anyone since that bitch Tia left him. I can tell he really likes you, Kaley. Please don't take this the wrong way... It's obvious you are still very much attached to your..." she hesitated. "Well—attached to Nathan. I hope I didn't offend you. I just care about my brother and don't want to see him hurt."

I wasn't offended. I appreciated her honesty and told her so. "I will always love Nathan, and if he were to walk through that door right now that's where I'd be. The fact is, he's gone; and he's never going to come home to Summer and me again."

After two years of crying, you'd think I'd be all cried out but no such luck. I was able to keep the tears at bay when discussing the good times, but referring to Nathan's death or the things we'd never do seemed to trigger the waterworks.

"I am so sorry!" Julia said. She crossed the kitchen and wrapped me in a motherly hug. "I never should have brought it up."

I shook my head, "No, it's fine." I backed away and reached for a paper towel from the roll near the sink to wipe my eyes.

"No, it's not. I should have been more sensitive toward you. I was too concerned about protecting my dumb brother to consider your feelings."

I tossed the paper towel in the trash and took a deep breath. "For what it's worth, I have no intention of hurting John. In fact, I never intended to date anyone ever again. John is an exception. I get that he's special, and I understand your need to protect him."

As if on cue, John poked his head around the corner. "Do you want me to carry Summer to the car?"

he asked. Then spotting my red eyes and blotchy face: "Hey, everything okay in here?"

Julia spoke up, "Yes—it was me. In all my infinite wisdom, I tried to warn her away from breaking your heart; and in the process broke hers by mentioning her dead husband."

"Julia! What the hell?" John said, shooting his sister a look. He made his way across the kitchen and wrapped his arm protectively around my shoulders.

"Well, this is embarrassing." I wiped my eyes again and turned to him, "she's making it sound much worse than it was. Really—I'm fine," I said, backing away from the two of them and into the safety of the living room.

"Kaley—" John started.

"If you could carry Summer to the car that would be great," I replied, opening his coat closet and reaching for our jackets.

He nodded and gathered my sleeping girl from the sofa.

I gently placed her coat around her and opened the door for John before racing ahead of them to open the car door.

Somehow, John managed to get her safely buckled in without disturbing her sleep. The kid didn't even stir.

Julia had followed us out and was hugging herself against the cold night air. "Again—Kaley, I am so sorry."

I waved away her apology, "It's all good. Please don't give it a second thought."

Her face was lit from the exterior lights above the garage; her brow was creased and her lips drawn up tightly.

"Really," I assured her. "It's fine. You're a good sister. Now go inside before you freeze to death."

"Yes—" John added, through clenched teeth. "Please go inside."

"It was really nice meeting you, Kaley," she managed to say before jogging back toward the front stoop.

John sighed and wrapped me in his arms. "I am so sorry for whatever she said. Her intentions are good."

I squeezed him tightly. "Really, it's fine. I like her."

"Well, that makes one of us," he grumbled.

We walked around to the driver's side, and John leaned down and kissed me gently on the cheek. "Call me when you get home."

"I have no intention of hurting you." I felt the need to tell him, even though I knew he didn't need to hear it.

"I know," he replied gently before I slid in behind the wheel.

∞∞∞∞∞∞∞∞

Once back home, I had a hard time settling down for the night. I went to the kitchen with the intention to make tea. The small room off to the left caught my eye; it had been Nathan's home office. I tried not to go in there too often, as the room was one hundred percent Nathan. The space was just one more reminder of what I'd lost.

Maybe it was because I was starting to believe I could have something with John, or maybe it was the fact that I'd gotten through another year without him—whatever the case, I found myself drawn to the room. I left the empty ceramic teacup on the counter and padded lightly across the tile, stopping short of the entrance. I inhaled deeply and made my way into Nathan's office. I didn't need to turn on the light; there was enough illumination from the kitchen to see. I sank into the sturdy fabric armchair in the corner. Nathan's duty coat was still slung over the back, where he'd left it. I curled up and rubbed the sleeve across my cheek as I'd done many times before. I knew at some point I'd have to clean out the room. It made no sense to waste the space on what was starting to feel like a shrine to my dead husband. There were times when I would inhale deeply and still pick up his crisp clean scent among the dust and memories. That was not something I was ready to part with. If there came a time when I could no longer sense his presence here, then maybe I would let it go.

"Hey, Nathan—" I said aloud to the empty room.

My greeting was met with nothing other than the hum of the heating vent followed by a whoosh of warm air.

I snuggled deeper into the chair. "I met someone, Nathan. I didn't plan it—it just sort of happened. He's really good with Summer too. You'd like him..."

I closed my eyes and continued talking to the empty room. "I almost forgot, you actually did meet him. He said you helped him with some of his football kids."

I recounted my dinner with John and drifted off at some point. When I woke a while later, it took me a moment to acclimate. I stumbled across the room to the pine computer desk. The small digital clock next to the monitor read 1:11 am. I contemplated still making the tea I'd wanted over three hours prior but quickly dismissed the idea.

I stretched, said goodnight to Nathan, and padded out of the office and out through the living room. Sargent Snuggles was with Shane at his house tonight. As I passed the dog crate to click off the floor lamp, I noticed something unusual tangled up in the dog's bedding. A white notebook partially covered by blankets protruded from the edge of the crate. I bent down to retrieve the chewed paper hoping it wasn't Summer's schoolwork. I flipped through the pages, silently cursing the beast. Aside from most of the cover missing and some chewed edges, the notebook seemed otherwise intact.

Upon further inspection, I realized it was filled with Nathan's small unsteady handwriting. I smiled at the familiarity. My husband was good at many things—penmanship was not one of them. I recalled teasing him regarding his terrible handwriting. Very few people could read what Nathan wrote. Where in the hell had the dog come up with it?

I turned page after page trying to figure out what I was looking at. At first glance, I thought maybe a journal but given Nathan's personality, that seemed unlikely. As I looked closer, I concluded it might be work-related. There were a lot of names listed and pictures of people I did not recognize taped inside. There were dates and addresses along with monetary values. The notebook was relatively full. There was no way I'd get through it all tonight, but I knew I wanted to investigate it further. I would need to mention it to Shane the next day. Maybe it was a case Nathan hadn't been able to close. Maybe with Shane's help, I could do that for him; and maybe, just maybe, if I could do that, I'd finally get some sense of closure too.

Chapter 17
MATT

My eyes burst open and my muscles tightened. The room was dark. The beating of my heart so fast the rhythm seemed to pulsate through my entire body. The only sound was that of my rapid breathing in the otherwise silent bedroom. I pushed myself upright and glanced at the clock: 1:11 am.

The soft touch of Aiyona's hand on my bare back made me jump. "Baby, what's wrong?" she asked.

Sweat beaded on my forehead as I fought to catch my breath, "Nothing, sorry I woke you."

"Did you have a bad dream or something?"

In the darkness, I felt for her hand, and gave her what I hoped was a reassuring squeeze. "Everything's fine. Go back to sleep."

"Matt?"

I swiped a palm across my damp forehead and resumed my position beside her. It still felt as though my heart was beating a thousand times faster than it should be. Aiyona snuggled back under the covers and rested her arm lovingly across my chest. I waited until I heard the soft sighs of sleepiness overtake her before extricating myself from her hold. Carefully, I crept from the bedroom and made my way to the kitchen for a glass of water.

The truth was, it was a dream that startled me awake but it wasn't necessarily bad. The dream was about Stone and his family. There was another guy in the dream too; but he wasn't familiar to me, at least I didn't think he was. I'd been at the diner where Stone and I first met. I was talking to the detective, about what I couldn't recall, when his wife and Summer entered the joint with the mystery man. Stone waved to them to join us, which, they did. The next part was what had left me feeling unsettled—Stone handed me his daughter and then fixed me with his piercing blue eyes, "Help them, Matt. You owe me," he'd said. Even as I'd come fully awake Nathan Stone's deep baritone voice continued to echo in my mind.

I told myself it was just my subconscious trying to find a way to deal with Layla's new friend. The mystery man was probably just a customer, someone I had waited on earlier in the day or some other random Round Rock resident I'd come across. I ran the tap again refilling the cup.

Feeling too amped to sleep, I crept back through the living room and closed the bedroom door. With that done, I was able to turn on a lamp without disturbing the girls. I retrieved the book I was currently reading. The newest in a series by my favorite author David Baldacci. Even reading was difficult, the words were just words, and I found myself unable to get lost in the story.

Before I knew it, the sun was streaming through the window and Aiyona was gently shaking me. "Hey, have you been out here all night?"

I stretched and looked around, feeling slightly off-kilter, "Yeah—I guess so."

She felt my forehead with the back of her hand. "You feelin' okay?"

She was treating me like a child, which I found slightly endearing and kind of annoying all at the same time. "Aiyona, I'm fine," I said, in what I hoped was a reassuring tone and not at all irritable. "I just didn't sleep well."

"Is it because of the phone call I got the other day?"

My dream about Stone had actually made me forget about the veiled threat, at least for the moment. "Surprisingly, no," I answered.

"Then what?"

"Can you just let it be?" I asked.

"Fine. Whatever," she said, storming into the kitchen. Aiyona proceeded to create quite a ruckus banging around pots, pans, and various kitchen utensils as she removed the clean dishes from the drying rack near the sink.

"You mad?" I called out.

My inquiry was met with a clattering sound that caused me to sink lower into the couch cushions.

The landline phone rang from the kitchen. Aiyona snatched it up before the ringing woke Layla. It was a rare weekend treat that the little one had slept past six am.

"Yeah, he can be there," I heard my fiancée say.

I cautioned a look through the peek window that separated our kitchen from the living room. "Where can I be?"

She replaced the handset back on the base, "Work." Turning her back to me she busied herself with the task of preparing breakfast.

"This isn't my weekend, though, I was planning on hanging out with you and Layla today."

She shrugged, "We need the money, Matt. And you're keeping things from me anyway. I'd rather you go to work than stay here and keep lyin' to my face."

"What am I keeping from you? I told you about the drugs. That's the only thing I kept from you, I swear."

She stomped into the living room and paused, placing her hand on her hip. "Then what about last night?"

I sighed, "It was a stupid dream. I'm not keeping anything from you. It wasn't even real."

"Well, it was real enough to upset you. It was real enough to keep you on the couch all night."

"I fell asleep reading. You're making a big deal of nothing."

Layla emerged from the bedroom and chose that particular moment to cannonball right into me on the couch. Her bony knees connected with a very sensitive area.

I let out a rush of air and doubled over. "Layla...honey," I choked out her name as I gritted my teeth. It was everything I could do not to cry out like a little girl. "I thought... we talked about... jumping on people. Especially—people who aren't expecting it."

"Sorry, Matt!" She giggled and skipped off into the kitchen to forage for food. Leaving me in the fetal position and groaning in agony.

Aiyona pointed her finger at me, "Serves you right! That's karma, baby," she said, with a satisfied chuckle. Then, she spun on her heel and tromped off in the same direction as her man-killing spawn.

"That's not karma," I moaned. "How does that even make sense, Aiyona? That's a sign Layla has too much sugar in her diet. That girl is too hyper."

"Sorry, Matt!" Layla called again from the kitchen.

"It's okay, Lay," I uttered as I limped my way to the bathroom to shower before work.

∞∞∞∞∞∞

The store was much busier than it had been all week. That's why my boss had called, they needed all 'hands-on-deck.' With the holidays just around the corner, things were starting to pick up.

"Hey, Matt," Dwayne greeted me cheerfully. "There's a guy who has some questions about those humidifiers we got in last week. Can you help him?"

"Yeah—give me a second," I said, as I made my way to the break room to hang my jacket and throw the hodgepodge lunch I'd created into the refrigerator. Normally, Aiyona prepared lunch for me, but she was still a little prickly before I left. Which meant I was on my own and resulted in a bunch of random plastic containers from the fridge hastily tossed into a grocery bag. I had no idea what lunch would be; but surprises were good, they kept life fresh, or so I told myself.

I exited the break room to track down Dwayne. It wasn't hard; he was waiting on the other side of the door for me. "Thanks for coming in, buddy. It's a madhouse in here today."

"No problem. You mentioned a customer...?"

"Yes. I think he's still in aisle eight. He asked for you specifically."

That seemed odd. I strode across the store to aisle eight. There was only one shopper, the cop from Stone's house. He was standing in the center holding the box for a room-size humidifier, mouthing the words as he read the information from the packaging.

"Any questions I can answer for you, sir?"

He turned with a smile, "Why yes, yes, you can but not about the humidifier."

"Okay," I said turning on my heel, anxious to move on.

"Hey, wait a minute, that doesn't mean I don't have questions."

I turned back. "There's something else?"

"Yeah—there's something else." He set the box down and considered me for a moment. "I knew you looked familiar when I saw you at Kaley's the other day. I assumed I'd just seen you around town, like here, ya know."

I didn't say anything. The silence prompted him to continue with whatever it was he had to say. "But then, I thought about it a little harder, and guess what, Matt?"

I shrugged.

"I did some digging, and now I'm thinking I recognize your face from my place of business—not yours."

Well, that answered one question, I thought. He didn't know anything about me through Detective Stone. Not if he had to go digging.

"I haven't been in any trouble here, and I plan to keep it that way," I said sincerely.

"That's good to hear. And I fully support reformed criminals. It's rare for them to actually be fully reformed, but I support the effort, nonetheless."

What a condescending ass. I thought the old Matt would have called him out on it, but the new Matt kept his mouth shut. New Matt didn't need any more problems, especially coming off the grocery store fiasco.

"Anyway, in your ongoing effort to be a pillar of our fine society, I'm going to offer a suggestion."

I sighed, "You want me to stay away from Kaley and her daughter."

"Ding, ding, ding," the cop remarked condescendingly. "You're pretty smart for a criminal. Maybe you'll make it on this side of the bars after all."

I said nothing. I wouldn't give the blowhard the satisfaction.

He slid the box he'd been examining across the floor with his foot. "Take this to the front for me. I got some shopping left to do."

"Absolutely, sir," I said with a nod of my head. "Is there anything else I can help you find?"

His eyes scanned me coolly from head to toe, "I doubt it," he said dismissively.

"Okay," I bent to pick up the humidifier.

"Just remember what we talked about, and we'll be simpatico." He gave my shoulder a hearty pat before brushing past me and out of the aisle.

The timeline was starting to make some sense now. The cop had just told me he'd been digging and Aiyona's call at work... most likely not a coincidence. Did the cop know he'd stirred a hornet's nest or was that simply a side effect?

Chapter 18
KALEY

It was my Saturday to have the gallery open. Summer and I got an early start. Summer settled herself at a table near the front of the store and was soon deeply engrossed in a watercolor project. This left me free to catch up on emails and go through online orders in my office in the loft area of the gallery.

The bell chimed, alerting me to the fact that someone had entered the store. That sound was followed by happy chatter and lots of giggling. I abandoned my administrative duties, grateful for any kind of distraction, and made my way to the main floor. Sargent Snuggles was eagerly licking his smallest human while Shane looked on with amusement.

"Hey, it's still your weekend. Don't try and pawn Sargent off early." The comment was made in jest. Truth be told, the dog had grown on me; and despite my initial resistance, I missed the furry guy when he was at his other home.

"Wouldn't dream of it," Shane replied. "Sargent Snuggles and I have big plans today."

"Doin' what?" Summer asked.

"Well, we just went to the hardware store to buy a humidifier. After we get that set up for Josie, we're going for a run. Then possibly some Christmas shopping."

"Big plans indeed," I agreed.

Sargent Snuggles was on his back, thoroughly enjoying the belly rubs Summer was offering up when Shane asked to speak away from little ears. I led him upstairs to my office under the assumption he wanted to discuss Christmas gifts; he didn't.

"Don't be mad..." he said cautiously. "But I did something you probably won't like."

"Oh, boy," I leaned against the desk and folded my arms across my chest, mentally preparing myself for the blow. "What did you do?"

Shane rubbed his scruffy chin and nervously avoided my eyes. "I know it's not my place, but I ran into Matt Pine at the hardware store."

"What do you mean ran into? I'm pretty sure he works there."

"He does, he does," Shane said, still avoiding eye contact.

I shifted uncomfortably. "Oh my gosh, you didn't go there to tell him to stay away from us... did you?"

"Well, yes and no."

"What does that mean?"

"It means I went there to buy a humidifier, but... I might have warned him away."

"Where do you get off?"

He held up his hands. "I know—like I said it isn't my place."

"Shane, the guy has done nothing wrong."

"Well... that's not necessarily true..."

"Okay, let's hear it. What did Matt Pine do?"

"Well, I did some digging—"

I held up my hand to stop him, "You know what, I don't want to know. He has his right to privacy. Just because you're a cop and don't like the way he looks doesn't give you the right. It's an abuse of power," I stopped, "unless he's a danger to Summer... Is he a danger to Summer?"

"I don't think so."

"Okay, then that's all I need to know."

"Kay, I just think—"

I pushed away from the desk and patted Shane on the shoulder in way of dismissal. "I don't want any part of this. I already told you, I'll make sure not to be home alone with him. That's probably an unnecessary precaution in itself." I brushed past him and exited the office.

Shane followed me down the few steps that led to the front of the store. "Look, I get it. I screwed up. That's why I'm telling you upfront."

I sighed and sat down at the edge of my large display cube at the center of the store. We were talking quietly enough so as not to be overheard by Summer. Not that she was at all interested in us anyway, not with Sargent Snuggles around. "What exactly did you say?"

"Not much," he looked around the gallery, focusing his attention anywhere but on me. "I hinted that I was aware of his past and asked him to steer clear."

"You didn't! Seriously? What did he say?"

"He said he would and was extremely professional."

"Shane! That's embarrassing. What if that affects the friendship between Summer and Layla?"

"I thought of that. That's why I asked to speak with his boss."

I jumped up, "You did what?"

"No, no, it's okay," he waved his hands urgently. "It's not what you think. I told old Ollie what a good employee he had. I said I was extremely pleased with his courtesy and knowledge and recommended he give him a raise."

"You did?" I asked skeptically.

"I honestly did, Kay. I knew you would be pissed when you found out. So, I tried to make it right."

"Well, that's something at least."

He backed off, seemingly pleased with himself. "I did good then," he stated rather than asked.

I laughed, "No Shane—you did bad. Really bad, but then... you slightly redeemed yourself."

He rubbed his hands together with pleasure and finally met my eyes. "That's better than I thought, so I'm good with that."

I rolled my eyes and debated about whether or not to tell him about Nathan's notebook. In a spur-of-the-moment decision, I decided to keep it to myself, for a little while anyway. As Shane had just shared, he could be impulsive, and that made me wary. I also wanted to explore the information further. I had no idea what, if anything, I had. If nothing else, digging deeper made me feel close to Nathan again.

Shane stood there grinning like an idiot, still feeling quite pleased with himself, I was sure.

"Can you stick around?" I asked. "There are some new pieces to put in the display cube, and you know what a pain that can be."

He nodded and gestured toward the odd multidimensional glass case beside me. "I remember helping Nathan pick that thing up. You hated it, remember that?"

I smiled at the memory, "Well, yeah, it was ugly and impractical."

"Nathan had a vision, though."

I admired the case for a moment before ducking behind the check-out counter to retrieve the pottery I wanted to exhibit. "Yeah, he fixed the aesthetic. It's still impractical, though."

"Why? Because you have to shimmy underneath to get anything inside?" he asked, raising his eyebrows.

I laughed, "Yep, and after that, you still have no idea how it looks until you can extricate yourself from the monstrosity."

"Well, it always looks impressive, so I'd say you figured it out."

"Thank you," I replied quietly, feeling my cheeks flush slightly at the compliment.

"So, how about I crawl underneath so you can hand off and direct," Shane suggested.

I happily accepted his offer. Working together we had the new display ready to go in under twenty minutes.

"Mommy, Uncle Shane, it's snowing!" Summer called from across the room. She'd abandoned her art to peer out the large storefront window, which offered a wide view of historic Round Rock's main street.

I joined Summer at the window where she had her face pressed up against the glass. Resisting the urge to do the same, I looked out onto Round Rock's main drag. Fluffy white flakes floated down from the sky giving the impression of being trapped inside a giant snow globe. Although snow is not my favorite, I had to admit the scene was beautiful.

"I hope we get enough to finally go sledding," she commented gleefully.

"If we do, I'm going with you, okay?" Shane said, squatting down beside her.

"Promise?" Summer asked.

"Pinkie swear," he said, offering her his little finger. My daughter laughed and reciprocated by holding out her own. After making it official, Shane stood and ruffled her hair. "Alright—we'll see you two later," he said, pulling Sargent Snuggles' leash from his coat pocket and hooking up the scruffy mutt.

As Shane made his exit, a gust of wind blew the flakes into the gallery along with a blast of arctic air. He made faces as he jogged past the window, causing Summer to squeal as we watched him go.

Chapter 19
MATT

My long, busy workday eventually came to a close. When it was time to lock up for the night, I realized I hadn't even had time for my mystery lunch. I still had no idea what I'd brought but thought it best to leave it in the staff fridge. There was a strong possibility I'd still be in the doghouse with Aiyona on Monday. I loved her like crazy, but the lady could hold a grudge like none other. There was no way I was going to tell her about the dream because then I'd have to explain the rest. Although I'd told her about the dealing, I didn't feel further details would be particularly helpful. Especially considering the guy who trusted me ended up with a bullet to the brain.

Along the same lines, I'd have to make sure to be busy on the days Layla would be with her new friend. I didn't want to poke the bear any more than I already had. All I wanted was to live a quiet, peaceful existence. What was it about me that seemed to attract trouble?

"Matt, great job today," Dwayne said, entering the break room behind me. He stepped around and reached for his brown parka hanging on the coat rack.

"Ahhh—thanks," I replied, having no idea what he was referring to.

"Not sure what you did, but that customer gave you a glowing review. Even asked to talk to Ollie about you."

"What customer?"

"You know—the guy with the humidifier, Shane Gavin."

I clenched my jaw and felt my muscles seize up, "Gavin asked to speak with the boss?"

"He sure did!"

That couldn't be good, "Is Ollie still here?" I asked, trying to keep my voice even despite my rising anxiety.

Dwayne scratched his head. "Yeah—I think he's in his office. Everything okay?"

I waved him off. "Oh yeah—I just have to touch base on my schedule that's all. Thanks for letting me know about that customer," I added.

Dwayne brightened, "You bet! See ya Monday," he zipped his parka and toddled off.

Once Dwayne was out the door, I made my way upstairs to Ollie's office, skipping steps in my haste. It was as I reached his office door that I hesitated, not sure if I really wanted to know what Gavin had said to my boss. However, I reasoned it was better to be prepared than not. I rapped lightly on the wooden door.

"Come on in!" came the muffled response from the other side.

I walked into the sparse office. It consisted of a moderate-sized metal desk and file cabinet. A window ran the length of the room and looked over the entire store.

Ollie was around sixty with a bald head and gold-framed spectacles. He was short, stocky, and wore a permanent frown that was completely misleading. When it came down to it, Ollie was an old softie.

"What can I do for you, Matt?" he asked, removing his glasses to wipe them on the hem of his red flannel shirt.

I didn't budge from the doorway. "Dwayne mentioned a customer asked to speak with you about me?" I shifted nervously waiting for a response.

"Ahhh yes—Shane Gavin—he said you were most helpful today." Ollie nudged his glasses back in place. "Shane commented on how polite and informative you were. He was very happy with your service."

I let out a breath. "Wow—okay. Thanks." I turned to walk away.

"Matt—" Ollie called me back. "You seemed surprised."

"Well... normally when a customer asks to speak to your boss—it's not good news."

Ollie chuckled, "True, true. People don't tend to share when they've had a positive experience, do they?"

"No, sir."

Ollie reached into his desk drawer and pulled out an envelope. "Here, Matt—I was planning on giving you this at the holiday party, but I'm guessing you could use it a little sooner. You need to make sure that little girl of yours has a good Christmas."

I liked how he referred to Layla as mine. Ordinarily, it was your stepdaughter or Aiyona's little girl; but Ollie had said she was mine. That felt good. "Thank you," I said, stepping forward to accept the gift. "You really don't have to—"

He cut me off, "Yes, I do. All my employees get a bonus this time of year. But Matt, if you could keep this to yourself, I'd appreciate it. You may have done a bit better than the rest," he said with a wink.

I wasn't sure how to respond, "Thank you." I said searching for the right words. "You have no idea how much this means."

He nodded, "I think I do. Anyway, we'll see you Monday. And bring Layla round with you. I got some new markers and coloring books for her in my desk," he said, patting the drawer to his right.

"Absolutely." I left with a bit of a bounce in my step. I had no idea what kind of game Shane Gavin was playing, but it didn't matter. For the moment, things were going my way.

Once I reached my Impala, I hastily wiped the snow away from the windshield with my bare hand before sliding behind the wheel to tear into the white envelope from Ollie. I was not disappointed. Five hundred dollars in cash! I felt a childlike giddiness wash over me. That amount hadn't even been on my radar.

I glanced out the partially snow-covered windshield, catching a glimpse of Ollie as he ambled out of the store toward his truck. I scrambled out of the Impala and sprinted across the parking lot toward him. Without thinking, I grabbed my boss in a giant bear hug that lifted him off the ground. I thanked him again and ran back to my car with a whoop, leaving Ollie in the parking lot laughing and shaking his head at his unruly employee. My behavior actually reminded me a lot of Layla. Thankfully, I hadn't accidentally kneed Ollie in the groin in my rush of enthusiasm.

Chapter 20
KALEY

John and I continued to see each other once to twice a week. Before either of us understood what was happening, we became a couple. I learned subtle and not-so-subtle things about his personality like: Sunday was for NFL and church only, no exceptions. I also learned, that in addition to being the high school football coach, he was the Assistant Athletic Director for the school district. I discovered that he did this nervous laugh thing when he was uncomfortable. I also noticed that people gave him a lot of attention; women were flirty and the men complimentary and both things brought on the nervous laugh.

He, in turn, learned not to talk to me when inspiration struck; and when that happened, I called it an 'artist binge.' He found out that I could be very antisocial and preferred a good book to the company of strangers. Most importantly, he understood that Summer came first, and he took my daughter into consideration when planning everything. He even became a pro at sneaking vegetables into Summer's food which even further endeared him to me.

As we approached the winter holidays, though, there was one glaring aspect of our relationship that might be an issue. Although I was starting to consider us a couple—we hadn't actually sealed the deal with a kiss. Sure, there had been affectionate pecks here and there but an actual full-on passionate new relationship kiss—that had yet to occur. It was not something I wanted to rush into. At first, the thought of kissing another man made my stomach churn. Then, I went through a phase where I just wanted it to happen if only to prove I could overcome that hurdle. When it still didn't happen, I wondered if John just wasn't as invested as I was. Perhaps he was looking for a way to let me down easy; he certainly had other options.

These were the thoughts running through my mind as I worked on an impressionistic painting of a lake scene. I found the painting to be uninspired and truly lacking. Perhaps a reflection of my current relationship? Needless to say, I was not thrilled to discover both my work life and love life were blah.

My gaze wandered from my easel to the large industrial clock that was visible from any spot on the main floor of the gallery. I still had an hour before I needed to pick Summer up from school. I decided right then and there that it was time to push John for better or worse. I locked up the gallery and fled for my vehicle not giving myself a moment to rethink the decision.

It was as I pulled into the parking lot and faced the sprawling brick school building that I realized I wasn't dressed for success. In my old paint-splattered overalls and ball cap, I couldn't hold a candle to the cute suburban moms that frequently fawned over John. The hesitation over my outfit was fleeting. I'd made a decision, and I was nothing if not stubborn.

I had to answer a few questions through a speaker attached to the exterior of the building before I was allowed to enter Round Rock High School. Once I was buzzed into the vestibule separating the academic environment from the rest of the world, the nervousness set in. With shaky hands, I pulled open the big glass door that led to a brightly lit office. Straight ahead was a tan reception desk that filled the majority of the room. I faked confidence as I approached the stern-looking woman seated behind it and proceeded to ask for Coach Kyler.

The secretary gave me a disproving look and dialed a number. "John—it's Mary Nicole. You have a visitor in the office... Just a minute." She held her hand over the receiver, "who shall I say is here?"

"Kaley," I replied.

She peered at me over the top of her stylish, smokey colored eyeglasses, "Just Kaley?"

"Yep—he'll know."

Her lips tightened down into a frown as she took her hand off the receiver to relay the information. I decided she was attractive but probably scared people with her ornery nature. The secretary ended the call and gave me a once-over. "He'll be here in a minute. Are you planning on going into the rest of the school?"

"Ummm, I don't know. I guess I hadn't thought about it."

"I need your license."

"Excuse me?"

She rolled her eyes impatiently. "If you plan to leave the office area, then I need to scan your license and issue you an ID badge."

I realized I hadn't thought to bring my purse. "I'll just stay here."

The side door that led into the rest of the school opened, and John stepped into the office looking professional and way overdressed in comparison to me. He was wearing gray trousers and a button-down shirt with a tie.

"Kaley—I didn't know you were stopping by," he greeted me with a warm smile. "Great surprise! C'mon' I'll show you around the school," he said, offering his hand.

"She can't." Mary Nicole said tightly, "no ID."

I shrugged, "Sorry. I didn't bring my bag."

"I'll vouch for her," John said, pulling me out into the hall before Mary Nicole could protest. "I'll show you my office."

We walked down a narrow, fluorescent-lit corridor and past the gymnasium. As we rounded the corner, I was caught off guard by a young guy and girl leaning against a row of lockers engaged in a salacious form of PDA.

"Hey!" John's voice had dropped a couple of octaves causing both kids to jump. "Get to class!" he snapped.

The kids mumbled apologies and avoided eye contact as they hurried away in opposite directions.

I suppressed a laugh, "Does that happen often?"

John looked at me quizzically, "Didn't you go to high school, Kaley?"

"Well, yeah. But I think I was older than those two!"

He chuckled, "That's just because we're old now."

"Speak for yourself! Anyway, I certainly didn't do that in high school—at least not out in the open."

He narrowed his eyes, sizing me up. "Really?"

My jaw dropped, "You don't believe me!"

He tilted his head, considering me for a moment: "No. Not really."

"Hey, I was a good girl!" I said, playfully slugging him in the shoulder.

"Sure you were," he joked, pulling me around the corner, preventing me from further defending myself.

We entered the gymnasium where a gym class was playing basketball. The sound of shoes squeaking on the hardwood along with the echo of voices bouncing off the concrete walls brought back memories of my own high school phy-ed experiences.

The rear of the gym opened into a suite of offices. The office off to the far right displayed a large gold nameplate that read John Kyler. John ushered me inside, pulling the door closed behind us. The office was small and cluttered. There were piles of paperwork everywhere and uniforms strewn across chairs, not to mention several equipment bags shoved up against the sidewall. A large window occupied the back wall of the room. Had the blinds not been drawn, the office might have felt bigger or at least cheerier. However, the lack of light made it feel depressing and cramped. A plug-in deodorizer protruding from a wall outlet did the job of replacing the odor of sweat with a light vanilla fragrance.

John perched on the edge of his desk and looked at me expectantly. "I'm guessing your unexpected visit wasn't brought on by a sudden desire to see my glorious workspace." He held his arms wide gesturing toward the mess as though it were some sort of prize.

I smiled, "No—although this is pretty amazing." My voice dripped with sarcasm.

He smiled at that, "Not that I'm complaining—but why are you here?" His hazel eyes searched mine.

I shifted uncomfortably. This seemed like a much better idea when I was painting in the safety of my studio, but it was time to put it all out there. "John— why haven't you kissed me?"

"What?" He laughed—his nervous laugh.

"Why haven't we kissed? I think we're dating... We always have fun, but you've made absolutely no move to kiss me."

"I've kissed you. Now, you—you are the one who hasn't kissed me." He was using humor to deflect. It was one more thing I liked about him. However, I'd come here with a goal in mind, so I plowed ahead.

"You know what I mean. I'm not talking about a peck on the cheek," I hesitated for a moment. "Are you just not that into me? You don't have to let me down gently just because I'm a widow... I mean, you could let me down a little gently—but I'd rather know the truth than not."

John did his nervous laugh again and swiped his hand down his face. "Are you done?"

Unable to make eye contact, I started to pick at the paint flecks on my fingers, "That depends..."

"On?"

"On what you have to say next."

He tossed his hands up in exasperation. "Kaley, what are you doing with me?" The question was unexpected. He was still perched at the edge of the desk, although he did not look as comfortable as he did initially. "I'm more than ten years older than you," he continued. "Not to mention the fact that I'm obsessed with a sport you can't stand, and I don't have the first clue about art. You're young, beautiful, and incredibly talented. You could do so much better than a hopeless bachelor."

I took a couple of tentative steps forward, situating myself in front of him. "Is that what you really think? Or are you looking for an out?"

"You think I want out?"

I shrugged, "Rumor has it women throw themselves at you. Maybe the question is—why would you settle for me?"

He looked away and chuckled, this time a genuine sound not brought on by nervous energy. Before I had time to contemplate the meaning behind the laughter, John grasped the straps of my overalls and pulled me close. He gently lifted the ball cap from my head and placed it on the desk. There was no time to worry about my crazy hat hair, as John tenderly took my face in his hands. The rough texture of his palms against my cheeks sent a shiver up my spine. John's lips brushed against mine and I melted into him. We spent the next several minutes in a heavy make-out session. Not to brag or anything, but I was quite certain the coach and I could put those horny hallway teenagers to shame.

John pulled away first. "I'd like the record to show," he spoke the words slowly and in a low hushed tone. "That I initiated the kiss."

I laughed and rested my forehead against his, "Duly noted."

His arms were wrapped around me and I wasn't eager for the moment to end. "Now, Kaley, just because we're making out after over a month of seeing each other, I don't want you to get the impression I'm easy."

"Ha! First off—Mr. Kyler, if you think that makes you easy... I have a lot to teach you. Secondly—why did it take so long?"

"First off," he repeated mocking my tone. "I can't wait for those lessons. And secondly—I didn't want to rush you. You set the pace, okay?"

"I appreciate that," I said, running my fingers through his unruly hair. "Think it's too soon to kiss you again?"

"Probably," he shrugged. "But I'll take my chances."

Our second kiss was even better than the first, with one exception. We were interrupted by a knock at the door. The sour-faced secretary poked her head in the office. "John... oh, I'm so sorry," she stammered, stepping back as she realized what she'd just interrupted.

I quickly backed away from John, allowing him to maintain some sense of professionalism. "It's okay, Mary Nicole. What can I do for you?"

The secretary reappeared in the doorway. "Mr. and Mrs. Bauer are here for the parent meeting you have scheduled."

John glanced at his watch and ran his hand through his hair, "Shoot—it's that late already?"

Mary Nicole nodded, "Do you want me to set them up in the conference room?"

"Yes, please. I'll be there in a few minutes."

She turned and quietly closed the door behind her.

"Kaley, I gotta run," he said apologetically. "Can I show you the rest of the school another time?"

"I got the highlights," I replied, reaching for my ball cap.

He smiled. "Can I take you and Summer to dinner tonight?"

"Only if you promise no fast food or bar food."

"Deal. Come on—I'll walk you out," he said, offering me his hand again.

Chapter 21
MATT

I waited nearly a week to tell Aiyona about the bonus from Ollie. I knew the vet clinic had been busy, and I hadn't been around much to help. Also, Layla had been kind of a handful with all the excitement of the holidays approaching. For once, I was able to get home early. It would be nice to share some good news for a change. Things were finally going well, and that was something to be celebrated. It was a challenge making it home before Aiyona started dinner, but I managed.

I flung open the kitchen door and made my announcement. "Load up, we're going out to dinner!"

Aiyona rounded the corner from the living room and narrowed her eyes at me.

I decided to move onto Layla instead. If there was anyone in the household that could match my enthusiasm, the little one was my best bet.

"Layla!" I called, bounding into the living room past my irritated fiancée, "I have a surprise for you!"

Layla came charging out of the bedroom at full speed. This time, I was prepared and scooped her up before she barreled into me. "What's the surprise?" she squealed.

"I'm taking my girls out to dinner. After that, we're going to write a letter to Santa so you can tell him what you want this year."

"Matt!"Aiyona snapped, from the edge of the room. "Have you lost your mind?" She lowered her voice. "We don't have money for that kind of stuff."

I set Layla down and crossed the room to Aiyona. If this news didn't soften her, nothing would. I handed her the envelope.

She peered inside, her eyes widening, "Matt! What the hell, baby! Where did you get this?"

I smiled, "Ollie—it's my Christmas bonus."

"Seriously?" She handed the envelope back and put her hands to her mouth, stifling a happy scream.

"Go get dressed," I prompted. "We're treating ourselves tonight."

The girls whooped and ran into the bedroom to change. "Where are we going?" Aiyona called out from the other side of the door.

"Anywhere you want!" I yelled back and laughed as they both whooped again.

∞∞∞∞∞∞∞∞

Aiyona picked a little restaurant she passed every day on her way to work. It was jam-packed, a good indication that it was probably better than anything we had in Round Rock. The joint had a classic supper club feel—dim lighting with lots of dark wood and a lot of red; red tablecloths, red velvet chairs, and where we were in the entrance—red leather benches. Layla did better than I did with the hour-long wait. The tantalizing smells of garlic, herbs, meats, and pasta permeated my nostrils and triggered loud, longing growls from my stomach which made me irritable.

Once we were finally seated, Layla started to shriek. It took me a moment to realize the sound she was making was a happy one. The little girl ran off, past the fireplace in the middle of the dining area to a table across the restaurant.

I started to follow but stopped short realizing the cause for her excitement.

"What is it?" Aiyona asked, coming up from behind me.

"Looks like she found her friend," I said, gesturing across the room toward the back wall where Summer was seated with her mom. From my vantage point, I could see they also had a dinner companion, a man; but I didn't think it was Detective Gavin.

"Oh! Is that Summer?" Aiyona asked.

I'd forgotten they'd only spoken on the phone and had yet to meet in person. "Yes, it is. You should go over and say hi," I suggested, making my way back to our table.

Aiyona grabbed me by the elbow steering me across the room instead, "Introduce us."

"Naw—I have to hold our table," I said, trying to pry myself from her grasp.

Aiyona nudged me forward, "Don't be silly. Our table isn't going anywhere. This will just take a second."

Before I realized it, we were on top of Stone's family. Kaley and her male companion had stood to shake hands with Aiyona. Kaley offered me a small wave, and I wondered if she knew about my conversation with Detective Gavin.

The man she was with reached past her and offered me a hearty handshake. It wasn't until he said his name and I, in turn, told him mine that I really looked at the guy. I knew him from around Round Rock—that wasn't the issue, though. The issue was that this was the guy from my dream about Stone.

Apparently, I was unable to hide my surprise because the man asked if I was okay.

I staggered back a bit not sure how to respond.

"Baby, are you okay?" Aiyona asked, reaching for my waist.

I tried my best to recover. "Ummm... yeah, I'm sorry," I said, shaking my head. "I haven't eaten all day. I'm just feelin' off."

"Are you sure?" the guy asked.

"Positive." I took a few tentative steps back. "It was really nice meeting you, sir," I said, as I continued to back up slowly. "And seeing you again Summer and Kaley," I added, before spinning around and smacking right into the table behind me. The couple seated there gazed up, wearing equally shocked expressions. I had rattled the glasses and knocked some silverware to the floor. I apologized as I retrieved the utensils and did my best to inconspicuously make my way back to our table. However, my behavior and overall aesthetic didn't really lend well to being inconspicuous.

Moments later, Aiyona and Layla returned. "Are you sure you're okay, Matt?" Layla asked, her little face scrunched up with concern.

I nodded and took a gulp of water, "I'm just a little dehydrated," I said and apologized again.

"It's okay," Aiyona said, patting my knee under the table. "We'll get some appetizers or something—it's probably my fault you feel this way anyway."

"Your fault?"

"Yeah—I haven't been the nicest to you lately. And haven't been packing your lunches or making sure you're eating healthy."

"It's okay," I stated, pairing it with my most sorrowful expression. However awkward the last few moments had been, it had worked in my favor. Not only was my fiancée no longer angry with me, but now she was blaming herself for my cringe-worthy behavior. I seemed to be racking up the points after all and excused myself to use the restroom before I messed up a good thing.

As I exited the bathroom, I was feeling more like myself. I stopped briefly in the dimly lit corridor and gave myself a once over, making sure I hadn't splashed water on my tan chinos or denim button-down shirt before returning to the dining area.

"Hey, Matt!" A feminine voice called from behind.

I turned to see Kaley. I hadn't noticed before, but she looked really good. It wasn't just the outfit, a snug black dress, and a short red faux leather jacket. She looked happy, relaxed, lighter than the last time I'd seen her.

"Hey," I responded, feeling uncertain if I should stay or bolt.

"Hey—" she said again, fidgeting uncomfortably with her hands. "I feel like maybe I'm the reason you weren't feeling so great back there."

I wasn't sure what to say. So I said nothing.

She looked uncomfortable and lowered her voice. "You know, because of what Shane said to you in the hardware store."

So, she did know. "I really didn't know your family would be here tonight," I offered. "I'm not following you or anything. I'm sorry I make you uncomfortable. I told your friend I'd stay away."

"This is so embarrassing. I didn't know Shane was going to do that. He had no right. You don't make me uncomfortable..." she paused. "Well, you actually do... but that's really more my problem than yours."

I tried to smile, "Well, at least you're honest."

"To a fault," she replied. "Look—Shane is very overprotective, which is comforting but unnecessary. Our girls are friends, and I want you to feel welcome to pick up Layla, okay?"

"Okay."

She tried to reassure me by giving my upper arm a friendly squeeze. "Wow! You have some serious muscle there—don't you. I mean—wow!"

This time it was easy to smile, "Thanks."

"See—honest to a fault," she repeated. "Anyway, I'm going back to enjoy my dinner. I hope you do the same. I look forward to seeing you again soon."

"Shane put in a good word with my boss so don't be too embarrassed," I said.

"Good to know. It still wasn't okay, though, and I told him so."

"Thank you."

"You're welcome," she stated and turned to leave.

"Hey—Kaley," her name sounded unnatural on my tongue. In my head, I'd always thought of her as Stone's wife or Summer's mom. "The man you're with... he looks familiar... would I know him from somewhere?"

"Oh—probably, he's the football coach at the high school, John Kyler. Maybe from there?"

Nope, I thought, that aint it; but to her, I said, "Yeah—that makes sense."

"Well, goodnight, Matt."

"Goodnight, Kaley."

Chapter 22
KALEY

As Christmas drew closer, it was the first time since Nathan passed that I wasn't dreading the holiday. Instead of drowning in misery, I found myself watching the activity of the season through the eyes of my daughter, and her excitement was contagious.

Not only had I fallen prey to Summer's holiday spirit, but John had as well. He spent an entire afternoon helping her craft a homemade gingerbread house, and not the kind that comes from a kit, either. From baking gingerbread to constructing the perfect edible frosting. They constructed the real deal.

After spending a half-hour scrubbing frosting from my daughter's hair, I tucked her in for the night. Then, I made my way to the kitchen, where John was still cleaning up the aftermath of the fun but very messy project.

"Where did you learn to do that?" I asked. "Seriously, you are amazing!"

He shrugged. "My mom used to make them with me and Julia when we were kids. It's always been one of my favorite Christmas memories. I thought Summer might enjoy it too. I made a call, got the recipe and instructions, and voila," he said, gesturing to their sweet creation occupying the center of our kitchen island.

"Impressive."

"My mom neglected to mention the mess, though," he added, taking in the assortment of mixing bowls, utensils, and sugary confections occupying every square inch of my kitchen countertops.

"Well worth it I'd say." I grabbed a dishcloth, preparing to take over for him.

He came up behind me and wrapped his arms around my waist, pulling the cloth from my grasp in the process. "Go, relax, I got this."

"Are you kidding me?" I exclaimed. "You cook and clean! Not to mention how good you are with Summer! I swear, John Kyler, you may be the perfect man."

He shot me a look.

"Too mushy?"

"You're walking a line, Kaley," he teased. "I'll let it slide and hope you remember how you feel right now."

"Why is that?"

He chuckled, "Because—come high school football season... you're going to think I'm the most unreliable, obsessed, and self-absorbed man you've ever met."

I shook my head, "I don't believe you."

"You just wait," he said, pointing a finger at me. "I swear to you—come August you are going to think I'm the worst boyfriend in the world."

My eyes involuntarily widened. John putting a label on our relationship suddenly made this whole thing very real.

John cleared his throat uncomfortably, "Well now, I realize I just made some pretty big assumptions..." His nervous laugh made an appearance. "And I didn't mean to imply anything. I just meant—I can be kind of an ass... I'm not perfect..." He let the sentence peter out and cleared his throat again.

It was painful listening to him wrestle with an explanation. However, I wasn't sure how I felt much less how to respond, so I stayed quiet.

"Kaley..." He said my name with caution. "I'm going to need you to say something here because I'm feeling just a tad vulnerable, and I mean that in the manliest way possible."

I smiled and met his eyes; he definitely appeared uncomfortable. In that moment, I realized that the label didn't matter. I didn't have to make any long-term commitments to ease his anxiety. John was living in the moment. All I needed to do was meet him there. "Ummm, John..." I started, wading my way through my emotions.

"Yes?"

"I don't like the term boyfriend. It makes us sound like we're teenagers dating. I certainly don't want to be called your girlfriend. There has got to be a better, more mature term."

He offered me a lopsided smile and turned back toward the sink full of dirty dishes. The awkwardness of the situation slowly faded away. "So then, Kaley, how should I refer to you?" He started scrubbing my mixing bowls as he waited for my reply.

I tapped my chin in quiet contemplation. "I'm going to have to get back to you on that."

"Well, alright then," he responded and placed the bowl in the wooden strainer next to the sink.

∞∞∞∞∞∞∞

After John finished cleaning, he joined Sargent Snuggles and me on the couch. We were in the process of going through our movie options when his cell rang.

John looked at me apologetically before answering. "This is Kyler.... Can you repeat that?" he asked. Suddenly, he was upright with the phone pressed tightly to his ear. He headed back to the kitchen for privacy.

I could hear his voice rising and bits and pieces of the conversation. Not enough to gather what was happening, but from his tone, I didn't think it was good.

He returned holding the phone down at his side. "Kaley—I'm so sorry. I have to go," he said. I wasn't sure if the other person was still on the line or not.

"Oh, okay…" I slid off the couch to retrieve his coat from the hooks in the kitchen. In the time it took me to do that, he'd already let himself out. I peered out the window just in time to see his truck pull away from the curb and onto the street. I looked at Sargent Snuggles, who appeared to be as confused as I was by John's rapid departure.

With my evening plans shot, I flopped back onto the couch, tossing John's coat to the side, "Well, I guess it's just us." I patted Sargent Snuggles on the head.

In response, he yawned and settled his head in my lap with a contented sigh. The dog was already over it even if I wasn't. I gave him a good scratch behind the ears before sliding out from underneath his large, furry head to change into comfy clothes. I didn't like the way John had left. His behavior was completely contrary to the relaxed, mild-mannered man I'd become accustomed to. I retrieved an old t-shirt and sweats from the bureau in my bedroom. After changing, I planned to watch a movie anyway. It was as I was walking out of the bedroom that the notebook on the nightstand caught my attention. It had been sitting there untouched since the night I'd discovered it in Nathan's office. It seemed like now might be a perfect time to dive into my husband's mysterious, hand-written notes. I carried the notebook back to the couch and settled in with the dog.

I started at the beginning. Looking again at the names and monetary amounts that I still didn't understand. Nathan had used a lot of shorthand that I had no idea how to interpret. A number on the last page looked like it might be a phone number but that was simply a guess as there were no lines or dashes separating the numbers. I was operating under that assumption only because the first three numbers were the area code for the Round Rock area. I reached for my cell phone and dialed. On the third ring a gruff voice said 'hello.' When I didn't respond right away the man repeated the greeting followed by the standard: 'anyone there?"

The twang of his Alabama accent was immediately recognizable, and I quickly ended the call.

My phone rang a few short moments after I hung up. I palmed my forehead at my stupidity. Of course Matt Pine's landline would have caller ID.

"Hello..." The greeting sounded much more hesitant than I'd intended.

"Kaley—it's Matt. You just called here."

"Ummm—yeah... Sorry. I wanted to check about a playdate. I didn't realize how late it was—let's chat tomorrow."

"Don't worry about the time. Aiyona is getting Layla ready for bed. I'm sure she'd be happy to call you back in a few minutes."

"Nah—we'll touch base tomorrow. Have a great night!" I singsonged and abruptly ended the call before things got even more awkward.

Why did Nathan have Matt Pine's phone number scrawled across this mysterious notebook?

I thumbed out a text to Shane. I couldn't keep my findings to myself any longer. Then, after waiting a few minutes for a response I sent a text off to John. I really wanted someone to talk to.

After an hour of waiting for one or the other of them to respond, I gave up and went to bed feeling more sad and alone than I had in a very long time.

Chapter 23
MATT

I wasn't eating. I wasn't sleeping. I was arguing with Aiyona a lot. Recognizing Kaley's dinner date from my dream had really creeped me out. Not to mention, all the crap with Shane Gavin. I felt like I was losing my grip. I knew I needed to turn things around but therein was the problem. I had no direction. Correction—I had direction but really didn't want to go there. The call to Aiyona's work, followed by Shane Gavin's veiled threats at the hardware store, and Layla's new best friend... The timeline was too coincidental and seemed to point in the direction of Stone's widow. I had a sinking feeling that whatever was happening stemmed from my recent involvement with Kaley. At least that's what my subconscious seemed to be telling me with all the spooky, supernatural-like dream shit.

"What are you still doin' here?" Aiyona entered the kitchen, where I'd sat sipping coffee for the past hour. I was completely oblivious to the time or even the fact that my fiancée was still home.

"Matt?" she snapped in my face. "You in there?"

I blinked a few times and absently nodded.

"Aren't you supposed to be at work?"

"Aren't you!" I shot back.

She jutted out her chin and crossed her arms in front of her. "Excuse me?" she drawled. It was easy to tell when Aiyona was angry because the Alabama in her came out.

I sighed and swiped my palm across my mouth. "Sorry, baby. I got a lot on my mind."

"Whatever," she replied, turning her back to me to wash up the few breakfast dishes littered around the sink. "Not that you care but I took the day off. I'm going to have lunch with Layla to celebrate her half-birthday."

"What's a half-birthday?"

Aiyona threw down the dishrag and addressed me as though I were a small child. "Matt—kids who have birthdays in the summer need to be celebrated too. Therefore, the class recognizes their half-birthday so they get a day to feel special."

"Seriously? That's a thing! I have a summer birthday. I was never celebrated during the school year. I managed to turn out okay," I grumbled.

"Ha! You are a reformed drug dealer with a record, living in Wisconsin, in a tiny little dump of a house. The best thing about you is me and Layla."

I couldn't help but smile, "Okay—you got me there. Screw the Alabama school system. If I'd had a half-birthday celebration, I'd be a millionaire. I would have invented some huge social media company or somethin'. We'd be living large!"

"You think you'd still be with me if you were a millionaire?" she asked doubtfully.

I grabbed her around the waist and pulled her playfully onto my lap. "Baby, you said it yourself—the best thing about me is you and Layla."

"That's right," she agreed with a curt nod of her head.

"Anyway, to answer your previous question… I have the day off cause I've covered so many extra weekend shifts lately."

"Then you can go to the school for lunch too!" Aiyona said, with an overly enthusiastic tone to her voice.

"Hell yeah!" I agreed, as she hopped off my lap. "Let's go celebrate Layla's birthday seven months early."

"Half-birthday," Aiyona corrected.

∞∞∞∞∞∞∞

I had no idea a school cafeteria could be so damn loud. It was fun to eat with Layla, but my ears were ringing by the time we exited the brown brick building. I dropped Aiyona off at home and told her I had some errands to run. When I added that she shouldn't expect me home for dinner, I thought she'd be upset, but she actually seemed pleased. My fiancée was ready to be rid of me for a while.

If I was serious about looking into Stone's death, I needed someone to give me some background on this crappy little city. I needed to talk to someone who wouldn't find it at all unusual I was asking questions. I had to find someone who I could trust if it came down to it, and most importantly, someone who wouldn't get me mixed up with the wrong people again. I was just driving past the hardware store when it hit me—the person I needed was Dwayne.

I quickly pulled into the back of the store and went through the employee entrance in search of my buddy.

I caught a glimpse of my co-worker's bright red vest as he turned up the electrical aisle. "Hey, Dwayne!" I called out.

Dwyane poked his head back around the corner and smiled. "Hey, Matt. What are you doing here on your day off?"

I shrugged, ignoring his question, and asking one of my own. "How long have you lived in Round Rock?"

He scratched his head. I was unsure if this was due to the uncertainty of his Round Rock timeline or because he was considering why I'd asked him in the first place. "Well... practically my whole life, I guess. We moved here when I was about four or five, I think."

So, it was the former. "What do you know about the Round Rock police department?"

If he had thought the question odd, he didn't show it. "Well, not a whole lot. What kind of information are you looking for?"

"I'm not really sure... I'm kinda wondering about the cops... like what kind of people they are. Did you grow up with any of them?"

He smiled broadly, "You thinkin' about becoming a cop, Matt?"

I laughed. That had to be a first. Most people would have jumped to the opposite conclusion. That I'd asked because I'd gotten into some sort of trouble but not Dwayne. Dwayne had immediately assumed I was interested in becoming one of them. "Naw, man. I was just thinking—that's all."

Dwayne scratched his head a second time. "That's an odd thing to be thinking about."

"Yeah," I agreed. "Just forget I said anything."

"Is this about Shane Gavin?"

I paused, "Why would you think that?"

"I don't know," Dwayne shrugged. "Because it seemed like he was giving you a hard time, and then he talked to Ollie about how great you were. I thought maybe you were just sorting through it—that's all."

"Huh..." Dwayne had noticed the behavior too.

"Huh, what, Matt?" Dwayne asked, his forehead creased in confusion.

"Nothing," I responded, before switching gears. "Did Shane grow up here?"

Dwayne laughed.

"Why is that funny?"

"Shane Gavin is Round Rock. He was 'the guy' when I was in school. High school quarterback, prom king, whatever—you get it. Dumber than a box of rocks too. The only reason he even got through high school was because his teachers made sure he passed. Can't play football without your superstar—you know the type. He had a ton of scholarships too, but old Shane would never leave Round Rock. Out there in the real world, he would be nothing. But here in small town USA he can continue to be everything."

"Huh, can't say that surprises me too much."

"Yeah—we don't really travel in the same circles, but I'm pretty sure he's still a jerk."

"It would seem so," I agreed. "What about his friend, Kaley Stone. Did you go to high school with her too?"

"I know her but not through high school. She's an artist. You should check out her gallery downtown; she's really talented."

"So she's not from around here?"

"Oh no—she is. She's younger than me, though, so we weren't in school together. Her grandfather owns Henry's."

"The bar?" I tried to sound surprised; but, of course, I knew the old man owned it. I'd actually spent quite a bit of time there upon my arrival in Round Rock. Not so much anymore, though. It was best to just stay away from anything that tempted me.

"Irish Pub," Dwayne corrected me. "Yeah, she used to wait tables there quite a bit, but I don't think she really does that much anymore."

I couldn't recall ever seeing her in there; but in the beginning, I wouldn't have been looking. "Kaley and Shane are pretty close you know."

Dwayne looked at me questioningly. "I do know. Her husband was a cop. He was Gavin's partner, but I'm not sure they were friends. I think Kaley and Shane became friends by necessity."

"Necessity?"

"Yeah. Her husband died in the line of duty. You must not have moved here yet—If you'd lived in Round Rock at the time you'd know. It rocked this community."

I stayed quiet.

"Despite Gavin's faults," Dwayne continued, "I think he was hit hard by the death. People say he's taken upon himself to be Kaley and her daughter's guardian. Probably the only good thing the guy has done in life."

"What people?"

Dwayne shrugged, "I don't know...people... Round Rock isn't really that interesting. People talk about people."

I rubbed my chin, "Interesting."

Dwayne paused, "Matt, why all the questions?"

I wasn't sure how to play it. I could shrug it off, pretend I was also a bored Round Rock resident interested in community gossip, or I could give it to Dwayne straight. Instead of doing either, I threw another question at him. "Did Kaley's husband... the cop who died... did he grow up here too?"

"No. I think he came to town when he was hired by the police department. He was a heck of a nice guy too. Not at all like his partner."

"So you knew him?" I asked.

"Dwayne shrugged. "Yeah, I knew him. He was pretty outgoing and liked to chat it up with people. I think anyone who worked in town probably knew him and liked him. You would have too."

I had no doubt.

"Why all the questions?" Dwayne asked for the second time.

"It's complicated," I answered truthfully.

Dwayne settled his big green eyes on me. His eyeglasses seemed to magnify them to twice the natural size, reminding me a bit of a cartoon character. "Matt, I know you've had some trouble in the past." His comment wasn't meant to be judgmental, but it caught me off guard.

"What are you saying, Dwayne?" I shot back defensively.

Dwayne seemed taken aback, "Sorry, Matt... I mean... It's not like... I just." He stopped stammering and looked down at his athletic shoes.

I regretted my behavior; Dwayne didn't mean any harm with his words. The guy was honest to a fault. He was just calling it like he saw it, and he wasn't wrong. "I've changed," I said quietly.

"I know," Dwayne responded. "I don't have a lot of friends, Matt. But I do consider you one."

I was genuinely touched by his confession. "Thanks. I feel the same way."

"If you need any help or need to talk about anything... I hope you know—you can tell me anything."

Oddly enough, I did know that. Even if I hadn't realized before, I did for certain now. "Thank you. I may just take you up on that," I responded, reaching out to give him a friendly slug to the shoulder.

We were interrupted by a customer ringing the bell at the front of the store for service. I hadn't even noticed anyone enter during our conversation.

"We'll see ya tomorrow," Dwayne said, before scurrying away to offer his assistance to someone else. He left me contemplating whether or not I should bring my 'friend' into the loop or not. I might do that eventually but not today. It was time, however, to have a heart-to-heart with Kaley Stone.

Chapter 24
KALEY

"Summer, please hurry!" I was standing by the front door with her backpack and coat, all I needed was the child to go with the items. "We're going to be late!"

"Coming, Mommy," she called out from her bedroom. A few more minutes passed. Just as I was on the verge of snapping, my daughter appeared. Summer skipped down the hallway without a care in the world.

"What were you doing? I've been standing here for ten minutes!"

"Lining my stuffed animals up by height. I forgot to do that last night."

"Of course! How can you possibly learn if your animals aren't arranged proportionally at home?" My irritation lent well to sarcasm.

"I don't know, Mommy?"

"Okay—" I sighed. "We need to get to school, and we need to rush," I helped her into her coat and then swore under my breath as we looked for her boots.

In the end, I squeezed her feet into boots from last winter. We hustled out to the SUV, which I had running and waiting in the driveway. I was about to help Summer into the backseat but stopped short noticing John's truck parked at the curb. He strolled up the driveway, completely distracting me from any concerns I had regarding my daughter's tardiness. I hadn't heard from him since he'd raced out of my house a few nights before. I'd called and texted numerous times; but both went unanswered, which seemed completely uncharacteristic.

He kissed me lightly on the cheek and leaned into the backseat to greet Summer. The entire interaction was so natural and lovely it caused me to push my concerns about his lack of communication aside.

"Aren't you running kind of late?" he asked Summer. His voice cheery and unruffled.

"Yes," Summer laughed.

"I bet your mom was being pokey, wasn't she?"

"Yes," Summer giggled again as he buckled her safely into her booster.

"And here she is, just standing around. Did you tell her school is about to start?" John teased, as he ducked back out of the vehicle and gave me a sly smirk.

"How long have you been sitting out here?" I asked, shutting Summer's door.

He checked his watch, "Not too long. I was hoping to catch you before you dropped Summer off," he paused, "you do know school starts in five minutes—right?"

"Yes, I know that!" I snapped. "Summer had to arrange her animals by height before we could leave."

He nodded, "Common excuse for tardiness."

"Aren't you running a little late yourself?" I asked.

"Nope—I took the morning off. Mind if I tag along for the ride?"

"Hop in." I gestured toward the passenger seat before making my way around to slide in behind the wheel.

John accepted the invitation, ducking into the other side of the SUV.

He chatted with Summer all the way to school. By the time we pulled in, we had missed the bell by nearly ten minutes.

"I'll take her inside," John offered.

"Really?"

"You bet. I'll tell them I'm the reason she's late. I can guarantee her tardy will be excused."

I eyed him skeptically, "How's that?"

John leaned in close. He smelled crisp and clean like a bar of Irish Spring. "I'll let you in on a little secret. I know you could care less about football, but to most people around here—I'm kind of a big deal."

"Is that right?" I feigned skepticism.

"Yes, ma'am," he said, tipping his head slightly. "Summer—you want me to walk you in? he asked, turning his attention to the back seat.

"Yes!" Summer shouted back.

"I'll be right back." He winked before exiting the vehicle.

My daughter gathered her things, and John hoisted her into his arms. He carried her into the school like a little princess.

'Right back' actually meant thirty minutes later. Apparently, John and Summer shared the same sense of timing.

"What took you so long?" I asked, trying not to sound irritated when John finally slid back into the vehicle.

"I had to sweet talk the secretary into excusing her tardy."

"Oh—you did, did you?" I replied suspiciously as I made my way out of the drop-off zone.

"Oh yeah," he nodded. "That and Summer wanted to show me around."

"Ahhh, and they had no problem with my already late daughter taking you on a tour?"

"They were thrilled as a matter of fact."

"Really?"

"As I told you—I'm kind of a big deal around here."

I shook my head in response.

"So where to now? Your gallery?" John asked.

"Ummm, no." I replied, looking down at my leggings and baggy sweatshirt. Not to mention the fact that I hadn't even combed my hair this morning but popped on a ball cap instead. "I need to go home and shower. Look at me, John—would you buy art from someone dressed like me?"

"Absolutely," he stated firmly. "Then again, I may be biased. I'd probably buy anything you were selling."

I raised an eyebrow.

"Don't look so doubtful, Kaley. In case you hadn't noticed, I've fallen kind of hard for you."

I debated for a moment whether to be cute and flirty with my response or just honest. Brutal honesty won out. "What if I am doubtful, John?

He turned toward me, his forehead creased with concern.

I sighed, "Ever since you rushed out of my house the other night, I've been leaving you messages—voicemail and text. Did you even think to respond? You really left me hanging."

He looked genuinely surprised, making me feel slightly foolish for even bringing it up. "I'm sorry. I guess I did do that—didn't I?"

I tried to wave it away, "It's fine. Obviously, something happened... I don't want to invade your privacy... I just hoped you'd reach out—that's all. Even if you don't want to talk about it—is it too much to ask that you at least let me know you're okay?" We'd reached our destination. I parked the vehicle and prepared to exit

"I'm sorry. I guess I'm not used to having someone worry about me. It won't happen again."

"Thank you," I said, reaching for the door handle. Even with his reassurances I still felt unsettled.

John reached for my hand. He opened his mouth to say something but must have reconsidered because he clamped it shut instead.

I dropped the handle and settled back against the seat, "What's on your mind, John?"

He rubbed his hand across his forehead. "I'm having trouble with some of my kids."

"I'm sorry...kids?"

John's somber expression changed as his lips turned up slightly in an amused smile, "Relax, Kaley. I'm talking about my football kids. I didn't forget to mention a hoard of children or anything."

"Whew," I said wiping my forehead in mock relief.

He chuckled uncomfortably and turned serious once again, "I'd like to tell you about it, but it's complicated."

"Okay..."

He leaned closer. "Would it be okay if we revisit this after I've had time to sort some things out?"

I reached for his hand, "I could help you sort through things."

"I'm sure you could. However, part of the complication is confidentiality."

"Ahhh, well, it's not like my husband was a cop or anything. I don't really understand confidentiality," I replied playfully.

John smiled, "Trust me—if I was going to talk to anyone, it would be you."

I shrugged my shoulders, "I'm here if you change your mind. How about some breakfast?" I offered in an attempt to steer the conversation into more comfortable territory. "We can swing into Henry's quick."

"Raincheck?"

I was confused by his response. "Sure... but I got the impression you were planning to spend the morning with me."

"I'm sorry; I'm all over the place. That was my intention, but something you said got me thinking... I'm actually going to head into work..." he trailed off and dropped his hand from my own.

I waited to see if he would elaborate. He didn't.

"Would you like to clue me in here?" I asked.

"Later," he replied brusquely as he pushed open the passenger side door, allowing the chilly morning air to fill the space between us.

I'd been fully prepared to move forward and forgive his lack of communication. However, his sudden shift in behavior had me rethinking everything.

"John!" I called out after him, practically chasing him down the driveway.

"I'll call you later, Kaley! And thanks again!" he called back before climbing into his pick-up and driving away.

"What just happened?" I found myself asking the question aloud as I stood confused and a little hurt at the end of my driveway. I spun around wondering if any of my neighbors had witnessed the perplexing situation. However, I found myself completely alone.

I let myself into the house through the kitchen and set my phone on the island when a text from Shane buzzed through. He wanted to meet up for dinner. With all John's weirdness, I'd actually forgotten to talk to Shane about Nathan's notebook. I quickly tapped out a reply with details.

The uneasy feeling about Nathan's notes returned. I tried to push it away, there would be time to explore it later over my dinner with Shane. Right now, I had to figure out what to do about John, not to mention it was time to open the gallery. So I pushed myself onward to do the one thing I had any power to control.

∞∞∞∞∞∞∞

By noon I'd come to a couple of conclusions. The first one being that John's uncharacteristic behavior was a signal that something was seriously wrong. The second conclusion had a lot to do with the first. If I wanted to be a part of John's life, I'd need to put in some effort. The result had me headed to Henry's to pick up a lunch order for John.

This time, I had my driver's license ready to go when I entered the school. I wasn't about to give that battleax of a secretary a reason to deny me access. I found Mary Nicole to be much more accommodating when I followed the procedure.

With my visitor ID stuck to my coat, I trotted down the hallway in the direction of John's office. Luckily, I remembered the way. In general, I'm direction inept; and the school, while beautiful architecturally, had many issues spatially. It had been built in the early 1900s; with so many additions put on throughout the years, it was an entirely different building than when I'd attended over fifteen years previously.

I entered the pod where John's office was located. It was much more active than on my last visit. His office door was shut. As I was debating whether or not to knock, it opened up, and a group of men poured out including Police Chief Logan Sterns. Logan was in his late forties with a nondescript face topped with a head full of black wavy hair touched with gray. The buttons on his white uniform shirt seemed to be stretched to their limit as they strained to stay closed over the chief's generous gut.

Logan smiled when he saw me. "Kaley, what a nice surprise." He wrapped a beefy arm around my shoulder and pulled me in for an awkward hug.

I gave him a customary back pat and caught John's eye. Judging from his tight-lipped expression, he was not happy with whatever business had brought the Chief to his office.

"How are you? How's Summer?" Logan continued. The chief was either completely unaware of the tension rolling off John or indifferent.

"Fine thanks. And I don't think we've talked since Summer's nighttime adventure. Thanks again for everything you did. It really helped knowing I had that kind of support."

He hitched up his pants, "Well, I'm just glad we found her."

I looked toward John. He was standing behind Logan with what I could only describe as a 'coaching stance', his legs shoulder-distance apart and arms crossed, the way I saw NFL coaches stand on the sidelines. Even with my limited football knowledge, I recognized the look. "Actually, John found her," I gently corrected.

"Well—is that right..." Logan replied, turning toward John. A look was exchanged between the two. It felt like Logan was baiting John. Even if that were the case, John wasn't biting. "I wasn't even aware you two knew each other," Logan added.

"No reason you should." John's tone was icy, which seemed unnecessary given the situation. Then again—I had no idea what the situation was.

"Well, Kaley here, is family." Logan clucked. "And we watch out for family. Just like football—right, Coach?"

Anger flashed in John's eyes, but he recovered quickly. So quickly in fact that suddenly his entire demeanor changed. In place of the scowl, there was now a big, mock grin plastered across his face. "Well—thanks for stopping by, Chief," John chirped. I'll take everything under advisement and get back with you."

Logan mirrored the disposition with his own phony smile. His reply was overly boisterous in nature, "Oh, don't waste your time here, Coach. As I said, things are taken care of. Just a little misunderstanding with the kids. No harm, no foul, right?"

John didn't reply.

Logan looked away from John and toward me again. "Kaley—again, so nice to see you. Take care of yourself, sweetheart."

I watched him walk away before turning toward John. "What did I just walk in on?"

John pushed the door shut and stomped back toward his desk where he dropped down hard into his chair, "That guy... That guy is an asshole!" he said, gesturing toward the doorway where Logan had exited.

I sat down on the edge of John's desk. "Want to tell me what's going on?"

He ran his hands through his hair. "I can't. Look—forget I said anything. I don't want to put you in the middle of anything, especially given the fact you seem to have a relationship with the guy."

"Hey," I said gently. "Logan was Nathan's boss; and he was good to us after Nathan died, but that's it. You're not getting in the middle of anything."

"Kaley—you don't have to say that. Anyway, what brings you by," he asked, abruptly changing the subject.

"Oh, I almost forgot!" I held out the white paper sack I was carrying, "tada—lunch!"

He smiled, "You brought me lunch?"

"I did. Henry's famous potato soup and breadsticks."

One of the guys who had been in John's office upon my arrival opened the door and poked his head in, "John," he said tersely, "we need to talk."

"I'll be there in a minute."

The man gave a curt nod and strode away leaving the door opened a crack.

John apologized, "I'm really swamped here. Can I call you later?"

I hopped off the desk, "No worries. Just make sure you eat."

"Absolutely. Thanks so much for this," he held up the bag.

"You are more than welcome. Call me later?"

"Count on it."

Once again, the situation left me with so many questions and no hope for answers.

∞∞∞∞∞∞∞

After picking Summer up from dance class, we headed to Culver's where I had arranged to meet Shane for dinner. Summer and I ordered and found a table.

As we waited for our food, I set my daughter up with my phone and some earbuds, that way I could talk to Shane uninterrupted.

Shane arrived bringing an unsettled energy with him. He roughly dragged an extra chair across the restaurant and plopped down between us. "Sorry I didn't get back to you last night. Is everything okay?"

Summer was completely engrossed with a game on my device and oblivious to Shane's arrival.

"I'm not sure…" I had photocopied the pages from the journal and tucked them into a manilla folder to share with Shane.

I slid the materials across the table to him. I studied his face as he opend the folder and started leafing through the pages. A small, sad smile crept across his lips, "Nathan and his chicken scratches. Who the hell could read any of this?"

I smiled too. That had been my first reaction too. Then, I watched as his smile faded, and Shane leaned in for a closer look. He started to turn pages more rapidly; and then without warning, he closed the folder and fixed me with a steely gaze.

A high school kid brought a tray with our food and set it down in the middle of the table. I gave Summer her chicken tenders and passed Shane the burger basket I'd taken the liberty of ordering him. I carefully unwrapped my own burger and waited for him to say something. He ran his palm across his face and pinched the corners of his lips.

"I found the notes a few weeks ago," I offered. "I really didn't look at them until last night, though."

"Where is the original, Kay?"

"Why?"

"Does anybody else know?"

I shook my head. "I've only shown you."

"Good," he nodded. "Keep it that way. In fact, forget you ever saw it."

I had anticipated a few different reactions from Shane, but this wasn't one of them. "It seems like Nathan was investigating something here, Shane. I can't just pretend I didn't see it."

His voice dropped an octave, and his tone was stern. "Nathan is gone; whatever concerns he had are moot. You bringing up any of this is a bad idea."

"But Shane—"

He cut me off, "End of discussion, Kay," he slid the folder off the table and onto his lap.

"Fine," I said, as Shane took a bite of his burger. "I'll just ask Matt."

He stopped mid-bite. "Matt Pine?"

I nodded. "Nathan had his contact information written in there."

"Contact information?"

"Yes. Stop repeating me. There was a phone number and I called it. It just so happened to be Matt's."

He set the food down. "Matt Pine is an ex-con. If Nathan recorded his number in his notes, I'm sure that's even more reason for you to keep your distance."

"What if Matt was helping Nathan with something?"

Shane choked on his food. He wiped his face, swallowed a sip of soda, and then spoke to me in a tone that can only be described as patronizing. "Kay, what could Matt possibly offer Nathan? I mean it's not like he was an informant or anything. I know Nathan had a registered informant and I know it wasn't Matt. If Matt's information is in there, it's because Nathan suspected him of something... something bad."

"Like the other people he noted?"

"Exactly. Now take my advice and keep this information to yourself. You don't want Matt or somebody like Matt to find out you have it. Better yet—give me the original—I'll hold onto it for you."

"That doesn't make sense, Shane. The police chief is mentioned in Nathan's notes a few times. Do you think Sterns is up to no good too?"

"No..." he replied carefully. "He's probably noted because he's the boss. I think there's a lot going on that you just don't understand."

"That's why I need you," I countered.

He stopped stuffing his face for a moment and reached across the table to grasp my hand. "Do you trust me?"

I looked into his eyes and searched for something that would make me question his sincerity. If it was there, I didn't see it. My friend had been with me to hell and back. I may not agree with what he was asking me to do but he was right—I didn't have all the information. "I trust you, Shane, and if you want me to let it go I will."

He gave my hand a squeeze and nodded, satisfied with my answer. The tension faded away. "The only good to come out of this is that it reinforces my warning to you."

I bit into a fry, "What warning would that be?"

"The one about Matt. He's definitely bad news. The guy has a rap sheet. Nothing around here, but he had some problems in Alabama. Drugs, car theft, and assault charges. Not great."

"I know I told you before that I didn't want to know, but I gotta ask... How old are the charges?"

"That's your question?"

"Well——yeah. You said nothing around here. People change so I'm just wondering how far in the past this is?"

"First of all, people don't change that much. And secondly, you need to watch your back. You can't be so trusting."

"Well, that's a crappy way to live," I stated.

"Kay—that's life!" Shane said in an exasperated tone. And it wasn't that long ago. The most recent charge was just over three years ago."

Okay, so it was more recent than I'd envisioned; but I was not going to give Shane the satisfaction of knowing that. "Well, you said nothing around here... right?"

"Come on, Kay!" he said, leaning back in his chair.

"Relax. I told you I wouldn't be alone with him. I won't let Summer go to their house. What else do you expect me to do, Shane? Tell the girls they can't be friends?"

"Well—maybe, yeah."

"Seriously? You saw them together. They would be crushed. What about the mom? Did you dig up dirt on her too?"

"No. Aiyona Green is clean."

"Soooo... I stay away from the boyfriend—the girls get to play—it's all good."

Shane looked doubtful. "I want you to notify me whenever the girls have a playdate."

I laughed. Shane did not. "You cannot be serious?"

"I'm not messing around here, Kay."

"So you're going to drop everything to come over when that little girl is playing at our house?"

"If you insist on continuing playdates, then yes—yes I will."

"Shane, that's over the top, even for you."

He ignored the statement and took a large bite of his burger. He glanced over at Summer, who was still fully engaged in whatever she was playing. "Take those things off her. I want to talk to the kid about her day before I have to run."

I rolled my eyes. "You better get yourself in a better place before you talk to Summer; you're ornery as hell."

He wiped his face with the napkin. "I apologize. Sometimes you drive me a little crazy."

"The feeling is mutual, pal." I tapped Summer on the hand. She took out the earbuds, "Uncle Shane wants to talk to you before he has to go."

Summer's face lit up. "Want to hear about the frog that got loose during math?"

"I sure do!" Shane leaned forward attentively. The animosity over the notebook and Matt faded away as he listened to my daughter recount the events of her day.

Chapter 25
MATT

As much as I wanted to leave the past buried, it seemed that was no longer an option. If I had any hope of figuring out what was going on, I would need to go to the source. Since Stone was dead, his wife was the next best thing. That's how I found myself waiting in the dark parking lot of the Culver's.

I watched from the warmth of my Impala as Shane Gavin exited and swaggered under the streetlamp toward a fancy newer model Mustang. He didn't drive off as I'd hoped but waited behind the steering wheel watching for Kaley and Summer to exit. As they did so, Shane jogged to their little SUV parked across the lot from him. Luckily, I'd tucked myself toward the rear of the lot squeezed between two diesel pickup trucks. It wasn't likely either of them would spot me.

Kaley and Shane exchanged a few words before she opened the back of her vehicle and helped Summer into her seat. Shane didn't move until Kaley had started her Honda and rolled out of the parking lot onto the street. Only then did the cop leave, robbing me of the opportunity to have a conversation with Kaley.

I weighed my options. Due to the subject matter of the conversation I needed to have with Kaley, it should be done in person. I'd already ruled out calling. Showing up at her house was a possibility but that possibility almost guaranteed another face-to-face with Shane Gavin. There was the option of holding off and trying to catch her at school; but that would require patience, which was a gift I'd never been blessed with. Or I could follow her and see if she stopped somewhere on the way home. I turned left and caught up to her little black SUV.

As luck would have it, Kaley pulled into a gas station. I slid my car into one of the slanted spaces outside the storefront and jogged over to say hello. The plan was to be as disarming as possible and give her a solid reason to want to hear what I had to say.

I called out to her before approaching, "Hey, Kaley!"

She slid the lever on the pump before turning my direction. If I had startled her, she didn't show it. She also didn't appear particularly pleased to see me. Which was a surprise as she'd been so welcoming the last time I saw her.

I stepped up on the concrete island and under the flickering light of the florescent. I slid my hands into my pockets. Again—trying to look as approachable as possible. "I'm glad I ran into you," I said casually.

She began to fill her tank and gave me a tight-lipped smile, "Why is that?"

I was caught off guard. I'd become accustomed to the nuances of Wisconsin small talk and had completely anticipated a friendlier greeting. In light of her response, I chose to plow straight ahead and hoped I could provide her with a compelling reason to stay after her tank was full.

"Well ..." she prompted.

I sighed, she obviously didn't want to linger and quite frankly neither did I. "I have a problem, and I think I need your help to figure it out."

She raised her eyebrows and finished up with the pump. She screwed the gas cap back on and retrieved her receipt before responding. "Is there a problem with the girls?"

"No—not at all." At the mention of Summer, I stooped down to wave in the window. Summer appeared to be playing a game on Kaley's phone and had absolutely no interest in me.

"What then, Matt?" Kaley sounded annoyed.

"I think I may have gotten your husband killed." And there it was. I hadn't meant to just blurt it out like that but what was done was done. "I think I'm the reason Nathan is dead," I repeated, quieter this time.

To her credit, she didn't balk. Kaley crossed her arms in front of her and narrowed her eyes at me. "I'm going to need some more information, Matt."

I squirmed under her glare and stammered a bit trying to find my words. "I knew your husband... He was a good guy... I think someone used me to set him up. I think he was investigating something that made him a target."

"My husband was shot in the line of duty by a low-life drug dealer. Nathan managed to take out the piece of shit on his way down. So—how do you fit into this scenario, Matt?"

I opened my mouth to say more but Kaley suddenly put her hand up and shook her head. "You know what... I'm not having this conversation with you. I'm calling Shane, and you can tell him whatever it is you have to say. I know about your past, Matt. I'm not comfortable talking to you by myself out here. So just head on back to your car over there and stay away from me and my daughter."

She started for the driver's side door. I instinctively reached out to try and stop her. My hand grasped her elbow with just enough force to completely freak her out.

"Don't you touch me!" she yelled. Luckily, at that moment, there were no other customers within earshot.

I raised my hands in surrender and took a few steps back. "I'm sorry. That was stupid."

Kaley said nothing; but she wasn't trying to get away at the moment, either, so I had a small window of opportunity.

"Please don't call your husband's partner," I hesitated before deciding to disclose my suspicion. "There's a possibility he was in on it."

"Now I know you're lying," she said tersely. "Shane would never hurt Nathan. He is the most loyal friend we've ever had."

"Why do you think that is, Kaley?" I gently prodded. "Is there a possibility your good buddy Shane feels guilty for what happened to your husband?"

Anger flashed in her eyes, "Stay away from us!"

Kaley yanked open the car door and slid in behind the wheel. I stayed planted in place as she started the engine and peeled out of the parking lot.

Something had changed. After our exchange at the resturant, I thought she might be receptive to hearing me out. There were so many missing pieces, but my gut told me Kaley could help.

Chapter 26
KALEY

The conversation with Matt was utterly unnerving. I wasn't sure what to do. Part of me wanted to hear him out, but Shane's warning flashed through my mind. Matt's statement—that he'd gotten Nathan killed— that scared me. Despite what Matt had asked, I sent Shane a text to call when he got the chance. Then I fired a similar text off to John.

I got Summer settled in for the night, which was sooner than I expected. She complained of a sore throat after dinner and didn't put up a fight about bedtime. I checked her temperature and was relieved to see she didn't have a fever. At least that was reassuring. It always made me nervous when Summer came down with something. Nathan had been so much better at that stuff.

I checked my phone after leaving Summer's room but hadn't heard anything back from Shane. John, on the other hand, had replied right away. His text was short and sweet:

In a meeting. Call you later.

With so much weighing on my mind and nobody to talk to, I found myself back in Nathan's home office. I sat down at the computer desk, not bothering to turn on the lights. I powered up the computer, the electronic hum filled the otherwise silent house. The glow emanating from the screen cast everything in an eerie blue light. After typing in the password, I stared at the image Nathan had chosen for the wallpaper. Our happy family. He had his arm wrapped around me as I held baby Summer. His blue eyes were smiling as he peered out at me from the glowing electronic device.

"Hey, Nathan," I whispered to the empty room. "I miss you."

I couldn't quite bring myself to take the next step and start exploring the files on the device. Instead, I slouched back in the chair wondering who I should trust. What if something Nathan had been investigating led to his death? Why wouldn't Shane want to look into that? I ran my hands down my face and questioned my next move.

"Tell me what I'm looking for, Nathan," I whispered. "Help me out here... If you can hear me, just send a sign. Point me in the right direction..."

"Kay?"

I jumped at the sound of my name.

Shane was outlined in the doorway. "You okay?" he asked, seemingly to have materialized out of nowhere.

"What are you doing here?" I snapped. "Can't I get any privacy? You come and go like you live here but guess what Shane—you don't, and I don't want you here!"

"I'm sorry," he replied softly. "I tried to call after I got your text, but you didn't answer. I decided to drive by, and when I saw all the lights off... well, it's early... I was worried, but I didn't mean to intrude."

I turned away and leaned forward onto the desk, burying my face in my hands, feeling embarrassed by my outburst. I wasn't even sure why I'd lashed out at him. Shane's duty coat, almost exactly like the one Nathan had left on the chair in the corner, made a rustling sound as he shifted. He was most likely debating whether he should stay or go. I made the decision easier for him.

"I'm sorry," I murmured, my face still buried in my hands. "I didn't mean that." My apology was met with silence. I turned to see if he'd left. He hadn't. Shane remained in the doorway, probably trying to gauge my emotional state.

Then, Shane surprised me, he slid down the length of the doorway and settled on the floor. He rested his arms on bended knees and sighed. "It should have been me, Kay. Nathan should be here with you and Summer. Josie would be just fine without me. Everyone would be just fine without me. I was the one on call that night. I should have died—not him. I'm the one who is sorry. I'm trying my best to fill a hole that realistically I can never fill. I am so sorry."

I wasn't sure how to respond. I knew Shane felt responsible on some level, but he'd never verbalized it. Despite what Matt had implied this wasn't guilt. Shane had been my rock. Albeit goofy, annoying, and self-righteous—a rock nonetheless. I had been so busy mourning my husband I'd never stopped to consider the hole Nathan had left in his partner's life as well.

I slid from the chair and inched toward him. "Shane—this is not your fault. Nathan shouldn't have been taken from us, but it would have been devastating to lose you too."

Shane hung his head. In the blue glow from the computer, I could see his eyes were closed.

I placed my hand gently on his knee. "Tell me what I can do?"

Shane swallowed, "The notebook you found... Nathan was investigating some shit. I told him it was a bad idea. I told him whatever he found to leave me out of it. I was too chickenshit to actually do my job. I was on call that night, Kaley, but nobody called me."

I replied hesitantly, "If you would just look at the notebook again... I think Nathan may have been suspicious of some of the other cops..."

Shane shook his head. "I know it looks that way but, Kay, I work with these guys. Logan can be an ass and he's not the best chief, but it's not a corrupt department."

"I'm not sure Nathan would have agreed with you."

Shane was silent for a moment before he replied, "He should be here with you and Summer. Given more time he would have figured things out. I'm sorry, I'm so sorry."

"I'm the one who should apologize. All this time I've been leaning on you, I never gave a second thought to your feelings. Shane—you put your entire life on hold to take care of Nathan's family. You didn't sign up for that. I gotta ask, what have I given you in return?"

A look of surprise registered on his face as he turned toward me. "A family, Kay. You and Summer have given me a family."

I scoffed, "You have a family."

"Not one that respects me. Not one that actually cares. Josie and me... well, we're nothing like you and Nathan were.

Shane rarely talked about his relationship, but I'd always assumed that was out of sensitivity for what I had lost. Despite my infidelity suspicions, it never dawned on me that he didn't talk about Josie because of marital problems. It never really occurred to me that Shane could have any problems. I was too busy letting him solve all mine.

"You and Josie okay?" I asked.

"Yeah—we're fine. We're what we've always been... whatever that is."

"I don't understand."

Shane scoffed, "You wouldn't. Like I said, my relationship is nothing like what you and Nathan had. I mean, Josie is beautiful, she's rich, and smart.

However, she's really self-absorbed and not always a very good person. We're a lot alike that way."

"Shane," I said gently. "You are so much more than that."

"I am now," he agreed. "That's because of you and Nathan. I want to be the man he needs me to be—that you and Summer need me to be."

"You are that guy," I assured him.

"I'm getting there. However, at the moment, I seem to be having an emotional breakdown in the middle of Nathan's home office."

"I'm glad you are."

"Thanks?" he replied sarcastically.

I laughed, trying to lighten the mood. "It gave us the opportunity to talk like this. I think it's probably long overdue."

He nodded, "Maybe you're right." Then he took in the room around us. "I don't think I've been in here since…" he trailed off.

"I know," I said, ignoring where his comment had been headed. "There is so much I need to go through, but I just haven't been able to bring myself to do it. Two years… and things are still exactly the way he left them. Except for the notebook I showed you earlier…" I let the statement hang there, wondering if I would get a different reaction this time.

He leaned his head against the wall. His gaze focused on something or nothing across the room.

I continued, "Matt approached me earlier tonight."

With this piece of news, Shane snapped back to attention. "When?"

"After we left the restaurant. I stopped to get gas, and there he was."

"He was there or he followed you?"

I shrugged, "Does it matter? He wants my help, Shane. He mentioned something about Nathan… Something that makes me question if my husband's death was indeed accidental."

Shane leaned forward anxiously, "What did you say?"

"Actually, I was a total bitch. I yelled at him to stay away from me."

At this Shane slumped back and resumed his position against the wall. "Good."

"Thing is—I think he might be onto something. What if the timing of the notebook and Matt approaching me means something?"

Shane eyed me suspiciously, "Like what? Nathan's trying to contact you from beyond the grave?"

"Would that be so crazy?"

Shane laughed and then realized I was being completely serious. "Holy shit, Kay! You can't possibly think...."

I shrugged, "I'm going to look into this, Shane. With or without your help."

He ran his hand through his hair and let out a sigh, "Do you trust me?"

"You know the answer to that."

"Do me a favor then—let this go. Give me the notebook, and I'll handle things."

"But—"

He held up his hand, "I'll make things right this time, I promise. Please let me do my job for you... for Nathan."

I nodded solemnly, not wanting to give Shane the notebook, but knowing he'd make far more headway in investigating than I ever could. However, it felt like I was letting go of another piece of my husband.

Shane, sensing my hesitation and the reason, gave my hand a tight squeeze. "I need to know what Nathan knew. I don't want to start from scratch."

"I get that... but maybe it would be better if I held onto it. You can look at it anytime you want. I already gave you copies."

Shane nodded, "I'll go through it and get it back to you as soon as possible. You have to promise not to let anyone else know, though. There is a possibility that whatever Nathan was investigating got him killed. We can't discount that."

I shivered involuntarily, "You think?"

"Anything is possible."

"I'll keep it safe—I'm not ready to part with the original."

Shane looked at me skeptically.

"What?"

He hesitated, "Just make sure this stays between us. Leave it be."

"I'll keep it between us and I'll try to let it go—for now."

Shane sighed, "Just don't act on anything without talking to me first."

"Only if you do the same," I countered.

"I'll share what I can."

That was probably the best I was going to get, so I didn't argue.

"And another thing," he continued. "Don't talk to Matt. Leave things the way they are for now. Okay?"

I let out a breath, "You sure have a lot of contingencies."

He ignored me and looked around the office. "You mentioned needing to clean out Nathan's stuff... Do you want help going through things?"

"That would be great. Only if you're up for it, though."

"I am," he stated. "It will be... cathartic."

I felt my eyes go wide, "Big word, Gavin!"

He smiled, "Thanks! I actually learned it earlier. I've been waiting all day to use it."

I laughed, "Are you serious?"

"I am!" he exclaimed. "Did I use it correctly?"

The way his face lit up led me to believe he was serious. In an effort not to ruin his moment, I managed to stifle the rest of my laughter and congratulated him. "Well done." Then, because I couldn't resist. "Did you get a word of the day calendar?"

"No," he replied, pushing himself up from the floor. "I heard it from a meth head I arrested this morning."

I laughed and accepted his hand as he pulled me up beside him. "So, what now?"

"Now, I'm going to check in on my favorite kindergartner before heading home to my shallow life." He gave me a nod and disappeared into the darkness of the hallway.

Chapter 27
MATT

After my interaction with Kaley at the gas station, I drove around for awhile. My wanderings led me to Stone's neighborhood. Eventually, I ended up parked on the street a few houses down. I turned the car off and did my best to keep warm. I was seriously considering whether or not I should try to talk to Kaley again. Given her reaction at the gas station, I was pretty sure showing up at her house was a bad idea. But most of my life decisions generally were... so what was one more?

I watched as snow shimmered under the light of the lone streetlamp. Slowly it blanketed the streets and bathed the neighborhood in a peaceful white glow. I was about to try my luck and see if Stone's widow had calmed down when headlights approached from the opposite direction. Instinctively, I ducked down as the lights cut across my Impala. I risked a glance and watched as a red pickup truck pulled into the Stone's driveway. Apparently Stone's old partner had ditched the fancy sports car for the evening and was driving a more appropriate vehicle for the weather. Gavin jogged the few feet from the driveway to the front of the house and let himself in. Luckily, the detective wasn't observant enough to notice me.

It appeared Kaley had run straight to her friend, even though I'd asked her not to. I guess in one way that was good. If things ramped up in the next few days, I'd know to look harder at Nathan's ex-partner. I waited a few more minutes. Kaley's house remained dark, which seemed odd but maybe not, maybe she did have something going with the detective after all. If that was indeed the case, he'd probably be there a while. There was no way I was going to approach the house with him there, so I sighed and turned the key.

The stillness of the winter night was broken as the engine clattered and hummed its way back to life. Snow crunched beneath the tires as I pulled away from the curb and maneuvered back onto the street.

Soon the comforts of suburbia were in my rearview as I literally made my way to the other side of the tracks—the south side of town, where my family lived in our tiny rental home. I wasn't ready to go inside yet, though. Instead of turning onto my street, I kept going. I drove straight out of town and into the county. After an hour of aimless driving and absolutely no better understanding of my situation, I made my way back home.

It was a little after 8:30 pm when I pulled into my gravel driveway. A dark sedan parked across the street caught my attention. The vehicle didn't look familiar, furthermore, the house there was abandoned. The car was just far enough away from the streetlight to make out the exact color, but it was definitely dark. Inside, the silhouette of a man was visible behind the steering wheel. Ordinarily, a strange vehicle on the street may not seem like a big deal. However, our home was on a cul-de-sac, and we didn't have many neighbors. I slid out of the car and trudged up the steps, pulling open the aluminum storm door, then unlocking the door that led into our kitchen.

Aiyona was busy cleaning up dinner, which I had obviously missed. "How was work?" she asked sharply, as she banged around various pots and pans. I knew from experience that missing dinner was a huge no-no. Especially missing dinner with zero communication beforehand. My night would now be spent trying to make up for my grievous error.

"Good," I answered, debating whether or not to ask her about the sedan. I decided it was a risk not to. "Hey, did you happen to notice the car parked across the street?"

"No. What car?"

"It's probably nothing," I said. "But somebody is just sittin', and I thought that was odd—you know—since nobody lives there."

"Did you make sure somebody didn't just park there and die?" she asked, without bothering to look up from her task.

That may seem like an odd conclusion to some, but Aiyona grew up in a rough neighborhood. She'd actually experienced people OD and die in their cars. Not just once, either. A few times.

"I don't think that's the case..." I replied hesitantly.

"But you don't know," Aiyona snapped, turning toward me with her hand on her hip.

"True enough. I'll go make sure the guy parked in the suburban Wisconsin neighborhood isn't dead of a heroin overdose," I replied sarcastically, pulling open the door to make my way back into the cold.

"Make all the jokes you want, Matt! Drugs are everywhere, even in little lily white Wisconsin suburbs! You should know that! Oh, I forgot—you were part of the Round Rock drug trade. Hell, you probably introduced some new shit," she yelled after me.

The door clanged shut behind me as I stomped back down the driveway, trying to ignore her dig. I tugged up the collar up on my flannel jacket to shield me somewhat from the sharp northern wind. As I reached the end of the driveway, the headlights flickered on, and the engine purred to life. The sedan zipped off past me and into the night.

From the brief glimpse I caught, it looked like an unmarked squad car. It could be nothing or more likely it was something, but I didn't know what. The whole thing was completely disconcerting.

Before opening the door, I paused to gather my thoughts. The vehicle had been there before I got home. Maybe it had more to do with Aioyna than me. Maybe I was looking at this all wrong.

The door swung open. "Why are you just standing there?" Aiyona asked, peering past my shoulder out onto the street. "Did they leave?"

"Yeah, whoever it was is gone now," I said, stepping into the warmth of the kitchen. The aroma of onions and meat permeated my nostrils.

"Huh—guess he wasn't dead then."

"Guess not."

"Well, wash up. I re-heated dinner for you."

She may have been annoyed with me, but I took it as a good sign that she still wanted to feed me.

Chapter 28
KALEY

The holidays came and went. Henry hosted a festive Christmas gathering at the bar. It was a mix of lovely and awkward, considering the guest list. Of course, there was Summer and me along with Ted, Macy, and a few other bar employees. John and his sister Julia came with her kids. Since Julia's husband was involved in a big trial, she stuck around through the weekend. Although they were older, it was nice for Summer to have other kids to hang out with. Shane and Josie rounded out the guest list.

Something had been bothering John, and I had a sneaking suspicion it had to do with Chief Sterns. Whatever I had interrupted in his office had him rattled; he hadn't been the same since. Every time I asked John about it, though, he skirted the issue. His behavior had me second-guessing my decision to get involved with someone.

Then there was the whole thing with Nathan's notebook. Shane had promised he'd look at the photocopies as long as I promised not to bring it up again. Keeping my end of the bargain was proving difficult, especially since Shane had shared absolutely nothing with me. I had to wonder—had he claimed to look into the matter just to shut me up?

Then, there was Matt. I found myself frequently reflecting on our interaction at the Gas n' Go. What if Matt was right? What if Shane was somehow responsible? Could he be part of some type of conspiracy or coverup? I found myself watching my friend more closely. He and Josie seemed to have their own private battle brewing, Shane denied anything was going on, but the tension between the two was palpable.

When I woke up on January second, I exhaled with relief. We made it through the most difficult part of the year. It was time a fresh start, and I'd made a decision. If Shane was going to continue to keep me out of the loop, I'd go it alone. It was time to finish what Nathan started. Feeling determined, I got myself ready and then headed to Summer's room to prepare her for the first day back to school after break.

I had to remind her several times to pack toys for after school. She'd be going home with Henry as I had a meeting scheduled with a new artist interested in renting gallery space. Henry was a wonderful great-grandfather; however, his apartment above the bar was severely lacking in kid-friendly entertainment. I sent a text off to Shane asking if I could swing by after dropping Summer at school. He replied yes and that he wasn't going to work until around ten.

∞∞∞∞∞∞∞

I parked in the driveway of Shane's two-story brick colonial. To my surprise, I was greeted by Josie rather than Shane. She pulled open the front door; beveled glass set in a red wood-grain as I reached the top step.

Josie looked like she was ready to head out, wearing a pair of skinny jeans and knee-high boots with a brown corduroy jacket. Her red hair flowed around her shoulders. Her big emerald green eyes were accentuated by long black eyelashes. My grandfather had once referred to her as an authentic Irish beauty. His label was spot on.

"Hey, Josie." I did my best to greet her pleasantly, wondering if she had been expecting me or not.

"Hi, Kaley," she smiled widely in response. "Shane had to run an errand quick. He asked me to entertain you for a few minutes. He didn't think he'd be long."

"Thanks," I smiled back, hoping it looked genuine. "You don't have to do that. I'll just catch up with him later."

"Don't be silly," she remarked, waving me inside. "Come in—get out of the cold." I stepped inside and was immediately greeted by Sargent Snuggles. It was comforting to have my furry friend around for what could be an uncomfortable few minutes. Josie led me into the sparsely decorated living room with vaulted ceilings. The furniture was all gray and matching. The space itself looked barely lived in. With the amount of time Shane spent at my house, I surmised that was a pretty accurate assumption.

I sat down on the stiff cloth sofa and declined her offer of a beverage. Josie sat down across from me and folded her hands gingerly in her lap while Sargent Snuggles rested his head contentedly in mine.

"Well, Kaley..." she began. "I'm actually glad for a little time alone with you."

"Oh?"

"I feel it's a good opportunity to set some things straight."

I took a deep breath. I had some idea where the conversation might be headed. Actually, I'd been expecting it for awhile. Despite what Shane said, his wife couldn't be pleased about the amount of time we spent together. Had the situation been reversed, I knew I wouldn't have been okay with it.

"It's about Shane—"

I held up a hand to stop her. "Josie, I know he spends entirely too much time with me and Summer. We have monopolized his time for the last two years. I get it... really, I do. He's your husband and we've taken advantage—"

Josie cut me off, "Kaley, it's fine. He was where he needed to be, but I got to ask... Are you sleeping with my husband?"

My eyes widened. "Oh my gosh, no! Josie—I have never nor would I ever—"

She nodded, "Okay, thanks. I had to ask. I mean a lot of nights he doesn't even come home, and it's not because of the job, either."

Although Shane wasn't sleeping with me and did spend some nights at our house, I wasn't entirely convinced he wasn't cheating on his wife. That was not something I'd share with Josie, though. That was their issue to work out and none of my business.

I felt my phone vibrate from my rear jeans pocket. I had forgotten to remove it when I sat down but was grateful for the distraction. I slid it out from underneath me—a text from Shane that he'd been delayed and would catch up with me later. When I looked back up, I caught Josie giving me a once-over. She smiled and tried to hide it.

"Was that Shane?" she asked. Her voice was a couple octaves higher and her phony smile just a bit wider.

I cleared my throat uncomfortably and peered back down at my now blank phone screen. "Yeah," I confirmed. "He's not going to make it."

"Well, at least I know I'm not the only one he stands up." She tacked on an insincere giggle.

"He's been great," I offered, uncertain of how to tactfully navigate the situation. "And as I said, we shouldn't take advantage. His place is with you."

She waved away my concern. "It's fine. Now that I know you're not sleeping together that is."

"Yep, I mean nope. We're not or won't… not ever." I bumbled, tripping over my words.

Josie's smile tightened, "It's okay, Kaley, relax. We're good. In fact, I was just thinking… maybe we could be friends? I mean you are kind of sharing my husband."

"Sure!" I offered, possibly a bit too enthusiastically. "You are always welcome to come with Shane."

"Great! And maybe we could grab a coffee or something sometime? Just the two of us?"

"Sure!" I repeated and managed to make my mouth turn upward. Sargent Snuggles grunted and sauntered off toward the open dining room area. The tension was too much for the poor pup.

"Fabulous, Kaley. I'm really looking forward to getting to know you better."

"Me too." *What else could I say?* "Well, since Shane isn't coming, I'll get out of your way," I said, doing my best not to bolt upright out of the chair.

Josie rose too. We practically raced each other to the front entrance.

"See you soon!" Josie's enthusiasm was at risk of boiling over as she ushered me back into the cold.

"For sure!" I responded, noting my cheeks felt numb from all the ridiculous smiling.

I had a feeling Shane was avoiding me. If he wasn't going to help me unravel Nathan's notes, then I'd do it myself. It was time for the second part of my new year's resolution. On my way to the car, I texted John and asked him to meet me at the gallery after work. I was going to get to the bottom of whatever his issue was. If John wasn't willing to give me something, then I had a decision to make.

∞∞∞∞∞∞∞

On impulse, I decided to stop by the hardware store on my way to the gallery. I had no idea if Matt was working, but I was determined to accomplish something. I was tired of reacting to everyone else's decisions regarding my life. It was time to take charge, and my gut told me that Matt Pine could provide some clarity.

Hardings Hardware, where Matt worked, shared that universal hardware smell—kind of a rubbery, metal scent, mixed with wood chips, and something unknown, a smell I'd always found comforting. I'd made it a few steps into the store when I was greeted by a heavyset blonde guy with glasses. I knew him by sight but not by name, "Good morning, can I help you with something?" he asked cheerfully.

I read his nametag, "Hi, Dwayne, I was wondering if Matt Pine is working?"

He gave me a once-over and scratched his head. Apparently, this wasn't a common question.

"I was hoping he could help me with something," I offered. "I own a gallery in town," I added. Although my visit had nothing to do with the gallery, it seemed to offer credibility to my presence.

"Oh, sure. I'll go get him," he said, scurrying off toward the back of the store.

I busied myself looking at keychains hanging near the register. When I looked up again, Matt was strutting toward the front of the store. His red polo shirt fit much differently on him than his doughy co-worker. The short sleeves bursting at the seams as they tried to contain the bulk of his biceps.

"Kaley?" he looked surprised to see me. Who could blame him? The last time we'd seen each other I freaked out on him.

"Hi," I forced my mouth to turn upright in a casual smile, although we both knew my visit was anything but casual. "Do you have a few minutes? I was hoping we could talk."

"Ummm, sure," he looked around. "Give me a moment to make sure it's okay with Dwayne." He instinctively touched my arm and then quickly withdrew his hand, probably thinking I'd go crazy and yell at him again. "Just don't go anywhere."

I nodded and went back to checking out the keychain display. After a few moments, Matt returned and led me to a small break room toward the back of the building. The room held a couple of round tables and chairs. A soda machine occupied the rear corner next to an ancient green refrigerator. The room seemed to vibrate from either the soda machine, refrigerator, or both. Matt politely pulled out a metal folding chair and offered me a seat. I accepted and sat down, anxiously tugging at the cuffs on my coat.

He sat down across from me, "I didn't mean to frighten you the other night," he offered apologetically.

"I know. I overreacted," I said, placing my arms on the table.

"No. Not at all. I wouldn't be happy if some meathead approached Aiyona at a gas station at night. That was a bonehead move on my part. You did the right thing."

I nodded, "Thank you." I looked up and made real eye contact with Matt, as though seeing him for the first time. His eyes were big, brown, and surprisingly kind. I thought that to be quite a contrast to the rest of his gruff exterior.

"I'm glad you came," he offered. I knew he was waiting for me to say something, but I didn't know where to start. My motivation for seeking him out was unclear even to me so how could I explain it to him.

I had to say something... the silence was getting uncomfortable. "Anyway, Matt..." I rubbed my palms on my jeans and took a deep breath. "What you said the other night was upsetting. More than upsetting, actually—shocking. You claimed to have had something to do with Nathan's death, how is that possible?"

Matt leaned forward and lowered his voice. "The fact that you're here leads me to believe I'm onto something."

"Why? And how did you know Nathan?"

He kept his voice low. "I got into some stuff when I moved here. Nothing big, but illegal, and I kind of narced out some guys to Detective Stone. Anyway, he really helped me, Kaley. Your husband was a good guy. He actually trusted me... If it hadn't been for him, I'm not sure I could have turned things around. I might have hurt my family, but I'm not a screw-up anymore; Aiyona and Layla can depend on me."

I could feel my eyes growing damp and wiped them with my sleeve, "Thank you for that, Matt. I won't ask for any details. Whatever happened was between you two. I'm just glad he could help. It's obvious you have a wonderful relationship with your family. What I don't understand is how helping you could have led to Nathan's death." I also didn't understand why Shane had said Matt hadn't had any trouble in Round Rock when clearly he had, but I kept that to myself.

Matt hesitated, "I asked Nathan to go to the bluff the night he was killed. I knew something wasn't right... but I did it anyway."

"What do you mean?"

"I gotta be truthful with you, Kaley. I'm not sure how much I should share."

"Well, so far you've told me pretty much nothing."

He looked away and folded his arms across his wide chest. "Thing is... I think we can help each other."

"Well, that's cryptic."

He surveyed me with an uncomfortable amount of intensity. "I need to know you're not going to go running to Shane Gavin with whatever I tell you."

"I can't promise that."

Matt rose slowly from his seat. "Then I'll have to go about this another way."

My pulse rate quickened, "We're talking about Nathan's last few moments on this earth. If you know something about how that time was spent, then you owe me an explanation."

Matt glanced down at the floor. "You're right," he said quietly.

"And..."

Matt wouldn't or couldn't reestablish eye contact. "I think they used me to set your husband up."

"Who, Matt?"

"I'm not sure..."

"If you don't know who—then tell me why. Why would someone want to kill Nathan, and why would they use you?"

He shook his head wearily, "I don't know."

I pushed away from the table. "I don't have time for this."

"Wait, Kaley—please. There's more."

I decided to hear him out.

"I'm trying to piece everything together," Matt admitted. Aiyona got a phone call at work a while ago. Actually, it was around the time the girls became friends. The caller warned her that I should back off. I had no idea what that meant. Then your buddy Gavin showed up at work and told me to stay away from you."

"What are you implying?"

Matt hesitated. "That maybe Shane Gavin isn't the person you think he is."

"Shane has nothing to do with your conspiracy theory or whatever it is. He warned you away because he's over-protective. I thought I might be able to trust you, Matt, but I won't make the same mistake Nathan did." I turned to leave.

"Don't you see?" Matt called after me. "I thought it was over the night your husband was shot. There were no more threats. No more ties. It was just over."

"Well, how lucky for you," I spat.

"No. Not lucky at all… just over… until now. Until I started talking to you."

"Me?" I had no idea what he meant by that.

"I'm not a hundred percent on this… but I think Nathan was onto something, and they wanted to shut him up. I think I could have helped your husband put the pieces together."

His words chilled me, I thought about the notebook but certainly wasn't about to let Matt know about that. "Well, Nathan's gone so whatever he knew died with him." I said abruptly.

"Are you sure?"

I narrowed my eyes at him. "What do you mean—am I sure?"

"Maybe you have information you're not even aware of, Kaley."

"Nathan didn't discuss his cases with me. Case in point, I knew nothing about your relationship with him."

"But they don't know that."

I threw up my arms in exasperation. "Who is this elusive 'they' you keep referring to, Matt?"

His voice softened, "I don't know. But I think I'm being watched. Maybe you are too. I want to help you, Kaley. I just thought you might want to help me too."

"You know what…" I stepped in close. "I think you feel bad for whatever role you played in Nathan's death, and I'm starting to think you should. I'm not willing to help you alleviate that guilt." I turned on my heel to leave for the second time.

"Kaley, please wait…" Matt pleaded.

Some unexplained force drew me back to hear what else Matt Pine could possibly have to say. I shoved my hands deep into the pockets of my peacoat and waited.

"I will never forgive myself for what happened to Nathan." His voice cracked as he continued. "So, I don't expect you to either. I think Nathan was killed to shut him up. I'm going to do what I should have done before. I could really use your help. If I'm right—Nathan was set up and they used me to do it. Will you help me find your husband's killer? Please? And that's all I can say unless I know you're in this with me... just you..."

Meaning he didn't want me talking to Shane. I chewed my lip and considered everything Matt had just divulged.

"Kaley..." His eyes met mine. Once again, I was struck by the softness there.

"I can't do this without Shane. If what you said is true, then he can help you."

Matt threw his hands up. "Or kill me faster!"

I shrugged and walked away, knowing I couldn't deal with any more of this today but deep down knowing that I wouldn't be able to let it go, either.

Chapter 29
MATT

I spent the rest of the morning overanalyzing my conversation with Kaley. Then, I clocked out for a late lunch. Making my way across the parking lot, I was so absorbed in my thoughts that I didn't notice the black Mustang GT. It wasn't until I was behind the wheel of my piece of crap Impala and ready to back out that I realized I was blocked in. It didn't dawn on me right away, but I knew the car.

As I prepared to confront the driver, I caught movement in my rearview mirror. Then as I watched Shane Gavin saunter toward my vehicle, I put two and two together. He was dressed like a wanna-be rockstar in jeans and a brown leather jacket with fleece around the collar. A pair of costly-looking aviator sunglasses topped off the look. I lowered the window, steeling myself for whatever was coming.

"We meet again!" he exclaimed with a cocky self-assured grin.

"You're blockin' my exit," I replied dryly.

The smile disappeared as he leaned in my window. "I have some questions for you, my friend."

"Well... we're not friends... And by the looks of your wheels, you're not here as a cop," I said, gesturing toward the Mustang.

"Cut the bullshit, Matt."

I took my hands off the wheel and shrugged. "No BS here, Detective. I really don't want trouble."

"You don't want trouble..." Shane parroted back at me.

I shrugged, "That's right."

"But that hasn't always been the case—has it?"

"You are well aware that it's not," I said, trying to keep my voice neutral. I was starting to get annoyed but did my best not to show it. Gavin was looking for a reason to bust me. I was not going to give him one.

"Did you know Detective Stone?"

"Yes."

"I'm glad you chose to be honest, Matt."

"I have no reason not to be."

"Are you sure about that?" the detective asked, raising his eyebrows.

"Look—you're obviously after something here, but I don't know what it is. I'd be happy to answer any questions you have, but I'm not great at guessing."

"Could you tell me why Nathan had your contact information?"

I wondered what, if anything, Kaley had told him about our conversation. It was clear she believed in the jackass, but I had to wonder if her husband had.

"I'm waiting..." Gavin drummed his fingers on the window frame.

I decided to go ahead and divulge the information. Maybe I could learn something from Gavin. "I was kind of like a CI for him."

I watched his face closely. I couldn't tell if this was new information or not. His lips stayed pressed together, and I couldn't see his eyes through the stupid sunglasses. "You were an informant?"

"Something like that."

"What exactly did you inform Detective Stone of?"

"Weren't you his partner? I feel like you should already know."

"I was and that's how I know you're lying," Gavin snapped.

"Or Nathan didn't trust you."

Gavin didn't seem to know where to go from there. He straightened up. "Don't think I'm done with you yet, Matt." He turned on his heel and sauntered back to his Mustang.

"Of course you're not," I mumbled under my breath. I watched him in the rearview as he hopped back into the car and tore out of the parking lot. The day just kept getting better and better. I pulled out and drove in the same direction as Gavin.

I thought about Detective Stone. I tried hard to recall that night. I was messed up; I knew that much. On what, though, I couldn't recall. That's the thing— I couldn't account for so much about that day. I'd worked hard to stay clean until that point. I didn't think I'd messed up at least not with anything harder than alcohol. Gavin's Mustang signaled and pulled to the curb along the main drag. The action distracted me from my thoughts.

Kaley was on the sidewalk in front of her gallery. I could see she was struggling to open the door with an armload of bags. Gavin jogged up to help her; and on impulse, I pulled into the space in front of his vehicle and got out too. I trailed the pair and reached the entrance door before it had time to swing closed behind them. The little bell attached to the front alerted them to my presence.

Kaley turned, "Oh, we're not actually open today..." She had taken the bags from Shane and set them near a large cube-shaped display case. "Matt?"

Gavin turned at the sound of my name. He didn't appear pleased to see me. "What the hell?" he said, yanking off his sunglasses with a sneer. "I thought I told you to keep your distance."

I laughed, "You're the one that came lookin' for me."

"Don't be a dumb ass, Matt. You know what I'm talking about," the detective took a step forward.

Kaley placed a calming hand on his shoulder and looked back and forth between the two of us. "Guys—I don't know what's going on, but someone should probably clue me in."

"Did you tell him about our conversation this morning?" I asked, gesturing toward the glowering Gavin.

"What conversation?" Gavin asked.

"I didn't have the chance yet." Kaley narrowed her eyes at me.

"What conversation?" Gavin asked again.

Kaley sighed, "When you stood me up this morning, I went to the hardware store to see Matt."

"You what?" Gavin's jaw tightened.

"Don't even, Shane!" Kaley exclaimed. "Did you harass Matt... again?"

"A—I didn't stand you up. And two—I have my reasons for going to see Matt again."

"I think you mean B," I said. Gavin just looked at me. "You said A and then two rather than B—" I tried to clarify, but he cut me off.

"You know what I meant."

I laughed, but it seemed I was the only one finding humor in the situation. Gavin was glaring so hard that I thought he might actually strain something.

"See, Kaley—" I started, "Shane says he doesn't want me near you and your daughter. He claims it's because I have a criminal history. But I think there's another reason he doesn't want me around."

"Go on..." Kaley prompted, shooting daggers at Shane.

I continued, "If I planned to harm you or Summer, wouldn't I have done it? Didn't I have the perfect opportunity the other night at the gas station? But you asked me to back off, and I did."

She chewed her lip and glanced away.

Gavin folded his arms across his chest and looked back and forth between Kaley and me. Before saying anything, he took a deep breath as though trying to channel a calmer version of himself. "Kay," he began. "I asked Matt to stay away from you because I think he could be a danger to you and Summer. Maybe not he himself but his choices, his lifestyle. I get that the girls are friends and there is bound to be some interaction there. What I don't get, though… is why you would go out of your way to seek him out."

Kaley scowled. "Because—Shane—you said you'd look into Nathan's death, and as far as I can tell you've done absolutely nothing. So, I went looking for answers myself. Like it or not, Matt is connected to Nathan."

Interesting… it seemed Kaley wanted the same thing I did. "I was his informant," I said, directing my attention toward Kaley and trying my best to ignore Gavin.

"So he says," shot Gavin.

I continued to ignore him and focused my attention on Kaley. "As I told you this morning—I think I was used to set Nathan up. I can't put the pieces together on my own but I think together—"

Before I could finish the sentence, Gavin grabbed the front of my jacket and shoved me hard against the gallery wall, rattling some of the paintings in the process. He was strong but I knew I could take him. However, I wouldn't give him the satisfaction of fighting back.

"Shane!" Kaley yelled. "What are you doing?"

"He's a lying son of a bitch, and I'm going to find out what he's hiding," Gavin sneered. The words meant for me rather than in answer to Kaley's question.

"Let go of him!" she yelled again. And when he didn't listen, she took it upon herself to try and pry her husband's partner off of me.

Another voice boomed through the chaos. "What's going on here?"

Gavin had me pinned pretty tight. It was difficult to breathe let alone see who had happened upon our altercation. With my luck, it was probably another cop.

"Will you help?" Kaley's voice sounded strained as I felt Shane's grip lessen. I used the opportunity to push off to my right and away from him. From my new vantage point, I could see it was Kaley's boyfriend John who had come to the rescue. He had pried Shane off and was holding him back from coming at me again.

I put my hands up in surrender. "I'm leaving now. I don't want to cause Kaley any more trouble." I turned toward Kaley, who looked extremely flustered at this point. "I didn't mean you any disrespect. I want you to know I'm not the man I used to be. Let me assure you I'd never do anything to hurt you or your daughter."

John spoke up now. "Did he hurt you or Summer? Because if he did…"

I mentally rolled my eyes. Poor Kaley had so much testosterone surrounding her it was a wonder the woman could even function "Give her some credit guys. The woman is quite capable. After only knowing her a short time, I can quite honestly say if I had done anything to negatively affect her or her daughter she would have handled me already."

Kaley looked at me appreciatively and tucked her hair behind her ear. "Thank you for that, Matt."

Both Shane and John shuffled around a bit, not particularly enjoying the fact that I'd shown them up.

"Anyway," Kaley continued. "Matt didn't do anything. Shane, on the other hand, is acting like a maniac."

"I'm gonna go and let you all sort this out," I offered, turning to leave.

Kaley stepped forward to stop me. "Not until you answer my question."

"And mine!" Shane piped up behind her.

Kaley shushed him and directed her attention back to me. "Why didn't you tell me who you were when we met?"

I struggled with the question. Why hadn't I told her when the girls became friends? I offered the most logical explanation I could come up with. "Because I knew your husband as a cop when I was—as your buddy would put it a 'low-life criminal.' I was afraid you would judge me, and Layla would lose her new best friend."

"Oh..." Kaley said quietly.

I waited, but she didn't offer anything further.

I slipped my hands into my pockets and shifted awkwardly, not sure where to go from this point. Hell—I wasn't sure where I was going from the beginning of this. It was an impulsive decision and one I was already regretting. "Anyway, I'm sorry. I'm going to go."

"Not yet!" Shane snapped.

I sighed, trying to hide my irritation.

"Let it go, Shane," Kaley said gently, reaching out to grasp his shoulder.

He shrugged her off and took a step forward, and I feared I was about to be manhandled for the second time. Lucky for me, Kaley's boyfriend stepped in again.

John positioned himself between me and the angry detective. He placed one hand on Gavin's chest and used the other hand to point at me. "Matt," John's voice sounded stern. I imagined it was the same tone he used on high school kids when he was about to reprimand them. "I think it would be best if you left now."

I threw my hands up in the air. "That's what I'm sayin." I turned to leave, finding it increasingly more difficult to keep my attitude in check. I gave a slight nod to Kaley and pushed my way out the glass doors.

Chapter 30
KALEY

I didn't think I'd ever been so angry with Shane. I waited until Matt was clearly out of earshot before rounding on my friend. "What was that about? What are you doing? You can't go around harassing people, Shane! And don't you dare say you were doing it for me."

Shane refused to meet my eyes. Instead, he scratched his scruffy face and looked out the window to where Matt's vehicle was pulling away from the curb.

I stepped forward, positioning myself right in front of him. "Shane!"

"Look, Kay, I have my reasons. I need you to trust me."

"Trust you? You're running around behind my back intimidating people on my behalf—and I'm supposed to what—just drop it and trust you?"

A look of defiance crossed his rugged features, "Yeah—pretty much."

"Well, I'm not okay with that."

"Tough!"

"Excuse me?" I crossed my arms and waited for a response. I was doing my best not to totally unleash on my friend.

John must have sensed I was on the edge. Before Shane had the opportunity to counter, he spoke up. "I think you two might need a break before someone says something they might regret."

My eyes locked on Shane's.

"John's right," he agreed.

I didn't say anything. I continued to stare Shane down. I could only hope he felt as uncomfortable as he'd made me feel.

Shane ran his hand down his face. "I'm not going to apologize for looking after you, Kay..." He struggled for a moment, trying to decide if he should say more or not. He went with the latter and turned hard on his heel, storming out of the gallery. The force of his exit knocked the welcome bells from the hinges, and they clamored to the floor with a crash.

"He's so damn irritating!" I exclaimed, bending down to retrieve the bells.

"Are you okay?"

"I'm fine," I replied, walking away from John and discarding the bells on the checkout counter before taking a seat on the stairs. "I'm glad you showed up when you did."

"Me too." He moved to join me, but I rose from my seat before he had the chance.

"Aren't you supposed to be at work?" I asked.

"I took the afternoon off. This time I'm actually going to use my vacation time too."

"And you what... thought I'd just drop everything to spend time with you?" I snapped, realizing it sounded harsh; but I was really tired of everyone making assumptions about me.

He frowned, "No... I didn't actually expect you to do anything. I got your message. I'm the one who dropped everything to come see you."

I folded my arms across my chest, physically closing myself off from him. I wanted to push him away—push all of them away. I didn't want John's affection. I didn't want Shane's friendship. I sure as hell didn't want Matt Pine in my life. I wanted everything to go back to the way it was before...

When I didn't say anything, John threw his hands up in exasperation. "Now that Shane's gone—you want to fight with me?"

I didn't want to fight with anyone; but I wasn't sure how to handle the overload of emotions, so I continued to give John the silent treatment.

"I don't know, Kaley... I thought that being part of a couple meant dropping everything to be there for the other person when they needed something. Clearly, I misread some signals. I apologize—I'm very rusty in this department."

I scoffed. "We're a couple? Cause ya could have fooled me!"

"What's that mean?"

"It means couples communicate. They are there for one another and share plans with each other. Something is going on with you, and you won't talk about it."

"I could say the same thing about you!" he retorted. "What the hell happened here today?"

"Which part?"

"All of it! You asked to see me; and when I show up, you treat me like dirt. That is, after I pried your friend off Layla's dad. None of that was just out of the blue. You've been keeping things from me too."

I nodded and tried to sort my thoughts, which were becoming increasingly more muddled. "I think I jumped into this too soon," I finally said.

"What?"

"I'm sorry, John. I think this is all happening a little too fast."

John scoffed, "Over two years, Kaley. He's been gone for over two years."

"I know how long Nathan has been gone! I don't need to be reminded of that!"

John ran his fingers through his hair and let out an exasperated breath of air, "I'm sorry."

I nodded. "I need you to go," I brushed past him toward the front door. I was fully prepared to usher John out onto the street and possibly out of my life. I needed to focus on Nathan's final project. I didn't have time for distractions.

John lingered in the doorway. "I really care about you, Kaley. I'd like to stay and work through this."

In response, I pulled open the door.

John gave me a swift nod, "Okay."

As I pushed the door shut behind him, Julia's plea rang through my mind. She had asked me not to hurt her brother, and I knew I'd done exactly that.

∞∞∞∞∞∞∞∞

I canceled my evening meeting and closed up the gallery. It was a good thing Henry had Summer because I was not in a good mindset to parent. At home, I crawled into bed with Nathan's notebook and snuggled up under the covers ready to do some digging. Some of the notes and abbreviations made sense. Other pages were more challenging to decipher.

Nathan used a lot of abbreviations and shorthand. I recognized some of it as his own, and others were more recognizable as law enforcement jargon. One thing was for certain, it would be a hell of a lot easier if Shane were here to help me decipher it. I considered calling him, but I was still a little too irritated about the way he'd handled pretty much everything.

I searched for some kind of thread to follow. What was Nathan trying to accomplish? Why did he have work notes at home instead of at work? I rubbed my palms down my face and read through his notes for what seemed like the hundredth time. I had to get out of my own head and look at this from a different perspective.

One page was laid out like a mind-mapping activity. I looked for that page again. I found it and noted Shane and Logan were both listed toward the center; branching out from there were names of other officers. Shane's name had a question mark behind it. Under each officer were notes about various cases and numbers. I assumed the numbers were case numbers that coordinated with the notes. The next section on his diagram contained boxes with a bunch of Round Rock businesses. A majority of the listed companies were family-owned. Among them was Hardings Hardware, where Matt worked.

I went back to Shane's box. Why the question mark? Had Nathan been unsure which cases Shane had worked? Or, as Matt had suggested—was Nathan suspicious of Shane? One other officer, Josh Mason, had a question mark too. I knew Mason had been newer to the department, but other than that didn't know much. Logan was circled—probably because he was involved with all the cases. He was the Chief, after all. Yet John had some issues with Logan, so could it be something more?

After that, it was just pages and pages of dates and notes that made absolutely no sense to me. The last page was full of names. A few I recognized, either the individual or at least the family name. Nathan had abbreviations or a series of numbers after each name. I used my phone to look up the individuals on a public website that provided access to open court action in Wisconsin. I was able to confirm some of the people listed had various charges against them. So what? I flipped back to the page with the officers again. Maybe Nathan needed more information from the arresting officers? Matt said he'd provided information to Nathan, but that was about criminals. Matt also seemed to believe someone used him to get Nathan to the bluff that night...

I had a sinking feeling that Nathan may have been investigating his own department. Perhaps I was just looking at the information wrong or letting Matt's suspicions cloud my judgment? Did Nathan really not trust Shane? My mind was racing. I closed the notebook and tossed it aside. Was it possible that Shane's attentiveness was not due to survivor's guilt but because he'd been instrumental in having Nathan killed? Is that why he was dragging his feet on helping me?

I pushed that thought from my mind. No way. Shane was my best friend. I was being paranoid and ridiculous. Then there was the chief. Logan had been so good to us. I couldn't discount John's feelings toward him, though.

I padded out to the kitchen and made myself a rum and coke, heavy on the rum, and returned to bed with the drink. I sipped, and curled my feet up underneath me, mentally reviewing Nathan's notes. A quick glance at the clock on my nightstand indicated I'd been at this longer than anticipated, I was officially late for picking Summer up. Drinking only served to compound the problem.

I reached for my cell phone and dialed up Henry.

"Hello, darlin'. Are you on your way?"

"Actually, no," I replied, gearing myself up to lie to my grandfather. "I'm not feeling very well. Would you mind keeping Summer overnight?"

"I'd love to keep my great-granddaughter; but if you're comin' down with somethin', I better come over and take care of you."

"No. It's okay. John's doing that," I lied again.

"Well, tell him thanks from your ol' grandad." I could practically hear the old man grinning through the phone. Which made me feel even worse.

I was about to say goodbye but instead decided to get my grandfather's opinion. "Hey, Grandpa... can I ask you something?"

"Shoot."

"I know Shane isn't your favorite person, but do you think he's a good guy?"

"Well, that's an odd question. Where is this comin' from?"

I decided to share just enough information to get Henry's take. "I found a notebook of Nathan's, and a lot of it doesn't make sense. However, it seems like Nathan may have been uncertain about Shane."

"Uncertain how?"

"I don't know... like maybe he didn't fully trust him... is that possible?"

My grandfather was quiet for a moment. I imagined him rubbing his chin in quiet contemplation. He let out a breath of air, "Darlin', that's a loaded question. Can you tell me a bit more?"

"I'd rather not. Not yet at least. Can you just answer the question? Do you think I've been trusting the wrong guy?"

"Now, that's a different question. As ya know, Shane has never been my favorite person. I think he's cocky, dimwitted, and could be better to that beautiful wife of his. Now, I don't know if Nathan trusted him or not. What I do know is this... he has been there for my girls; and for that, he gets my complete admiration and support. Don't ya dare go tellin' him that, though."

I laughed as I felt the tension drain from my body. I took a swig of my drink and relaxed against the pillows. "Thanks, Grandpa."

"You bet. Now get some sleep, darlin'. And you tell John to take good care of ya."

Again, the pang of guilt from lying. "Goodnight," I said, as I ended the call. If my grandfather wasn't suspicious of Shane, then I certainly shouldn't be either. I had to go at this from yet another angle.

Chapter 31
MATT

I woke in a cold sweat. The room was dark and silent. I pushed myself upright, not quite sure what had roused me. As I leaned against the pillows, I could hear the rhythmic breathing of Aiyona beside me. I crawled to the end of the bed and peered down at Layla's sleeping form, and gently touched her cheek. The motion caused her to stir slightly. Her movement reassured me. If all was well, why did I feel so off-balance?

I crept from the bedroom into the kitchen, choosing to keep the lights off, and retrieved a glass from the cupboard nearest the sink. As I ran the tap, waiting for the water to cool, a car engine roared to life out on the street. Setting the glass aside, I turned toward the kitchen door. I peered out the curtains covering the small pane of glass at the top. The streetlight illuminated the dark SUV as it pulled away from the curb. Was it my imagination, or had it been parked in the exact same place as the dark sedan from before? We lived in a quiet, blue-collar neighborhood. The few neighbors we did have were sound asleep and would wake with the sun. The SUV speeding down the street in the middle of the night was out of place. It was getting more and more difficult to chalk up recent events to a series of coincidences. But why? Could it really be because of Kaley?

"Because of me," said a voice from inside my head. Not my own voice—a deep baritone. I looked around the kitchen, half expecting to see Nathan Stone standing behind me.

"I'll make this right," I said, my voice sounding oddly out of place in the stillness of the night. "I promise, Nathan. I'll do right by you."

"Who's Nathan?" asked another voice. This one not from my head but from the living room and belonging to my sleepy-sounding fiancée.

I ignored the question. "Sorry. Did I wake you?" I whispered.

"I woke up and you weren't there," Aiyona said as she padded into the kitchen and wrapped her arms around me, resting her head on my shoulder.

I inhaled the fruity scent of her shampoo and pulled her closer. "Sorry, baby. I was havin' trouble sleepin'."

"Who's Nathan?" she asked again.

"Nobody."

"He must be somebody if you're makin' promises to him in the middle of the night."

"Just a ghost," I whispered.

"Matt," she whispered back. "I think you're crackin' up."

"I think you're right," I agreed and scooped her into my arms to carry her back to the bedroom before she could ask any more questions.

Chapter 32
KALEY

I showered and changed into pajamas, which consisted of a pair of ratty old sweatpants and a tank top. I padded into the kitchen to make a sandwich. I'd need some brain food to power through the rest of Nathan's notes. After pulling out all the necessities to accomplish the task, I scrolled through my phone apps, looking for music or a podcast to listen to while I prepared my food. The phone rang in my hands, startling me enough that I almost dropped it. I fumbled around with the device and saw that it was Shane. I had no idea how to feel about him at that moment, so I took the call. Perhaps talking to him might help me sort my feelings.

"Hey, ready to apologize?" I said by way of greeting. I set the phone on the counter and pushed the speaker button as I continued to prepare my sandwich.

"Apologize for what?"

"Really?" I set down the butter knife.

"Look, I just called to let you know I'm out of town for the night."

"Everything okay?"

"Yeah, Josie went to Minneapolis to shop. When she was ready to come home, she couldn't get the Mustang started."

"Oh, oh, I hope it's nothing major."

"It's not," he snarled irritably. "She left the damn dome lights on and drained the battery."

"Sorry."

"It gets better. She decided we should stay over and got us a stupid, expensive room at some fancy hotel."

"Poor baby," I teased.

"I'm not amused, Kay."

"I can tell. Just try and relax. Have some fun with Josie."

"Josie is probably back in Round Rock by now."

"What? I thought you said—"

"Yeah—we had an argument. She said she was going down to the bar for a drink. I waited for over two hours, and when she didn't come back, I started to worry. I called her and guess what—she left me here."

I sighed, "I really am sorry, Shane. That was pretty shitty of her. What were you arguing about?"

"It doesn't matter."

I wanted to point out that if his wife was angry enough to ditch him in another state—it probably did matter. However, knowing Shane, it wouldn't help to point that out. "What are you going to do?"

"Well, she paid for this ridiculous room so I'm going to try to make the best of it."

"Good for you," I stated, wondering why he seemed so irritated by the expense. Shane rarely mentioned money. It was my understanding that Josie's parents had passed on, leaving her with a large inheritance. From the stories Nathan had shared, Shane could have actually quit the department and comfortably lived off his wife. The concern made me wonder if perhaps the relationship was indeed coming to an end. Maybe Shane was losing his sugar mama, and he'd have to once again worry about pesky financial responsibilities. Probably a good thing he'd held onto his job.

"If you want to get Sargent Snuggles from my

house, I'm sure he'd appreciate it," Shane continued. "I was going to call you earlier to get him—when I thought we'd both be staying overnight but..." he trailed off.

"I'd rather not run into your wife," I replied truthfully.

"Can't say I blame you there, but I would feel better if you and Summer had the dog with you."

My hand clenched the phone. "Are you using our dog in a roundabout way to warn me about Matt again?"

He sighed, "That guy is bad news."

I paused my sandwich-making process and leaned on the counter, contemplating where to go from there. "You know, Shane... I think there are some bad guys out there... I don't, however, think Matt is one of them."

There was a long silence and then: "I don't agree with you on that."

"What does that mean?"

"It means—I just need more time, okay?"

"Time for what?"

Another pause.

"Shane?"

"We'll talk tomorrow."

"Sure," I replied flatly and ended the call.

Suddenly my sandwich didn't seem as appealing. Maybe I should just pick up Sargent Snuggles and get out of my own head for a bit. I'd only drunk about half of the rum and coke and over an hour had passed. Besides, my conversation with Shane had been very sobering. I cleared the countertop, putting everything back. Then, retrieved my parka from where I'd earlier discarded it over one of the kitchen chairs. I zipped it up over my tank top and sweats. Lastly, I slipped my feet into a pair of faux fur boots next to the back door. I'd need to go straight to Shane's and home again. I did not want to be caught in public in this particular attire. Hopefully, Josie would be okay with me taking the dog. Thankfully, my keys were hanging on the key hook by the door, so I didn't need to hunt them down for a change.

As I started out the kitchen door, I remembered my cell phone on the counter. Later I would recall the chill that had run the entire length of my spine when I reached across the counter to retrieve it.

Before I could fully process, something clamped firmly over my mouth. I tried to call out, but the knit fabric from a glove pushed further against my lips. As I tried to pull away, a strong arm encircled my waist and lifted me off the ground. I struggled and kicked as I felt the sensation of being lifted, and my legs were grabbed out from underneath me by what must have been a second person.

My heart felt like it might thump right out of my chest. I tried to sink my teeth into the glove, but it was too tight against my lips. They carried me through the kitchen into my dark bedroom, where I was flung like a ragdoll onto the bed. I wrestled to get away as my parka was ripped off. My boot must have managed to connect with a soft spot on at least one of the intruders as I heard a grunt. I made it off the bed, dragging my comforter with me. Unfortunately, I was only able to make it as far as the bedroom doorway before I was tackled from behind. My body hit the wood flooring hard. Someone wrenched my right arm out from underneath me. I felt a sharp pinch followed by some stinging near my shoulder. I had an immense fear that I had just been injected with something. I cried out but was unable to move as the two very strong bodies held me in place. I clawed at the floor, trying to get out from underneath the hold. A warmth filled my torso, spreading out to my extremities.

"What do you want?" I asked breathlessly, ceasing to struggle, at least for the moment.

I heard voices but I couldn't make out the words. They seemed to be talking to me or each other, but it felt like my head was underwater. My fear had been confirmed. I'd been drugged but with what and why? Thank goodness Summer was with Henry. That was the last thought I had before a slow fog started to fill my head.

Chapter 33
MATT

Aiyona and Layla were out the door before me the next morning. I didn't have to be at work until ten, so I made up for the lost hour of the night by sleeping in. Even with my delayed start to the day, I was still ready by eight-thirty. It was as I was drinking my second cup of coffee that the idea hit me. I should talk to Kaley's boyfriend—the high school football coach guy. I couldn't get to Kaley without Gavin getting all up in my face, but maybe I could get to her through the coach. Wasn't it possible that he'd have some insight into Round Rock as well? I grabbed my coat and keys and headed over to the high school.

∞∞∞∞∞∞

The office woman peered over the top of her reading glasses. She had asked me a lot of questions and even scanned my driver's license, but despite all this, it didn't look like I'd get any further than the front office. She asked me for the third time what business I had with Coach Kyler.

"As I told you before ma'am, it's personal. I just need a few minutes of his time."

She pursed her lips and scowled at me.

"Please," I tried.

She picked up the phone and dialed a few digits. "John—you have a visitor in the front office," she said, keeping her skeptical blue eyes focused on me. "No, I will not send him your way... Because he doesn't have any reason to be in the school. He says it's personal business."

I drummed my fingers nervously on the counter as I waited for the outcome of the call. The secretary, whose nameplate read Mary Nicole, didn't seem to like that. She narrowed her eyes, and I stopped. I bet she scared the hell out of the kids here.

Mary Nicole hung up the phone and stood. "Mr. Kyler will be with you momentarily. I'll show you to one of the offices where you can wait."

"Naw, that's fine. I'll just wait here."

She was about to protest when the door that led from the hallway to the office swung open, and an older kid raced into the office and proceeded to vomit all over the floor.

"Lovely, Max," Mary Nicole murmured with distaste.

The pale boy looked away from her and toward a room on the right with a placard reading NURSE above the door.

"Well, go on in," the secretary said, shooing the kid away as the putrid scent started to waft across the room.

My stomach started to churn as I looked away from the soiled area. "On second thought—I'd like to wait in that office area now," I managed.

Mary Nicole smiled for the first time since I'd walked in the door. "I bet you would. First door on the left," she said, pointing me in the opposite direction.

I made a rapid exit as I heard her call for a custodian on the loudspeaker.

The room where I'd been directed was cramped; it contained a desk, a small round table, and a large bookcase that took up an entire wall. There was one tiny window with the blinds pulled so tightly shut there was no hope of any natural light creeping through. I had a feeling the secretary had sent me to the room that was designated for in-school suspensions and whatever other forms of behavior modifications the school district implemented. I was familiar with these types of designated areas, which made me feel all the more cramped and sweatier, so I opened the door. Fortunately, there was still enough distance between me and the putrid smell.

The office door opened again. Coach Kyler breezed in, wearing a light blue button-down shirt with tan dockers. He was carrying an accordion folder under his arm and looked very harried. He gave Mary Nicole a curt nod.

"Watch your step, John," she warned, pointing to the ground in front of him.

"Well, that's gross," he stated simply, as he caught my eye and continued in my direction. "You might want to call a custodian," he offered.

The secretary rolled her eyes and turned back to her computer.

Working in a school was decidedly very different from working in a hardware store.

"Matt—" John offered his hand.

I grasped his hand firmly, feeling very adult with the formality of the greeting in the school office.

"Thank you for seeing me."

"Would you like to sit?" he asked, gesturing toward the blue plastic chairs pushed in under the table.

"Ummm, no thanks. I prefer to stand."

John closed the door and waited for me to say more.

"I'm sure you're wondering why I'm here..."

John set the file on the table and folded his arms across his chest, rocking back slightly on his heels as he responded. "Does it have anything to do with whatever happened at the gallery yesterday?"

"Somewhat... I'm not sure how much Kaley told you about my ummm..." I stammered, trying to find the right word. "I guess relationship is the best way to put it..."

He furrowed his brow, "Your relationship? With Kaley?"

"Ummm, no, her husband."

He raised his eyebrows. "Nothing."

I started to sweat again, the space feeling even tighter than it had originally. How was John going to react to my confession? Would he jump all over me the way Gavin had? Why had I thought this was a good idea?

"I think I had her husband killed, and I need her help," I blurted out.

John's eyes widened. "What the hell, Matt?" He yelled louder than I think he intended because he shook his head and lowered his voice before repeating, "What the hell, Matt?—"

I cut him off, "Not that I actually had anything to do with Nathan being shot, but maybe I made a bad decision. A decision that led him to the bluff, you know..."

"I don't know. I have no idea what you're talking about. Or why you've come to me, but this sounds like something you need to talk to the police about."

"I can't. That's why I'm here. Shane Gavin has it out for me—he's turned Kaley against me too. If you could just talk to her—"

John held up a hand to stop me, "Kaley and I had a disagreement, and I haven't heard from her since yesterday morning. She's not returning my calls or texts. If you're here because you think I can help you with Kaley... you've come to the wrong place. You'd probably have better luck with Shane Gavin."

"Freakin' Gavin again! I told you he has it out for me. Why does everything always come back to him?"

"Look, you've just made a very alarming statement. I don't know what the deal is between you and Shane—"

A light rap on the door prevented John from saying more. "Sorry to interrupt," Mary Nicole stuck her head in the door. "But the elementary school is on the line for you. Summer Stone had an accident on the playground. The nurse wasn't able to reach her mother, so she called the emergency contacts. One of the girl's contacts is a detective who is currently an hour away. He's coming but he asked the nurse to notify you."

"Tell them I'm on the way," John said, rushing out of the room. He turned back suddenly, most likely realizing he was walking out in the middle of our conversation. "Matt—"

"Yeah..." I motioned for him to go. "This can wait. Summer is more important. Let me know if I can do anything."

He nodded and then sprinted out of the school.

I was suddenly worried about Kaley and Summer Stone.

Chapter 34
KALEY

"Kaley ... Kaley ... Can you hear me?"

Someone was trying to wake me. I managed a groan in response. I felt achy and kind of sick, the last thing I wanted to do was wake up.

"Honey, the cops are on the way; but I really need you to wake up and talk to me... okay?"

Cops? Why were the police coming? And why was whoever being so insistent I get up?

"Kaley, do you know what happened?"

I opened my eyes but had difficulty focusing. The outline of John sitting on the edge of my bed swam across my vision. I couldn't really recall what had happened, there was just an overwhelming sense of dread or fear... I was having difficulty identifying the feeling.

"Kaley?"

I pushed myself upright and felt John fold over me like a security blanket. I let him hold me as I tried to comprehend the situation. When I finally pulled away, I took in the state of my bedroom. It had been completely ransacked. My closet doors were open with clothes strewn about everywhere. The dresser drawers were emptied, the contents scattered on the floor. The nightstand nearest the door had been toppled and partially blocked the entrance.

"What happened?" I asked.

John shook his head. "I was hoping you could tell me. Your entire house is a wreck."

I looked around in disbelief, "And I just slept through it?"

"I don't think so..." John hesitated. "I think someone knocked you out or something... You were difficult to wake. I don't think you were just sleeping..."

A hard rapping at the front door startled me. "That's probably the police," John said. "I called them when I got here." He rose from the bed, "I'll be right back."

Knocked me out? I racked my brain trying to remember. A hazy memory of Shane's phone call came back to me, and then struggling with someone... Maybe more than one person?

Moments later, John was back with Chief Sterns hot on his heels.

I looked back and forth between the two as a wave of nausea hit me. I rubbed my palm across my damp forehead, "I think I need a minute, guys."

John turned back to Logan, "Can you wait in the hall?"

It didn't appear Logan was going to budge. John positioned himself between me and the police chief, "A moment, please."

Logan nodded and backed out of the room, allowing John to pick up the toppled nightstand and close the door behind him. That done, John lowered himself to the edge of the bed. His thick brows furrowed with concern.

"I don't think I was knocked out..." I rubbed my right arm. I recalled feeling the poke of a needle. "Is it possible I was injected with something?"

John didn't respond; he remained quiet as I continued to sort things out.

"I wasn't in bed..." I rubbed my eyes as I tried to clear my vision and my mind. "I was trying to leave,

John... Then—two people came in through the kitchen door." As I spoke, the fog started to clear. However, it all felt kind of like an out-of-body experience.

"Two men came into the house?" John asked.

I shivered involuntarily, "I think it was two men... I don't know—I couldn't see them, but I don't think there was more than two."

John gently took hold of my arm and studied the spot I'd been rubbing, and then pulled one of the blankets from the bed and wrapped it around my shoulders. "That's good you can remember that," he took my hand as a show of support. "Anything else?"

I nodded and gave myself a minute to try and recall the events with more clarity. "I was trying to leave because Shane called."

John leaned closer. You were going to meet Shane? I don't understand..."

I shook my head, "No... I don't know... Did something happen to him?"

John reached out, sliding his hand down my cheek to wipe away a tear. Until that moment, I hadn't realized I was crying.

"It's okay," he said reassuringly. "Shane is fine. I talked to him earlier."

I nodded.

"We'll figure this out." John released my hand and looked around my mess of a bedroom. "How about we find something a little warmer for you to wear before Logan comes back?"

I nodded again.

John rifled through the piles and produced a black sweatshirt that I slipped over my head; but instead of walking over to the door to let Logan in, he resumed his position beside me. "Look... Kaley..." he cleared his throat. "I'm not really sure how to ask you this..."

"What?"

He looked extremely uneasy. "You said you were getting ready to go somewhere. It's pretty cold outside, and you're not wearing much…"

It seemed like an odd question given the circumstances. I had just been terrorized, and he was worried about weather-appropriate apparel. I was about to snap at him when a fuzzy memory of being pulled out of my coat made its way to the front of my memory.

"Oh, no… I had my parka on over my pajamas. I remember someone pulling it off and then getting stuck."

"Stuck? As in drugged?"

"Yeah… injected with whatever…"

"You were going out in your pajamas?" John asked.

I nodded, "I think so…"

"Do you remember anything else?"

I pressed my fingers against my eyes. My head was pounding, and I couldn't get a full grasp on anything. John appeared anxious. I could tell he wanted to know more. So did I, but there was nothing more to tell.

"Maybe I should talk to the cops now?" I offered.

John nodded and stepped gingerly over my belongings to open the door. Maneuvering through the disaster was not easy for a man of his stature. It was as he reached for the handle that I remembered Nathan's notebook.

"Wait…" I said, throwing aside covers and taking a shaky step onto the floor. "Something's missing."

John shifted uncomfortably. "Kaley, I'm afraid you probably have a lot of things missing. I believe you were robbed."

"No. Not like that. I had a notebook with a white cover. I need to find it."

To his credit, John didn't ask any questions. He just started helping me move things as he joined in my frantic search.

A sharp knuckle wrap on the bedroom door interrupted the mad search. "Don't go movin' anything in there," Logan warned. "Remember this is a crime scene."

John didn't miss a beat, "We're just looking for some clothes for Kaley."

"Okay... try not to disturb anything."

"Thank you," I mouthed to John before getting down on my hands and knees to look under the bed. There, in a tangle of sheets and blankets, the corner of the notebook was visible. I pulled it out and handed it to John. "Nobody can know about this."

Without a word, he lifted his shirt and tucked the bottom of the notebook into his waistband before adjusting his shirt back down around it. He held his arms out to his sides for inspection, "Can you tell?"

"No." Still feeling dizzy, I took two giant, unsteady steps over all my crap to reach him. I wrapped my arms around him, resting my head against his chest.

He squeezed me gently, causing the notebook to crinkle slightly under the pressure. Before we could say anything else, Logan knocked again.

"Ready?" John whispered.

I nodded and pulled away to navigate my way back to the edge of the bed. Hopefully, getting off my feet would aid with the dizziness. While I tried to quell another sudden wave of nausea, John made his way back across the room and pulled open the door.

Logan entered, trying not to step on anything as he shuffled into my bedroom. "Are you okay?" he asked. A genuine look of concern crossed his normally brusque features.

"I think so... Thank you," I replied shakily.

He looked back and forth between John and me before continuing. "There's an ambulance crew out front. They're ready to take you to the hospital."

I waved away the suggestion, "I don't think that's necessary."

"Kaley, you think someone shot you up with something," John gently reminded me. "I think you need to be seen, at least to determine what's in your system. If you don't want to go by ambulance, then I'll take you."

Logan's eyebrows shot up. "Injected you?"

"I think so..."

Another officer entered the room. "I'm glad you're okay, Mrs. Stone," he offered before turning toward the chief. "Gavin is on his way with the little girl."

"I don't want Summer to see the house this way," I interrupted.

John gave my hand a squeeze. "I'll head them off. Just so you know—Summer jumped off the top of a slide at school today."

I gasped, "I'm sorry—she what?"

"She's fine. She twisted her ankle. Just to be sure, I took her to be checked out."

I nodded, doing my best to absorb everything, "How did you know?"

When the school couldn't reach you, they called Shane; he had them get in touch with me. That's actually how I ended up here," he explained.

I nodded again.

John must have sensed how overwhelmed I was feeling and took charge. "It's all going to be okay, Kaley. You tell the chief everything you told me, and I'll have Shane get Summer situated in my truck. Then, I'm going to pack a bag for her and you. You'll both be staying at my house for now."

Logan scowled. "I don't think that's necessary. We can make accommodations—"

I cut him off, "Thank you, Logan. I think I'd feel better if I stayed with John."

"Good," John responded. "Take your time. We'll leave when you're ready." He brushed past Logan and left the door open on his way out.

I took a deep breath and relayed to Logan everything I could remember. It was basically the same thing I'd told John. Logan jotted down notes in a small spiral notebook as I spoke. I was just finishing up when Shane burst into the room.

"Kay! What happened?" he asked, sweeping me into a suffocating hug. "The house is a disaster! I mean what the Fu—"

Logan coughed, cutting him off, "I was just trying to figure that out. If you don't mind, Gavin."

Shane loosened his grip and sat down next to me "Sorry, Chief. Please proceed."

Logan set his notetaking materials on my overturned nightstand and pointed a stubby finger at Shane. "Gavin, you do not give me direction. I give it to you. Understand?"

Shane's jaw twitched before he responded with a sharp, "Yes, sir."

"Now, you're interrupting an interview," Logan continued. "I suggest you step out and leave Kaley and me to continue."

"Since when do you do interviews?" Shane asked.

Logan's face reddened. "Since the victim is Stone's wife," he spat. "Why don't you see if you can be of use with some of the inventory and clean up."

Shane didn't move.

"I'd be more comfortable if he stayed," I said, still feeling a little unsteady.

Logan reacted as though my request was an act of insubordination from either me, or Shane, or both. You could practically see the steam rising from his head. "Nobody tells me how to run an interview, not my detectives or the victims."

"I don't like being referred to as a victim—and frankly, Logan—you're making me feel extremely uncomfortable right now. I'd prefer to talk to someone else."

Logan placed his hands on his hips. His beady little eyes moved back and forth between Shane and me. Nobody spoke for a few beats. Then, Logan looked down at the floor and let out a breath of air. "My apologies, Kaley. I'm taking this particularly personally as I'm sure is Detective Gavin. I want to catch the son of a bitch responsible for breaking into your house and drugging you."

"You were drugged?" Shane asked in alarm.

"She was," Logan answered for me. "Now let's start over," the chief stated, picking up his notebook and pen again and looking at me expectantly.

"Chief—" one of the officers called out from somewhere down the hall. "Can you come out here for a minute?"

Logan looked hesitant but stepped out of the room anyway.

With Logan finally out of earshot, Shane turned toward me, "What happened?"

"I really don't know, Shane. I remember talking to you, and then I got ready to leave... but I can't remember where I was going."

"To get Sargent Snuggles."

"That was it! How could I have forgotten that? Yes, to get the dog," I confirmed. "But I never made it out the door. Someone came in through the kitchen and grabbed me from behind. There were actually two of them. We struggled. I took a needle to the arm and that's it. Next thing I know, John is trying to wake me up."

He shook his head in disbelief. "How come Henry didn't come looking for you?"

"He wasn't expecting me. The original plan was for Summer to stay the night there."

"I'm so sorry, Kay. If I hadn't been stuck in Minneapolis..."

"Don't do that."

"What?"

"You know what. You could have been three blocks away and still had no idea."

He swiped his hand down his face and stood to survey the damage. I hoped the rest of the house didn't look as bad.

"I bet Matt Pine had something to do with this," Shane muttered under his breath.

"You need to let that go."

Shane ignored me and scanned the disaster, "Do you think Nathan left anything other than the notebook behind?" he asked.

"You mean besides me and Summer?"

He gave me a pained look, "I'm sorry—that didn't come out right. I mean—it looks like someone was looking for something here. Where's the notebook?"

"Safe," I responded, before Logan marched back into the room.

"Kaley, let's get you over to the hospital for a check-up, okay?" Logan barked.

"I'm good, really. That's not necessary."

"Yes, it is," Shane responded, planting his hands on his hips. "I'll stay here and take inventory."

I opened my mouth to argue, but Shane cut me off before I could begin. "Non-negotiable. We need the record of the hospital as part of the investigation."

"Come on, Kaley," Logan held out his hand to help me across the mounds of my belongings.

"Fine," I agreed, but made my way out of the room without accepting help from Logan. "Please try and find my phone. I really don't want to be without that."

"I'll catch up with you in a bit," Shane promised, as he knelt to pick up a picture of Nathan and me that lay smashed just below his boots.

I looked away and tried to disregard the state of my home.

Chapter 35
MATT

It didn't matter what side of the law I was on. The end result was always the same. Even though it had been a while since I'd experienced the inside of a jail cell, the feeling was familiar. Cold concrete and the smell of steel and urine permeated my nostrils as I waited.

Gavin accused me of sticking Kaley with some kind of animal sedative or medication or something. Worse than that, his theory involved Aiyona stealing the drug from the vet she worked for. So, to keep Aiyona out of harm's way, I did something stupid. I told Gavin that Aiyona had nothing to do with it. I got the sedative from another source. Only after that did I realize how crazy my white lie really was. Apparently, Kaley had been attacked in her home by masked intruders. It hadn't been a solo job either. So, it's not like my lie had eliminated Aiyona as a suspect.

My predicament was bad. I tried to straighten things out with Gavin, but he wasn't about to listen. What I needed was an advocate. Someone who might have some pull with the cops here. Since I'd started poking around and solicited help from Kaley, things seemed to be ramping up at an alarming pace. If my investigation was tied to what happened to Kaley, then it wasn't a far stretch to think Aiyona could be a target as well.

The sound of heels clicking down concrete echoed off the walls and I recognized the sound of the purposeful gait. I was quite certain Aiyona was making her way toward the block of holding cells, specifically to cell number three where I was currently holed up. Frankly, it scared me more than anything else. There was a strong possibility that Aiyona was going to kill me before I could work out any of the aforementioned problems.

"Matt! What have you gotten yourself into?" Aiyona shrieked from the other side of the bars. "I mean—what the hell, baby!"

I leaned my forearms on my knees and hung my head low. Even though I wasn't responsible for attacking Kaley Stone, I was pretty sure I was the reason.

"Matt! Look at me," Aiyona demanded.

I stood and made my way toward my fuming fiancée. When we were just a few feet apart, I grasped the bars and grappled with the best way to appeal to her sensitivities. "I didn't do whatever it is you're thinkin'."

"You have no idea what I'm thinking!" she snapped back.

"Alright, then—tell me." I concentrated on keeping my voice calm so as not to poke the bear aka my lovely bride-to-be.

She tapped her foot and then looked both ways before responding. When she did, she lowered her voice to a hush and leaned in as far as the bars would allow. "I think the stuff you told me about the other night... you know... about the drugs and stuff. I think your activities upon our arrival here just came back to bite you in the ass. I know you didn't do anything to harm Kaley Stone, but I do believe you have some idea why she was targeted. And I think it may be connected to all your little secrets."

I opened my mouth to say something, but no words came out.

Aiyona narrowed her eyes and gripped the bars, placing her hands just below mine. "How am I doin' so far?"

I nodded, "Remarkably well."

"So, Matt, we have some things to sort out—after you get outta here. My next question is—how can I get you outta here?"

Another set of footsteps echoed down the hallway, not nearly as loud or as purposeful as Aiyona's. However, the sound indicated that our short visit was about to come to an abrupt end.

"Should I try to get a lawyer?" Aiyona asked quickly.

I shook my head. We both knew we couldn't afford that. I needed to finish my conversation with John Kyler. Although I wasn't sure I could trust him, I knew he'd be a better bet than Gavin. He also had respect in the community, and I needed an ally.

"Matt…" Aiyona waited anxiously for my response, but the cop had arrived. He was a young muscular guy with a military haircut and a no-nonsense attitude. He made a motion that our conversation was indeed done.

"Get a hold of John Kyler," I said, in a rush of breath as Aiyona stepped away from the cell. "He's the man we met with Kaley a while back at dinner."

Both the guard and Aiyona offered me a quizzical look.

"He works at the high school," I added.

"I remember," Aiyona replied uncertainly.

"Tell him I need to see him. Tell him it's urgent."

I knew she had a million questions, but we both knew she didn't have time to ask even one.

"I got this, baby; sit tight," she said instead.

I shrugged my shoulders and threw my hands up as if to say, 'do I have a choice?'

"Your time is up," the guard announced.

"Can we get just another minute?" I asked hopefully.

"No."

"Don't worry, Matt," Aiyona stated reassuringly. "I'll find this Kyler guy and have you out before dinner." With that, she gave the guard a once over and then spun hard on her heel and tromped away with the beefy man in tow.

Chapter 36
KALEY

It turned out that I was shot up with a drug called Ketamine. The doctor explained that it was used as a sedation drug in a medical setting and also known as a 'date rape drug' in a recreational setting. Shane mentioned it was used by veterinarians. After a thorough examination, I was given the all-clear. I'd come out of the incident with only a few bumps and bruises and a very hazy memory of the incident. Other than that, I was completely unharmed. Which was a huge relief considering I couldn't remember much.

Shane thought Matt was behind the incident, no surprise there. I didn't know if he was or wasn't. All I knew was that I needed some rest, so when Shane offered to take Summer to his house for a while, I didn't hesitate.

Even though John had the most comfortable king-size bed I'd ever experienced, it was impossible to get any sleep. Every time I closed my eyes, I felt the sensation of being seized from behind, which was not at all restful. My eyes wandered around the bedroom. It was completely devoid of anything personal or really anything at all. There was nothing on the walls other than a very large flat-screen TV. The nightstand on the right was empty, whereas the one on the left side of the bed held a pile of books and a small reading lamp.

My observations were cut short by a hard rapping sound coming from the front of the house. It took me a moment to register the sound—someone was knocking on the front door. John's harried footsteps were barely audible as he rushed past the closed bedroom door.

Moments later, the sounds of hushed voices wafted down the hallway. Although the words were muffled, I was able to determine John was talking to a woman Her voice was familiar, but I couldn't quite place it.

The volume increased, making it much easier to eavesdrop. "I don't give a rat's ass what her cop friend thinks," the woman shouted. "What do you think? More importantly, what does Kaley think?"

I crept out of bed and opened the door just a crack.

John's sigh was audible, "I don't know what to think. Kaley has been kind of out of it since the incident so I'm not sure she knows either."

"I'm telling you, Matt is not responsible for this, but I think he has information that could shed some light on the situation."

The voice belonged to Aiyona Green, Layla's mom. I silently complimented my fuzzy, over-taxed brain for piecing the situation together.

"For whatever reason, he thinks you'll be able to help him, Mr. Kyler." Aiyona continued, "Please, please, just go down there and hear him out."

"Didn't Matt confess?" John asked.

That was news! Shane hadn't said anything about a confession.

"Only because Matt's a damn fool!" Aiyona exclaimed. "Matt thought a confession would keep your biased cop friend from comin' after me!"

"After you?"

"Yes—look—go talk to him, Mr. Kyler. He can explain all his boneheaded decisions better than I can."

"I'm not leaving her," John responded. "Especially if there's any truth to what you're saying. If it wasn't Matt—then who?"

"I don't know," Aiyona growled. "Which is why I'm askin' you to talk to him. If it makes you feel any better, I'll stay here with your girlfriend while you're gone."

"Frankly, Aiyona—that doesn't make me feel better. Not at all."

"Why? You think I'm gunna finish her off while you're gone?" Aiyona spat sarcastically. "Stupid dumb jocks. You're all the same. I bet if Matt was some good ol' boy you wouldn't think twice about talkin' to him. You probably would have pulled some strings— reached out to your football cronies—got him a 'get outta jail free card' or something."

"What I do for a living has nothing to do with any of this." John's voice had dropped an octave. I could tell he was starting to get frustrated. "And I don't appreciate any of your insinuations. I have no idea what's going on. What I do know—is this—I'm not leaving Kaley vulnerable, not now, not ever again."

"Aww, that's sweet," Aiyona cooed mockingly. "You are such a stereotype, Coach. You can't keep her safe; you're not some superhero, and furthermore, you are refusing to talk to the very person who could actually help."

I didn't know a lot, but I was pretty sure Aiyona was right. I didn't think Matt Pine had anything to do with what had happened. It was time to crash the conversation. Padding lightly down the hallway in the same joggers and sweatshirt I'd thrown on earlier, I came up behind John, placing a hand gently on his shoulder.

Aiyona was standing just inside the doorway in John's tiled foyer. Her hardened features softened considerably as she caught my eye.

"She's right," I nodded toward Aiyona. "Matt didn't do this."

John appeared skeptical, "You've been through a lot. Right now, we need to concentrate on getting you back on your feet; everything else can wait."

"Wait?" Aiyona snapped. "While Matt sits in a jail cell and the real criminal gets away with almost killin' Kaley! Bravo—fantastic plan, meathead!"

John turned back to Aiyona. We were all tense, and I wasn't sure what his reaction to the insult might be.

I jumped in: "I think Aiyona's right."

"She just called me a meathead," John said, with an amused smile.

I laughed nervously, "Yes, she did. That's not really the part she's right about, though."

Aiyona stayed quiet during our exchange.

"Will you please go talk to Matt?"

"Kaley, I'm not leaving you alone."

"I'll be fine."

He still looked uneasy.

"If you don't go—I'm going to take your truck and go see Matt myself."

John considered this.

"You think I won't."

"No...I'm pretty sure that's exactly what you'll do," he admitted, rubbing the back of his neck in quiet contemplation. "I'll go. But don't you move a muscle while I'm gone." He disappeared into the kitchen and came back with his cell phone. "Since your phone was taken, you'll have to use this. I have my work cell—the number is saved as that. Any issues you call, okay?"

I nodded. Silently relieved that I didn't have to demonstrate the great lengths I was willing to go to get what I wanted.

Aiyona looked around John to where I stood, "Thank you. I can stay with you if you want?" she offered, her voice soft and sincere.

"Not necessary, but I do appreciate the offer."

"I'm glad you're okay, Kaley," she added.

"Matt doesn't think this was just an ordinary break-in, does he?"

John responded first, "I don't think any of us thinks this was an ordinary break-in."

Chapter 37
MATT

"Get up!" There was an edge to John Kyler's voice that cut through the stale air and rattled my sleep-deprived brain. I pushed myself away from the cold, concrete wall I'd been sitting against, and made my way to standing.

"Is Summer okay," I asked realizing the last time I'd seen him he was rushing off to the school due to an accident. Had that only been this morning? It seemed months ago.

"She's fine," he replied curtly. "I doubt that's why you wanted to see me. Why am I here?"

"Thanks for coming," I said as I lumbered toward him, getting as close as the accommodations would allow. "I didn't do anything to hurt Kaley. Quite the opposite. I've been trying to help her."

The man didn't say a word. Instead, he fixed his eyes on me with a hardened stare.

"I hope you didn't buy into Detective Gavin's BS too."

John shifted his weight but didn't offer anything in the way of words.

I steepled my fingers together and brought them to my forehead. As though the gesture might actually assist me in coming up with a quick explanation. I had a feeling I wouldn't be able to hold his attention long. "Look, I'm going to lay something out for you."

He shrugged in such a way that implied he didn't much care what I had to say.

I took a deep breath and dove in, "Look, I think Kaley's husband was onto something big. Whatever happened at her house last night... it wasn't me. I also don't think it was random. I think Kaley was targeted... Are you with me so far?"

Finally, John spoke, "You admitted to drugging her, Matt!"

"Only because Gavin was tryin' to pin the ketamine on Aiyona. It's one thing for him to harass me—I panicked—I said I got it somewhere else."

"Where?"

"What?"

"Where did you say you got it?"

"I didn't."

"You didn't offer up another source, Matt? Shane didn't ask?"

"Of course he didn't ask! Why would he? I gave him what he wanted! Meanwhile, the bad guys are still out there."

John shook his head, "Did you recant your statement?"

"I tried! Gavin won't see me. He's either stupid or in on it. I haven't decided which."

"In on what exactly?" John asked, a scowl creeping across his face.

"I don't know yet, but I think it has something to do with Nathan."

"Kaley's husband?"

"I think there's some big-time shit going on behind the scenes. But I can't talk about any of it here. It's why I came to you this morning."

"Okay... why me?"

I shrugged, "This morning—because you have influence with Kaley. Now—because you have influence in the community."

"Are you trying to talk your way out of jail? You might have the wrong impression, Matt. I don't have any power to help you out of your current predicament. In fact, if you had anything, I mean anything, to do with drugging Kaley and ransacking her house, I will bury you."

I clenched my fists in frustration.

John continued, "Shane believes that—"

"You're not hearin' me! I don't give a shit what Gavin believes!" I tried hard not to yell but it wasn't working. "Don't you see—they're after something? Information of some sort."

That seemed to get his attention. "Looking for something like what? A notebook?"

It was an odd question and one I was not at all prepared for. "Not what I was thinkin'... but yeah, I guess it could be... why?"

John looked around before lowering his voice and leaning closer toward the bars. "Let's say you're not to blame."

"I'm not!"

John held up a finger to silence me. "If you didn't do this, who did and why?"

I spoke through gritted teeth. "I don't know, but I'll tell you what I told Kaley—if we work together, we might figure it out."

"You told Kaley?" He asked, clearly confused.

I nodded.

"There's more going on here isn't there?"

I gave him a look that clearly said duh. I wasn't in a great position. And it looked like my only hope was currently resting in the hands of a dumb jock. I sensed a pattern with the guys Kaley Stone chose to hang out with. Her husband seemed to be the exception to the rule.

"If I get you out of here," John continued. "And I'm not saying that's possible—but if I do. Then you'll fill us in?"

I nodded. "I will fill you and Kaley in. I don't want Gavin involved."

He looked like he was about to protest but then thought better of it. "I can't promise Kaley will keep anything from Shane, but you have my word, for now."

I breathed a sigh of relief, "Thank you."

John looked around, "We need more privacy."

I threw up my hands in frustration, "I think I pointed that out already."

Without another word, John turned on his heel and brusquely walked away from the hall of holding cells.

"Guess we're done then..." I called out after him. He didn't bother to acknowledge.

"Great, good talk!" I added for good measure.

Chapter 38
KALEY

After John and Aiyona left, I crawled back into bed. This time I easily drifted off to sleep. When I woke, it took me a moment to get my bearings. The room was dark, and the numbers on the digital clock on the nightstand glowed orange. It was 1:11. Judging from the darkness, it was morning rather than afternoon. And I was still in John's big, cozy bed alone. Alone? I panicked. Where was my daughter? How could I have slept through an entire afternoon? I threw the covers back and was about to leap from the bed when I felt something cold and wet against my arm. Sargent Snuggles barreled into me, causing me to flop back onto the pillows. If the dog was here, then certainly Summer was here too. John wouldn't have retrieved the dog and left my kid. I rubbed his ears affectionately as he nuzzled his nose against my neck.

I stifled a laugh, "What are you doing?"

In response, he ran his huge, slobbery tongue across my face.

"Yuck, Sargent!" I whispered and used my sleeve to wipe my cheek.

Gently, I pushed the lug of a pup off me and crept from the room. The guest bedroom was just down the hallway. I cracked the door a bit and poked my head inside. Summer was slumbering away contentedly, a night light plugged in near the bed bathed the room in a comforting, soft light. Quietly I pulled the door shut again and wondered where John was.

The answer became apparent as I rounded the corner to the living room. The large wall-mounted TV was flickering with the volume turned low. John was passed out on the sofa as sports highlights scrolled across the screen. His long legs were hanging off the edge and he was still wearing the same blue button-down shirt and khakis he'd been wearing all day. It appeared Sargent Snuggles and I had taken over his bedroom. I crept quietly across the room and positioned myself on the floor next to him.

John didn't stir.

I stroked his cheek lightly, causing his eyes to blink open.

"Hey, you…" He rolled lazily onto his side, so we were face to face. "I thought you might sleep forever."

"I thought I did," I said, pulling my legs up underneath me. "I didn't mean to kick you out of your room. I'll bunk with Summer so you can get some sleep."

"I'm fine here. You need the rest more than I do but since you're up, I'll grab a change of clothes. I didn't want to disturb you earlier."

I reached for his hand. "I was sleeping pretty soundly. I don't think I would have noticed. Now that I'm up, you should go enjoy your bed. Friendly warning, though—there may be a stinky four-legged creature under your covers."

"Duly noted," he yawned. His eyelids were heavy, and I couldn't help but feel responsible for his exhaustion.

"How did things go at the police station?" I asked. "Did you talk to Matt?"

"I don't think he was the one at your house, Kaley," John said, stretching his arms above his head with a sigh. "Matt seems to have an idea of what's going on with you, though. Which means he's way ahead of me."

I looked down, unable to meet his eyes, "I'm sorry."

"It's okay," he said gently. "We don't have to talk about this now."

"Thank you," I replied. "Thank you for being so understanding... and for everything. I have no idea what I would have done without you."

"No thanks necessary. I'm just glad you're okay." He pushed himself upright and did a few neck rolls to loosen the muscles.

"You scared me today," he continued. "When I showed up at your house and the door was partially open... I was concerned; but when I saw how the place was ransacked, and you were just lying there... I can't recall ever feeling that level of fear."

I ran my hands through my hair and looked away, feeling extremely uncomfortable. "I'm just glad you were there," I said simply. Then, hoping to maneuver the conversation back to more comfortable territory, I asked to raid his kitchen.

"I'll do you one better—I'll make you something to eat," John said, pushing himself off the couch.

"You don't have to do that."

"I know I don't have to—I want to," he replied. "What are you hungry for?"

"Anything... everything."

He laughed, "I can do that."

I padded after him and into kitchen, where he pulled out various pots and pans and then proceeded to start peeling potatoes.

"I didn't expect you'd prepare a gourmet meal," I joked.

"I'm just going to fry up some steaks and make mashed potatoes. It's hardly gourmet."

"Says you," I replied playfully as I pulled out one of the three bronze metal stools on the other side of the counter. The position offered me a great view in which to watch John work his magic.

"While I make you this 'gourmet meal'... he did air quotes to mock me. "Why don't you tell me why Henry was under the impression I was with you last night."

I felt the heat rise in my face; quite certain I was turning red while being called out on my fib. "Did you tell him you weren't?"

He continued to move about the kitchen with practiced efficiency while we chatted, "No. I played along. I told him I left before... well, you know... I figured you had your reasons. He's been beyond worried about you and Summer. I assured him I'd take care of you both. And I will... for real this time."

I looked down and traced the swirl of marble on the counter with my finger. "I'm sorry. I shouldn't have put you in that position. I just wanted some time alone and didn't want to explain that to Henry. So, I faked being sick to get him to keep Summer overnight. I said you were with me so he wouldn't rush over to play caretaker."

"I see. Any reason you wanted to be alone?"

I shrugged.

John stopped what he was doing and leaned on the counter across from me, "Did your need to be alone have anything to do with what happened at the gallery? Things got out of hand between Matt and Shane. Then there was the way we left things..."

"It had nothing to do with you, John. I was unfair; and again, I'm really sorry."

"Trivial. However, I would like to know what's going on. I'm getting bits and pieces, so I've got my own theories. If you don't want to talk about it now—I understand."

I didn't want to talk about any of it, but it might be better to just get it over with.

"What have you concluded?" I asked.

He sighed, "I don't want to guess here, Kaley. I also don't want to push you."

"I could say the same about you."

He nodded, "Fair enough."

It seemed like this might be my only opportunity, so I forged ahead, "What's going on between you and Logan?"

He pinched the bridge of his nose. "I don't like the guy."

"Yeah... that much I gathered."

John placed both hands on the counter and inhaled deeply. "Okay, a few of my football guys have been walking a fine line these days. And it seems our police chief, and my boss, who is the school superintendent, have an agreement of some kind that I'm not privy to. Long story short... the guys should be suspended from the game at the least. But because of how they play and who their families are... let's just say there are different standards."

Now things were falling into place. "Is Logan's son one of the boys walking the line?" I asked.

"I've probably already said more than I should... If it's okay with you, I'd rather not name names."

"Of course, what kind of fine line?"

"There is drug and alcohol activity, which is against the athletic code, not to mention illegal."

"Logan's looking the other way?"

"Not only Logan, but as I said, the superintendent and I think other school officials too but..." he trailed off. "It's probably better you don't know."

I nodded, "Okay, thanks for trusting me."

"It was never a matter of trust, Kaley. I don't want to put you in an uncomfortable position with Logan. I also don't want to break any sort of confidentiality or betray my team. Not to mention burdening you with one more thing"

"Thank you," I replied quietly.

"How about you, Kaley? You seem to have a lot of secrets. At some point, you'll need to decide if it's worth letting me in or not."

"Okay."

He waited, but I didn't offer anything more.

John raised an eyebrow, "That's it?"

I studied him carefully, trying to gauge how much I should share. It wasn't a tough decision. The way he'd shown up for me today. The way he'd taken care of my daughter, especially considering how I'd treated him at the gallery, I wanted to tell him everything.

John seemed to misinterpret my silence. He looked away, "Okay then." He pushed away from the counter and went back to meal preparation.

"John, I want to tell you everything. I just don't know where to start."

"Well, how about telling me about the notebook I smuggled out of your house?"

"Did you look at it?"

"Nope. None of my business."

"Where is it?"

He pointed with his wooden spoon in the direction of a small credenza in the far corner of the kitchen, "Top drawer."

I slid off the stool to retrieve it. "It'd be better if you read through it and gave me your opinion."

He furrowed his brow, "Why is that?"

"I don't want to influence your thoughts, and I'd really like to get your take."

His face softened as he appeared content with my response, "Okay."

"The notebook belonged to Nathan," I said, sliding back onto the stool with the notebook in hand.

He was faced away from me as a sizzling sound emitted from the pan on the stove. He paused briefly and then: "Okay."

"Okay." I parroted back at him.

He smiled in response, "While you eat, I'll read."

"Shouldn't you sleep?"

"Nah, I'll be good."

I raised an eyebrow at him but didn't voice my doubt. "Fair warning—Nathan had absolutely terrible handwriting. Don't feel bad if you can't read portions of his notes."

"I work with high school kids. I'm sure I'll manage."

Again, I had my doubts; but again, I kept them to myself.

John served up New York Strips, mashed potatoes, and garlic bread. I ate while he paged through Nathan's notes as promised.

"You realize that was a lot of food, right?" I said as I leaned back in my chair, uncomfortably full. John hadn't said much while I shoveled food into my mouth. He'd been so busy pouring over the notebook that he didn't bother to respond.

"I'm not one of your football players—you know," I said, pushing away from the table.

He glanced up, "Is that your way of saying you enjoyed it?"

"I enjoyed it very much. I'll have to skip eating tomorrow to make up for the calories, though."

"Naw. You're too skinny anyway." He had spoken the words without even bothering to glance up.

My eyes widened in response. Of course, he was oblivious to my reaction as his attention was deeply focused on the notebook.

"Did you just comment on my weight?" I exclaimed. "You realize that's never okay, right?"

He tore his attention from the notebook and furrowed his brow, "I thought it was a good thing to call a woman skinny?"

I laughed and tossed a napkin at him. "No. Never comment on anyone's weight. Nobody wants to hear they're too big or too small or even too tall."

"Well, I'd never call you too tall," he remarked off-handily.

"Hey!" I threw another napkin at him and threatened to throw a plate next.

"This was my grandmother's china, so if you break it, I'm pretty sure she'll haunt you for eternity."

"Ha! Thanks for the warning."

"I'm serious," he said, once again so absorbed in what he was reading that he didn't bother to look up.

"So, what do you think?" I asked, turning serious again.

John sighed and leaned back, clasping his hands behind his head. "I think there's a strong possibility that Nathan was investigating some dirty cops."

I nodded sadly, "Well, you came to that conclusion much faster than I did. I think Matt was helping him somehow?"

John raised an eyebrow, "He does seem to think if you two put your heads together, you can sort this whole thing out."

"What do you think?"

"I think you should turn this over to another department and leave the digging to them. Round Rock appears to be very corrupt. I had my concerns about Logan before reading Nathan's notes... this... this pretty much reinforces my opinion."

"You think Logan's running a dirty department?

John nodded solemnly, "I've suspected."

"How deep do you think it goes?"

John ran his hand down his face and stifled a yawn. "Can it wait until tomorrow? There's a lot here to digest, and I'm about shot."

"I know. I'm sorry."

"Stop apologizing," he said, standing up to collect my empty dishes.

"What about Shane?" I asked, following him over to the kitchen sink.

"I don't know, Kaley." John turned on the water and started rinsing pots and pans. "It appears Nathan was undecided on the loyalties of his partner. What do you think?" he asked, turning off the water and turning to face me.

"I think—I don't want to talk about this anymore. I also think we should leave the mess until morning."

"That is a fantastic plan. I'll just grab a few things, and you can have the bedroom."

"Or..." I said, taking a step toward him. "We could share your bedroom."

"I like that idea," he said, reaching out and placing his hands on my hips to guide me closer.

I stood up on my tiptoes and wrapped my arms around his neck.

John had to stoop slightly to make up for our height difference. Then, he brushed his lips against mine.

It wasn't long before we were reenacting the heavy make-out session we'd had in his office. Only this time, there was nobody to interrupt us.

Without thinking, I started to unbutton his shirt.

John stopped me. "Is this really what you want?" he whispered.

"Yes." I was surprised to realize that I really was prepared to move forward. Then, I realized that although I was ready mentally, I may not be ready physically. I stepped away from John. "Except—I haven't showered in over twenty-four hours."

He chuckled, "Now who's the charmer? Believe it or not, Kaley I don't care." John reached for my hand and led me down the hallway. I was relieved to see the dog was no longer on the bed.

Once we were in the bedroom, I realized maybe John wasn't ready for this step in our relationship. This time I put on the brakes. "We don't have to do this. I mean just because I'm ready..."

"I've wanted this since the night I met you in the bar."

Despite everything that had transpired, for the first time in a long time, everything felt right.

Chapter 39
MATT

After one night in lockup, I was a free man. I wasn't sure if I had John Kyler to thank for that or simply the fact that I hadn't done anything wrong—except lie. Either way, no formal charges were brought even though I didn't think Gavin was above manufacturing evidence.

Although my night in the cell was no picnic, the greeting I received in front of the cop shop from my irate fiancée was worse.

I walked out of the Round Rock police department and spotted Aiyona across the street in the parking lot leaning on her little red Toyota Corolla. Her posture was easy and relaxed, but experience had taught me not to be lulled into a false sense of security when it came to Aiyona. Her mood could change on a dime.

I made my way across the street to the lot and Aiyona lept into my arms. She wrapped her long denim-clad legs around my torso, melting me with a sweet, lingering kiss. Then, she hopped down and slugged me surprisingly hard in the chest. Not unexpected but still startling.

"What the hell, Aiyona?"

She tromped away, her black heeled ankle boots clicking angrily across the asphalt. "I'm mad at you!" she shouted back over her shoulder.

"Well, I gathered that," I retorted, reluctantly following her to the car.

∞∞∞∞∞∞

We didn't talk for the rest of the day. Then, at eleven o'clock that night, Aiyona started talking. The silent treatment had been manageable; but she hadn't fed me either, and that was wearing on me.

The living room was lit with a single lamp in the corner that allowed just enough light for conversation, but not enough to read by. From my position on the couch, I'd been watching Aiyona pace the room anxiously nibbling at her fingernails for at least ten minutes. I found myself longing for the solitude of the cell I'd left in the Round Rock police station.

"I don't understand, Matt!" She wasn't shouting because Layla was sound asleep; but I could tell she wanted to. Thank goodness for sleeping children—her tone was biting enough—I couldn't imagine it at a louder volume. "It's like you're living a whole other life I'm completely unaware of!"

I opened my mouth to speak; but before I could get the words out, she was on top of me, her finger just inches from my face. "Don't you dare try to defend yourself!" she snapped. "I don't want to hear a damn thing out of your mouth unless it's the truth. The whole truth!"

I started to speak, but once again, I was shut down.

"We vowed not to keep things from each other. Clearly, you've been keeping a lot from me! What did you really do when we moved here, Matt? Who did you piss off? How does Kaley Stone fit into any of this, and why the hell would lie about drugging her?"

"Look, Aiyona—"

"You shut-up!" She was in my face again. "Did I say you could talk yet?"

"Well, you asked me a series of questions and did say I could talk if I was going to tell you the truth," I offered with a shrug.

"Don't get smart with me, Matt Pine."

I said nothing. It just seemed safer that way.

"Well..." she waited, tapping her foot impatiently. "Spit it out."

"I have permission to speak?"

"Yeah—dummy, but only if it's the truth."

I reached for her hand, but she batted me away. "Look, baby, all I've ever wanted is to provide for you and that amazing little girl in there." I nodded toward the closed bedroom door. "I may not have been smart about how I went about that, but I assure you my intentions were good."

"Mhmm."

That was all I would get, so I continued, "I didn't drug Kaley. You know that. I was with you. I only said I did it because that detective—Gavin—he has it out for me. He was tryin' to use you to get to me. I guess I played into his hands."

She raised her eyebrows at me.

I continued, "Aiyona, I told you what I did when we moved here—I got hooked up with a dealer in Round Rock. I moved some stuff. Nothing hardcore—just some prescription drugs—a little weed here and there. I didn't do it very long. People I was dealing with were into stuff I was not okay with."

"Like what?"

"I mean, the guys at the bottom seemed okay. Up the chain—things got a little uncertain."

She motioned for me to keep going.

I sighed, "They were bad people, Aiyona. They were trying to move harder and harder stuff and diversify."

"Meaning?"

"Meaning they were talking about moving things other than drugs... weapons... possibly people..."

Aiyona gasped involuntarily, "Matt—you didn't—"

I cut her off, "No, I didn't! You know me, Aiyona—I would never. I'm not a great person but I'm not a monster either. I hung in just long enough to get us out of our financial hole. Once we both found solid work, I got out. Not only did I get out, but I worked for the right side of the law for once too. I narced out everyone I was working with. I did everything I could to shut that operation down."

Aiyona moved to sit on the opposite end of the couch. "How does Kaley Stone fit into all this?"

I took a deep breath. "It's hard to sort out."

"Then we'll sort it out together." Her voice had softened slightly, but it still had an edge. My lady was not messing around.

"The cop, the detective I was working with was Nathan Stone, Kaley's now-dead husband."

"Okay..."

"He was a good guy, Aiyona. He helped me out. He gave me money and kept my name out of all of it—at least I thought he did."

"And now?"

"And now—now I'm not so sure. Somebody seems to have figured out the connection. Who am I kidding? Someone knew back then too."

"What are you talking about, Matt? You're not making any sense."

"The phone call you got at work. Things heated up when I started connecting with Kaley Stone. Her house getting ransacked. It's all a way to keep Kaley and me apart."

"What do you mean by that?" Aiyona leaned toward me. The fire in her beautiful brown eyes now replaced with a look of genuine concern.

"I think Kaley knows something that she might not even necessarily know."

Aiyona shook her head in confusion. "That doesn't make sense."

"The night her husband was killed... I made a phone call."

"Okay..."

"Let me back up. I was at Henry's Pub drinking."

Aiyona narrowed her eyes at me.

"I know, I know. I told you I'd stay clean and sober the day we moved to Round Rock. I slipped up a few times. But baby—I swear to you. That night was the last slip up."

I wasn't sure if she was buying it or not. Her expression hadn't changed. I was telling her the truth. I hadn't had a drop in over two years and planned to keep it that way.

"It was late, and I was a little plastered I'm ashamed to admit," I continued. "This chick walks in and takes the stool next to mine. She tells the old bartender that she'll have what I'm having."

Aiyona narrowed her eyes even further. "Maybe you better back up and tell me about this 'chick.'"

I waved away her concern. "She was flirty, but I wasn't playin'. Anyway—this chick is pissed off. She had a fight with her boyfriend or husband or whatever. Anyway, we're both drinking, and she starts to get loose lips and tells me about her husband being into some bad stuff."

"Bad like what?" Ayiona asks.

"Like the stuff I'd gotten out of. Apparently, I didn't clean up Round Rock as well as I thought I had."

Aiyona looked at me skeptically, "You really thought you had the power to clean up a whole city?"

"Well—it's not a big city."

Aiyona rolled her eyes, "You are the most naïve man—" she waved away the rest of her own comment. "Anyway, why would this woman tell you?"

"I don't know, Aiyona. She was angry and drunk, and I was a sympathetic ear."

"How sympathetic?" she asked suspiciously.

I sighed, "I told you already—she might have been interested—but I was not."

She settled back against the couch and allowed me to continue.

"I asked some questions. I got some information and found out her husband—boyfriend, whatever, was going to the bluff to meet up with some underage girls."

"The bluff where Kaley's husband died?"

I nodded, "Wanna guess how Detective Stone ended up there?"

Aiyona put her hand on my knee. "You passed on the information."

"I passed on the information," I repeated, confirming her statement. "If I hadn't made that call, Stone wouldn't have gone to the bluff. He'd still be here with his wife and kid." I rubbed my hands down my face, trying my best to hold it together. It was one thing to think I'd been responsible but to say it to Aiyona made it so real.

"Matt, his death is not on you. He died doing what he was trained to do."

"No. See, it is on me because I was doing something I promised you I wouldn't, and it impaired my judgment. I also knew something wasn't right, but I ignored my gut and dragged Stone in any way."

"What wasn't right?"

I shook my head trying to clear my brain. "Why would this woman approach me? And the other thing... I don't remember drinking that much, but I felt like I was plastered."

"You think someone slipped you something? The woman?"

I stood up and clasped my hands behind my neck, trying to remember. That night was so fuzzy. "I don't know... maybe... Who would know to use me to set up

Detective Stone? He kept my name out of it—he said he did."

"Who was the woman? Have you seen her before or since? Round Rock isn't a big city, Matt."

"I don't know. She had a ballcap on. I didn't really look at her face."

"What about the rest of her? What was she wearing?"

"Black—all black...like leggings and an athletic jacket."

"Her body type?" Aiyona asked.

I looked at her out of the corner of my eye. Was I about to fall into one of my fiancée's traps? "Goodish..."

Aiyona rolled her eyes, "So, she was hot. Fine. Anything else?"

"She was white," I offered, shrugging.

Aiyona smiled, "So, not your type."

I returned her smile with one of my own, "Definitely not my type."

"Would you recognize her again if you saw her?"

I shook my head, "I don't think so. I've wondered that before. You know me—I'm terrible remembering names and faces."

She nodded in agreement, "You're the worst."

"You're asking me a lot of questions about her, Aiyona."

"Because she set you up!"

"You think so too?"

"Yeah—Matt, I do."

I sat back down, this time in the wooden rocker beside the couch. "Stone called me a week before his death and asked me if I knew of any cops that might be involved."

"Involved in what? Dealing or selling?"

I shrugged, "Both."

"And what did you say?"

"I told him the truth. I didn't know."

"And?"

"And a week later the guy is dead after a phone call I made based on a tip from a disgruntled woman in his grandfather-in-law's bar."

Chapter 40
KALEY

I liked waking up next to John. Although we hadn't been together long, it felt familiar, safe. I also didn't feel like I was being disloyal to Nathan. I actually felt there might be room in my heart for both Nathan and John.

The buzzing sound coming from John's side of the bed interrupted my introspective moment. He responded by grunting and then turning away to tap the cube-shaped alarm clock on his nightstand. The noise or movement or both alerted Sargent Snuggles, who had apparently crept back into bed with us. The crazy beast responded to the movement by assaulting John's face with his tongue.

Although he was turned away from me, I could tell how he was reacting to my furry family member. John's back muscles flexed as he tried to push himself away from our eager morning companion.

I couldn't help but laugh as I sat up preparing to fend off the furry mutt, should he point his mug in my direction.

John turned to face me, shielding his face from the dog. "Until I heard you laughing, I'd convinced myself it was your tongue all over me and not his." His voice was gravelly from sleep. With the morning light starting to peek through the curtains, I noted he was completely disheveled and incredibly handsome.

Sargent Snuggles scurried over top of John and started in on me. I squirmed back underneath the covers, continuing to laugh as I felt the dog bounce around the bed in excitement. After a few moments, the bouncing stopped, and I risked a peek. John had gently ushered the beast to the floor. The gentle clicking of Sargent's nails hitting the hardwood confirmed he'd left the bedroom.

"That's one helluva wake-up call!" John exclaimed, as he wiped away the remnants of dog slobber with the back of his arm.

I shrugged, "You get used to it... sort of..."

"Hmmm, we shall see," he remarked.

I wasn't sure how to respond so I didn't. John must have mistaken my silence for discomfort, reminding me of the girlfriend slip at Christmas. It must have reminded him, too, as he fumbled with the covers and muttered what sounded like an apology.

"John, it's all good." I tried to reassure him.

"But I did it again... I made an assumption..."

I ran my hands through my hair. "I like that you're thinking about the future—about our future. This is all still new to me. I had no intention of being in a relationship again, and I was okay with that. Summer is enough for me. Loving Nathan was enough for me. I never anticipated you. So, sometimes what we have just catches me off guard but not in a bad way."

He scratched his head, "So you're okay?"

"I'm perfect," I smiled.

In response, he sat up and brushed his lips against mine just as his alarm started to buzz again. He leaned over to silence it. "I have work," he said apologetically as he climbed over me and out of bed. "I'm going to shower and take Summer to school."

I threw back the covers, preparing to get up as well. "You don't have to do that. I can take her."

John shook his head and tucked the covers back over me. "The only place you're going is back to sleep.

Shane is bringing your vehicle over later this afternoon, so you don't feel stranded." He stopped, "unless you aren't comfortable with that... Do you trust Shane? I mean after our conversation last night—"

I cut John off, "I don't think Shane had anything to do with what happened at my house," I said, snuggling back against the pillows. "Nathan may have had doubts about his partner; but he didn't know Shane the way I do."

"Well, that's good enough for me," John stated. "There's a duffle bag full of your clothes in the room Summer is using."

I relaxed and sank deeper into the fluffy pillows as John turned and grabbed a few items from his closet and dresser drawers before quietly slipping out of the room to prepare for the day.

"John," I called before he closed the door.

He turned back expectantly.

"Thank you." The words felt impossibly inadequate in light of everything. However, for now, they'd have to suffice.

Chapter 41
MATT

"Matt... Maaattt... Maaaatt..." A little voice whispered in my ear.

I'd learned from experience that ignoring Layla wouldn't work. She didn't care if I was sleeping or not. When she wanted something, she was relentless, and at that moment, she wanted me awake.

"What's up, baby girl?" The question came out as more of a jumble of sounds than actual words.

"I wanna Pop-Tart. Mama's still in the shower."

I fluffed the pillow back up under my head. "She'll be out soon. I'm kinda sleepin' here, kiddo." I hoped the explanation would satisfy her.

Ollie had gently suggested it may be good for me to take a few days off after being hauled into the police station. I knew the time off wasn't really for my benefit but his. Ollie feared I might not be the reformed individual I claimed to be. So since I wasn't working, I planned to take full advantage of the situation and sleep in. However, my plans did not meet with Layla's approval.

"Matt... Maaaattt ..." she was at it again.

I grabbed one of Aiyona's pillows and held it firmly against my head. Layla just tugged it away and was back in my ear within moments.

"I'm hungry, Matt," she pouted. "And I can't reach any food without you."

I slowly opened my eyes. Her little face was so close to my own that she looked distorted. "You're not gunna let me sleep, are ya?"

"Nope." She smiled and skittered off the bed to allow me space to move.

I stretched and shuffled out behind her as she pranced her way to the kitchen.

"Hey, Matt—" she said as she took a seat at the worn wooden table. "You know what?"

"What, Lay?" I grumbled, reaching up into the cabinet for a breakfast pastry.

"Sometimes your breath is kinda bad in the morning."

I raised an eyebrow at her. "Thanks for telling me."

"Sure," she smiled up at me. "If you brush your teeth before you talk to people that will probably help."

"I'll keep that in mind," I replied dryly. I looked at Layla and then back at the toaster. "You can reach the counter, right?"

She laughed, "Yes, silly!"

I nodded, "Great, then you take it from here, okay?"

"Okay, Matt!" she hollered back in response.

Why was she shouting? It was only seven-thirty in the morning. I patted her on the head and shuffled back to the bedroom, hoping I'd be able to get back to sleep without any more interruptions.

That hope would not become a reality. No sooner had I started to drift off when the phone rang. I once again took the pillow and pressed it hard up against the side of my head. I could still hear Layla's muffled voice joyously announcing that she would get it. I pushed myself out of bed to close the bedroom door, wondering why I hadn't just done so in the first place.

Layla's laughter echoed through the house, and I heard her exclaim, "You're not my daddy!" I stopped dead in my tracks. "Matt's gunna be my daddy," Layla announced proudly to the caller.

I raced to the kitchen to grab the phone, but Aiyona beat me to it.

Wearing her bathrobe and dripping wet from the shower, she yanked the phone from Layla's grasp. I came up behind her as she put the receiver to her ear.

"Who is this?" Aiyona demanded. "Hello... hello... is anybody there?"

I gently grasped her shoulder and she startled at my touch. I held out my hand, and she willingly passed the phone to me. I listened for a moment before returning the handset to the base.

"What's wrong, Mama?" Layla asked, clearly confused by her mother's reaction. Aiyona bent down next to Layla and held her firmly by the shoulders. "Who was on the phone, Layla?"

Layla just shrugged, "Don't know. He didn't say. What's wrong?"

"What did the man say to you?" Aiyona tried again. "I heard you tell him he wasn't your daddy."

Layla giggled, "Oh that! The man was being silly. He asked who I was, and I said my name then he said..." Layla lowered her voice in an attempt to impersonate the person she'd heard. "Layla, I'm your daddy. I laughed cause Matt's gunna be my daddy. Right, Matt?"

I nodded, "That's right, baby girl," I confirmed. "Why don't you finish your breakfast and get ready for school," I added.

"Okay." She skipped away, oblivious to the possible dangers that lurked just outside our little home.

Aiyona stood and chewed her lower lip, "There's no way he could know... let alone find her... right? I mean he's in prison, Matt."

"Come here." I held my arms open; and she folded into me, resting her wet head on my shoulder. "I think someone is trying to scare us away."

"It's working," she murmured into my neck.

"Go get dressed. I'll take Layla to school."

Aiyona pulled away from me. "I don't think she should go." Her eyes darted back and forth.

It pained me to see her look so frightened. "She'll be okay. I'll even hang out at school if it will make you feel better."

Aiyona smiled, "I don't think they're just going to let you hang out at school."

"Why, because I'm laid off from work due to my night in jail?"

"I'm pretty sure the school frowns upon people in general just hanging out. And yes, Round Rock is small—I don't think your recent stay behind bars is going to win you any favors."

I took a deep breath, absorbing her scent of jasmine and citrus. "It's going to be okay, Aiyona. I'll make sure of it."

She pulled away and fixed me with a steely gaze. "And what if the Round Rock police department thinks you're a threat again? Then what, Matt? How are you going to make sure of it from behind bars?"

"That's not going to happen."

She shoved me in the chest, not causing pain but definitely some discomfort. Aiyona wanted me to feel her point. She took a step back. "You watch yourself, Matt Pine, and don't you go makin' promises you can't keep."

"You have my word."

"Ha! Your word isn't meanin' as much as it did—now that I know about all your little lies."

My fiancée knew how to push all my buttons. "Aiyona! Damn it! I came clean with you. Doesn't that count for something?"

Before she could answer Layla came bounding out of the bedroom dressed and ready for school. "Don't be a potty mouth, Matt," she warned, galloping her way through the living room toward her backpack and coat that hung on the pewter coat hooks by the kitchen door.

Aiyona smiled, "That's good advice right there." She pointed toward her daughter and winked before padding away toward the bathroom.

"Let's go potty mouth, Matt!" Layla bellowed from her spot by the kitchen.

I looked down at my attire—bare feet, boxer shorts, and a plain white t-shirt. Not exactly the best choice for public let alone a January morning in Wisconsin. "Can I change first?"

Layla sighed and put her hand on her hip, "Not unless you want to tell the school lady why I'm late."

I considered my options and pulled on my heavy waterproof snow boots by the backdoor along with my parka. I prayed this wouldn't be a day that Gavin messed with me. I held out my hand, "Let's go, baby girl."

Layla put her tiny hand in mine, and we opened the back door to a blast of arctic air. I involuntarily shivered. "You probably should have worn pants," Layla pointed out before she dropped my hand and skipped down the length of the driveway to the car.

Lord help me, this kid was a mini version of her mother. And heaven help anyone who dare try to mess with either of them.

Chapter 42
KALEY

The house was quiet after John and Summer left for school. I took a shower which was probably the best shower I'd had in my lifetime. Then, I scrounged through the bag John had thrown together from my house. Surprisingly, he didn't do too bad a job of packing. I pulled out a pair of jeans and a t-shirt and then grabbed one of John's football hoodies to ward off the chill.

I'd just finished blow-drying my hair when the doorbell rang. The sound sent Sargent Snuggles into a barking frenzy. I cautiously crept into the guest bedroom where there was a decent view of the front porch. I parted the blinds just enough to see without being seen. From my viewpoint, I could see Logan standing at the front door. His hands were shoved deep in his pockets, and he was staring straight ahead. I snapped the blinds back in place and coaxed Sargent Snuggles out the patio door and into John's fenced-in backyard. I debated about ignoring the unwanted visitor. However, I decided against it. Even if I was suspicious of Logan, it wouldn't be good to let on. Besides, if he did intend to do me harm, he certainly wasn't going to do it now. All eyes in our tiny community were already watching due to the break-in. The doorbell sounded again so I jogged the last few feet through the living room to greet the impatient police chief.

"Kaley," he offered me a huge smile that didn't seem all that genuine, but maybe I was imagining things. "How are we doing this morning?" he continued, peering past me into John's empty living room.

"Better. Thank you." I crossed my arms in front of as the arctic air coursed through the open door and sliced through my defenses.

"Is John here?"

I hesitated, "No... he went to work for a bit, but he'll be back soon."

Logan scratched his head, "You two seem pretty tight these days." He nodded toward the oversized Tiger Football sweatshirt I was sporting like it was some proof of intimacy.

"He's a good guy. I'm happy."

Logan rubbed his chin as if contemplating my opinion of John. "You know, Kaley, people don't always turn out to be who you think they are."

"Isn't that the truth." I knew he was taking a shot at John, but I took the comment to mean more about Logan than anyone.

"Suppose I could step inside for a minute? It's pretty chilly out here." Logan started rubbing his hands together, as if his visual display of warming might accentuate his point. He wasn't really dressed for the weather, wearing blue jeans and a navy-blue windbreaker with the Round Rock emblem emblazoned on the breast. He had his badge clipped to his waistband, and I could tell from the extra bulk around his middle he had his duty belt concealed under his clothing.

Again, I hesitated but didn't want to raise any red flags, so I stepped aside allowing the large man to lumber up the step and into the foyer. As he pulled the door shut behind him, I suddenly became aware of just how quiet it was in John's house and how vulnerable I'd suddenly become. Then, I chided myself. Logan had been nothing but kind to my family the last few years. If Nathan had indeed been suspicious of his boss, it was due to unscrupulous work practices not that he was actually a danger to anyone.

"Kaley—are you alright, sweetheart?"

I had totally spaced out on the guy. Good thing he didn't try to attack me. He'd have succeeded while I was busy contemplating how trustworthy he was. "I'm fine," I responded curtly, inwardly cringing at being called sweetheart.

Logan looked down at the ground and shuffled his feet a bit. His black boots making a squeaking sound on John's tiled foyer.

"Is there a reason you stopped by?" I prompted.

He met my eyes and tilted his head slightly, as though confused by the question. "I came to update you and, of course, to check on your welfare."

"You have an update?" I asked anxiously.

"Well, no new information really... Shane took inventory, and it seems they were interested in electronics only. Your phone, laptop, computer, some gaming system—they all appear to be gone."

"Okay... well, you didn't need to take time out of your busy day to tell me that, but I appreciate the thought." I started to reach for the door handle, ready to usher the police chief back outside.

Logan stepped in front of me, blocking my reach. "See the thing is, I need to share some sensitive information with you; and I thought it would be better in person."

"Okay..."

Logan cleared his throat and continued, "I'm concerned John might be involved in what happened."

"In breaking into my home and drugging me?" I squinted in confusion.

"Possibly. Yes."

"If John wanted to get into my house all he'd need to do is ask."

Logan stepped closer, completely invading my space. I tried to inch backward, but unfortunately, I'd positioned myself with the entryway closet behind me. "I have concerns about your new boyfriend, Kaley."

I narrowed my eyes, "As he does you."

Logan chuckled, "Really? Please share—what exactly are the coach's concerns?"

I shrugged, "You'd have to ask him. All I know is what I've observed."

"And that is…"

"You two clearly don't like each other."

Logan reached out and grasped my shoulder. "Kay," he cooed gently. I did not like him using the name that only Shane had ever called me. He was trying to force an intimacy that we did not share.

"If it comes down to choosing sides," Logan continued, "I need to know where you stand."

I tried to casually step to the side and out from under his hold. It didn't work. Logan took a hold of my other shoulder, leaving me firmly under his grasp.

I wasn't sure whether the vibe he was going for was intimidation or concern. Either way, he wanted me to view him as the alpha here.

I tilted my head up slightly. Our eyes locked. "Since I have no idea what your issues are with each other that's a difficult question."

He pursed his lips and gave a slight head nod as though he understood.

"We've been through a lot together, Logan."

He still had an uncomfortable hold on me and at my words, he gave my shoulders a strong squeeze. I believed he was trying to pass the gesture off as compassion, but I recognized it for what it was—an exertion of control.

"However," I continued. "If I had to make a choice I'd have to go with John."

My response triggered the reaction I expected. Anger flashed across Logan's features. "And why is that?" he snapped.

"That is actually none of your business."

"I have taken care of you and your daughter for the last two years. You have no idea what I've done for you!"

"Then tell me?" My heart was racing, but I did my best to hide my unease.

He brushed the hair away from my face with his thick fingers. "You have no idea what is going on, Kaley."

"I'm starting to get a pretty good idea."

He snarled, "You are in over your head."

We stood there in a silent standoff for a moment. Logan still gripping tightly to my shoulders and me doing my best to stare him down. He must have realized that his position was precarious because he eventually averted his eyes and loosened his grip. "I just want to keep you and Summer safe." His voice had softened, and he patted me with an uncharacteristic gentleness as he took a step back.

I wasn't going to let him off easy, "Like you kept Nathan safe?" I shot back.

Logan looked away and swiped his palm across his mouth. "Like I kept you safe from Nathan," he said the words in a quiet, resigned sounding voice.

"Ha! If you are going to try and spin this—you're going to have to do better than that. Nathan was one of the best people I've ever known. He was by the book, Logan. And he was investigating a dirty department. A dirty chief. You knew he was onto you. You took him out before he could blow the whistle on you."

Logan's face hardened as he closed the distance between us again. This time, he kept his hands to himself. "Nathan was an excellent cop!" Logan exclaimed. "That is until he met Matt Pine."

"Ha! You expect me to believe that Matt turned Nathan? That doesn't make any sense. Why would Nathan risk everything?"

"Because of you."

I backed away from Logan and folded my arms across my chest, "Well, this ought to be good. How exactly did I turn my husband into a dirty cop that you needed to protect me from?"

"Kaley, sweetheart…"

"Don't call me sweetheart, Logan."

He ignored me and continued, "You're a very talented artist, but did you really think you could make enough to get out of the financial hole? Your gallery was a drain. Yet, you were coming out ahead."

Logan's comment gave me pause. Nathan had taken care of the financials—that was until he was promoted to detective and had less time. At that point, Grandpa Henry took over. Henry liked keeping the books for the bar, so it was a no-brainer to take him up on his offer to help at the gallery. If Nathan had been padding the books somehow, Henry would have caught it. Logan was just trying to get in my head, and I wasn't going to let him.

"You know I'm right," Logan said. "I'm so very sorry. I didn't ever want you to find out. Then you found the notebook…"

This caught me off guard, "How do you know about that?" I snapped.

"Gavin told me you had some suspicions and about the notebook you'd found."

"He said we were keeping that a secret."

"It seems the people in your life are not at all who they seem to be."

I shook my head in response, "I knew Nathan inside and out. And I know Shane too—"

He cut me off, "And John Kyler? Do you think you know him too, Kaley? Because you don't."

"The only person I don't trust right now is you."

Logan balled his fists at his sides.

"I also trust Matt Pine a hell of a lot more than I trust you," I added, just for good measure. If I was going to push the man, I might as well push all the way.

The statement did exactly that. Logan was pissed. A darkness crossed his features. He moved quickly, his large hand grasped firmly around the back of my head, pushing my face so close to his that his features were blurred. "I'm the damn police chief, Kaley! I protect this town! I protect you! Maybe someone oughta show you what gratitude is."

I said nothing for fear of feeling the full impact of his rage. I could hear Sargent Snuggles barking at the back door and pawing to get in. Hopefully, he would attract the attention of the neighbors. Suddenly, there was a clatter as John's only piece of artwork, the ugly beach painting tumbled off the wall behind us.

The action startled us both. Logan let go and stepped away. He wiped a bead of sweat from his forehead, "I'm sorry."

"I think you should go." I brushed past him and pulled open the front door.

Logan didn't move. "You need to drop this now. I can't keep you safe if you insist on moving forward."

I shrugged, "Well, you certainly didn't keep Nathan safe, so I wouldn't expect anything less."

"You have no idea what you're doing."

"Now that's where you're wrong. For the first time, in a very long time, I know exactly what I'm doing."

Logan stepped toward the door, "Don't say I didn't warn you."

"And don't you ever come back here or lay hands on me again."

Logan laughed, "Don't worry. You're on your own now, *sweetheart*." He emphasized the 'sweetheart' to undermine me before he stalked out the door.

Once I shut and locked the door behind him, I ran to the patio door and let Sargent Snuggles in. The dog ran straight to the living room window, barking and growling as Logan made his way down the driveway.

"Atta a boy you tell him," I said, wiping away a few tears that had involuntarily fallen. I watched as Logan ducked into his SUV and sped away down the quiet residential street.

Although Logan's visit was disconcerting, it did give me a kind of clarity I'd been lacking. I took a deep breath. It was time to make some phone calls.

Chapter 43
MATT

I wasn't sure what to expect after Kaley's cryptic phone call. Whatever I thought, though—I wasn't even close. Kaley opened the front door to John Kyler's home and invited me inside. We walked through the dull living room that seemed like one white and beige blur and into an impressive kitchen. Here, Gavin and John were seated across from each other at an oval wooden dining table. The tension in the air was thick, makin' me feel as nervous as a long-tailed cat in a room full of rockin' chairs.

Gavin's back had been to me, but as soon as I walked toward the table and into his line of sight, he rose to protest. "Awww, hell no! What are you thinking? No—just no, Kay."

Before Kaley or I had a chance to say anything, John's voice boomed through the house. "Shut-up and sit down, Shane! If you don't like the way Kaley has chosen to handle this, then get out!" He pointed toward the door.

Gavin shot daggers at John but reluctantly took his seat back at the table.

"Have a seat, Matt," Kaley said, calmly gesturing toward the table, completely unfazed by the interaction between John and the detective.

I sat. There was no way I wanted to set off any of the people in this room. With that in mind, I took a chair at the head of the table to avoid sitting next to either Shane or John. Kaley took the seat to my left beside John.

Once we were all in place, Kaley began to recount the visit she'd received from the police chief. He'd implied that Nathan had been a dirty cop and that I had somehow been the cause of Nathan's illegal activity. She described how the police chief had been physically aggressive under the guise of protecting her.

With the day's events still fresh in her mind, Kaley's voice was understandably shaky. John looked away as she spoke; I wasn't sure what he was thinking. I was angry, I couldn't imagine what I'd do if the police chief had gone after Aiyona that way. Gavin twirled his wedding band as she spoke. The lack of reaction from either John or Gavin gave me the sense that they had already heard the story and Kaley's recount was solely for my benefit.

When she finished, I thanked her sincerely for bringing me into the loop.

"I still think it's a bad idea to include him," Gavin murmured under his breath.

John shot him a menacing look.

In response, Shane stood and kicked the chair away from the table.

"Sit down, Shane!" Kaley snapped, and surprisingly enough he did so without hesitation.

"Now," Kaley continued "We all have one thing in common and that's Nathan. I think, at this point, we can agree his death was not an accident."

I ventured a look at Gavin and then John; they were both nodding in agreement. I found myself joining in.

Kaley took a deep breath, "Okay, then, like it or not we need to work together."

"Not all of us," Gavin huffed, crossing his arms in front of him.

John threw his hands up as though exasperated by the cop. I knew how he felt. "You're free to go, Shane," he offered.

Nobody said anything for a beat, and Gavin made no move to leave.

Deciding to move past the interaction, Kaley turned and focused her attention on me. "Matt, you tried several times to reach out. I'm sorry that I continually dismissed you. It's been a lot for me to process. However, I would very much appreciate any information you can offer."

I wasn't sure what to say. The whole situation felt a little surreal. Although I was finally getting what I wanted, I wasn't sure where to begin, especially given the fact that I didn't feel comfortable sharing anything with Gavin.

Kaley slid a white notebook across the table to me. I hesitated to reach for it.

"We believe that notebook is the reason Kaley's house was ransacked," John explained. Someone was looking for it, and we're all pretty eager to get your take."

"I gotta warn you, though," Kaley added. "My husband had terrible handwriting. "You might need me to decipher some things."

I looked at it and then looked up at three faces looking back expectantly at me.

Gavin grumbled, "I don't like this."

Kaley ignored him, "Take a look, Matt."

I opened the cover as John nodded approvingly, and Gavin scoffed.

"While you're doing that, I'm going to pick Summer up," Kaley rose from her seat.

John stood too, "I'll get her." I noticed how he considerately pulled her chair out giving her room to maneuver.

"It's okay. I want to do something normal."

"Are you sure?"

I tried not to intrude on their private moment, but I couldn't help it. My thoughts wandered to Nathan. I'd bet he'd be happy to know Kaley and Summer had a guy like John in their corner. I knew if something ever happened to me—which let's face it—was incredibly likely given my current circumstances, I'd want Aiyona and Layla to have someone like that to count on.

I turned my attention back to the table as John walked Kaley to the door.

"I don't trust you," Gavin snarled.

"Well, guess it's an even playing field then, Gavin."

"I saw the way you were looking at her just now." He leaned forward, closing the distance between us. "For all I know, you knocked Nathan off to have a shot at his wife."

I laughed, "Good one, detective. You have me all figured out."

Shane slammed his fist down hard on the table. "You may have fooled those two, but you don't fool me."

John returned and slid into his seat. "Knock it off! Like it or not we need each other. And Matt, I'm going to save you some time. Kaley was not exaggerating when she said his handwriting is terrible, so you won't understand most of it. Feel free to look anyway, but here's what it boils down to... Nathan seemed to trace illegal activity back to the police department. Your contact info is in there. From the information you shared, we believe you were Nathan's CI, although he chose to not make you official."

Gavin interrupted, "We know you weren't official cause there's no paperwork leading back to you."

John ignored Shane and continued, "As you know—Nathan was killed before he could figure all this out. And what Kaley failed to mention about her visit from Chief Sterns is that he knows about the notebook. That would be in thanks to our friend Shane over here." His jaw tightened as he looked across the table toward the other man.

Shane narrowed his eyes and looked at John with a look of repulsion. "As I told Kay—talking to Sterns about the notebook was the right move. Kay trusts me—maybe you should too."

"Under normal circumstances, I would agree with you. However, she's been under some stress and may not be thinking clearly. And if I recall correctly, Kaley agreed to disagree with you on that judgment call?"

I had to interject, "Meaning what exactly?"

"Meaning Kaley and I both believe Sterns is in this up to his eyeballs," John responded, sounding tired and defeated.

Gavin shrugged, "I don't know, man. I think you're barking up the wrong hole."

I half coughed—half laughed. They both turned their attention toward me. "Sorry—Gavin, it's tree. You meant barking up the wrong tree," I corrected.

"I'm pretty sure it's hole, dumb ass," Gavin shot back. "And I trust Kaley to know what she's doing."

"How can a dog bark up a hole? That doesn't even make sense—"

John cut me off. He completely ignored the whole tree versus hole discussion. "So, Matt, what can you add? Kaley mentioned you feel responsible for Nathan's death. Why is that?"

The guy did not mince words. I sighed and slouched back in my seat. I told them how I'd been the guy to make the phone call. The phone call that led Nathan to the bluff. The spot that would be his final resting place.

John reached out and gripped my shoulder supportively, "You couldn't have known."

"I don't get it—how can you just blindly buy what he's selling?" Gavin shouted, gesturing wildly in my direction.

"And I don't get how you just blindly trust Chief Sterns!" John shot back.

"Ha! Really?" Gavin raised his eyebrows. "Maybe because he's a freakin' police chief and Matt is a criminal... seems pretty cut and dry, my friend."

"Does it?" John asked.

I stepped in before the detective could reply. "You know what—this back and forth does us absolutely no good. How about we take it to the source."

"Who? Sterns?" Gavin asked.

"Yes, Sterns," I replied, then turned to face John. "As long as you can put your game face on. You can't go after him for what happened earlier."

John said nothing. Gavin, on the other hand, had plenty to say. "You guys have no idea what you're talking about. Confronting Sterns is about the stupidest thing you could do. Say you're right about him. Paying him a visit will just tip him off. And although I feel differently about Sterns than you do— I'm not at all okay with the way he handled things with Kay. He needs to know—"

I cut him off, "He needs to know what? What exactly would you say to Logan? After all, he's the police chief, not a lowly criminal like me. I'm sure whatever happened with Kaley was just misconstrued," I said sarcastically, mocking the asshole.

John stood abruptly, "Matt's right. Let's go to Sterns."

"What? You mean now?" I asked, pushing out of my seat. It didn't seem wise; however, I was prepared to follow.

"Yes, now." He turned to Gavin. "You in?"

The detective remained seated. "No. This is a bad idea. What would you even say? What information do you hope to obtain?"

"We'll wing it," John shrugged.

"Wing it?" I asked. "Don't you think a plan might be a good idea?"

"We can't plan for this," he remarked. "I agree we should stay quiet about Kaley, though. Feel him out—see what he offers up..." John trailed off as he turned and walked out of the kitchen.

Gavin stood too, "Well, don't look at me, criminal. This was your idea."

"Are you coming?" John called.

Gavin grumbled and pushed away from the table, "Guess I'm going to have to go. I can't let you two go off half-cocked."

With that, we followed John out the front door and piled into his truck.

Chapter 44
KALEY

After picking Summer up from school, we swung over to the bar to visit Grandpa Henry. I was trying very hard not to feel like a victim. Although I knew it wasn't their intention, that's how I felt when I was with the guys in John's kitchen. Like with all uncomfortable situations, I'd strive to avoid it as long as possible.

"There's my favorite girls!" Henry exclaimed as we entered the office. My grandfather was seated at his desk with papers strewn out around him. Although he looked to be in the middle of something, he appeared happy to have a distraction.

Henry spun on the chair and held his arms out to his great-granddaughter. Summer joyfully ran to him and was rewarded with a giant bear hug.

Henry pulled Summer onto his lap and then looked to where I still stood in the doorway of the dated office space. "What brings ya by?"

"We just wanted to check on you," I said, taking a few steps further into the room. "You know—make sure you're staying out of trouble."

Henry chuckled, "Always. How about you?"

"Me?"

"Yeah—you. Trouble seems to be your middle name lately."

Summer laughed, "I thought your middle name was Harper like mine?"

"It is. Grandpa's just teasing."

Summer laughed again and hopped off the old man's lap. "Can I have some cheese curds?"

"You betcha," Grandpa replied. "Go out to the bar and tell Ted that his boss wants him to fix you whatever you want."

Summer took off at a sprint. Luckily, I was able to intercept her before she made it through the doorway. "No. You politely ask Ted if you can please have cheese curds. Then, tell him it's okay with grandpa—if he has time."

"Bleh—" Henry motioned toward me with disgust.

"Hey—I'm trying to raise a decent human here," I said in response. "You could actually help instead of whatever it is you're doing."

He waved me off again.

"Can I go, Mommy?" I still had a hold of Summer.

"Only if you promise to be polite."

"I will."

I let go and watched as she bolted toward the dining area.

"How ya doin, kiddo?" Grandpa asked, sliding his reading glasses off his face and settling his pale blue eyes on me.

I flopped onto the nearby sofa and sighed, "I've been better."

"I can imagine. What can I do for you?"

"You're already doing it. You're here and available to Summer. What more could I ask?"

"Well, you never ask for much; but I do feel like you're holding something back..."

I didn't want to worry my grandfather by mentioning the incident with the police chief or Nathan's notebook. Not to mention the unlikely partnership currently taking place in John's kitchen.

"Kaley..." he leaned forward, waiting for my reply.

"I'm just feeling emotional," I offered a half-truth. "So, I'm resting up at John's and sorting out my feelings."

"Feelings about what?"

I hadn't expected him to press. Usually, any mention of feelings and he was out. The old man didn't like having them much less discussing them.

"You know—my house getting ransacked and moving on without Nathan. Little things like that," I joked.

He seemed satisfied with my answer and grabbed his cane from beside the desk as he hoisted himself out of the chair. "Come on then, darlin'. Let's make sure my great-granddaughter isn't eatin' too much cheese." He limped over to the sofa and offered me his hand.

I accepted and walked alongside Henry down the hallway. "I don't think Summer could ever eat too much cheese."

"Ahhh, you'd be wrong about that. She'll eat too much and won't be able to poop for a week."

I grimaced at the unexpected remark, "Personal experience?"

"Well, sure."

"Nice, Henry."

"Don't you go callin' me Henry, now. It's grandpa to you. And don't you go scoffin' at this old man's advice. You benefit greatly from the wisdom I bestow on you."

We'd reached the dining area. Across the room, Summer was perched on one of the high wooden bar stools. Ted was nodding animatedly as Summer happily bent his ear about something.

"What great wisdom have you offered me?" I asked Henry.

He stopped and leaned on his cane rubbing his chin pensively. "Well, I do recall putting ya in a pretty good position with a certain coach."

"Ha! You set me up in an embarrassing situation with a certain coach. Thanks for that!"

"I handpicked him for ya and ya know it. Someday you'll admit I know whatcha need better than you do."

He may have had a point, but no way would I give him the satisfaction of acknowledging that. Or any encouragement for him to further meddle in my life. So instead, I just called him a crazy old man and joined my daughter at the bar, leaving Henry sniggering in my wake.

Chapter 45
MATT

Never could I have imagined a scenario where I'd be teamed up with a football coach and a detective. Yet, there I was in Chief Logan Sterns' office with John Kyler and, even more surprising, Shane Gavin. The biggest shock, though, was that nobody tried to arrest me for anything.

Upon arrival, Gavin had us all buzzed in. He left John and me in the entryway while he tracked down the chief. He wanted to give the man ample warning before our little trio descended on him. I don't think John was keen on the idea of Gavin having a word in private with Sterns first. However, he didn't want to negatively affect Gavin's position with the department so he grudgingly agreed.

Sterns led us into his spacious, orderly office. The interior wall was all glass which allowed him a clear view of the squad area filled with cubicles. Logan's office was filled with various plaques and accommodations along with framed photographs of the man himself posing with local officials and celebrities. None of them all that impressive.

There were two mesh office chairs on the other side of his desk for visitors. John and Gavin each took a seat facing the chief. Sterns didn't offer to bring in an additional chair, so I stood behind John. Gavin turned and narrowed his eyes at me before settling into his seat. The detective wanted me to keep my mouth shut, and I was happy to oblige. The less talking I did the better off I'd be.

The beefy chief folded his arms across his chest and leaned back in his oversized executive chair. "Now, gentlemen, Detective Gavin shared that you all had concerns about my visit with Kaley this morning."

John's head snapped in Gavin's direction. I could only imagine the look he shot him. Since I was behind them both, I couldn't confirm, but Gavin's posture changed. He slouched and leaned in the opposite direction of John. The move was slight but enough to determine I was right; there was no love lost between my new partners.

John cleared his throat, "While that is a concern... I was actually hoping to talk to you about something else."

The chief lifted his chin. He appeared intrigued. "And what might that be?"

"The notebook that belonged to Nathan Stone."

The room was quiet except for the low hum of people working from the squad room on the other side of the glass walls.

John continued, "I think you might have a problem in your department here, Logan. If I'm right, I believe the break-in at Kaley's was an attempt to clean up some of that problem."

Sterns eyes flashed with something... amusement, annoyance, anger? I didn't really know. The guy wasn't an easy read, but there was definitely something there. "Are you telling me the notebook that was in Kaley's possession was taken during the break-in?"

Before John could respond, Shane jumped in. "She can't find it, so I'm guessing it was. I mean, it was more sentimental than anything, so of course, I didn't list it with the inventory."

The chief rubbed his chin in contemplation. If he had something to do with the break-in at Kaley's house, then he'd know Gavin was lying.

Sterns leaned back and casually pulled open a desk drawer, "If Kaley told you about my visit this morning, then, I'm sure she shared with you my concerns about Nathan."

The three of us stayed quiet and waited to see what Sterns would say next.

"I want to show you something," the chief produced a manila folder and handed it to his detective.

Gavin opened the folder revealing a handful of papers. "Evidence logs? Why are you giving me pages from old evidence logs?"

Sterns made a point of looking at each and every one of us before responding. I got the feeling he was about to feed us a big load of bullshit.

"Nathan wasn't the only one doing a little investigating," Sterns announced with a smug smile playing across his lips. "Unfortunately, I was starting to notice some missing inventory here and there. Nothing major at first, an ounce of marijuana, a gram of coke... I didn't suspect sticky fingers—not in my department. I assumed it was logging errors or general disorganization. Don't get me wrong, that's completely unacceptable too, but better than the alternative. Then there were weapons that couldn't be accounted for and other things as well..." He paused, "let's just say—I had a problem on my hands. And I know what you're thinking..."

"I'm thinking dirty cops." I blurted out somewhat involuntarily.

Gavin extended his arm far enough that he was able to lightly backhand me in the stomach. "Shut up, criminal."

Sterns stood and extended to his full height, which wasn't nearly as impressive as I believe he thought it was. "No, Matt's right. I was concerned there might be a dirty cop here, but that's no longer the case."

John pointed his finger at the chief, "Don't you dare try and blame this on Nathan Stone."

Gavin's head snapped to his right so fast I thought there might be a possibility of whiplash. "Chief, you can't possibly think—"

"Really, Shane?" John interrupted. "Can't you see what's happening?"

Shane appeared dumbfounded as he turned back toward the police chief for guidance, "Nathan would never..."

"I'm sorry, Shane," the chief nodded sadly. "You're holding some of the proof right there. The dates correspond with missing items from the evidence room."

Shane glanced down at the folder clutched in his right hand.

"Now, can you see the predicament this presented me with? I started getting suspicious around the time... well, you know... Poor Kaley and little Summer... The truth would completely destroy them."

I couldn't contain myself any longer, "What a load of BS!" I shouted. "Nathan was not a dumb man! If he was trying to cover up his activity, he would have done it. He wouldn't have signed his name to his crimes, if you know what I mean."

The chief smiled at me maliciously, "Matt, we know he paid you off too. We know you were taking bribes from Detective Stone."

"What?" I asked, feeling genuinely confused.

"Pictures of him paying you off at Luke's Diner." The chief said matter-of-factly. I couldn't help but notice the sparkle in his eye. The fat bastard was actually enjoying this.

"You have no clue—"

John cut me off, "Shane—I want to see those logs."

Shane handed them over. He'd barely looked at the papers himself.

"I believe Nathan pulled them out of the log to cover his tracks," Logan started to explain, "They were found when we cleaned his desk."

I peered over John's shoulder as he leafed through the pages. There seemed to be a whole slew of logged-in weapons and narcotics, with Nathan's signature documenting the process.

"I didn't want these to ever see the light of day," Logan said. "That family has been through enough. There is no use in pursuing this. Now, you're here, though—what am going to do?" Sterns slapped his thighs and situated himself at the edge of his desk.

"You're sure Nathan Stone was the one that logged and signed this evidence?" John asked.

"You can see for yourself—it's his clear as day."

"Clear as day?" John repeated the chief's phrase.

"Let me see those!" Gavin snatched the papers from John's grasp, causing some of the sheets to flutter to the floor.

"You stupid bastard!" Shane exclaimed, "This couldn't be Nathan."

Logan dropped his confident air, "Look, Shane, I know this is difficult news but..."

I looked at John, wondering if he was feeling as confused as I was.

"If it's legible, it's not Nathan's signature," John explained.

"That's right!" Gavin jumped on John's statement. "Nathan had terrible yet very distinct handwriting. If you can read it—like this," he said, holding up the paper as proof. "Then this was not written or signed by Nathan. Go look at any of the reports he signed off on. The writing won't match."

Logan and Shane locked eyes. The chief tried to stare down his subordinate. To Gavin's credit, he was not backing off. Finally, the chief was the one to break the long uncomfortable silence. "What are you suggesting, Shane?" The chief asked through gritted teeth.

"I'm not suggesting anything, Chief. I'm simply stating facts."

"And those facts would be..." Logan asked, clasping his hands in front of him, waiting patiently for a response.

John gave him one, "Somebody set Nathan Stone up. From the looks of the log pages here, they did a poor job of it."

Sterns turned to Kyler, "That's a pretty serious accusation."

"One you certainly didn't seem to mind making when it was Nathan."

"That's right!" Shane exclaimed, agreeing with John.

"Because that's where the evidence pointed," the chief said sharply.

"And now..." John continued, "now that the evidence seems to be pointing in another direction?"

"I'll look into it," Logan responded. "A word of advice gentlemen—you may want to reconsider your stance."

"Why is that?" Gavin asked, folding his arms in front of him.

"You all have something to lose here. If I start to look into this again, I'll go where it leads."

"Isn't that what you're supposed to do?" I asked.

Sterns offered a low chuckle. Clearly, he was the only one in on the joke. "Right now, this issue is settled. Done."

"Blame conveniently placed on a dead man," John muttered under his breath.

Sterns gave him a steely, side-eyed glance before continuing. "Let's face it—you all gained something with Nathan's death."

Gavin was pissed now. "I gained nothing! How can you say that!" He sat forward on the edge of his chair and lowered his voice, "If I find out—"

Sterns straightened, "If you find out what?"

John stood abruptly and grasped Gavin's shoulder. "We appreciate your time. We trust that things will move forward from here."

I wanted to say I didn't actually trust that at all. But I kept my mouth shut.

Logan seemed caught off guard by the about-face. He stammered around a bit before telling John he would look into things. I couldn't help but wonder what he meant by that.

John nudged Gavin out of the office and down the hall. I trudged along silently behind the pair. John still had his hand on the crackpot's shoulder and was saying something to him in a whispered tone. Gavin pulled a card from his pocket and swiped the electronic box by the exit. Moments later we were in the vestibule between the station and freedom. Then, we pushed through the last set of doors. These were glass and much more welcoming than the steel gray we'd passed through to get into the building.

I inhaled the cool, crisp air trying to get the sterile scent of bleach and Pine-Sol to clear from my passageways.

Gavin rounded on John, "Why didn't you let me finish?"

"Because—I had no idea what you were about to say to your boss. I'm not sure you even knew what you were going to say! Since this was my idea, I feel a certain obligation to keep you out of trouble."

Gavin shrugged, "Wasn't that your whole plan anyway... wing it?" Gavin started to stride toward John's truck. "What's the next move then, coach?" he yelled back from several yards away.

We caught up to Gavin, and I answered his question. "We go back and regroup. I get the feeling the chief has something on all of us. Let's get that out in the open and go from there."

"He doesn't have a damn thing on me," Gavin stated.

"Well, he thinks he does," John replied. "And as we just witnessed, he doesn't have any problem manufacturing evidence to support his theory."

At that, Gavin tipped his head back to the sky and exhaled sharply, his breath visible in the crisp Wisconsin air.

I stopped beside the detective while John continued toward the truck.

"What is it?" I asked.

Gavin gave me a sideways glance, "He's not an idiot," he mumbled.

"Who?"

John had backtracked and stood several feet away listening.

"The chief," Gavin replied. "I mean, he might be an idiot but not like this."

"What?"

Gavin turned to face me, "Jeez, criminal, do I need to spell it out for you?"

"Apparently," I snapped back.

"The evidence logs, Nathan's signature, if he truly wanted to set him up—wouldn't he at least attempt to forge his writing?"

Gavin had a point.

"Which leads me to believe that either someone else messed with the logs to test the chief or the chief is testing me."

We all stood there for a moment mulling it over.

"Come on," John said after a moment, "Let's get out of here."

Gavin moved ahead quickly and hopped into the truck, shutting the door behind him before I could climb in back. The vehicle had a backseat but just the two doors for entry.

I walked around to the driver's side just as John shut his door.

I debated for a moment if I actually wanted to ride with two of them, or not.

I had not yet come to a conclusion when the driver's door opened, and John slid out, "Matt! Get your ass in the truck!" he bellowed.

So, the decision was made for me. I shuffled forward closing the gap. "The three fuckin' amigos," I murmured.

"Yeah—something like that," John replied.

Chapter 46
KALEY

Henry ended up tagging along to John's house. He claimed it was to make sure I wasn't lying to him again. Couldn't blame him for that.

We entered through the garage door, which led to a small mudroom where Summer quickly discarded her winter gear and backpack. She had spied Shane's truck parked at the curb and was excited to greet both Shane and John. She charged full force into the kitchen as Henry struggled to bend over to retrieve her coat from the floor.

"I got this, Grandpa. I know you're just as excited to see Shane as Summer." I nudged him slightly, offering him a wink.

Henry handed the coat to me so I could hang it from one of the many black hooks that lined the wall. "I was going to be a gentleman and help ya get all this crap picked up. Since you decided to be such a wise-ass—I'm thinkin' you can handle it on your own."

I shook my head as he limped off into the kitchen to join the gang.

"Hey, old man!" I heard Shane bellow in way of greeting. "They know you escaped from the home?"

I sighed and hung the rest of Summer's things. Then, took a seat on the bench that ran the length of the mudroom and started to dig through her backpack to make sure there weren't any notes that required my immediate attention. No matter how unfamiliar life seemed, it was comforting to experience familiarity in routine.

"Gavin, you son of a bitch," Grandpa growled from the other room.

"Seriously, does Kay know you're here? Or is she out issuing a silver alert?" Shane continued goading my grandfather.

"Now you listen here, ya little cock sucker."

I bristled at the sound of grandpa's voice echoing through the kitchen. Whether he realized it or not, Henry had just added a new term to my kindergartner's vocabulary. I squeezed my eyes closed and took a deep breath, giving myself a minute before confronting the two of them.

"You, okay?" John's voice resonated in the small area.

I didn't hear anything else and cautiously opened one eye and then the other, slowly bringing his fuzzy form into focus. He'd shut the door, which explained why I could no longer hear the back and forth between Shane and Grandpa.

"Kaley, are you okay?" he repeated, shifting from one foot to the other.

I offered up a smile, "Fine. Thanks. It's just those two sometimes."

"Do they always go at it like that?" he asked, jabbing his thumb over his shoulder toward the kitchen.

"No, it's usually much worse."

"Summer didn't seem to notice, if it makes you feel any better. She ran right off to the spare bedroom with my iPad to play games. I hope that's okay..."

"It's great. Thanks. Now I don't have to explain what a cock sucker is later."

John chuckled and slid onto the bench beside me. We sat in silence for a moment.

When John spoke again, his voice was lower and uncharacteristically soft. "We went to see Logan today."

"What?" I exclaimed, shifting my position on the bench to look at him. "Want to tell me about that?"

"You're not going to like it..."

"Not surprising. Go on."

"Long story short—Logan fabricated evidence against Nathan. In fact, it appears he's prepared to pin all of our suspicions on Nathan."

My body tensed, "He alluded to Nathan being dangerous earlier too but he can't possibly..."

John rested his hand on my knee reassuringly. "We aren't going to let that happen. The fact that he was prepared tells us exactly what we need to know."

"What do we need to know, John?"

"Logan's done, Kaley. Nathan started this and now we're going to finish it. His boss is dirty, and he tried to bring him down. He died protecting our community and the people in it. We won't let that be for nothing."

My eyes started to sting. I hadn't been fully aware of how much weight I'd been carrying until it started to lift. At that moment, John was offering to help carry the load. Shane and my grandfather were terrific, but their idea of support had little to do with what I needed and everything to do with what they felt I needed. I used my sleeve to wipe the dampness from my eyes.

"Why are you doing this?" I asked.

"Because it's the right thing to do and beyond that—I might like you just a little bit."

I nudged him with my elbow, "Just a little bit."

He pinched his thumb and pointer finger together to demonstrate.

It was at that moment that the door squeaked open, and Summer chose to grace us with her presence. "Why are you crying, mommy?"

I pulled her onto my lap, "I'm just feeling grateful for John. I'm not sure how he came into our lives at the exact right moment... I guess we're just lucky." I couldn't look at John while I tried to explain my emotions to my daughter. I was feeling vulnerable and awkward, so I kept my focus on Summer and just kept talking. "His friendship makes me feel overwhelmed, and when I'm overwhelmed... sometimes I cry."

She wrinkled up her little nose, "That's kinda weird."

The statement made John chuckle which loosened some of the tension. "Sometimes adults are weird when they have feelings," he offered.

I kissed the top of her little blonde head, hoping we'd answered her question adequately. Summer looked back and forth between the two of us. Her little features were scrunched up in concentration... or confusion... I wasn't entirely sure which.

"No—not that part," Summer said. "The part about not knowing how we got lucky."

Now I was confused, "What do you mean, honey?"

Summer sighed like an exasperated parent. "I mean—it's not luck that brought John to our family. It's Daddy. I already told you this, Mommy. Remember—the night Sargent Snuggles and I went out at dark. I told you, Daddy sent a new friend to keep you safe."

I did remember. And yet, I was not at all prepared for my daughter's nonchalant response about communicating with her dead father.

"I swear, Mommy. I gotta repeat stuff to you all the time."

I looked at John for guidance.

He shrugged, "Way out of my league here."

Summer slid off my lap and gently tugged on John's pant leg. "May I please have one of those string cheeses?"

John smiled, "You bet. Do you need help?"

"Nope," she pulled open the door and started to skip away.

I called after her, "Summer…"

"Thank you, John!" She called back over her shoulder.

John chuckled, "You're welcome, Summer." Then he turned his attention back to me. "Pretty great kid you got there."

"Yeah… a little odd but I'll keep her."

He raised his eyebrow, "Odd? Because of her statement about Nathan?"

"Ummm, yeah. That's not exactly normal is it?"

John leaned back against the wall. "I don't think it's abnormal. Summer misses her dad. Kids have active imaginations. It kind of makes sense that she made Nathan into this all-powerful being that makes her feel safe and watched over… right?"

"Well, when you put it that way, it does make sense."

"What does?" I glanced up to see Shane standing in the doorway. He was munching down on his own string cheese.

"How long have you been standing there?"

"Not long," he turned to John and held up the cheese. "Hope you don't mind."

John waved away the question. "Not at all, help yourself to whatever."

"Thanks, man. Anyway, what's weird?"

I stood and stretched, "Oh, nothing, really. Summer just said something about Nathan that struck me as strange, but after talking it out—maybe it isn't that odd."

Shane tilted his head, "Oh, you mean like her ghost dad thing?"

"Her what?"

"Ghost dad. That's what I call it anyway. Nathan tells her shit all the time." Shane took another bite of cheese.

"Like what?"

"I don't know, Kay… like—you're going to be okay. That John's a good guy. That he loves the name she chose for the dog. And he tells her to help you out around the house and stuff. Normal dad things."

I felt my eyes widen, "Except her dad isn't alive to tell her stuff. How often does she have these conversations?"

Shane shrugged, "I don't know… couple times a month maybe…"

Now I wanted to know more. "How long has this been going on?"

He shrugged, "I don't know. I guess I don't recall her not doing it so… since he died maybe…"

"And what's your take on it?"

"On what?"

"What do you mean on what? On Summer talking to her dad."

"Shane shrugged, "I think it's nice Nathan can communicate from the other side. I hope he doesn't try to talk to me, though… that crap freaks me out." He shuddered and started to walk away—then thought better of it and turned back. "What are you guys doin' in here anyway?"

I looked at John, "Hiding from you," he offered.

Satisfied with the answer, Shane nodded and sauntered off.

"What do you make of that?" I asked John.

John stood and slipped his hands into his pockets, "Well, I think your daughter is just fine; but that guy may be slightly crazy."

I laughed nervously, but John's expression was solemn. It had been a long day, and neither of us had gotten a lot of sleep. Was that it or something more?

"Can I ask you something?" he asked hesitantly.

"I'd think by now you'd know you can ask me something, without actually saying, can I ask you something."

He turned to face me, "Fair enough. If you don't want to answer or I offend you, just tell me."

"Another thing I'd think you'd have learned by now—if I'm upset or offended... I'll just tell you."

He nodded, "Okay, then... We've decided Logan is not to be trusted, along with some of his department, correct?"

"Yes..." I responded cautiously, wondering where he was going with this.

"Where does Shane fall? Cause' if I'm being honest with you, Kaley. I just don't know. I can't read the guy. He could be playing us for information. He pulls off loveable dope really well with you but when you're not around..."

"What?"

John shrugged, "I don't know. He's just different. And part of me wonders if he's playing us for fools."

"He's not." I was quick to defend Shane, although I had to admit some of his decisions had given me pause as well. Like telling Logan about Nathan's notebook and my house being hit when he was conveniently out of town. Then, there was the question as to where he was the night Nathan died. Was there more to that than just survivor's guilt?

John studied me carefully, "You sure about that?" he asked, as though he could see inside my thoughts.

"I really need a nap," I said, abruptly changing the subject. I punctuated the point with a yawn.

John seemed to accept the response as we prepared to exit the safety of the tiny mudroom to whatever craziness was taking place with the three men in the kitchen.

"You have a way of always making me feel better," I remarked.

"That goes both ways."

His words stopped me dead in my tracks. "How on earth do I make you feel better? Look at all the drama and chaos I've brought into your life."

"My life needed a little chaos." He nudged me forward through the kitchen to the dining table. Grandpa, Matt, and Shane stopped their conversation and looked at us expectantly.

"But, I'm not sure my life needed this motley crew," John said, gesturing toward the table.

"Great band!" Shane piped up.

Chapter 47
MATT

After returning from the police station, we didn't get much accomplished. John wanted to go to the DA. Gavin, on the other hand, seemed to be having a hard time wrapping his head around the possibility that he was part of a corrupt department. He insisted we obtain some kind of concrete evidence before bringing anyone else in. I agreed with both of them. Nobody was going to listen to anything we had to say until we had something solid. John seemed to think Nathan's notebook was enough. It wasn't. I only hoped that Gavin was actually with us rather than trying to deceive us.

Once Henry showed up, any progress was abruptly halted. We weren't sure how much Kaley wanted her grandpa to know. The man was already overly concerned about her and his great-granddaughter—understandably so. Even though I hadn't made the headway I'd hoped, I tried not to feel disappointed as I trudged up the few steps leading to our kitchen entrance.

It was a little past six, so I expected to be bowled over by sweet smells wafting from the kitchen. I found myself once again disappointed. The kitchen remained dark, and not a single pot or pan had been displaced from the rack above the stove.

"Aiyona!" I called out, deeply unsettled by this huge disruption in my familiar routine. When she didn't answer, my mind flashed back to what had happened to Kaley only a few short nights ago. That sent my thoughts spiraling. My pulse rate quickened as I pushed through the kitchen and into the darkened living room.

"Aiyona!" I called again.

The house was empty.

I ran to the landline and quickly tapped out the digits to her cell. It went straight to voicemail.

"Baby, I need you to call me right away. I'm not sure where you are and I'm freakin' out a little bit..." Unsure what I could add to that, I placed the handset back on the base and looked around the house.

Nothing appeared out of place. I went to the bedroom next, and again—things seemed normal. But Aiyona always kept me apprised of her whereabouts. I raced back to the kitchen to check the dry erase board stuck to the refrigerator. If she or Layla had an appointment, there would be a note scrawled on one of the oversized squares labeled with the days of the week. I told myself I was probably overreacting, and I'd soon be reassured by a beautifully handwritten notation under today's date. Again, nothing.

I spun in a circle wondering what to do next. Was her car here? I sprinted back out the kitchen door to the one-car detached garage and lifted the door. I was relieved to see the space that normally held her little red Toyota was empty. Wherever she was she most likely left of her own accord.

I ran back into the house, worried I'd miss her call; but an hour later when I still hadn't heard from her, I started to panic. I needed to call someone. But who? Certainly not the cops but Gavin... maybe?

The phone ringing through our otherwise silent home made me jump, even though the sound was what I'd been waiting to hear. I cautiously picked up the handset, fearing it wouldn't be Aiyona. "Hello…"

"Matt, I'm so glad you're home!"

The relief at hearing Aiyona's voice washed over me. The feeling didn't last long, though. It was quickly replaced by irritation. How could my beautiful bride-to-be leave me hanging like that? With everything going on she'd have to have known how worried I'd be.

"Matt? Did I lose you? Are you still there?"

"I'm here," I replied flatly, trying to suppress a surge of emotions.

Then my Aiyona did something she rarely did. She completely broke down. "I didn't know what to do," she cried into the phone. "I was so scared, and you weren't home. I just took Layla and ran. I didn't have a way to get a hold of you, and I was afraid if I left a note someone might see it. They might get into our home like what happened to Kaley."

"Aiyona… slow down, baby. What happened? Why are you freakin' out on me?"

"There was a letter tucked in the front door. It said to back-off or Tyrone Braxton won't be your biggest problem."

My heart felt as though it might beat right out of my chest. Adrenaline coursed through my veins. "Tyrone is in prison, Aiyona. He's not even a problem. That message was meant for me. Someone is trying to get me to back off and they are using you to do it. Tyrone can't hurt you or Layla."

I was met by silence on the other end of the phone.

"Aiyona—just come home. I promise you'll be safe." I could imagine her chewing her lip on the other end in quiet contemplation.

"Where are you? I'll come to you if you prefer…"

I waited patiently for her to respond. Usually filling the silence when Aiyona was thinking was the wrong move. I'd learned to not fill the void with my own chatter, and sooner or later she'd come around.

"Matt… what are you supposed to back off of?"

"Come home and I'll explain. It's been a weird day."

"Could you just check? I mean, is there a way you could make sure Tyrone is still behind bars without someone clueing him in?"

I sighed, "I know a guy, and there's no way to trace it back to us." Guess I'd be calling Gavin tonight after all.

"You sure?"

"Positive. Now, tell me where you are."

"I'm not really sure... I just kept driving. We're way out in the country. I'm headed back toward town now. I didn't realize how spotty cell reception could be out here. Layla fell asleep in the car. I just kept driving away from home."

Well, that explained why she didn't pick up when I called. "Glad you're coming back. I have a lot to fill you in on."

"Yeah? Including Tyrone's status?"

"Absolutely," I reassured her. Now, I'd just need Gavin to come through for me.

"Thank you," she said softly.

"You don't need to thank me. It's the least I can do. After all, you're in this mess because of me. You trust me day in and day out with your life and Layla's. I'm going to prove someday I'm worthy of you both."

"You've done that time and time again, Matt. There's nothing left to prove."

"Maybe not to you but definitely to myself." *And possibly Nathan*. I kept the latter to myself.

"I love you, Matt."

"I love you too, baby. See you soon." Aiyona would never fully appreciate how much I cared. I slipped the proof of my devotion out of my pocket. Gavin had scrawled his number on a post-it note back at John's place. I'd soon find out if we were all truly in this together. I took a deep breath before dialing the asshole's number.

Surprisingly, he picked up immediately, "What?"

"Do you always answer your phone like that?"

"I put your number in my phone, so I knew it was you."

Didn't fully answer the question but okay... To him, I said: "I need a favor."

"What do you want, criminal?"

I ignored the slam and continued, "My fiancée is concerned about an ex... "

"Okay..."

I wasn't sure how much to share so I stuck with the basics. "She was involved with a pretty bad guy several years ago, and someone implied that he might be an issue. He's supposed to be in prison, but if we could just get some confirmation that would be helpful."

Gavin laughed, "Sounds like she's got a type, criminal."

I gripped the phone tighter. Perhaps going to Gavin was a mistake. "Look, you don't like me. I don't like you, but I know you have a heart. I've seen you with Kaley and Summer. Layla thinks you're pretty great too. So, I'm asking for Aiyona and Layla. Will you please make sure this guy isn't a threat to them?"

The line was quiet for a beat. When the detective spoke again his voice was quieter, his tone genial. "What's the name?"

"He can't ever know we were checking up on him..."

"Name," he repeated.

"Tyrone Braxton."

"From Alabama too?"

"Yep, he should be at Kilby, unless something changed."

"I'll get back to you."

"Thank you."

"I'm not doin' it for you, criminal."

"And here I thought we were starting to connect."

There was no response and I realized Gavin had already hung up.

Chapter 48
KALEY

I tossed and turned most of the night. When I finally rose, John's bedside clock read 9:00 am. The night before, John announced he would again be taking Summer to school. He also said the offer was non-negotiable. I was so mentally and physically exhausted that I didn't have the energy to protest. Somehow, I slept through the whole morning routine.

My inner voice was nagging me to get up and open the gallery. It seemed important to try and regain some sense of normality. However, I wasn't feeling particularly motivated or creative. John's observations regarding Shane were weighing on me. It didn't help that we'd barely had a minute alone since the break-in.

I showered and dressed in jeans and a sweater. Forty-five minutes later, I was pulling into Shane's driveway. I'd already driven past the police station and verified neither his Mustang nor truck were in the lot. Which most likely meant he was still home. He usually started as late in the day as possible. Nathan had always been an early riser, I knew Shane's chronic morning tardiness drove him crazy.

Before I could put my vehicle in park, I was startled by a tapping on my window. I involuntarily let out a little scream. Shane had appeared from out of nowhere. I lowered the window, "You scared me half to death!" I chided him. "Where did you come from?"

"Park your car around the block on Orchard Street. I'll pick you up." And just like that, he was gone again.

I followed his instructions. Less than a minute later, Shane drove up in an unfamiliar black sedan. He pulled alongside my vehicle and waved his hand, beckoning me to climb in. Quickly, I retrieved my handbag and hopped from my vehicle to the passenger seat of the sedan. Shane drove around the block in silence. It wasn't until we pulled up to the curb on a side street that he made any attempt at conversation. I couldn't help but notice, our parking spot offered a perfect view of the front of his house.

"What are you doing, Kay?" he asked sharply.

"What am I doing? What are you doing?" I shot back.

"What does it look like?"

I looked him over, not sure how to respond. He was dressed in jeans and a black t-shirt with a black puffer jacket, unzipped, giving a clear view of the badge hanging around his neck. "It looks like you're working your neighborhood... specifically your house... Josie? Whose car is this anyway?"

"I borrowed it," he said offhandedly, his attention alarmingly focused on his house.

"You're watching your wife?" I asked hesitantly.

"We need to get you a new phone today," he responded, completely disregarding my question.

"Great. That sounds great. But how about we talk about what's happening right now?"

He ran his hand down his face. "I told you Josie and me... we're not anything like you and Nathan."

I waited patiently for him to continue.

He didn't.

I tried my best to navigate the situation. "Are you watching the house because you're worried Josie's cheating on you?"

"Funny you came to that conclusion so fast," he said dryly. "And I'm not worried that she might be... I know she is."

"Do you think he's there now?"

"Yep," Shane replied in a low growl.

I didn't ask how or why. Instead, I asked, "What can I do? You want me to go up to the door and pretend I'm looking for you?"

He raised his eyebrows and shot me a look that said, 'really?'

I threw my hands up, "Well, I don't know. It seemed like a good idea to me."

He said nothing and set his attention back on the house.

"Do you want to know why I'm here?" I finally asked, hoping to re-direct Shane's attention, at least for a little bit. The intensity in which he was watching his house was a bit unnerving.

He leaned against the driver's door and slouched back in his seat a bit; still looking straight ahead he replied, "You're doubting me. You're doubting yourself, you're not sure who you can trust. So you came to feel me out. Probably because John or Matt or both made you question my motives."

I swallowed hard. How could he possibly know that? He had rendered me speechless.

Shane finally turned to look at me, "How am I doing so far?"

I chewed my lip, "That pretty much sums it up."

The vinyl interior creaked as Shane shifted his weight to the side. "I never told Logan about the notebook."

"Then why did you say you did and how does he know, Shane?"

"I didn't tell Logan, but I did tell someone; and it got back to him. I didn't deny it when he asked."

"Why would you tell anyone?"

"You wanted me to help, right? I thought that's what I was doing."

"Are you covering for someone?" I was having trouble making sense of my friend's confession.

"Look, I know you, Kay. And you know me... probably better than anyone. Some of my decisions may seem questionable, but I need you to know I have my reasons."

I started to respond when movement caught the corner of my eye. Shane's garage door slid up. A black Chevy Tahoe backed slowly down his driveway.

Shane noticed, too, and hit the steering wheel hard.

"Maybe it's not what you think—"

"Get low," Shane interrupted. He yanked my shoulder, pulling me down with him. We hid from the SUV that would most likely pass by Shane's borrowed sedan in a matter of moments.

"What if he goes the other way and spots my Honda parked around the block?"

"He won't," Shane grumbled.

"How do you know?"

Shane ventured a peek, "Because he's already at the stop-sign behind us."

I risked a look too. I peered through the back window just in time to see Logan Sterns turn right and exit Shane's neighborhood.

"It makes sense," Shane said, resuming his position behind the wheel.

I sat back up too. "How does Logan sleeping with Josie make any sense?" I exclaimed.

"One more thing you're going to have to trust me on," Shane responded. He put the vehicle in drive and expertly maneuvered back onto the residential street.

Chapter 49
MATT

Gavin called me back to confirm Layla's father was still behind bars. Surprisingly, he went above and beyond too. The detective revealed that with Tyrone"s criminal history there was no need to worry; he assured me Tyrone wouldn't be going anywhere anytime soon.

I ended the call with a sigh of relief. The note, the phone calls, it was all just somebody's way of trying to scare me off. I was ashamed to admit, but it had almost worked. My first reaction had been to pack up camp. Although I was able to rationalize the situation, convincing Aiyona that Layla's bio dad wasn't an actual threat was easier said than done.

Aiyona spent half the night tossing and turning. Every bump and creak led her to believe something or someone was out to get us. Her paranoia lasted well into the morning when she announced she was keeping Layla home from school.

"Aiyona, I told you my information is solid. Tyrone doesn't know anything about anything. Someone is using your past to get at me."

"What if you're wrong?

"I'm not. I have the facts to back it up."

She crossed her arms in front of her defiantly, "Cause that cocky cop checked it out for you?"

"Well... yeah ..."

"He's probably in on it, Matt. Why you trustin' him anyway?"

I stepped forward and rubbed her shoulders, "Well, Kaley trusts him."

"That's it? Because a woman we barely know thinks he's a stand-up guy? I hate to break it to you, baby, but you are crackin' up! I'm callin' in sick and keepin' Layla home today."

"No. You're not. One of us needs to be working. Since I'm laid off—that honor goes to you. I know you have sick time, but you should save it for when you need it. Besides, Layla likes school. She's not going to want to stay home all day."

"Since when do you order me around?"

"Since I'm the one with my head on straight."

She was about to protest, but I quieted her with a kiss. "Please, Aiyona—don't argue with me today. I got this."

To my shock, my fireball of a fiancée backed down. She threw her hands up in defeat. "Fine, Matt. You win. But if I'm going do it your way, then you're going to adhere to my wishes."

I couldn't help but smile. I'd actually won a disagreement with Aiyona. It was definitely a first. "Please, tell me your wishes." I bowed dramatically before her.

Aiyona laughed, "Well, first you're going to get Layla to school."

"Not a problem."

"And then—since you don't have anything better to do—you're going to sit your ass in the parking lot all day and make sure you're just a few steps away in case..."

My smile faded, "Aiyona," I groaned. "Who says I don't have anything better to do?"

She pointed her finger in my face, "You sayin' you got better things to do than make sure our baby is safe?"

I sighed; guess I didn't win the disagreement after all. "No. If you need me, I'll be in the parking lot of the Franklin Elementary school for the foreseeable future."

Aiyona spun on her heel and trotted into the kitchen. "You better get a move on, Matt. You know what a beast Layla is to get up in the morning."

"Yep," I turned and shuffled off in the opposite direction. It seemed it was time to wake the sleeping beast.

"Matt..."

I turned back.

Her smile had faded, and I saw the look of fear once again in her big, beautiful brown eyes. "Promise me it's going to be okay."

"I promise."

Chapter 50
KALEY

Shane refused to talk about Josie and Logan. Under normal circumstances, I'd completely respect my friend's desire to wallow. However, this was more than just an extra-marital affair. If Logan was heading up a corrupt police department and sleeping with Shane's wife, there could be so much more going on than any of us could have imagined.

I'd give him some space, but time wasn't something we had a lot of. The guys already stirred a hornet's nest with their visit to the police chief.

It was time to pick Summer up from school. I parked my SUV in front of Franklin Elementary and was preparing to walk toward the entrance when a tan Impala caught my eye. I made a slight deviation in my route and tapped gently on the driver's side window of Matt's sedan.

He seemed to startle awake. The guy practically jumped out of his skin. Guess I couldn't blame him. By the looks of it, I'd just woken Matt from a pretty deep slumber. I could imagine how disconcerting it would feel to wake up and find someone peering in the window at you. I backed up allowing him room. He pushed open the car door and quickly scrambled out.

"Hell! You scared me, Kaley!" Matt exclaimed, shutting the door as he joined me in the chilly lot.

"I'm sorry. I didn't realize you were napping at first. Everything okay?" It was a stupid question. I realized it as soon as I said it. Like anything was okay these days.

Matt didn't seem to notice. Instead, he pulled a black stocking cap out of his pocket and tugged it over his bald head with a sigh. "Yeah, Aiyona asked me to stake out the school lot. She's worried about some trouble with Layla's dad."

That was unexpected. "Want to tell me about it?"

He looked around, left then right, anywhere other than at me. "Gavin didn't mention anything?"

"No..." I replied slowly, "should he have?"

Matt seemed to make an effort to avoid eye contact. Instead, he focused his attention on his well-worn work boots. "Naw, I just figured he would," he responded.

I shrugged, "He's got other things on his mind."

I hoped Matt would offer up an explanation, but instead, he asked a question. "Are you a good judge of character?"

"I'd like to think so," I responded, taken aback by the direction of the conversation.

"Do you think Shane is a good person? Because I have serious doubts about him."

First John now Matt. I didn't mention that he wasn't the only one with doubts. Instead, I responded in the best way I could. "He feels the same way about you."

"And you, how do you feel?"

"I think you're both good people, but you're too bullheaded to admit you're wrong about each other."

He chuckled and looked up, meeting my eyes. "Thanks, that helps."

"Yeah?" A loud electronic ringing sound cut into our conversation. The bell had just signaled the end of the school day. "The girls will be here soon. Anything you want to share before we're bombarded?"

Matt shifted uncomfortably, "Layla's dad is a pretty bad dude. He doesn't know about her, and we'd like to keep it that way. Anyway, Aiyona and me... we've been gettin' these calls. Calls that he's out of prison and coming for her. The calls started soon after I met you. I asked Shane to look into it."

I reached out and gently grasped his arm in what I hoped he'd see as a show of support, "What did Shane say?"

Matt shrugged, "He pretty much confirmed what I already knew."

"Which is?"

"It was nothing but an empty threat. Unless your buddy Gavin is lying."

I released my hold on Matt's arm, preparing to defend Shane. "He's not. He wouldn't do that to you."

Matt nodded, "I sure hope you're right. Anyway, I spent the day in the parking lot to make sure Layla didn't have any unwanted visitors."

Things had started to make a little more sense. "Pretty hard to watch the school through your eyelids though, right?" I couldn't help but rib him for his mid-afternoon nap.

Matt smiled, "There's that."

The sounds of happy little voices wafted through the air. Students spilled out of the brick building, eager to put their day of academics behind them.

"Well, time to find our little minions," Matt commented, as he started in the direction of the school.

I fell in step beside him just as my phone buzzed in my back pocket. Noting it was Shane, I asked Matt to nab Summer too, so I could take the call.

I walked in the opposite direction to be heard over the rising throng of students. "Hey, Shane, what's up? How are you doing?"

Ignoring the first two questions he rapid fired two of his own. "Where are you? Do you know what's going on with John?"

I stopped dead in my tracks, "What do you mean what's going on with John?"

"So you don't know?"

"Know what?" I asked, my voice involuntarily rising an octave.

"There's some kind of investigation going on at the high school."

"Could you be any more vague?" I snapped.

"Probably. Anyway, you should get in touch."

And with that, he was gone.

I stood there staring at the phone for a minute as Matt ambled up with the girls.

"You okay?" Matt asked. I surmised I must be wearing my feelings on my face again.

"Yeah," I replied, waving away his concern.

"Mommy, can I play with Layla now?" Summer asked, tugging on the sleeve of my coat.

I was about to object, but then an idea formed in my overtaxed brain. "Ummm, maybe..." I replied. "Let me talk it over with Matt. "Why don't you two play on the playground for a couple of minutes while we chat."

"Okay, Mommy!" The girls ditched their backpacks and took off hand in hand toward the monkey bars. I was about to call out after them to watch for cars; but thankfully, they had already made it safely to the play yard only a few feet away.

"What's going on?" Matt asked quizzically.

The wind was starting to pick up. I brushed the hair from my eyes, wondering if what I was about to ask was a good idea or not. I knew Shane certainly wouldn't think so, but I thought Nathan would. "So, something's come up.... Do you think Summer could hang out with you for a bit? I mean the girls want to have a playdate and if it wouldn't be an inconvenience..."

He nodded enthusiastically, "Sure, not a problem. I'd be happy to watch Summer but—"

I cut him off, "I know it seems odd given our history. However, I wouldn't ask if I didn't trust you, and I've decided that I do. I realize this is awkward and sudden and—"

This time he cut me off, "No need to explain. I appreciate the opportunity—more than you know. You seem flustered, though—you sure everything's okay?"

I shifted my weight, debating about what to tell him. It's not like I could really answer that based on the information I had. "I don't know... John could be in some trouble."

He looked surprised, "Trouble? Would it have anything to do with our conversation with Logan?"

"Possibly. I really don't know yet, but I'll keep you posted," I offered.

"Yeah. Thanks," he replied, shoving his hands in his pockets.

I got the impression he wanted to ask more but he didn't. Instead, he asked me for my car keys so he could grab Summer's booster while I let Summer in on my afternoon plans.

Oddly enough, I felt a sense of calm, unlike anything I'd felt in a while. Given everything that was happening.... calm was really the last feeling I should be experiencing.

Chapter 51
MATT

I hoped everything was okay with Kaley and John. Although, secretly, I was happy to have earned her trust. Yet, I couldn't help but wonder if it was the circumstances rather than an actual newfound comfort level that compelled her to ask. Whatever the reason, I'd make for damn sure Summer was happy and safe. That's why it took longer than normal to reach our little rental home. After we stopped for ice cream, I drove slowly and cautiously. I avoided the main route, opting for a more scenic way to entertain the kids.

Aiyona was particularly pleased to arrive home from work to find Summer and Layla building a blanket fort in the living room. It was the first time Layla had entertained a friend in our home. Due to our lack of space, Aiyona and I both had concerns about her inviting kids over. We worried that kids might question Layla about why she didn't have her own room as well as the lack of toys and outdoor play space. Thankfully, Summer didn't even appear to notice. They pulled out games, art supplies, and then blankets. Both kids seemed happy.

"Did Kaley say how long?" Aiyona asked as she pulled her hair up into a ponytail before starting dinner preparations.

I shook my head, "It was kind of a last-minute deal, as I said."

"Okay, well, I'll just plan on Summer staying for dinner. If Kaley does call sooner, we'll just let her know. It will be nice for Kaley not to have to fix dinner, right?"

I stood up from where I'd been seated at the kitchen table. I enjoyed watching Aiyona shuffle around grabbing pots, pans, and various ingredients. I crossed the room to give her a gentle kiss on the cheek. "You're amazing, you know that?"

She shooed me away. "Don't go all mushy on me, Matt. All I'm doing is settin' an extra plate for a little girl."

"You're still amazing," I said and then ducked in case she decided to swat me away. The move was the right one as she backhanded the air where my chest had been a few seconds earlier.

I love my girls, but they are both equally and unintentionally abusive.

A quiet knocking sound interrupted our banter. We looked quizzically at one another. I cautiously made my way to the door off the kitchen. I peered through the curtain covering the window. Perhaps Kaley didn't trust me as much as I thought.

"It's fine," I said to Aiyona. "It's just Kaley's cop friend."

She folded her arms across her chest and leaned back against the countertop. "Well, are we lettin' him in or not?"

I bowed my head and sighed, "We're lettin' him in."

On the other side of the door was Shane Gavin. He was bracing himself in the doorway. His hands gripped the peeling trim on either side. He leaned forward, his powerful form filled the entrance. I surmised it was an attempt to create a larger presence.

I was wrong.

In actuality, he was attempting to hold himself upright.

"Don't call 911 and lock the doors behind me," Gavin directed in a rush of breath.

"What the—"

He stumbled forward. I managed to catch him before he hit the ground. The old aluminum door creaked behind me as I pulled the detective inside.

Aiyona shrieked.

It all happened so fast. Thinking back, I'd realize he didn't look quite right when I'd opened the door. At the time, it just didn't register how badly Gavin had been injured.

Chapter 52
KALEY

John didn't answer his work phone, and I still had his personal cell. I went back to his house hoping to find him there, but he wasn't. When I went to the school, Mary Nicole seemed eager to help. The secretary stood and smoothed out her gray pencil skirt. She came around the broad reception desk and motioned for me to follow. She led me down an open corridor to a narrow room on the left.

She quickly closed the door and lowered her voice, "I'm not one to gossip or spread news... You understand that, right?"

I nodded and jammed my hands into the pockets of my black peacoat. I took a deep breath, steadying myself for whatever information Mary Nicole was about to share.

"Well, now, Principal Hanawall is looking into some allegations. Allegations that were made against John by some of his players."

"Okay..." I did not like the direction of the conversation.

"The students reported to the principal that John was supplying them with things."

"Things?"

Her voice dropped even lower, "Like drugs and alcohol."

"That is ridiculous!" I exclaimed.

She motioned for me to lower my voice.

"That's ridiculous," I repeated, this time in a whisper.

Mary Nicole pursed her lips, "I know. I agree. However, the administration has to look into it. They can't ignore such a claim."

"Yeah, of course, who were the students?"

She replied in short, clipped sentences, "I can't tell you that. I'm sorry. Confidentiality."

"Sure..." I was probably lucky she'd shared as much as she had with me. "Where is John now?"

Mary Nicole shook her head, "I don't know. After his meeting with the principal and superintendent, he signed out."

"Are the police involved?"

"Not officially... not as far as I know anyway."

I furrowed my brow, "Not officially. What does that mean?"

She looked around the tiny, cluttered space as though she was concerned someone might overhear. "Look, Kaley, John likes you. I can tell. I shouldn't have shared so much with you. However, John is a good man. I don't believe for one second he'd do what they're saying. Even so—I've said enough. I bet you're a smart woman. I don't think John would be dating you if you weren't."

I squinted in confusion. It seemed Mary Nicole had just said a lot without saying anything at all. "Ummm, thank you..."

Mary Nicole opened the door and motioned for me to exit. "The parents of the students were notified."

"Kyle Sterns," I said under my breath.

Mary Nicole raised her eyebrows.

"Do you have any idea where I might find John?"

"My guess is he'll find you."

Seeking guidance from Mary Nicole was like asking a magic eight ball or a fortune cookie for solid answers, "Okay..." I responded doubtfully.

She buzzed me back out of the building. I tried Shane as I made my way back to the parking lot. His phone went straight to voicemail.

Chapter 53
MATT

I managed to lower the detective to the floor. The motion was awkward and uncomfortable for both of us. Once on his back on the linoleum, I got a better look at the guy. His skin was taut and alarmingly pale. But other than that, I didn't see any outward signs of injury.

"I've been shot," Gavin gasped.

"Shot?" I asked in alarm.

"Get his coat and shirt off, Matt," Aiyona directed from behind me.

"Uncle Shane!" Summer came running full bore into the kitchen.

Aiyona caught her and quickly scooped her up. The little girl kicked, screamed, and tried her best to claw her way away from Aiyona.

"I'm okay, kiddo," Gavin managed through gritted teeth.

I unzipped Gavin's coat and saw the blood seeping through the left shoulder of his gray sweatshirt. I quickly grabbed a towel and pressed it over the wound.

Summer broke free of Aiyona's hold and lowered herself down next to the man. She took a hold of his hand in both of her tiny ones. "Not like daddy, please not like daddy," she repeated over and over again.

I turned back toward Aiyona for help. She was busy trying to comfort Layla who had also entered the room and was crying hysterically.

"Fuck," I muttered under my breath. The situation was really difficult enough without throwing two traumatized kids into the mix. I did my best to ignore the wailing. The situation would probably require some time and therapy down the road. However, we could worry about that later. Right now, I had to keep the asshole from dying in my kitchen in front of them.

I hopped up from the floor and grabbed a pair of kitchen shears from the knife block on the counter. Hastily, I cut through the fabric of the shirt and tore it away, relieved to see a bulletproof vest underneath. It appeared he'd been shot multiple times and had it not been for the vest, he'd have probably died before reaching our front door. I could see a clear perforation right in the center. I removed the vest and set in on cutting away the black t-shirt underneath, causing Gavin to yelp. His rib cage was swollen and starting to bruise. It was easy to determine where the bullet had hit the vest. With the outer layers of clothing removed, I could also see the source of bleeding. I used the towel and swiped at the blood oozing from his shoulder. The more I cleaned the easier it was to see where the bullet had entered. I wondered if I should check for an exit wound or if this was the exit wound. The thought caused my stomach to lurch a bit.

"Keep pressure on that shoulder with the towel, Matt!" Aiyona called over the noise of the kids.

Grateful for the instruction, I did as she suggested.

"Summer," Gavin said.

The sound of his voice suddenly quieted the child. Aiyona had managed to get Layla into the living room. With the absence of the auditory chaos, I was finally able to focus.

"Summer," Gavin repeated. He was doing his best to put on a brave face for the little girl. I could tell it was hard for him to articulate, but he was doing a good job, considering. "I need you to go back into the other room and help your friend, okay?"

Summer shook her head vehemently, "I need to stay with you."

"Layla's parents need to help me, and she's super scared. You can help her with that."

"I need to help you," the little girl cried.

I was about to step in.

I didn't need to. Gavin finally found a way to ease Summer's fears. "Your dad is right here with me, Summer. Whatever happens, he's got this. He's got all of us, okay?"

Chills went up and down my spine. Had Gavin been communicating with his dead partner too? Maybe I wasn't as crazy as I thought.

Summer nodded and kissed Gavin gently on the forehead before running out of the room to tend to her friend.

I piled another towel on and continued to hold pressure, "Do you believe that?" I asked.

Gavin was still unnaturally pale. He didn't move a muscle, but his steel-gray eyes turned toward me. "Believe what?" he murmured.

"That Nathan is looking out for you?"

He closed his eyes. "It's a thing Summer does. She has a ghost dad. It helps."

"Oh..." So I was crazy.

Aiyona came back into the kitchen and grabbed a bag of frozen vegetables from the freezer. She knelt next to me and gingerly applied an ice pack to Gavin's rib cage.

"Matt, go take care of the girls. I got this."

"You know what you're doing?" Shane mumbled.

"Unfortunately, yes," Aiyona replied. "Lucky for you this isn't even close to the worst thing I've seen."

"Thank God," Shane exhaled and closed his eyes.

There would always be things about Aiyona that she'd probably never share. I realized and accepted that for what it was. However, it didn't mean I wasn't caught off guard when her past bubbled to the surface. There would always be moments of surprise when I'd catch a glimpse of who Aiyona had been and the reality she'd grown up with.

Chapter 54
KALEY

As I pulled out of the high school parking lot, John's phone started to buzz. I quickly slid the device from my coat pocket and answered without even glancing at the screen.

"Who's this?" snapped the female voice from the other end.

I pulled the phone away from my ear and focused on the incoming caller information. It was John's sister Julia. I wondered how much she knew, if anything, about the current situation. "Hey, Julia—this is Kaley. I have John's phone."

"What is going on with him?" she hollered. I had to move the phone away to ease the noise.

"What do you mean?" I asked, hoping to gain some insight.

She was quiet for a minute and then: "You don't know?"

"Do you?" I countered.

Julia sighed audibly on the other end, "Here's what I know. He called me from work this morning and left me a cryptic message. He said he had an issue that might require an attorney. He asked if my husband, Ben, could help. I thought maybe it was the same situation as before—you know—like with that Matt guy."

"Okay."

"Well, I called him back, and he didn't answer. I called the school, and they said he was out for the day. Then, I called his cell, which is apparently you."

Okay, my turn to share. "A lot has happened recently..." I purposefully paused to see if she would fill the silence. It worked.

"I know. I should have reached out after the break-in at your house, Kaley. I'm so sorry. That had to be terrifying. Honestly, what is the world coming to? I'm glad you and your daughter are staying with John for a while."

"It's fine. Thank you." So, she knew a little bit.

"Wait! Is that what this is about? Was John accused of the break-in? Because that is just crazy!"

I closed my eyes and tried to keep my anxiety at bay rather than rise to her level. "No, Julia. John was accused of something at work."

"At work? He's great at his job. He would never do anything inappropriate—" she gasped. "Are they accusing him of sexual harassment or something? Because—"

I cut her off, "I need you to stop jumping to conclusions. Let me fill you in." For two people who looked so much alike, they had decidedly different personalities. If John were anywhere near as high-strung as his sister, we'd not be together.

"Well, okay—go ahead." I sensed quite a bit of attitude in her words.

"John was accused of pushing drugs and alcohol to some of his players."

"He would never!" she declared, her voice rising several more octaves.

"You're right. He would never. That's why I'm trying to track him down. We'll get this sorted out, but you might want to fill your husband in. John is right to seek legal help. You know what allegations like these can do to a person, true or not."

There was quite a bit of shuffling and crackling coming through the phone. It sounded like she'd just opened a bag of chips or something. Who knew? Whatever she was doing was very distracting.

"Julia," I said... "I'm going to find your brother. I'll have him call as soon as possible."

"I'm coming," came the harried response from the other end.

"You're what?"

"I'm coming to Round Rock. I'm on my way."

"Oh... I'm not sure that's a good idea."

"I'll meet you at John's house."

"Julia, I'm sure he appreciates the support. There's no need for you to make the trip, though. I'm sure he'll be in touch shortly."

"Don't you dare tell me what Johnny needs!" she snapped. "I'm on my way."

"Well, I'm sure you know best." The statement came out much snarkier than I anticipated but oh, well. That's where we were.

"I do. Thank you," she responded curtly.

Leave it to me to make things even worse for John. Speaking of John, where the hell was he?

Chapter 55
MATT

Aiyona must have worked some kind of magic because a few hours later Gavin looked much better. Still not great, but I was no longer concerned he was in imminent danger of dying. Our kitchen, however, not so much. I know this sounds lame; but without the adrenaline coursing through my veins, the blood was a lot more difficult to stomach.

Gavin was leaning back in a kitchen chair wearing one of my t-shirts, his long legs outstretched in front of him. At least he was still wearing his own jeans. Don't get me wrong, the guy still looked extremely uncomfortable; but at least he had some color in his face again.

"How's Summer?" he asked.

"She's okay. The thing you said about her dad really seemed to chill her out."

Gavin nodded, "Your girlfriend is amazing."

Although I wholeheartedly agreed, I did not like the way he said it. It sounded somewhat flirtatious to my ears and most likely to Aiyona's. I noticed that she turned away shyly.

I took a seat next to Gavin, "My **fiancée** is the best!" I confirmed.

The twinkle in his eye and the smug smile on his face confirmed that he did not miss my emphasis on the word fiancée. He was definitely feeling better, and I wasn't altogether sure I was happy about that.

"Don't do that," Aiyona said, as she set Gavin's tactical belt down on the table in front of him.

"Do what?" I asked innocently.

She narrowed her eyes at me, "You know what, Matt Pine."

The response caused the detective to chuckle and then immediately grab his chest in discomfort.

"And you—" she pointed at Gavin. "Don't goad him."

"I don't know if it's because you healed me or if it's because of the way you carry yourself—but, Aiyona, I think I'm in love with you," Gavin proclaimed dramatically.

My fiancée giggled. She actually giggled like a schoolgirl. Here he was shot up, his blood on my kitchen floor, and he was flirting with Aiyona in front of me.

I slid off my seat and slowly rose to standing. Daring the man to say one more word.

"Sit down, criminal," Gavin directed, "I'm just messing with you."

Then he turned to Aiyona, "But in all seriousness... thank you."

She nodded, accepting the compliment in the nature in which it should have originally been given. "I still think you should go the hospital."

"Not an option," he replied.

Aiyona nodded and changed the subject. "I cleaned your belt. Not sure it does you any good without your gun, though."

Gavin pursed his lips together tightly. "Yeah, they got my gun, but I still have my knife and cuffs. Would you help me get this on?" he asked with a wink.

"No. She won't," I replied. I grabbed the belt from the table and roughly pulled it around the detective's midsection.

He grimaced, which gave me at least a bit of satisfaction.

"I trust you can buckle it yourself?"

He nodded. Aiyona ignored the whole exchange as she set in on cleaning the blood off the kitchen floor.

I sat back down, "Now we need to talk."

Gavin took a sip of whatever was in the mug Aiyona had given him. "Yes, we do. Apparently, you shot me, Matt."

Chapter 56
KALEY

Shane's phone continued to go straight to voicemail. I was running out of options. Maybe I'd just need to drive the streets of Round Rock in search of Shane and John.

The words from the school secretary floated around in my head—she said he'd find me. Was she just making an off-handed comment, or did she know something more? I started in the direction of Matt and Aiyona's. I needed to pick up Summer. She wouldn't mind driving around for a bit. Then, if I still hadn't located anyone, I decided I'd go back to John's to wait. From the sound of it, his sister would be there eventually. Maybe Julia had some kind of twin telepathy we could use to locate her brother. I was really reaching now.

The wail of a siren surprised me. A glance in the rearview quickly confirmed the squad car approaching at a rapid speed. The blue and red strobes seemed to light up the dreary evening sky. I didn't think I was speeding... Most likely they were headed to an emergency. I pulled to the shoulder, expecting the police SUV to fly right past. It didn't. Instead, I watched as the vehicle slid in behind me and the driver's door opened swiftly.

I rubbed my hands down my face. Great, it was really the last thing I needed. I glanced back up and saw the familiar stalky form meandering up to my vehicle.

I lowered the window, "What do you want, Logan?"

He gripped the edge of my window and leaned in, bringing his face uncomfortably close to mine. "Well, I noticed you driving by and thought perhaps you could help me with something."

I shied away, resisting the temptation to close the window on his portly fingers. "You could have called instead of chasing me down—lights and siren."

He shrugged.

"I'm on my way to get Summer."

"Well, that might have to wait."

I knew it wouldn't do any good to get in a power struggle. That would just drag things out. Instead of the million things running through my head, I smiled and said: "How can I help?"

Logan seemed pleased with my attitude. He backed away from the window and scanned the area. "I'm looking for two men that seem to be very attached to you, Kaley."

"I'll save you some time—I have no idea where to find Shane or John."

He sneered, "Why would you assume that's who I meant?"

I shrugged, "The only other two guys attached to me would be Henry and Sargent Snuggles. And if you were looking for Henry, I'd suggest the bar. If it's the dog you're looking for... I have several questions."

He tapped the window and chuckled, "I always have enjoyed your sense of humor."

"Thanks," I replied dryly. "Can I go?"

He shook his head, "I'm afraid not. You see, I really need to find John and Shane. We both know they'll be in contact with you sooner or later."

"Well, I'll let you know if I hear from them."

He resumed his position at my open window, "No you won't."

I raised my eyebrows but said nothing.

"So…" he said tugging open my car door. "I'm going to need you to come with me."

Chapter 57
MATT

"Shot you? I didn't shoot you!" I exclaimed. "I was at the school the entire day."

"Easy, criminal," Gavin patted the air with his hands. The gesture meant for me to take it down a notch. It didn't work.

"No! You just accused me of shooting you! What's your game here, Gavin?"

"No game. I was purposely lured to your neighborhood and then shot. You want to know why?"

"So they could blame it on Matt," Aiyona answered for me.

Gavin shot her an appreciative glance, "Smart too."

They shared a look and Aiyona offered him a warm smile.

Well, that shit had to stop, but I'd worry about that later. "Someone is trying to set me up?"

"Yep, we stirred up the birdcage."

"Hornet's nest," I corrected.

"What?"

"It's stirred the hornet's nest."

He looked back at me blankly.

"You know what... never mind."

"Who shot you?" Aiyona asked from across the kitchen.

"We gotta find a place to lay low," Gavin said, dodging the question. "I'm pretty sure I'm supposed to be dead; and Matt, you my friend, have been set-up to have murdered me."

"You think they'll be coming for me?"

"Well, yeah... for both of us once they realize their plan failed." Gavin made a move to get up and winced, causing Aiyona to rush to his side.

I shooed her away, "I got Gavin. You get the kids ready."

Aiyona must have been frightened because she actually listened to me for once. Gavin must have been in quite a bit of pain because he didn't try to piss me off.

"Any idea where we should go?"

He nodded, squeezing his eyes tight as he braced himself against the table. "I gotta get in touch with Kaley."

"You think she could be in trouble too?"

"It's a concern... someone is tying up loose ends."

"Do you know who?"

Gavin nodded, "I'll fill everyone in at the same time. Right now, though... I'm going to need your help. Let's go for a ride in your piece of shit car. Or I could ask your lovely fiancée to give me a hand if you prefer."

And he was back.

"You know..." I said, "If I'm going to be framed for your murder anyway..."

Gavin smiled and then grimaced as he clutched his side.

I took a hold of him by the waist and allowed him to lean into me, "Easy, Gavin. You probably broke a few ribs when you went down too."

He nodded, "Thanks."

I called to Aiyona to meet us in the garage. Then, in another scenario I never imagined, I loaded Gavin into the passenger seat of Aiyona's little red Corolla.

"Sorry to disappoint you," I said to the detective, "but we're going to take Aiyona's ride instead of mine. If your theory is right, they'll be on the lookout for my car."

Gavin leaned his head back against the seat and closed his eyes, "Good thinking."

I was about to shut the car door when he spoke again, "You know what—you're okay, criminal."

"Thanks." I wasn't about to return the compliment, but it was nice to hear... sort of... I'd prefer he stop referring to me as criminal.

I retrieved Summer's booster and tossed it in the backseat before climbing in behind the wheel to wait for Aiyona and the kids.

"So, what's the plan here?"

Gavin shifted slightly to look at me. The action caused him to wince. "It depends..."

"On?"

"If Logan arrested John on some bogus charge."

"Why would he arrest John?"

"For selling drugs to high school football players."

"For what?" I exclaimed. "No way! He seems straight as an arrow!"

Shane raised his eyebrows, "That's why I said bogus. Sterns is trying to clean things up again."

"Again?"

Aiyona opened the back door and the girls scrambled into their seats.

Summer leaned over the seat and wrapped her arms around Gavin's neck. "Are you all better now, Uncle Shane?"

"I sure am, kiddo," he reassured her.

"You won't leave us like daddy, right?"

I caught the detective's eye. He hesitated for a moment and gave Summer's little hand a squeeze. "I don't ever want to leave you, Summer. Know this— every day I'll do my best to make sure I don't."

Aiyona didn't give Summer the opportunity to mull over Gavin's words. She coaxed her into the booster and then squeezed herself between the two girls. We were off to wherever Gavin directed me.

Chapter 58
KALEY

I wasn't sure what to do when Logan pulled open my car door. So, like an idiot, I just sat there.

"Come on, Kaley."

I squinted up at the man looming just outside my SUV. "Go where? How does going with you help anything?"

He sighed. It was an exasperated sound. Similar to the sound I'd made numerous times when trying to deal with one of Summer's irrational tantrums.

"Based on my knowledge of the law," I continued, "Which I'll admit, is not very vast, I'm pretty sure I don't have to go anywhere with you."

In response, he leaned into the car and unclipped my seatbelt. Before I could protest, Logan took a stronghold on my elbow and forcibly removed me from the SUV.

I tried to pull away, causing Logan to lean in closer. I must have been putting up enough of a struggle as his breaths were coming out in short, quick puffs fueled by overexertion. His breath was hot on the side of my face, his mouth just inches from my ear. He growled, "Don't make me inject you again. There's no telling what I might do this time."

I stopped. The admission made me lightheaded. Logan wasn't simply an asshole he was dangerous.

Logan took my momentary lack of resistance as a sign of compliance. He was wrong.

"Did you have Nathan killed?" my voice sounded shaky to my own ears.

"No. I've done a lot of stuff, Kaley, but killing Nathan was never my idea."

"But you knew about it?"

In response, he tugged my arm harder and started to drag me toward his running squad car.

I stomped hard on his foot. The action caused him to relax his grip just enough. I used the opportunity to pivot and bring my knee up hard. He let out a rush of air as I connected with a very sensitive area.

Logan released his grip entirely, and I ran back to my vehicle.

He caught me by the hair before I managed to duck back inside. I covered his hands with mine in an effort to force his release. The pain seemed to radiate through every nerve ending.

"You know, Kaley," he tried to sound commanding; but it was difficult given how short of breath he was. "I now have it within my rights to arrest you...." He sucked in some air and continued, "for assaulting a police officer."

I didn't respond.

He yanked me to the front of my vehicle and pushed my head down hard on the hood. He may have been out of shape, but he was strong. The powerful blow caused my ears to ring, and my vision momentarily blurred.

He tugged my arms behind me, and I heard the metallic clanking sound before feeling the pinch of the cuffs being clamped around my wrists. Logan pulled me up again, this time by the collar of my coat. He prodded me forward, using his knee against the back of my own, and had the gall to Mirandize me on the way to his squad car.

He heaved open the back door and shoved me sideways into the backseat. The overwhelming smell of disinfectant with an undercurrent of something vile permeated my senses. I tried to relax as much as possible to conserve energy for whatever was coming next. At that moment, I couldn't see any possible way of escape. If I stayed in the position in which I'd landed, maybe he'd believe I was injured or had given up. It was the only thing I could think of that might allow him to drop his guard, if only for a moment or two.

Logan was breathing heavily and coughed as he put the car in gear. He didn't say anything more. We drove in silence for a good ten minutes.

We weren't going to the police station, that was for certain. Had that been the plan, the drive would have only taken a few minutes. I wished he'd actually arrested me because that would have given me some sense of what to expect, and a possible opportunity to summon help.

From here on out, I would need to be extra cautious and think everything through. If I didn't play this right, there was a strong possibility that Summer could end up without either of her parents. I loved my grandfather, but I didn't think he was up to raising yet another granddaughter.

The car slowed as we moved through bumpier terrain. I glanced up at the canopy of trees. My heart caught in my throat. I knew where we were. I used to love it here—it had been one of my favorite hiking spots. I hadn't been here in years, though. I didn't think I'd ever return to Maple Bluff, as it was the last place Nathan had walked on this earth.

Chapter 59
MATT

The first part of Gavin's plan was to find a safe place for Aiyona and the kids to lie low. At this point, he didn't trust anyone in the department. The guy also didn't seem to have any friends, so that left it up to me. I, on the other hand, had precisely one friend.

I pulled up in front of Dwayne's modest ranch home. I'd dropped him off several times but had never been inside. Dwayne lived on a quiet residential street a few blocks from the hardware store. I left the rest of my gang in the car while I tested the waters of my friendship.

I rang the bell. The sound of quick, heavy footfalls came from somewhere on the other side of the steel front door. Dwayne's face brightened when he laid eyes on me. He offered me a wide smile and beckoned me inside. "Hey, Matt! What a pleasant surprise."

He might not feel that way in a minute.

Dwayne's house looked pretty much as I imagined. The living room was small and tidy with brown, dated carpeting. The carpet stretched to the threshold of a neatly organized kitchen, where the flooring morphed into a gold linoleum.

I couldn't think of a good way to start the conversation so I didn't think. I just spoke. "Dwayne, I have a huge favor to ask."

His smile widened, not the type of reaction I'm accustomed to, but it worked in my favor.

"Whatcha need, Matt?"

I ran my hand across the top of my head, "Well, it's complicated... I need to take care of something; and I need a safe place for Aiyona, Layla, and Layla's friend to stay."

His brow furrowed, "You're not in trouble with the law again? Are you?"

Funny he should jump to that conclusion when the bad guys seemed to be in the Round Rock police department, but I wasn't going to share that. "No, Dwayne, I'm actually working on the right side of the law for once. Although I can't say it's any safer."

"I don't know what that means," Dwayne replied, scratching his head.

I gave him a hearty pat on the shoulder, "You know what, buddy? When this is all over, I'll tell you exactly what it means but for now..."

"For now, your family and whoever is welcome to stay here," Dwayne declared.

I nodded, "Thank you."

"You're welcome, Matt." Dwayne crossed back over to the front door to wave my crew inside.

While Aiyona helped the kids out of the vehicle, I noticed Dwayne squinting to get a better look at Aiyona's car.

"Is that Shane Gavin with you?"

"Yep, told you I wasn't doing anything illegal."

Dwayne turned to me, "Are you sure? He doesn't look so good?"

I stepped up beside him and peered out the door. Dwayne was right. Even from a distance, you could see something wasn't right. Gavin was slumped inside the vehicle, his complexion waxy and unnatural in appearance.

"He's fine," I assured Dwayne, as Aiyona and the girls reached the top step.

Aiyona and Layla both knew Dwayne, but I quickly introduced Summer.

Dwayne seemed thrilled to open his house to the kids and Aiyona. He shuffled the girls inside and whisked them away to see some model train set up he had. I was grateful for the opportunity to have a moment alone with Aiyona.

"What's the plan here, Matt?" she asked.

I took her hands in mine, "I don't know yet. Gavin seems to have one, though."

She raised an eyebrow and scrutinized me for an uncomfortably long moment.

I turned away, catching a glimpse of Gavin. He was no longer reclined but looking toward the house. No doubt, he was impatient for me to return.

"I know this seems like a bad idea, but I feel like I need to see this through," I answered honestly.

She squeezed my hands. "What that boy really needs is a hospital. What if he's tryin' to set you up? Once it's just you and him—you don't have back-up."

"I have to do this."

"You don't even know what THIS is!" Aiyona exclaimed.

"Maybe not, but I do know it's a means to an end. I need to finish this with him."

"Why?"

I stroked her cheek gently, "You know why."

"I'd feel a lot better if I knew where you were headed."

"You and me both," I agreed.

"Just be careful and check in with me as soon as possible."

"I will. I promise—" We were interrupted by the shrill sound of a horn honking. Gavin was done waiting.

Chapter 60
KALEY

We sat there for a good ten minutes. I wasn't sure what Logan was doing, but he eventually inhaled sharply and blew out his breath with a loud puff of air. The car shifted slightly as he heaved himself from the vehicle, shutting the door solidly behind him.

I counted to sixty, three times before venturing a peek. When I turned my head, Logan's face filled the rear window. His hands were cupped as he peered down at me from outside the glass. If I hadn't already been disturbed by the situation, this visual would have definitely gotten me there. I shivered as he pulled open the door then yanked me upward into a seated position. It all felt impossibly awkward and startlingly rough with my hands still cuffed behind my back.

"Quit playing games with me, Kaley," he snarled.

"Me? You made a bullshit arrest then drove me out to the bluff. I'm not the one playing here."

"Get out!" He pulled me from the vehicle.

I did my best to stay upright as he prodded me forward. The ground was covered in snow, making it difficult to walk, especially considering I was wearing two-inch ankle booties. In my defense, I did not plan on being taken hostage or forced to hike through the snow-covered woods when I chose my clothing for the day. Logan was much better equipped for the weather than I was. He easily marched us forward in his boots and cargo uniform pants.

"Are you going to kill me?" I asked without preamble.

He stopped and swiveled his head in my direction. Logan legitimately appeared startled by the question.

"I mean you killed Nathan," I continued, "and you took me to the same spot so it's not much of a stretch... Right?"

His brows furrowed, "I told you I didn't kill Nathan, and I'd certainly never pull the trigger on you."

"Well, whoever did your dirty work then... Are they going to kill me?"

He jerked me forward shaking his head. "You really don't know what's happening do you?"

"I know you're dirty."

Logan chuckled, "Enlighten me, please. How am I dirty?"

"Nathan discovered things missing from the evidence locker. And the heightened drug usage among high school kids around Round Rock doesn't appear coincidental, either. I believe Nathan started an informal investigation that led him straight to you." I didn't wait for a response. "Nathan's knowledge didn't die with him. He left a trail that I picked up. That's why I'm here."

Logan didn't respond in any way. We kept trudging onward as the darkness slowly crept in around us.

"Then there's John. He couldn't tell me about the conflict with you. Obviously, he cares more about his career and our community than you do; but I'm pretty sure I understand now. You are pushing product to kids. Maybe even using your son to do that."

I gave him a sideways glance. Still no reaction—nothing, not even at the mention of Kyle.

I continued to ramble. I didn't think there was anything to lose at this point. "John caught on, didn't he? So, you had to figure out what to do about him.

Then John shows up at your office with Shane and Matt. Suddenly, it's not just one detective on your ass but a detective, a respected football coach, Nathan's former informant, and, of course, me."

Logan stopped for a moment. Maybe I'd finally hit a nerve, "Okay—I can see where you might think that. But, sweetheart, you are in the dark about a lot. My advice—you stay that way."

He could dish out as much advice as he wanted. I wasn't going to take any of it. "Who was with you the night you broke into my house?"

Logan started trekking us forward again.

"What was the purpose of the break-in? Was it the notebook, you were after? Or were you trying to scare me off? If not me—someone else... Shane or John?"

He wasn't talking.

However, I wasn't deterred. I continued to rapid-fire questions at him. Hopefully, something would land. "If it was the notebook, you didn't succeed. Shane has copies—did you know that? Did you ask Shane?" *Or Josie?* I kept the latter to myself. I wasn't ready to reveal the fact that I knew about the affair, not just yet anyway.

"So, Logan, what's the plan here?"

"You don't want to know," he mumbled.

"Why? I mean you're probably going to kill me soon anyway. Isn't it fair I know what I'm dying for?"

He stopped, "You, my dear, are untouchable."

"Why is that?"

"Because my boss would never lay a hand on you."

"What?"

"You think I'm running this whole operation?"

This time I was the one to stay quiet.

"You have no clue. I almost feel sorry for you," Logan shook his head sadly. "Come on," he beckoned me forward.

I didn't move.

"Come on, Kaley. We have things to do."

"Who is your boss?"

He sighed, "You might not believe this, but you really don't want to know. Don't dig any deeper. Despite what you think of me, I'm not a monster; and I really liked and respected Nathan. He was a good guy. He didn't deserve what happened to him. None of you did."

This was the Logan I knew. The other guy—the guy that framed my husband, the guy I saw in John's office, the guy that got physical with me—that guy was a stranger.

"What?" Logan asked as I studied his features.

"You. What happened to you? I doubt you got into law enforcement to break the law. What happened?"

"We're not talking about this."

"Maybe I can help you?" I tried.

"And why would you do that?" Logan snapped.

"Because, the only thing I care about, is finding Nathan's killer. If helping you gets me answers, then maybe it's a small price to pay."

"What if helping me means hurting Shane or John? Is that a small price, Kaley?"

Of course, it wasn't, but Logan was finally talking. "Why did you break into my house? Why did you drug me?" I tried again.

"For information."

"You drugged me for information? Did you get what you needed?"

"Ha!" Logan exclaimed. "Well, we're here so what do you think?" With that, he nudged onward.

It was difficult to keep my balance with my arms still bound behind my back. I fell. Not just fell but fell hard, faceplanting in the snow. My ears were ringing, and my head hurt. I'd hit something sharp.

"Shit," Logan muttered under his breath. He knelt down next to me and wrapped his arm around my waist assisting me to my knees, "You're bleeding." He swiped at my forehead with his coat sleeve.

"You know—it would be a lot easier if you took the cuffs off," I snapped.

"I can't," Logan replied. "I have something to take care of. I need to make sure you don't interfere."

"Why?" I shouted out in frustration.

"You'll try to stop me, and I can't let you do that."

Chapter 61
MATT

We weren't able to track down Kaley. Gavin directed me to an old gravel road. It went straight uphill and then made a sharp curve to the left. We drove on a little further, reaching what appeared to be more of a path than an actual road. I hesitated. The route had been plowed recently, so it wasn't snow-covered, but it was extremely narrow.

Gavin pointed me onward. I, in turn, looked at him doubtfully.

"Trust me, criminal. It's wide enough for your little sedan."

"Trust you, huh?" I stopped the car. "I'm not quite there yet. And if I'm not mistaken, we're on the other side of the bluffs from where Nathan was killed."

Gavin pushed himself up in the seat, wincing a bit as he did so. "You're not mistaken, and I think you trust me more than you care to admit."

He was right. I would never have helped him, much less let him direct me out here, if I thought he was up to no good.

"What now?" I asked.

"Keep going. It's just a little further to the cabin."

"Whose cabin?"

"A friend of a friend. Why does it matter?"

I shrugged, "And then what?"

Gavin turned his head gingerly so as not to disturb his injuries. "Then, you lucky bastard, you get to see what it's like to be me?"

I gave him a once over, "Well, that does not sound lucky at all."

"Shut up and drive."

Despite my reservations, I did as directed. We were about a mile into the woods when the little cabin came into view.

I parked Aiyona's car a few feet from the front door of a well-kept log cabin. The wood was a yellow pine with teal trim. No doubt someone's home away from home. The teal front door opened. A man in a black hooded sweatshirt and ball cap stepped onto the front porch. It took me a minute to recognize the tall, athletic form; but as the man jogged down the front steps, I knew for certain who it was.

I turned toward Gavin, "What's going on?"

The detective nodded at the figure striding toward the car, "John will fill you in."

I pushed open the door as John stepped to the side. He rubbed his hands together vigorously in the cold.

"Gavin's going to need some help," I said, making my way around the car.

John didn't say anything but watched as I awkwardly ducked into the vehicle to assist the injured man.

It wasn't until we emerged from the vehicle that John actually said anything, "Are you okay, Shane? What happened?"

I held Gavin around the waist so he could lean into me as we made our way toward the cabin.

"Completely fine," Gavin grunted sarcastically. "The criminal and I are dating. So, this is how we roll now."

I had to admire the guy's wit. I felt kind of bad for John, though. I decided to fill in some blanks "He's been shot and probably broke a few ribs. We're going to need some help on the stairs."

"Shot? Who shot you?" John asked, as he positioned himself on the detective's other side.

"We'll talk inside," Gavin huffed, sounding slightly out of breath.

We made it up the stairs surprisingly well. At least in my opinion. Gavin might have had a different take on it.

The cabin was dim but as tidy on the inside as it was on the outside. An impressive fire was blazing away in the wood-burning fireplace that occupied the back wall. Once inside, we assisted Gavin in situating himself in one of the matching forest green recliners. I took a seat on a nearby loveseat with the same plushy fabric.

John stayed standing, "Well, first things first, how did you get shot and why aren't you at a hospital?"

Although it sounded like a question for Gavin, John's gaze was focused solely on me.

I threw my hands up in frustration. "I have no idea who shot him or why he chose to come to me for help instead of a trained medical professional."

The detective rolled his eyes before replying to John, "We both know I can't go anywhere until this is done. But believe me, that will be my next stop. Until then—Matt's beautiful girlfriend did an extraordinary job of removing the bullet and patching me up."

"Fiancée," I corrected.

Everyone seemed to ignore the correction.

John folded his arms across his chest, "It seems like things have escalated too quickly. I think it's too late for our plan."

They had a plan? That was news to me.

"Did you fill Matt in?" John asked, tipping his head in my direction.

"Not yet," Gavin responded. "We haven't had a lot of alone time, and I'm not feeling that great."

"Understandable. So, who shot you, Shane?"

"I'd love to know the answer to that too," I chimed in.

"If I had to guess, I'd say Logan. Who by the way is also sleeping with my wife."

John's eyes widened, and he lowered himself into the other recliner, "What?"

Gavin ignored the fact that he'd just dropped a pretty big bombshell and continued, "I gotta be straight with you guys. Until tonight, I wasn't really sure who was on the up and up."

I felt my jaw go slack, "You actually believed Nathan could be a dirty cop?"

Gavin held up his hand to silence me, "No. I never believed that. There was never a doubt in my mind that Nathan was solid. However, I did not believe the chief was involved as deeply as he seems to be."

I sat forward in my chair, "Really?" My voice was much louder than intended. It was difficult to hide my shock. Was the detective really that naïve?

"What changed your mind?" John asked. His tone was much more even than my own. If he was surprised by Gavin's confession, he didn't show it.

Gavin shifted slightly in the recliner, causing him to wince, and then he continued. "Well, finding out he was having an affair with Josie definitely elevated my suspicions but getting shot really sealed the deal."

"And how exactly did that happen?" John asked. From the moment Gavin had literally dropped in on me and Aiyona, it was the one question he had yet to answer.

"The chief sent me to the wooded area in the criminal's neighborhood."

"He has a name, Shane," John interrupted.

Gavin gave me a sideways glance and started again, "I was sent to **Matt's** neighborhood," this time he overemphasized my name. "There was a supposed tip about some kids in the woods. I was told that you, John, had supplied them with party favors."

"That's when you called and gave me the heads-up?" John asked, the question filling in some more blanks for me.

Gavin nodded, "Yep, Logan was ready to pick you up. He was sending guys to the school while he was sending me after the kids."

"There weren't any kids though, were there?" I asked.

Gavin shook his head, "Nope. Just a set-up. When I arrived in Matt's neighborhood," he used my name again without prompting, "Logan's car was parked just up from Matt's house, on the end of the cul-de-sac. The chief's driver's side door was wide open on the SUV but no sign of him. His light bar was also off, which was odd. I drew my weapon and headed to the trail entrance a few feet from the chief's vehicle. I didn't hear or see anything... until I did."

I found myself on the edge of my seat as Gavin recounted his steps. "How far into the woods did you get?" I asked.

"Not far. I didn't hear anything. But I felt like I was kicked in the chest by a mule or something. I went down hard. After that, things are kind of hazy, but I have flashes of clarity. I hit the ground and realized I'd lost my weapon. I remember rolling onto my stomach and feeling around for it. I remember seeing a pair of department-issued boots, like my own. As they entered my field of vision, the boots stomped down hard on my hand. Then, another burst of pain but not from my hand."

"The other shot that hit you in the shoulder?" I asked.

"I think so... If not Logan—someone under his direction. I blacked out briefly. When I came to again, there wasn't anyone else around. I'm sure Logan tried to kill me the way he killed Nathan."

"Why didn't he finish the job?" I asked.

"I think he thought he did," Shane replied, before continuing where he left off. "I crawled into the underbrush and made my way through the woods. When I reached the street again, my vehicle was gone, so I made my way toward Matt's house. I don't remember much about that except the fact that I was in quite a bit of pain."

"You knew exactly where my house was?"

Gavin looked at me out of the corner of his eye, "Well, yeah, dummy. You don't think I took it upon myself to find out everything about you when you started sniffing around Kaley and Summer?"

The confession made me uncomfortable, but I understood where he was coming from. A realization hit me. "You were watching my house, too, weren't you?"

"I made sure all my bases were covered," the detective replied. "Anyway, I'm pretty sure he lured me out to your place to frame you for my murder."

I smacked my hand against my forehead, "Our visit to the police station played right into his hands. We let him know we were all working together."

Shane nodded, "We gave him a common thread to tie my murder to Nathan's."

"Me."

"Yep, you," Shane confirmed. "I told you it was a bad idea," this time his comment directed toward John.

"I'm sorry," John apologized, "I didn't know where your loyalties were. I thought putting you in that position would push you one way or the other."

"And how'd that work out for us, coach?"

"It gave Logan a reason and a mode to get us all out of the way."

"Sure did," Shane agreed. "John, I believe Logan wants you to go down as a kiddie dealer. While Matt goes away for murder, and me, well, I'm supposed to be dead."

I had to admit it made sense—except for one thing: "What's my motive?" I asked.

"Money and power. Is there anything else? You, Matt, are a convenient scapegoat. An out-of-town criminal—the moment you arrived in Round Rock—things went to hell. Luckily, though, we have our esteemed police chief. He gets to play the victim as he buries another one of Round Rock's finest. And then, hero, as he puts away the bad guy and cleans up the entire community."

"He thinks he's getting us all out of the way," I said, shaking my head in disbelief.

"Almost all of us... when was the last time you talked to Kaley?" John asked in alarm.

My pulse rate quickened, "We haven't! She left Summer with me this afternoon to go find you! Shane and I tried to get a hold of her but—"

John jumped to his feet, "When was that? I've been trying to call her, but I can't get any service here."

I started to pace, "I don't know.... three maybe four hours ago."

"Shane?" John asked.

Gavin looked panicked, "Around the time I caught wind of the allegations against you. I called Kaley to see if she knew anything. That would have been about the same time Matt was with her at the school. Like he said, we looked for her but with our current phone situation..."

"I don't understand how you could just continue on with our plan, Shane?" John shouted. "Kaley's safety has always been the priority."

"Right after his own," I grumbled.

"No—criminal!" Shane shot back. "I wasn't thinking clearly. This is bad!" he clenched and unclenched his fists.

John looked at his watch. "We have thirty minutes."

"We'll find her before the buy is supposed to go down. We have to." Shane responded.

"What buy?" I asked, looking back and forth between the two.

"That's not important right now. I need to get someplace where there's service." John grabbed his keys off a nearby end table and took off. "I'll be back," he shouted over his shoulder. The door slammed shut behind him.

We sat in silence. The only thing audible in the shelter of the cabin came from the crackling fire and a ticking clock from somewhere unseen.

Gavin steepled his hands and rested them against his forehead. "Logan wouldn't hurt Kaley. He's capable of many things, but he wouldn't take both Summer's parents."

I wasn't so sure, but I murmured my agreement anyway. "So, tell me about your plan," I said, trying to get our minds off Kaley.

"John got us in the door to make a score. I wanted to use you for that, but John was concerned that might mess up the progress you've made."

I was touched that John, and in his own way, Gavin had considered my wellbeing.

"He had to use high school kids to get the information we needed," Gavin continued. "If you can believe that?"

Actually, I could, but I stayed quiet.

"We're supposed to meet the supplier at the top of the bluff at six-thirty.

"Where Nathan was killed," I stated.

Shane shuddered, "Not like we could change the location. Anyway, the plan was for me to bust the guy when we got there. We need the supplier to give us a thread—just need enough to get started. Something that can point me in the direction of Logan."

"If you think the cops are behind this, though... wouldn't they recognize you?"

Shane shook his head, "Obviously Round Rock's finest aren't the one's taking meetings, criminal."

"Oh. You were hoping someone would name names, though."

Shane considered me for a moment. "You weren't a very good criminal—were you?"

I nodded, "I did get caught for a lot of stupid shit."

Shane rolled his eyes, "I just need enough to bring to someone higher up the food chain. Hopefully, enough to launch a federal investigation. However, John's right—this situation has escalated so quickly that I'm not sure our plan is still workable."

"And—you're not really in any shape to play cop tonight."

The corners of Gavin's mouth turned up slightly, "As I told you in the car, you have the honor of pretending to be me."

"Ahhh, perfect. I'm gunna be a cop."

"But if something happens to Kaley..."

"She'll be okay. You said it yourself. Logan wouldn't hurt her."

Chapter 62
KALEY

Logan's destination had been a picnic shelter at the top of the bluff. We waited in silence. I had no idea what we were waiting for, but I hoped it wouldn't be much longer. The night wind was blustery, causing the trees to creak as it blew through the woods. I shivered as the temperature dropped even lower. My jeans were crisp and frozen from falling in the snow. My head was pounding; at least the blood had stopped trickling from the wound. With my hands bound behind my back, there wasn't much I could do about it.

Logan removed his coat and draped it over my shoulders. As much as I wanted to wiggle my way out of the thick nylon material, the warmth was something I did not want to give up. At this point, I knew Matt and Aiyona must be worried about me. I hoped they'd reach out to Shane. Another concern was John. Where could he possibly be?

Almost as though in response, a familiar jingle filled the air. Logan leaned forward and dug John's phone from the pocket of the coat he'd just placed around me. He held it up with the satisfied grin of a Cheshire cat. The words *'Work Phone'* flashed across the screen. "I'm guessing this is your boyfriend calling."

I didn't respond.

"Hello, coach!" Logan answered the phone in an overly boisterous tone. "Sure took you long enough to call," he taunted. "Poor Kaley's just about frozen to death out here. I mean—really, what's been keeping you? We've been waiting for you to reach out."

Logan was quiet for a moment. His grin widened as he listened to John's response. "Oh, don't you worry, coach, I'm keeping her nice and warm." He wandered away from the shelter as he spoke. At one point, he looked in my direction; but in the darkness, he was nothing more than a shadow. His tone, however, indicated that smarmy Logan was back. I shivered from cold and disgust.

"Well, I think that can be arranged..." I heard Logan say as he wandered even farther away.

I stood on shaky legs. I was prepared to make a run for it when Logan started to trudge back. He was swearing under his breath as his boots crunched through the snow.

I lowered myself back to the picnic bench just as he reached the shelter.

Logan's fingers tapped away at the screen. "Call dropped," he offered.

Logan raised the phone back to his ear, "North trail top of the bluff fifteen minutes. I have a job for you, coach." He ended the call and slipped the phone into his cargo pants.

He crouched down in front of me, "This is almost over, Kaley." His tone was grim. The way he said it led me to believe he was trying to reassure himself rather than offer me any type of timeline.

"Please don't hurt John. He's a good guy. Summer loves him. She can't lose someone else. I can't lose someone else. You will destroy us."

Logan's posture slackened. "I have no intention of killing John," he almost sounded sympathetic. "I do plan to expose him for what he is, though." Logan stiffened and stood with a grunt. He rubbed his hands together and pulled his phone from his other pocket. As he checked the time, his face glistened in the light emitted from the screen. He was sweating profusely despite the cold.

"You're scared," I commented quietly.

"It's almost over," he repeated under his breath.

Chapter 63
MATT

Gavin and I went through the gun safe in John's absence. I sure hoped whoever the 'friend of the friend' was wouldn't mind that we were borrowing their weapons. Gavin had just settled himself back in the recliner with a .30-06 bolt action Remington when the cabin door flew open. John rushed into the room, "Logan has Kaley!" he shouted.

Gavin struggled to sit forward. "What do you mean he has her?"

"Is she okay?" I asked.

"Logan answered her phone, well, my phone, that she had. There was some innuendo about keeping her warm." John was pacing as the words spilled from his mouth in quick succession. "He said he has a job for me. Get this—top of the north trail in fifteen minutes... well, ten now."

Gavin laughed, gripping his side.

John and I both turned our attention his way. "How is this funny?" I asked.

"Don't you see? The buy John set up... the job Logan has for John..."

I smacked my forehead, "He's going to have John make the sale, but he doesn't realize we set it up."

"Yep!" Shane replied. "So, John, I recommend you try to record the conversation. Plan A seems busted, but let's proceed as planned. Maybe Logan will have someone else in place. The criminal can still go in as me, and I'll back him up. Maybe we'll still have an opportunity to bust someone—fake or not."

John looked at him skeptically, "Shane, you can barely move."

In response, Gavin heaved himself from the chair with a groan, "I got this."

I raised my eyebrows at him, "Really?"

"I'm extremely motivated. However, if this cabin has a liquor cabinet somewhere—I think some liquid encouragement would go a long way."

"I think the phrase is 'liquid courage' but—" I stopped myself, "liquid encouragement makes a lot more sense."

"Nice, criminal," Shane muttered as he hobbled off toward the kitchen.

John looked at me, "You good, Matt?"

"You bet."

"Look, the most important thing is we get Kaley out of there safely, okay? I don't care what happens to me."

"That goes double for me," Gavin said emerging from the kitchen. He held a drinking glass a quarter full of a tan liquid which he downed surprisingly smooth.

"We're all on the same page here, guys," I said.

"Good," Gavin responded, setting his glass on the fireplace mantel. "John, you take your truck. We'll give you a few minutes before going in. I'll hike up the back of the bluff from here."

John looked doubtful.

"Or... Shane, you could just drive in as originally planned, and I'll hike to back you up," I offered.

"Don't be stupid, criminal. I've been drinking. I can't possibly drive."

I swiped my hand down my face in frustration.

John raised his arms as though about to deliver a locker room motivational speech. "Shane is in no shape to be seen. One look at him and whoever is going to bolt. This is what's going to happen... I'll head to my meeting spot. Matt—you help Shane come in undetected from the backside. Then, haul ass back here to get your car to go in as Shane."

Gavin and I nodded in agreement.

"And Shane, John added, "If you have any way to get Kaley out, just do it. Don't worry about backing us up. I'll leave the keys in the truck for a quick getaway."

"I'll do the same," I added.

"Good luck," John said.

"Do you have something... just in case?" Gavin asked.

By something, I was pretty sure the cop meant a gun. In response, John disappeared into the back room and reappeared a moment later with an old Smith and Wesson revolver.

"Good, I hope you know how to use that," Gavin remarked. "It's a little different than tossing a football to kids."

John rolled his eyes, "Little late to ask me that now?"

"Fair enough. Carry on," Gavin said, with a wave of his hand.

"Your friend certainly has a lot of guns," I remarked under my breath.

"The criminal is right," Gavin stated, "I mean it works in our favor now, but the collection is much more extensive than it probably should be... I have concerns."

John sighed and shifted his stance, "Really?"

Gavin held up his hand, "I know—not the time. We'll visit the issue later."

"Let's just hope there is a later." With that, John stalked off, looking like a man ready for a fight.

"Ready?" I asked Gavin.

"Go to the back bedroom. Grab my duty coat and cap on the bed." I left Gavin to struggle with the rifle sling on his own.

I did as he asked. The Round Rock police-issued nylon coat was tight across my arms and shoulders. There was no way I'd be able to zip it. The strain of the material made me feel restrained and uncomfortable.

"You look ridiculous, "Gavin commented as I stalked back into the main room.

I shrugged, "Some of us workout."

Gavin sneered and made his way clumsily toward the door. I had to give the guy credit; he certainly was tough and determined.

"Hang on," I stopped him before we stepped out. "If anything happens to me—I need to know that—"

"It won't," he said, reaching for the handle.

I grabbed his forearm to really get his attention. "If something happens to me, I need you to look after Aiyona and Layla. They don't have anyone."

"Yeah, yeah, yeah. I got it."

I didn't release my grip, "I'm serious, Gavin. There are people out there that could do a lot of damage to them. Aiyona has had a hard life. I need to know someone has their back."

Gavin slowed down. He met my eyes. "I promise, Matt. I will look after them. You can count on me."

I sighed—for a guy I didn't trust... I had entrusted him with everything. The funny thing was, I believed he meant every word.

Chapter 64
KALEY

Logan left me in the shelter with my hands cuffed behind my back. For extra measure, he'd chained my ankle to a picnic table so I couldn't go anywhere. I was cold, dizzy, and really scared. I knew he'd set a trap for John, but there was nothing I could do about it.

In the distance, a pair of headlights flashed through the trees. Probably John coming into the park. I waited but didn't hear or see anything more. I hoped I'd be able to call out to warn him before he approached.

My fingers were numb from cold and lack of circulation. Even trying to rub them together wasn't doing much. The sound of footsteps crunching across the hardened snow was distinct in the clear night air. It was impossible to tell which way they were coming from. There was a moment or two of silence, and then the sound of voices wafted through the air. I was sure one of them belonged to John. I inhaled sharply; the frigid wind caught in my throat causing me to cough. Before I could call out, another sound caught my attention. Again, the sound of footsteps crunching through the snow. This time, I could tell the sound was coming from behind me, and at a much slower and uneven pace. I turned to my left, catching a shadow from the corner of my eye.

"Kay, don't yell," Shane whispered.

Relief washed over me, "Logan is setting John up. He has some kind of plan. They are near the north trail," the words were spilling out of me in a rush. "You need to get over there."

"It's okay," Shane said, his voice hushed and manner undisturbed. "John's setting Logan up. It's all under control." Shane had stopped just short of the shelter. I couldn't tell exactly where he was, but he was near, and John was prepared for Logan. The game was changing.

"Can you come to me?" Shane asked, his voice still quiet.

"If I could move, don't you think I would have done so?" I snapped.

"Why can't you move?"

Of course, in the darkness, Shane couldn't see the restraints. "I'm chained to the post, and my hands have been cuffed behind my back for hours. I can't even feel my fingers at this point," I managed, through chattering teeth.

"Shit, okay."

I heard some rustling beside me then felt Shane fumbling with my cuffs. "Do you have a bobby pin or something?"

"Really?" I snapped.

"Naw, I'm just messing with you. I have keys."

I sighed with relief. The cuffs gave way, and I felt Shane brush against my legs as he worked the restraint on my ankle.

"Terrible choice of footwear for hiking," he commented.

"If I wasn't half-frozen, I'd kick you for making bad jokes right now." I shivered.

The chain made a clanking sound as it hit the concrete. I was free but didn't quite trust my legs to hold me up. Shane was moving very slowly as he pushed himself up from the ground, making an odd groaning sound.

"You, okay?" I asked.

"Not really but we'll talk about that later. Right now, we gotta go."

Chapter 65
MATT

I parked Aiyona's car on the opposite end of the park from John's truck. That way we had escape vehicles at either end. I retrieved the holstered Ruger 9mm from the passenger seat and tucked it into the back of my jeans. I let my sweatshirt fall over the top. It felt odd. The cold handle pressed up against the small of my back; like my old life and new life had collided to bring me to this moment.

Using the small penlight I'd found in Aiyona's glove compartment, I trudged through the ankle-deep snow across the hillside to the woods. I met the north trail midway and climbed my way to the top. As I came to the clearing I surveyed the area. Nobody was there. I took a deep breath and waited.

"Up here," John's voice came from a few yards further up the trail.

I didn't respond for fear of screwing something up. I wasn't sure if John was now working under Logan's direction or not. I also had no idea who might be with him. I continued onward stuffed into Gavin's too-tight police coat.

John's boots crunched through the snow as he took a few tentative steps in my direction. I knew Logan wanted him to go down for this, but I had no idea how. Should I expect to try and pull off being a cop or prepare to fight actual cops? Was it just John up there, if so, what was the point of any of this? If the point had shifted to just getting Kaley back, then I didn't need to be dressed as Gavin. There was a strong possibility someone was just waiting to pop us all too. One thing was certain, though—I should have asked more questions.

"To your left!" Someone shouted. The voice did not belong to John or anyone else on the trail. This voice came from my head. I spun quickly to see another form moving through the trees in that direction. Based on the agility of the movement, it probably wasn't Logan. Someone else was out here among the shadows.

I felt for the weapon in my waistband.

A bright light flashed in my eyes.

I held up my right arm to shield my vision. What happened next is kind of a blur. There was a cracking sound above my head. I tumbled backward. My ears were ringing, and it was difficult to tell which way was up. Thankfully, a clump of brush and weeds piled along the trail were enough to stop my downward descent.

"Matt, stay down!" The command was once again internal rather than external. I belly-crawled through the cold, wet snow.

The air around me erupted in gunfire as I found cover behind a large tree stump.

I thought I heard John call out from somewhere above, but I wasn't sure. The sound was muffled, like swimming in a pool just below the surface. I took a quick peek but couldn't see a damn thing. Who was firing and why? I waited. It was quiet once again. All except for the ringing in my ears. I waited a little longer, for what I wasn't sure. My heart was racing, my breath escaped my body in short panic-induced puffs.

In the distance, a vehicle fired up. I watched but didn't see headlights, at least I didn't think. My vision was spotty. However, since the shooting had subsided, I surmised that they were retreating.

"Matt!" This time I was sure I could hear John over the ringing in my head. "Matt, you okay?"

"Yeah." I poked my head around the tree, but the view hadn't changed. I was surrounded by darkness. "How about you?" I called back.

"Yeah," came the muffled reply from somewhere above me. "I think Logan took off."

I moved out of the crouched position, brushing snow from my sweatshirt and jeans. I trudged back up the path in the direction of John's voice.

"How many do you think there were?" I asked. I tried to keep my voice hushed, but I had no idea if I was quiet or not.

"I thought just Logan, but someone else was obviously out here!" John was shouting. That much I could tell.

I trudged the last few feet to meet him, "Do you think they had Kaley with them?"

"Logan has her. I have no idea where, though. He walked me through the deal I was supposed to make. He also had me keep my phone in plain sight—so no recording. Logan said if all went well, I could see Kaley before he carted me off to jail."

"How nice of him," I spat sarcastically. If it were Aiyona in that position, I'd have been going out of my mind. John was doing a good job of holding his shit together.

"Why did you start shooting?" John asked.

"Me? I didn't fire a single shot. It was whoever was in the woods."

"Damn it!" John exclaimed. "Why would they fire?"

"I'm guessing to kill us," it was hard to keep the sarcasm out of my voice.

John ignored the comment, "We need to find Shane and regroup," he said.

"Hopefully, he wasn't hit again..."

"Where did you two set up?" Either my head was starting to clear, or John's voice was getting considerably louder with each word.

I shushed him before moving closer, "We don't know how many people Logan has out here. Follow me."

We continued up the path to the small clearing where John said he'd met with Logan. I did my best to stick close to the tree line for cover. John was tight on my heels. We made it to the next grove where I'd left Gavin. There was a stump that he'd planned to use to set up with the rifle. I explained this to John, who suggested we circle the area. I wasn't too keen on the idea. If there was still a chance Gavin was working for the other side, we'd just made ourselves prime targets.

"Well, what are we going to do, Matt?" John asked, "just leave him out here injured?"

"No," I relented, "I guess not. But let's stick together, and don't let your guard down."

The snow was at least a week old, and because the bluff was a popular hiking spot, there was no way to know which footprints belonged to Gavin. We moved as stealthily as possible through the snow-covered woods using the nearly full moon as a guide. It didn't take long to widen the circle and come to the conclusion that Gavin was gone.

Chapter 66
KALEY

Something was very wrong with Shane. We started to make our way back down the bluff. It was the same way Logan and I had trekked earlier. The wind had picked up causing the trees to bend and creak above us. My face and extremities were numb from the elements, and I felt unsteady on my feet. Shane seemed to be having issues of his own, needing a short break every few feet.

"Lean on me," I offered.

"What? Why?" he snapped.

"Ummm... because you're moving about as fast as—"

Bang! I didn't have the opportunity to complete my smart-ass remark as a car backfired nearby. That was what I originally believed anyway. Shane tugged me down behind a nearby tree. He pulled the rifle that was strapped to his back free and pointed the gun in the direction we'd just come. Shots continued to perforate the night air.

Then, just as suddenly as the gunfire had erupted, it ceased completely. We waited, silently, for what felt like forever. In actuality, it was probably only a few minutes.

"Let's move out," Shane whispered.

I nodded and slowly stood. I offered Shane my hand which he accepted without argument and helped him to his feet.

I waited for Shane to secure his weapon, then, we started moving again. This time, however, I wrapped my arm around his waist allowing him to lean on me as we moved. He didn't resist or try to stop me as we hobbled farther down the hillside. We passed the spot where Logan had parked. His police vehicle was no longer there. I made mention of this to Shane.

"That's good, Kay, but it doesn't mean we're out of the woods—literally. I don't think Logan was working solo."

"I didn't see anyone else. If there was someone working with him, they came in a different way."

"I'm sure they did," Shane grunted.

We'd reached the bottom of the bluff, and Shane pointed to the right. "Matt should have parked his vehicle somewhere over there for us."

"Matt!" I exclaimed. "I left Summer with Matt. How can he possibly be out here?"

"His fiancée has the kids. It's a long story but trust me, Summer is in good hands."

We'd made it to the red Toyota parked away from the trails, obscured by a small outbuilding not far from the park entrance.

"Want me to drive?" I asked.

"Yeah, probably." Shane leaned up against the passenger door. "The keys should be in it ready to go."

I moved quickly around the car. The dome light came on as I pulled open the driver's side door.

Shane cursed Matt's name as he maneuvered himself into the seat. "Shut the door quick. That damn dome light is going to give us away."

I stole a glance in Shane's direction before yanking the door shut and submerging us in darkness once again. He didn't look right. Shane's skin was ashen, and his breathing appeared somewhat labored, but there wasn't time to contemplate his health. The keys were hanging from the ignition as promised. I fumbled around with the seat in the darkness.

"Drive, Kay."

"Where?"

Shane directed me out of the park and down a series of winding backroads. He kept checking the rearview mirror to make sure we weren't being followed. Once he was sure that we weren't, he asked me to drive back toward Maple Bluff. It seemed like an odd request, but I didn't question it.

"Logan admitted that he broke into the house and drugged me," I said, not taking my eyes from the road.

"I'm sorry, Kay. I should have caught on sooner. I just—" he stopped mid-sentence and pointed to a barely visible side road. "Turn here," he snapped.

I followed his direction and waited for Shane to continue with what he'd been saying. He didn't. My concentration turned to navigating what appeared to be a private driveway hidden among the trees. Shane turned the heat on high. The warm air forced its way through the vents, obscuring all other noise inside the vehicle.

The path narrowed as I made my way around a bend in the road. It wasn't until the path straightened out that I caught a glimpse of light. I drove just a little farther to confirm what I thought I was seeing. Once I was certain, I stopped the vehicle and turned toward Shane.

"Son of a bitch!" he exclaimed.

Red and blue strobe lights were bouncing off the treetops. Wherever we were headed, it appeared Round Rock PD had beaten us to it.

"Can you back out fast?"

I nodded and threw the car in reverse. "Where are we going?" I asked. Thankfully the vehicle had a backup camera to assist me in keeping the car on the path.

He didn't respond.
"Shane!" I snapped.
"I don't know," he finally said.

Chapter 67
MATT

When we didn't find Gavin, John and I made our way back across the bluff to his truck. He drove me to the lower end to see if Aiyona's vehicle was still there. It wasn't. Which was good. That most likely meant that Shane had found Kaley, and hopefully, they'd made an escape.

We headed back to the cabin. We'd made it halfway up the drive and just around the bend when we spotted the blue and red strobe lights. John quickly reversed direction, and we hit the open road again at a high rate of speed.

"How did they figure out we were using the cabin?" I asked.

John shook his head, he seemed genuinely bewildered, "I have no idea."

"Gavin said the cabin belonged to a friend of a friend. Could that person have given you up?"

Again, he shook his head, "It's my brother-in-law's hunting cabin. It's not a secret or anything, but I have no idea how they thought to look for us there."

"You didn't ask your brother-in-law if we could borrow his guns?"

John narrowed his eyes, "Of course not, Matt. Nobody knows we were there. I'm not an idiot."

"Oh..."

John glanced at me, "Oh what?"

"Well, if you didn't ask, then we just broke into a cabin and stole a bunch of guns. I mean, I didn't realize we were doing that, so I think I have plausible deniability. Who would have thought I'd be the good one in our little scenario?"

John scoffed, "We didn't break in. I have a key in case of emergency, you know—because I live nearby."

I nodded, "I realize it's isolated, but maybe a passerby saw some activity and thought that was odd. I mean, you did put a fire in the fireplace—perhaps the smoke? Maybe the cops are there because of that? What if one has nothing to do with the other?"

John shrugged, keeping his eyes on the road, "Possible but not likely."

I peered out the window and noticed we were coming up on John's street. "You think it's wise driving over here?" I asked.

"Just a quick pass. I need to see if Kaley and Shane came back. I hope they didn't get caught at the cabin."

"Naw, they're good."

John eyed me suspiciously, "How can you be so sure?"

I had no idea why I'd said that or stranger yet... why I felt so strongly that they were fine. Nathan? I shrugged off the idea. I was crackin' up again. "Gut feelin'," I responded.

John gave me an odd look.

"We should probably ditch your truck," I said, changing the subject. "I'm guessing it won't be long before the cops hit the streets looking for you—maybe they already are. Do you have another vehicle somewhere?"

"What the hell?" John exclaimed.

I realized his response was not due to anything I'd said. We'd slid up to the curb outside his house. A tan SUV was parked in the driveway, but the house appeared dark. John pulled his phone from his pocket and placed a call, "Julia?"

I wondered who Julia was and why John picked this particular moment to call her.

"Why is your car in my driveway?"

Well, that answered part of my question.

"So where are you?"

John was quiet for a moment as he listened. Then he groaned and pinched the bridge of his nose. "What did you tell them?"

I strained to try and hear the other end of the conversation. Whoever he was talking to was clearly animated, but I couldn't make out the words.

"Jules, you have no idea what you've done..." John stated quietly.

From my end, things didn't sound very good.

"Okay... Don't say anything to anyone. And don't go anywhere with anyone.... I don't care if they are police officers... just don't.... I'll be in touch soon." John tossed the phone onto the center console before turning toward me.

"Well, Matt, I know how they figured out the cabin so quickly."

"This Julia person?"

John nodded, "My sister."

"Her husband's hunting cabin, then?"

"Yes. A couple of officers showed up at the house looking for me. Apparently, they found Julia. I have no idea why she's even here. Anyway, they told her they were trying to help me."

"And she believed them."

John nodded, "She doesn't know what's going on."

"So... where's your sister now?"

"The police station." John ran his hands down his face in frustration.

"In her defense, she couldn't possibly imagine the scope of things," I said. "She probably believed they wanted to find you to clear up the misunderstanding too."

John didn't respond.

"Anyway, we can't just sit here. Do you think your sister left her keys behind?"

"I'm not sure…why?"

"I propose we ditch your truck and take her SUV. We'll be able to fly under the radar a little longer that way."

"Good suggestion. Where should we ditch the truck?"

"Back at the bluff? Then they'll waste time tromping all over the park looking for you. Maybe they'll think they missed it the first time."

"Think they're that stupid?"

I shrugged, "Or maybe they'll think you went back to look for Logan."

"I guess it's as good a plan as any." John backed into the driveway past his sister's vehicle and pushed a button near his rearview mirror to open the garage.

He parked and lowered the garage door again. "Wait here, Matt; I'll be right back."

I decided to call Aiyona while I waited. I reached for John's phone in the center console and realized it was password protected. Guess I'd have to wait. It had been hours since I dropped her and the kids off at Dwayne's house. I hoped she wasn't too worried.

The truck door opened and a big, scruffy, slobbering dog joined us. John situated the dog in the backseat as I pressed myself against the passenger door trying to put space between us.

"What's with the dog!" I exclaimed as John slid back behind the wheel.

"Sargent Snuggles. He's friendly—relax, Matt."

"Why are we bringing a dog?"

"I have no idea when we might get back here. I can't leave him alone."

"Yeah, you can. He's a dog. If he has to pee or somethin' you can just clean it later."

John patted me on the back, "He's a gentle giant. You're fine." After he unsuccessfully reassured me about the dog, he handed me a set of keys.

"You found your sister's keys?" I asked, trying to ignore the rapid panting sound coming from just behind me.

"She left them on the kitchen counter. I'll follow you."

"And then what?"

"I honestly don't know, Matt. It's hard to believe in this day and age we only have one phone between the four of us. There's no way for us to reach Kaley or Shane."

"Will we leave the dog with the truck?" I asked hopefully.

John shot me a sideways glance, "Why would I get the dog from the house just to leave him in a truck in the woods?"

"Never mind..."

Sargent Snuggles barked. I jumped and wondered, not for the first time, what the hell was I doing.

Chapter 68
KALEY

I had no idea where I was supposed to go. Shane was slumped in the passenger seat uncharacteristically quiet.

"What's wrong with you?" I asked timidly, secretly afraid to hear the response.

"I was shot," he mumbled.

My foot slipped off the gas, "I'm sorry—you were what?"

"I'm okay, Kay. Watch where you're driving. It's already been a rough day; I'd rather not drive into a telephone pole to top it off."

I focused back on the road. "I'm going to need a little more information."

He sighed, "I figured you would. Keep driving north; and when we hit Shale Creek, we'll find a place to pull over and call John and Matt."

"How are we going to do that?"

"Well, we'll have to make up a story and borrow a phone at a bar or something."

"That's not what I meant, Shane. I don't have John's number memorized, and Logan has John's personal phone."

"Do you have any numbers memorized?"

"Do you?" I shot back.

"Fair enough. We'll figure out something. Just keep driving for now."

"Okay... can you fill me in on the getting shot part?"

Shane filled me in on everything since he'd called me at the school. Then I shared the events that had transpired on my end, starting with Logan pulling me over.

I glanced in his direction, but his thoughts were unknowable in the darkness of the night.

"Are you sure you're okay?" Shane asked.

"Well, better than you."

"Not by much..." he replied softly.

We drove in silence for a bit. Both of us processing information in our own way.

"Kay...." Shane finally broke the stillness. "You said something about Logan not finding what he was looking for..."

It took me a moment to figure out what he was referring to. However, when I did, things seemed a little clearer. "Yeah, he did. When he admitted to breaking into my house and drugging me. He said he did it for information. I asked if he got what he came for... He laughed and said something like—if he had, he wouldn't be doing what he was doing."

"Well, that explains some things," he said.

"What do you mean?"

"No offense, but you're kind of small. We already know one of the guys was Logan, right? If they just wanted to steal stuff, Kay, they didn't need to drug you to do that."

I was starting to see what he was getting at.

Shane continued, "Ketamine is used in sexual assault crimes due to the effects it has on its victims. It can cause sedation, immobility, and amnesia. We know you weren't sexually assaulted."

"So, I was drugged for information..."

"But you didn't give them what they needed."

"So?"

"So... I think Nathan had proof, and we blew it."

I threw my hands up in the air. "What the hell, Shane? What am I supposed to do with that?"

"Put your hands back on the wheel and calm down."

"That's great advice, thanks," I replied sarcastically.

"Actually, just pull over!" Shane shot back irritably.

I wasn't sure how long I'd been driving, but I was certain we were in the middle of nowhere. We hadn't passed another vehicle for miles. I pulled over to the shoulder, noting that if not for the snow-covered farm fields we'd be surrounded by darkness.

"Thank you," Shane said gently.

I scoffed in response.

"Now, Kay, you said Logan mentioned something about a boss... And that you were untouchable, right?"

"Yes."

"That confirms Logan isn't top dog," Shane stated. "I think he's just the tip of the mountain."

"Iceberg," I corrected.

"What?"

"Never mind," now wasn't a good time to distract him by correcting his metaphor. "What makes you think that?"

"The police chief can't be running around selling drugs, guns, and whatever else."

"Well, it seems like other cops are working with him."

"Again, the police, no matter how high or low the ranking, can't be seen engaging in illegal activities. Also, where's the money trail? They are getting help and funneling things through somewhere."

"Like the local businesses Nathan had listed in the notebook?"

"Exactly."

"Do you think Nathan had it figured out?"

"I don't think they would have killed him if he didn't."

I shivered at the thought of my husband shouldering this burden alone. Why hadn't Nathan confided in me?

"Kay…" Shane said softly. "I think we need to go to the gallery."

"The gallery? Why?"

He hesitated, "I can't say right now. I hope I'm wrong but if I'm not…"

"Shane?"

"Please."

I pulled out onto the country road and awkwardly managed a y-turn, pointing the vehicle back toward Round Rock.

Chapter 69
MATT

After leaving the truck at the bluff, we hit the road again, this time in John's sister's car. It was getting late. I asked John if I could use his phone to check on Aiyona and the kids.

"Absolutely," John unlocked and handed me his device.

Aiyona answered before the phone even rang, at least on my end; I wasn't sure how that was possible. But there you go. "Hey, it's me. How are you and the kids?"

"Oh, Matt, I've been so worried." I could hear the relief in her voice. I felt guilty for putting her and the kids in that position. If it hadn't been for me, everyone would be safe and warm at home.

"Matt?"

"I'm here, sorry. I'm okay. How are y'all holdin' up?"

She hesitated, "Ummm, fine..."

"You sure?"

"Hang on..."

I heard her mumble something to one of the kids or Dwayne and then some shuffling. I guessed she was moving into a different area of the house.

"Okay, Matt, I need to get real here."

"I wouldn't expect anything else."

"Summer isn't doin' so hot. I think that little girl is traumatized. She was fine for a bit, but now she's real quiet and keeps crying for her mama. She's worried about Shane too. I think Kaley needs to come get her."

I ran my hand over my head, "Well, that's not good."

John shot me a glance. I turned away and faced the window. We must have driven outside of town when I wasn't paying attention. There wasn't a house or business in sight.

"I have no idea where she is, Aiyona," I replied. "There's a possibility she could be in serious trouble."

"Can you at least put Shane on the phone? It would help if Summer could talk to him."

"I'm not with him anymore."

"Well, where the hell are you then, and whose phone are you callin' me from?"

"I'm with John Kyler. I'm using his phone."

"Matt... I don't understand what you're involved in?"

"That makes two of us."

"Not helpful!" she scolded. "Look, we can't stay here much longer. Your friend is nice and all, but we ran out of things to talk about like three hours ago. And what am I goin' to do with these little girls? Layla is tired and wants to go home, and poor Summer needs her family."

I sighed, "I don't know. I'm sorry."

John looked over at me again, "Hang on, Aiyona." I set the phone on my knee and whispered so as not to be overheard. "I think we gotta pick up my fiancée and the kids."

John raised his eyebrows, "And have them ride along with us? We can't even figure out what we're doing. I don't think adding your fiancée and two kids to our situation will help."

"I know," I agreed. "But Aiyona said Summer is pretty messed up. I'm sure after losing her dad and then seeing Gavin collapse and bleed all over my kitchen floor didn't help."

John snapped his head in my direction, "What now?"

"Oh... maybe we forgot to fill you in... After Gavin was shot he collapsed in my kitchen. Summer witnessed the whole thing. Gavin did his best to reassure her... It wasn't good."

John looked at me in disbelief, "Yeah, it seems you and Shane left a few things out."

"So... what now?"

"Now, now I'm going to get Summer. That just became the priority."

I told Aiyona we were coming, and then directed John to Dwayne's neighborhood. We made sure to park around the block, just in case the police thought about us using Julia's car. The three of us, John, me, and Sargent Snuggles, walked in silence. The air was brisk, and I wished I had my parka instead of the too tight police jacket. I couldn't even zip the damn thing.

I knocked lightly on the door, and we waited. There was a sound of footsteps moving across the floor inside.

Dwayne answered the door. I gotta say, the poor guy looked frazzled, but that didn't stop him from greeting me with his usual toothy grin, "Hey, Matt. I'm awful glad to see you." He ran his hands through his thinning hair.

I gripped his shoulder in appreciation as he stepped aside to let us in. "What are you wearing, Matt?"

I struggled out of Shane's jacket and handed it to Dwayne in a crumpled ball of fabric, "Think I could trade you for a hoodie or somethin'?"

He accepted the wadded-up material without question and nodded, "Sure, I'll find you something."

I made hasty introductions and noticed that the house smelled like Aiyona's enchiladas. Which led my stomach to rumble. I couldn't remember when I'd last eaten. John had a similar reaction and commented on the aroma.

Dwayne patted Sargent Snuggles on the head and grinned sheepishly, "Your girlfriend sure knows how to cook. She sent me to the grocery store with a big list. The kids and I ate way too much."

"That sounds about right," I commented. "I'll reimburse you."

Dwayne waved away the offer, "Are you kidding! I should pay Aiyona for cooking. I haven't had a meal like that in... Well, I was going to say forever but actually ever would be more appropriate. Better watch it, Matt... I might want to steal your girlfriend away from you," he said, elbowing me jovially.

"Fiancée," I corrected. And then: "Get in line." I added dryly.

"Speaking of Aiyona and the kids," John spoke up, "Where are they?"

"Oh, downstairs. I have a rec room with a pool table and board games. The kids had fun hanging out down there. Well, for a while anyway... Summer is feeling pretty upset... I don't really know what to do about that..."

"I think this guy can help," John said, patting the dog on the head. "Do you mind showing us to the basement?" he asked Dwayne.

"Oh, sure. Follow me. Dwayne led us through the living room and to the kitchen. He pulled open a dark-stained wooden door revealing a carpeted staircase. The carpet was a shaggy orange and brown. I'd bet it had been brand new in 1970 something... The sounds of the kid's voices mingled with a TV got louder as we descended the stairs. The carpet continued into the dark, musty space. I felt slightly claustrophobic and looked over to see if John was feeling it too. He was a tall man, and the dropped ceiling hung just inches above his head. He seemed much too focused on Summer to notice.

John and the dog made their way across the room to the child. Summer was seated cross-legged on the floor in front of an old, gold sofa, a game board of some sort between her and Layla. When John knelt next to her, Summer abandoned the game to wrap her little arms around his neck and started to cry. The dog nuzzled her blonde head with his nose.

Aiyona turned from her position on the couch and looked over her shoulder toward me and Dwayne. She said something to Layla and made her way across the narrow room to join us.

"You picked a good place for us to hang," she said, glancing over at Dwayne and offering him a little wink. "The kids had a blast, and Dwayne here is a wonderful host."

Dwayne turned several shades of red and looked away in an 'awe shucks' sort of manner.

"Thanks, Dwayne," I said, causing his ears to redden too. "I mean it."

"No need to thank me. It was fun, and like I said, your girlfriend made me a delicious dinner."

"Fiancée," I corrected him a second time before adding: "Is there any left, dinner, I mean? We probably won't be here long but if it's not too much trouble..."

"Say no more, Matt. I'll heat some food for you and John." He scampered back up the stairs, seemingly eager for a task.

Once he was gone, Aiyona reached for me. I leaned forward, resting my forehead on her shoulder. The activity of the day was finally catching up with me.

She wrapped her arms around me and spoke softly, "Can you tell me what happened?"

"Not yet," I mumbled.

"So it's not over?"

"Not yet," I repeated.

We stood there quietly for a beat before the room started to get to me again, "Aiyona?"

She gently massaged the back of my neck, "What, baby?"

I nuzzled into her and closed my eyes, "It smells funny in here, and the ceiling is too low. I don't like it."

She laughed softly, "I know, baby. I know."

Chapter 70
KALEY

Shane dozed off just outside of town. I reached the gallery and pulled into a narrow ally, where the side door to the building could be accessed. As soon as the car stopped, he seemed to be back on high alert.

"Hey, Kay, we probably shouldn't park Aiyona's car right outside the gallery. I'm assuming they'll be looking for any and all vehicles associated with the four of us."

"Does it matter if Aiyona's car is here? If they're looking for us, they'll end up here eventually—car or no car."

"I know but if it buys us time…"

I sighed, "I'll let you off. There's an apartment building a few blocks away. I'll hide this in the lot and run back."

Shane nodded, "Good idea. But you're not making your way back here by yourself."

I gave Shane a once over, "No offense—but you'll just slow me down."

He moved slightly to protest and grimaced, "You're right. I'll wait just inside the door and watch for you. Don't go through the front. Come back around to the side here, okay?"

"Okay, okay… Do you remember the code to get in the building?" I asked, nodding toward the large steel door with the attached keypad for entry.

"Yeah, I got it." Shane struggled to push himself forward.

I was concerned that not heading straight to an emergency department was causing more harm than good. Once he managed to swing his legs out of the car, he moved a bit faster; but if we had to make a run for it, we'd be screwed.

I waited until he was inside before pulling back onto the street. I made my way to the apartment complex where I managed to find a spot between two large pick-up trucks. I hoped the larger vehicles would somewhat obscure the smaller Toyota. Once parked, I made a run for it.

I didn't see a single car as I made my way back to the side of the building. Shane was ready and waiting as I reached the door. It felt good to be in a familiar space again. We walked down the hallway to my suite.

"You don't by chance have the key to get in the gallery, do you?" he asked.

"Maybe... My handbag is still back in my SUV. Do you think they left it there, or did Logan have someone move it?"

"I'm guessing they moved it."

I crouched down and retrieved a key from under the 'welcome' mat just outside the door.

Shane shook his head, "Super secure."

I shrugged, "The outside of the building is. I've forgotten my keys so many times I needed a backup. I'd think you'd be grateful for that right about now."

"Yeah, yeah, yeah—I am. Now, can we go inside?"

I opened the door and hit the switch just inside the doorway. The way we'd entered brought us to the elevated portion of the gallery. The loft space contained my office, workspace, and a small bathroom.

I bent down to return the key under the mat, but Shane reached out to stop me. "I've already been shot once today, Kay. Maybe you hold onto the key tonight... Let's not make it too easy for Logan to murder me."

I held up the key before slipping it into the pocket of my jeans, "Good point."

Shane shut and locked the door as we stepped fully inside. "Don't turn on any more lights, okay? From the street, you can't see these lights, but we certainly don't want to draw attention by turning on more."

"Makes sense." I walked into the small office and made a beeline for the desk in the rear corner. I pulled out the white, high-backed desk chair and sank into the comfort of the imitation leather.

Shane stopped in the doorway. He was leaning on the frame for support. His skin looked ashen under the overhead lights. I realized he should be the one taking the breather not me. I started to rise from the chair, "Get over here and sit down. You don't look so good."

The corners of his mouth turned up in a sad smile. "Thanks; I could say the same to you." He gestured for me to remain seated while he stayed planted in place.

I brought my hand to my hairline. My hair was hard and matted near my left temple. I'd nearly forgotten about the injury.

"Kay?" Shane said gently. "What happened to your head?"

"I fell hiking with Logan. I think I hit a rock or something." I realized then that I had a headache. It was more likely due to the stress of our situation than an actual head injury.

Shane hobbled further into the office, "How do you feel? Does it hurt?" he asked, stopping just short of the desk.

"I think I feel fine."

"You think?"

"Well, Shane," I snapped, "There's a lot going on! It's kind of hard to determine just how I feel."

"Okay... okay... I get it," he backed off.

I brought my hand back up to the clump of sticky matted hair. "This feels gross," I commented.

"It looks that way too," he agreed.

I scoffed, "I'm sure your wounds are much more attractive than mine."

He hobbled over to the corner of the desk and stopped, "Go get cleaned up."

I stood, assuming he'd decided to take a seat after all. Perhaps sending me off to the bathroom was his macho way of doing so.

We traded places; but instead of relaxing, Shane turned on the computer and started riffling through the drawers.

"What are you doing?" I asked.

"Do you have a safe or something around here?"

"Well, yeah... why?"

"Because I'd like to look in it while your computer is booting up."

I ran my hand across my forehead... thinking it hurt. "What?"

"Just tell me where the safe is," Shane snapped.

"Okay, jeez!" I pointed to the corner on the other side of the desk. There was a glass-top table with a medium-sized floor safe tucked snugly underneath. "If you're looking for money, there won't be much in there. I don't do many cash sales, and Henry stays on top of deposits. I'm guessing only about a hundred dollars in there."

It took him some effort; but Shane had moved from the desk to the corner, where he squatted before the metal object. "Combo?"

I rattled off Summer's birthdate, but the safe didn't open. Shane tried again. Nothing. I sighed and made my way to the corner and nudged him out of the way.

"When was the last time you were in here?" he asked.

"I don't know," I responded irritably. "I rarely use the safe."

"But Henry does?" Shane asked.

I tried the lock as well but didn't have any better luck than Shane. "He uses it more than me, I guess. He must have changed the combo."

The sound of a key turning in the back door caught our attention.

Shane reached behind his back and winced. He grunted quietly under his breath as he retrieved a pistol from underneath his jacket. He'd left the big gun in the car. He raised a finger to his lips to quiet me. As if I'd choose to make a sound at that moment. I watched as he stayed low and awkwardly brushed past me to venture a peek at what or who might be entering the gallery.

Chapter 71
MATT

I scarfed down an enchilada with some Mexican rice. John declined all offers of food, which perplexed Aiyona and Dwayne. That led to me explaining, multiple times, that food is not everyone's go-to in stressful situations. They didn't get it.

I made sure Aiyona and Dwayne were okay with the current arrangement before returning to the basement from hell for John. Dwayne was thrilled by the prospect of overnight guests. Aiyona was not. I'd just have to ask for forgiveness later. As I reached the bottom stair, I realized the basement hadn't improved during the time I'd spent upstairs. In fact, as I walked further into the room, I concluded it was actually worse than my initial impression. I'd owe Aiyona big time.

Summer had fallen asleep on the couch. Her head resting comfortably in John's lap. "Do you think you can extricate yourself from this situation so we can head out to look for Kaley and Shane?"

John nodded, "I don't want to leave her down here alone, though."

"Can't say as I blame you for that," I murmured.

"I think we should drop her off with Henry."

"We could, but she's probably safer here where nobody would think to look for her."

John squeezed his eyes closed. "I don't know what to do, Matt. She was so upset. How can I leave her again?"

"Maybe you shouldn't..."

His eyes widened in surprise, "What about Kaley? I can't just hide here while you three are taking on Logan and whoever else."

"You're not hiding, John. You're taking care of a traumatized kid. Your relationship with Kaley makes you Summer's father figure. You should probably start thinking like a dad. Kaley has me and Gavin. Aiyona is great, and she'll protect Summer like her own, but she's not. Summer needs a parent. Like it or not—you're the closest thing to that right now."

John nodded and looked down at the sleeping figure. "You think I should stay here, then?"

"I do."

"You'll need a phone. We need to be able to communicate."

"I'll take Aiyona's—be back in a minute—we'll need to exchange numbers."

"I'll need frequent updates," John added.

"You'll get them."

I went back upstairs to straighten things out with Aiyona and retrieve her phone. It didn't go as smoothly as I'd hoped.

"You can have my phone, but I come with it," Aiyona informed me.

I eyed her skeptically, "I don't think that's a good idea. What about Layla?"

"Layla is sound asleep, and she has John and Dwayne to look after her. You, on the other hand, don't have anyone to look after you."

I geared up to argue, but I'd just be wasting my breath. I knew from experience when Aiyona had something in her head, it was pointless to disagree. "Let me talk to John and Dwayne. You sure Layla will be alright?"

She crossed her arms in front of her and narrowed her eyes, "They're your friends, Matt. Is there a reason the girls wouldn't be okay without me here?"

"No, of course not. I just—"

She didn't let me finish, "Well then, quit stalling, and let's get a move on."

"I don't even know where we're going."

"Lucky for you I'll be there to help figure that out."

Chapter 72
KALEY

"Kaley!" A familiar voice called out, "Are you here, darlin'? I've been looking all over for you."

I scrambled out from behind the desk. What on earth was Henry doing here? I didn't want the old man near any of this.

"I'm here," I rushed out of the office to head him off.

"Well, thank goodness!" he proclaimed. "I've been trying to reach you all day. I finally told Ted he'd need to hold down the fort while I..." Henry trailed off as I stepped into the open area of the loft. "What in the tarnation happened to you?"

I wasn't sure how to explain my appearance. Quite frankly, I had no idea how bad I looked. Judging from the expression on Henry's face, it was worse than I thought. "I'm okay," I responded numbly.

The old man hobbled forward and reached for me. I was enveloped in a strong sense of nostalgia as I folded into his arms. Feeling very much like the young motherless kid I'd been when I'd first arrived to live with Henry. We stood there for a moment in silence.

Grandpa was the first to speak, "Did Logan do this to you?"

The question surprised me in both the nature and manner in which it was asked. Grandpa's voice sounded stern. His words clipped.

I stepped away from my grandfather, shocked to see his features had hardened and reflected the quality of his words.

"Why would you ask me that, Henry?"

The door to the hallway swung open again. This time, Josie stepped into the threshold of the gallery. "Oh, thank goodness you're here, Kaley!" Her voice was perhaps a pitch or two higher than her baseline and much too sugary.

"What are you doing here?" I took another step back from the duo. Wondering why Shane hadn't made his presence known.

"As I started to tell ya," Henry said. "I asked Ted to watch things so I could go lookin' for ya. Josie turned up at the bar worried about Shane, so we thought we'd team up. Most likely the two of you'd be together."

"Uh-huh," I replied.

"So have you seen him?" Josie asked, batting her eyelashes.

I ignored her and turned my attention back to Henry. "Why did you ask me about Logan?"

The two briefly exchanged a look. I didn't understand the intention behind it, but there was definitely a look. Perhaps Grandpa knew about the affair?

Henry sighed, "Darlin'; we have a lot to talk about. Why don't ya go get yourself cleaned up, and we'll go from there."

I stayed planted firmly in place.

"Kaley?" Grandpa leaned forward on his cane.

"I heard you."

Josie swiveled her head between the two of us. She opened her mouth to speak, but Henry held up his hand to silence her.

"How did you know I was with Logan?" I tried rephrasing the question to my grandfather.

Henry shook his head, "Oh boy… okay. You're not going to let this go are you?" One look into my eyes, and he knew the answer. "Well, come on then, darlin' let's have a seat in your office and chat."

I folded my arms across my chest, "No. Right here is just fine."

Henry sighed, "All I ever wanted was to protect you. After we lost your mom, it was up to me to make sure you had everything you needed in life."

I had no idea what this had to do with Logan.

"You were only ten at the time," he continued. "Your deadbeat dad wanted nothing to do with you."

"Hang on," I shifted my attention toward Josie. "You don't really need to be here for this. If I see Shane, I'll tell him you're looking for him."

Josie reached out and touched Henry tenderly on the arm, "Would you like me to stay?"

He nodded.

What was happening? Was she sleeping with my grandfather too? "You know she's having an affair with Logan, right?" I blurted out.

Josie took a step forward, "You arrogant little bitch. So, it's okay for Shane to mess around with you but—"

"Enough, Josie." Shane had emerged from the office, letting his pistol lead as he made his way to my side. I wasn't sure why he felt the need to confront Henry and Josie with a weapon, but I wasn't about to second-guess him.

"Shane, honey, you're not looking very good," Josie said, with a twinkle in her eye and more than a touch of amusement.

"I don't feel very good, either. That tends to happen when you've been shot and left for dead."

Josie gasped as her hand fluttered over her mouth. A complete overdramatization in my opinion. The way her lips curled up in a wry smile let on to the fact that she was not at all surprised that Shane had been shot. Perhaps the fact that he was alive, but not at all by the fact he'd been injured.

"I'm sure Logan told you all about his plan to get rid of me," Shane commented.

"Ha! You always were a sexist pig, Shane. Of course, you would think it was Logan," Josie spat.

Henry chuckled in amusement, "Settle down now, Josie. There will be time for you and your husband to have it out in a bit."

"No," Josie shot back. "He needs to hear this now! I'm with Logan because I can't get what I need from you."

"Nice, Josie," Shane replied dryly.

"You were supposed to be my in at the police department. Not Logan. However, it was very apparent you were not man enough to do what needed to be done."

"What? Man enough for what?" Shane shouted. "To open the way for Round Rock to be a pipeline for illegal drugs, guns, and human trafficking? Is that what I'm not man enough to do? Or is it taking product off criminals only to turn around and put it back on the streets for profit? Or something more personal, Josie? Please tell me—what is it exactly that I'm not man enough to do!"

"All of it, Shane!" Josie screamed. "People are going to do what they want to do. Why not profit off the stupidity of others? We didn't force anyone to do anything. If we didn't take charge, someone else would."

I pressed my palms against my eyes trying to sort out what was happening.

"Stop!" Henry shouted. This isn't getting us anywhere."

"Are you sure about that, Henry! Because I'm learning quite a bit right now!" Shane hollered back.

"I need time with my granddaughter," Henry snapped. "You two can work out your marital differences later."

"Kay, I'm so sorry," Shane said. His tone had softened considerably. "Logan said that you were untouchable, right?"

I took my hands away from my eyes and really looked at my grandfather. The realization hadn't changed him, but it did change me. He was still the charming, social, overprotective man I'd grown up with, but perhaps those traits took on a different meaning now.

Henry tilted his head slightly, his expression pained, "Darlin', there is so much we need to talk about."

I waved my hands in protest, "No, no, no, no. This can't be true. You would never do anything to hurt Nathan. You wouldn't destroy my family like that."

"I didn't do it to destroy you. I did it to protect you," Henry replied gently.

I turned toward Shane. He didn't look surprised.

"This is what you suspected. This is why you didn't tell me. Isn't it?"

"I'm sorry, Kay."

"Is this why you tried to stop me from the beginning?"

"No... I put it together after..."

"After what?"

"After what happened tonight. After what Logan said to you. After thinking about Nathan's notes. Even then I was just acting on a hunch."

"So you suspected Henry. How did that lead us here?"

"He's looking for proof I've been funneling money through the gallery," Henry said.

My shock was slowly being replaced by anger. "You what!"

"And he's not going to find it," Josie piped up. "Nathan already found the ledgers, and we have no idea where he hid them."

Shane turned toward me. This time he did appear surprised.

"Don't look at her, Shane," Josie continued. "She doesn't know, either. Logan and I tried to get it out of her the night we broke into the house." Then to Henry: "I told you that your ridiculous old school accounting system would be a problem—"

Shane interrupted, "You purposely lured me to Minnesota to ditch me that night!" Shane exclaimed. "Josie! What the hell!"

Josie shrugged, "No offense, Shane. It didn't have anything to do with you. It never did."

My eyes were burning as I strained to hold back my emotions. "You drugged me to find out where Nathan may have hidden evidence?"

"Well, yeah," replied Josie. "Once you found the notebook and started talking to Matt Pine, we figured it would only be a matter of time before you put two and two together. We searched the house and questioned you. You were most unhelpful I might add."

I stepped toward my grandfather but felt Shane grip my arm to stop me. "Did you know?" I asked.

Henry leaned on his cane and focused his gaze downward, unwilling to meet my eyes. "I didn't know exactly what they had planned; but yes, I knew. With Summer staying at my place, it seemed like the perfect opportunity."

"But you thought John was with me..."

He finally looked up. His lids were heavy and his shoulders drooped. "We knew that he wasn't, darlin'. We checked. The lights were on at his place, and there was no truck at yours."

My knees felt weak, "How could you let them do that to me? Do you have any idea how scared I was? I don't feel safe in my own home, Henry! Which is nothing compared to what you did to Nathan." I felt like I was going to be sick, but I had to know. "Did you kill Nathan or was it her?" I pointed toward Josie.

The room was hauntingly silent.

"I set him up, Kaley," Josie finally said. "I used Matt Pine to lure him to the bluff."

"And then what?" I asked. My voice shaking.

Henry cleared his throat, "We questioned him."

"Who? You and Logan?"

"Yes, along with some of the officers Logan had recruited."

"What other officers?" Shane wanted to know.

"It doesn't matter," Grandpa replied. "He was onto us, so we offered him some options."

I could only imagine what kind of options.

"I'll give him credit though, Kaley," Grandpa continued. "He didn't want to hurt you. He had more than we were even aware of, but he planned to tell you before he moved forward."

"Cost him his life," Josie interjected.

Henry shot her a look, and she sunk back into the shadows. "I gave Nathan the opportunity to join us," my grandfather continued, "he could have done that. It was really the only option that would have kept him from hurting you. He, however, refused."

"So you killed him!" I screamed. "You killed Summer's dad, My husband! Nathan was part of your family! For what, Henry? Money, power, what?"

"Assurance," Henry replied. "Everything I did was for you and Summer. No matter what, you girls would always be taken care of. If you got cancer like your mom, or God forbid, Summer needed something. I'd be able to get you what you needed. Your poor mother, Kaley...the bills... the treatments. I couldn't afford any of it. I could never let that happen again."

I almost felt sorry for the old man. Almost. I couldn't imagine what it was like for him to watch my mother waste away and how powerless he must have felt. There was nothing he could do to ease her pain and suffering.

"Kaley?" Grandpa took a step toward me.

"Did you tell Nathan any of this?"

"I did. He gave me a window to come clean."

"But you chose to kill him instead."

The sound of sirens filtered in through the walls of the gallery.

"Logan's coming," Josie interjected.

Chapter 73
MATT

The streets were quiet as the clock ticked toward eleven. Julia's SUV was nice. Certainly nicer than anything I'd ever owned. Aiyona took advantage of the seat warmers. She had borrowed a dark parka from Dwayne. She was hunkered down in the seat with the hood cinched tight. Given our ominous situation and her glowering attitude, it felt a little bit like riding around with the grim reaper. I pushed the thought away as it was more than a little unsettling.

I drove past John's house again. It was still dark. I also took a chance driving past Kaley's. It, too, was dark. I had some idea of where Gavin lived and toured his neighborhood as well. There was no sign of Kaley, Shane, or Aiyona's Toyota.

"Maybe head back toward downtown," the grim reaper directed from the passenger seat.

I followed her suggestion and made my way toward the historic center of Round Rock. The old architecture of the main street took on a gothic feel as the structures stood silent and foreboding in the moonlight.

"Slow down," Aiyona leaned forward in her seat, squinting out the front windshield. "The next block up, in front of Kaley's gallery, I think that's a cop car out front… If they're on a call, shouldn't the lights be on?"

"Yeah, something feels off."

I rolled ahead to the stop sign separating the blocks. There was no traffic this time of night, so I was able to linger without pissing anyone off. Sure enough, at the end of the next block, the building that housed Kaley's gallery, along with a few other shops, appeared to have two squad cars parked along the curb.

"I think we should park and walk up. See what we can see."

I agreed with Aiyona and looked for a place to stash the SUV. We settled on an apartment building not too far away. I wanted to ask Aiyona to wait in the vehicle while I checked things out, but I knew that would just lead to an argument.

She peered over at me from the depth of the hooded parka. "You're thinking about telling me to stay here while you scope out the situation. Aren't you?"

I shook my head and chuckled under my breath.

"I knew it!" Aiyona declared. "You know we're stronger together! Splitting up is just stupid—"

I cut her off before she went off on a full-blown tirade. "Aiyona—I get it. I thought about asking you to stay but realized the error of my ways before you even spoke up. Now, are you coming? Or what?"

In response, she pulled open the door and hopped out of the safety and warmth of the little SUV. I took a deep breath and followed suit.

We made our way across the parking lot of the apartments toward an alleyway. Aiyona reached out to stop me as we passed the last row of vehicles. "That's my car."

I turned in the direction she was pointing. Sure enough. Nestled between two large pick-up trucks was the little Toyota.

"So, maybe Kaley and Shane saw the cop cars and did the same thing we did," Aiyona suggested. The cold air whisked away her words. The frigid temperatures made her breath visible under the glow from the lamp posts.

I jogged forward and felt the hood of the car. It was just as cold as everything around it. I hustled back to Aiyona. "Nope. Your car has been here a while.

"You think the cops tracked them here?" she asked.

"I do. I don't know why'd they'd come here, though."

I reached for her hand, "I have no idea what we're walking into, Aiyona."

She took my hand and squeezed. "It's okay, Matt; I got your back."

Chapter 74
KALEY

Logan entered the gallery accompanied by two young officers. "Detective Gavin!" Logan exclaimed. "I'm surprised to see you here." He turned toward Josie and lowered his voice. "It seems you left out some information in your text."

"Did my wife forget to tell you that I'm not dead in the woods, Chief?" Shane replied sarcastically. "Her communication skills are really lacking lately. For example, she forgot to tell me that we're parking our trucks in the same garage!"

I watched the faces of the stoic young officers Logan had brought with him. One I recognized as being a new hire shortly before Nathan died. The other I didn't recognize at all. I wondered if they knew what was going on. Were they in on it?

Logan laughed; but there was no amusement behind the sound, "Funny, Gavin, very funny."

"Are you here to finish the job? Or will you have Mason and Dell do it?" Shane asked, gesturing toward the officers flanking Logan.

The acknowledgment of their presence caused both men to look away. The fact that they were looking anywhere other than in Shane's direction led me to believe they knew exactly what they were party to.

Logan tipped his head slightly, studying Shane before venturing to speak again. "I didn't try to kill you, and neither did anyone else in the department. Not that we wouldn't, or more accurately, that we still won't. Since you were wearing a vest, I'm guessing that doesn't come as a surprise. However, there is someone much more motivated than any of us."

"Nothing personal," Josie said from the shadows behind the men."

Henry stepped forward, "Come on, Kaley. Let's get you home and let these folks sort out their business."

I stood there dumbstruck as Henry offered me his hand.

Logan cleared his throat, "No offense, Henry, but we have passed that point. She's in, or she's not."

My grandfather whirled on Logan. "You don't give me orders! Frankly, Logan, the need for you has passed. You have turned my whole business into a shitshow. I'm taking Kaley home, and then I'll be back to clean up the mess you've made."

"You think I'm going to leave and let you kill Shane like you killed Nathan!" I shouted at my grandfather.

"Enough!" Josie hollered in response. She stepped forward and touched Henry lightly on the shoulder. "Henry, you had a good run. You were right to bring me in as your right-hand woman. Things didn't work out as planned, but we had a good time; we made some money. I think now would be the perfect time for you to retire. You have plenty of funds to take care of Summer and never have to worry about soiling your hands again."

Henry turned toward Shane's wife, "Don't you forget who's in charge here, darlin', you know what I'm capable of."

She nodded, "And you know what I'm capable of."

They stood there, locked in a visible struggle for power, the bull versus the matador.

While the attention was focused on my grandfather and Josie, Shane reached out and took my hand. I clasped my fingers around his, and for a moment it felt like the earth stood still. Then, Shane pulled me toward him as the air erupted around us. Henry was yelling. Logan was yelling. Hands grabbed at us from all directions. Josie shrieked and somehow we ended up on my office floor. Shane kicked the door closed behind us and scrambled up to push the lock and hold it tight.

"Barricade it, Kay!" he shouted.

I grabbed my filing cabinet and pushed it up against the door. That done, Shane struggled to push my desk across the room. I helped him shove that against the door too.

"Now what?" I asked breathlessly.

"Call 911," he directed. "Tell them to send the county and anyone they can from outside Round Rock."

My office phone had fallen to the floor when Shane moved the desk. It took me a moment to realize the receiver had come off the base, and I'd need to hang it up and start over for the phone to function.

Meanwhile, Shane had opened the single window on the back wall and forcefully removed the screen.

I barely had time to tell the dispatcher what Shane had told me to say before he was yelling more orders. I tried to focus inward as the world around me collapsed.

Shane grabbed the phone from me and identified himself followed by a string of short, clipped pieces of information that I wasn't quite following. He was yelling to be heard over the shouting and pounding in the hallway. Our barricaded door was about to be breached. It was the last thing he said that caught my attention, whether to the 911 operator or me, I wasn't sure—but the meaning was clear: "We're going out the window."

Shane took hold of me, and together we pitched forward through the open window.

The drop wasn't too steep, and Shane had cushioned my fall as we landed in the packed snow below the gallery window.

Chapter 75
MATT

Aiyona took off at a sprint. It was everything I could do to keep up with her. I had no idea why we were running. It soon became apparent as the sound of gunshots rang out through the still winter air. I picked up the pace and pulled Aiyona into the nearby alleyway outside the building that housed the gallery.

The explosive sounds ended just as quickly as they had started. The only audible noise was that of our rapid inhalations. We leaned against the solid cover of the brick, trying to catch our breath.

"Who was shooting?" I asked Aiyona. "Did you see where it was coming from? Is that why you took off like that?"

Aiyona shook her head, "No, the window above the entrance. I thought I saw someone fall. Then the shooting started."

"Are you sure?" I asked. "I didn't see anything."

Before she could reply, a door further down the alleyway flung open, slamming against the bricks. The sound echoed, bouncing off the buildings.

I pulled Aiyona back around the corner, so we were on the sidewalk again. We hugged the nearby building, doing our best to blend into the shadows so as not to be seen from either the side or front of the gallery. There was the sound of footfalls moving rapidly toward us. I ushered Aiyona back further, and we ducked behind a half wall at the entrance to the building next door.

Aiyona crawled forward on her hands and knees and looked out from behind the wall. Completely covered in the ridiculously large parka, I was confident she would not be seen in the darkness of the night. There was a bunch of shouting. The words were indecipherable as they were swallowed by the night.

"Oh, shit, Matt!" Aiyona exclaimed in a hushed tone.

I crawled next to her to see what was happening. There was a group of people struggling in front of the gallery.

"Whoever came out that window—they are in trouble."

A vehicle came down the street, the brightness from the headlights momentarily lighting the site in front of the gallery. The SUV pulled to a stop. It appeared to be another cop. The sound of a woman calling for help was instantly recognizable.

"Got your gun, Matt?" Aiyona asked.

"Yep."

And she was off again. I pushed off the ground and took off after her. I was running for our lives, which was probably the only reason I managed to pass Aiyona. My mind was moving a mile a minute. My brain unable to process the situation as quickly as it was unfolding.

Gavin was on the ground. Kaley was doing her best to shelter him from the group surrounding them.

Two cops, no three, one was next to Kaley and Gavin. Did that include the cop we'd seen pull up in the SUV?

Another woman was there too. I didn't see her right away.

The police chief, he was the one next to Kaley. She was screaming, and they were in a full out brawl now.

Guns were drawn.

Aiyona ran full speed, boring into the smallest of the cops from behind.

Before I could reach for my weapon, she elbowed the second officer in the face. Even over the yelling, I heard the nauseating, cracking sound resulting from the connection. Before he could recover from the blow, Aiyona's foot snapped out, striking him in the groin.

The first officer was scrambling to his feet, and I could see he was reaching for the gleaming object sticking out of the snow.

I clocked him in the back of the head with the Glock from the cabin. He went down again.

A shot rang through the air, and we all stopped.

The woman stepped forward. She'd fired her gun, but I wasn't sure if she'd hit anything. She stepped forward and wrapped her left arm around Kaley's neck and held the gun to the side of her head with the other hand.

"Drop your weapons! Everyone!" she screamed.

I held my hands up and slowly lowered my gun to the ground. I got a look at Gavin as I did so. His breathing was extremely labored, and his eyes were closed. Had I not been able to hear the wheezing as he struggled to take in breath, I would have sworn the guy was dead.

"You, too, Logan," the woman demanded.

The police chief scoffed but then quickly changed his disposition as the woman narrowed her eyes and removed the safety.

Kaley's eyes were wide with fear. Her normally pale skin now as white as the fallen snow. I could hear sirens in the distance. We were already outnumbered, bringing more dirty Round Rock cops to the scene would not improve our odds.

"Josie, please," Kaley pleaded with the woman. "Shane needs help—he's not going to make it. He's still your husband—"

"Shut up!" the woman, Josie, screamed. Kaley started to shake.

Gavin's wife? Things were falling into place.

The sirens were getting closer. We didn't have much time.

Josie turned her head in the direction of the sound. Gavin took the opportunity to reach for the weapon the police chief had dropped just short of the detective's practically lifeless body. I followed his lead and knelt to retrieve my own.

Gavin yelled something, and I saw Kaley lurch forward.

The woman raised her weapon, and I raised mine. I couldn't say which of us fired first.

Something slammed into my chest, and I fell back into the snow. I was suddenly engulfed in silence as pain radiated from my core to my extremities. A weight settled on my chest, forcing the air from my body. The world around me moved in slow motion. Aiyona's face floated in front of me. She was yelling, but the words were carried off with the wind.

She was so beautiful, I thought, and then I closed my eyes and let the darkness fold in around me.

Chapter 76
KALEY

I covered my head with my hands and fell to the ground. My ears rang in the silence that followed. I felt weighed down, but I didn't know by what. I felt wet and so cold. Colder than I'd ever thought possible. I couldn't stop trembling. I wanted to move, to see what was happening; but I was paralyzed to do so.

"You're okay, Kaley." I heard his voice clear as day.

"Nathan!" I called out.

"You're okay," he repeated. "I got you."

A sense of calm washed over me, replacing the fear and cold. The sensation, unlike anything I'd ever experienced or can actually even describe. "Nathan!" I called out again.

"It's okay," the same words, but this time in a different voice. "I got you, Kay."

I opened my eyes. Shane and I were huddled together against the wall outside the main entrance to the gallery. The night was pulsing as the red and blue strobes bounced off the snow and the buildings around us. More emergency vehicles wailed onto the scene. The block filled with the various departments and emergency personnel that had been summoned by our call to 911.

I pushed myself up to a seated position. The rawness of the elements and the situation started to settle in on me. Shane was propped against the outside wall, his legs splayed out in front of him. We were a few yards from where we'd landed after our exit through the window, but I didn't know how. The drop hadn't been too steep, and Shane had cushioned my fall. The moments were revealed in a series of flashes. Someone had fired at us. Shane had struggled to get up after the fall. He'd told me to run, but I wouldn't leave him. Then Logan and the cops came, followed by Josie. I closed my eyes and started to tremble again. This time, it was harder to control my body. My teeth were chattering so violently I feared they'd break right off.

I closed my eyes, willing myself to fall back into the dreamlike state where Nathan had the ability to comfort me. No matter how hard I tried, I couldn't will Nathan back. However, another thought occurred to me. I turned to Shane, "I know where Nathan hid the financial books you were looking for and whatever evidence he'd collected."

"What? How?" he asked his voice sounding raspy.

"I just do," I couldn't explain it. I just knew Nathan had tucked them inside my display cube. The cube he'd found and so proudly restored. The shallow compartment underneath. I'd teased him that he'd bought me a drug smuggler's hidey-hole. How ironic that seemed now. I stood on wobbly legs and made my way back toward the gallery.

"Kay, hang on. You can't go back in there. It might not be safe. Just wait. Soon this place will be crawling with cops."

"That's why I need to go now." I moved as quickly as my shaky legs would allow.

Shane called out again, but I ignored whatever he said. I tried the front door, but it was locked. I moved to the side of the building and punched in the code. Once inside, I noted the door to my gallery stood open. I stepped forward hesitantly. Maybe Shane was right.

Maybe it wasn't safe. I slowed my gait and continued ahead cautiously.

The loft area was quiet. I was clipped by a cold breeze. Most likely from my office window, where Shane and I had exited. I didn't stop to look. A strong feeling of urgency propelled me forward. As I reached the bottom of the stairs, the cube seemed to beckon me forward. The street lamp shone through the storefront window. The cube actually seemed to sparkle under the ray cast by the light.

I knelt next to the cube. My hand slid across the smooth glass. In order to reach the compartment, I'd need to shimmy underneath, which would be easier if someone was here to tip it up a bit. However, if I waited, they may not allow me to access whatever Nathan had hidden. My body felt so battered, bruised, and frozen that movement was difficult. Once on my back, I pushed underneath the cube and reached up, clicking the small clasp on the hatch to the right. I felt around inside and pulled out three leather-bound books.

The bell above the door jingled, and I caught a light move across the floor from a flashlight beam. I called out as I made my way back out from underneath the cube.

"Kaley Stone?" a woman's voice called.

A mega flashlight stream swept across my face. "Yes," I replied, shielding my eyes with my hand. "The light switch is near the door," I offered.

She kept her light trained on me as someone else, most likely her partner, switched on the overhead lights. Being suddenly bathed in light after spending so much time moving through the darkness lent a surreal quality to the situation.

"Your friend Detective Gavin told us you were in here. They are trying to get him into the ambulance, but he's not doing anything without you."

I nodded and made my way toward the exit.

"You look like you could use some medical attention too," the officer stated after giving me a once over.

I ignored the comment. "You're not affiliated with Round Rock are you?"

Her partner scoffed.

"No," she replied firmly.

"Good," I handed her the journals. "My husband left these for safekeeping."

The officer looked confused, but I didn't think she would be for long. My part was finished. I pushed past the cops, making my way back into the cold. I didn't know what had happened to Henry, and I didn't care. I needed to get Shane to the hospital and find Aiyona and Matt. They'd saved our lives. I hoped it didn't cost them theirs.

Chapter 77
SHANE

A lot can happen in 30 seconds. You can run 200 meters, send a text, kick a winning field goal. Life and death decisions are made in 30 seconds. How long did it take for that son of a bitch to make the decision he did? Goes to show you—you really never know what people are capable of. My wife tried to kill me, and the criminal saved me. Stupid Matt Pine. The guy made so many wrong turns. Wasn't he due to take a right one?

Matt managed to get off two shots. One hit Logan in the back. The chief would be fine, at least medically. However, being a cop on the other side of the bars did not bode well for him in the long run. The second shot hit Josie. Ironically enough, it was a GSW to the heart that ended her life. I recognized the poetic justice in that but didn't know how to feel about it. I knew we had issues, and I recognized my faults as a husband. That didn't change the fact that I loved Josie, or at least the woman I had thought she was.

Josie got off one shot. Her bullet found its mark and lodged itself in Matt's upper abdomen. He'd almost bled out on the way to the hospital. He made it to surgery, but things didn't look good. When I promised Matt I'd look after his family, I never thought I'd have to follow through.

I bowed my head and talked to God, to Nathan, to whoever in the universe would listen to an asshole like me. I'd trade places with the guy in a heartbeat. Aiyona and Layla needed him. I didn't want to be a fill-in for another good man taken too soon. In the dimly lit hospital chapel, I rose from the wooden bench and used my good arm to grab the crutch from where it leaned against the railing. I was told my shoulder wound would heal. Aiyona had done a good job of removing the 9mm slug. I'd broken two ribs on my left side and fractured my right ankle from the window escape. I knew how fortunate I was.

I hobbled to the front of the church room and paused in front of the wooden cross, backlit and glowing amidst the blue velvety fabric. I didn't come from a religious family. I could count the number of times I'd attended church on one hand. However, being here now was the only way I could think of to help Matt.

"If you help him survive," I said, looking toward the wood-beamed ceiling, "I promise I'll look into this church thing, or read the bible, or whatever. Please, don't let another family suffer like Nathan's has..."

The sound of a door creaking open filled the otherwise silent chapel. I turned to see Aiyona. She stopped just inside the stained-glass doorway.

"Do I need to cross myself or something?" I asked. "I don't want to do it wrong."

She shook her head and came to stand beside me. "You'll have to do it now. You know that, right?"

I offered her a blank look.

"Church. You promised you'd go to church if Matt makes it through."

I swiped my hand across my face, "Oh, yeah, that. I also offered to read the bible, so that seems like a more realistic option—but whatever it takes."

She smiled wearily. "Thank you."

"No, thank you. If it weren't for you and Matt, then Kaley and I wouldn't have made it through this night. I mean it, Aiyona, thank you."

She nodded this time, holding back tears. She wiped her eyes with her sleeve before continuing, "Have you seen Kaley?"

"Not since our ambulance ride. I know she's staying the night for observation. John is with her."

"I can't believe they aren't holdin' you here too."

"They tried. I signed myself out against medical advice."

She raised an eyebrow at me and ran her hand across the cloth sling supporting my injured shoulder, but she didn't offer any opinions on the matter.

"They found her grandfather," I told Aiyona. "He was near the window in her office. Single gunshot wound to the head. Apparently, his faithful employees turned on him too."

Aiyona buried her face in her hands, "She's going to be devastated. Summer is going to be devastated."

I reached out and pulled her close, "They'll be okay. We're all going to be okay." More than anything, I wanted to believe that.

Chapter 78
KALEY

I'd lost all sense of time. Upon waking, my mouth was dry and my body aching, battered, and bruised. It was daylight, that much was for certain. The sun shone brightly through the long, narrow window of the hospital room.

My dreams had been vivid and strange. Given my recent reality, one might think it would be difficult to determine what was real and what was actually a dream. However, it wasn't hard at all. The nightmares, the shooting, the loss, that was the reality. The dreams were where I wanted to stay. In my dreams, Nathan and I were restoring the gallery; and Henry was a good man, helping oversee the details of the project. In reality, a sheriff's deputy reported that Josie had shot my grandfather. He'd bled out on my office floor. I didn't ask any questions, but I answered all of theirs.

"Hey, you're awake," John entered the room. He was holding a disposable coffee cup. By his rumpled appearance, I surmised he'd had a rough time of it too.

"What time is it?" I asked groggily.

"Around three in the afternoon." He slid a chair next to my bedside, "My God is it good to see you," he smiled. I noted the dark circles under his eyes. I didn't even want to consider my appearance.

"Is Summer here?" I asked. Ordinarily, not knowing my daughter's whereabouts would send me into an automatic tailspin, but I trusted John had everything under control.

"She's with my sister. She and Layla both. Julia has them at your house—I hope that's okay. I thought she'd feel most comfortable there."

I nodded, "Thank you." I pushed myself upright and was surprised by the tug on the inside of my elbow. I hadn't realized I was hooked to an IV. I glanced at the tubes entering my body and then at John. "Can you call someone to disconnect me or whatever?"

He appeared puzzled by the request, "I don't think that's a good idea. You were pretty dehydrated. They also gave you some medication to help calm you. I think you're getting an antibiotic through there too."

They'd given me something? I could sort of recall that. It explained why I felt so mellow. I thought it was due to exhaustion coupled with acceptance, but medication made more sense. I thought about the interview with the deputies and the news about my grandfather. Bits and pieces floated through my memory on a continuous loop. Then, I recalled medics rushing Matt through the Emergency Department, and holding Aiyona as she had a full-on meltdown. I'd been where she was. I wouldn't wish that on anyone, much less the person who'd just saved our lives. There was a difference, though. In my situation, I'd been offered no hope. Nathan was gone. Matt had been hanging on.

"Kaley?"

"I need to check on Matt and Aiyona," I said, swinging my legs off the side of the bed.

John stood to stop me. He gently tucked the covers back over me, "Later," he said. "There's no news at the moment. I just saw Aiyona; I brought her coffee."

"He can't possibly still be in surgery. Why is there no news?"

John sat on the edge of the bed, "It's complicated. While the surgery to remove the bullet from his abdomen went well, he also suffered a serious brain injury from the impact of the fall. Matt's in a medically induced coma. They are trying to reduce swelling on his brain."

"Will he wake up?"

John reached for my hand, "I don't know."

I shook my head, "That can't be. Why is this happening? I need to be with Aiyona." I said once again, trying to make my way out of the bed.

John eased me back again, "Shane is with Aiyona. She's in good hands. How about you rest and take the second shift?"

I pushed John away, "Why isn't Shane in a hospital bed too? He's in much worse shape than I am."

"Shane signed himself out against medical advice. He has a whole herd of nurses angry with him. I suggest you cut everyone a break and do the opposite of that." John's tone had an edge to it.

I stopped fighting. It was time. Instead of pushing him further, I eased my head back onto the pillow.

John's posture relaxed, and the tension in his jaw eased.

"You should rest too," I stated. "You look absolutely exhausted."

He ran a hand through his hair, "I'm fine."

I patted the small space beside me on the bed.

Without another word, he managed to squeeze his large frame onto the bed next to me.

I nestled against him and did my best to ignore the electric hum of the environment around me and the powerless feeling inside of me.

Chapter 79
MATT

It's interesting how people process trauma. I'm not sure if it's due to my injuries or some kind of breakdown of my mental psyche, but I have difficulty remembering that night. Aiyona, however, seems to remember every minute detail. I imagine that's quite a burden to live with. Although the night of the shooting is mostly a blank, waking up in the hospital is not.

I woke up to freakin' Shane Gavin keeping vigil at my bedside. Of course, that's how life rolls for me. Five days in a medically induced coma, and instead of being welcomed back to the world by my beautiful, kick-ass fiancée, I opened my eyes to see his ugly mug.

Not that I'm complaining. Shane, Kaley, John, and Dwayne really stepped it up for me and my family. Aiyona told me that between the four of them she didn't have to worry about anything. Although he won't admit it, Shane was a huge advocate for me. He was my voice when I couldn't speak, only better, because people listened to him in a way I wouldn't have been heard. Gavin used his life-long citizenship of Round Rock, along with his legendary status as a hometown hero, to make sure I was taken care of. All that, and he rotated childcare and hospital duties with Aiyona. I couldn't wrap my brain around the fact that the guy who once loathed me had done so much for me. Whatever the reason, I was and still am grateful.

So much so in fact, I'm waiting for my best man to pick me up for the most anticipated day of my life.

It's a perfect, warm, and sunshiny afternoon. The only reason I can endure the brutal Wisconsin winters is that eventually, they melt into beautiful summer days. It's been five months since the shooting. After a lot of physical healing and personal growth, I'm ready to fully embrace the person I've become.

A horn honks outside. I take one last look in the bathroom mirror to adjust my yellow bow tie. I must say, I clean up well for an ex-con living the good life in hodunk Wisconsin.

The horn sounds again. I make my exit, grabbing the tuxedo jacket from a nearby hook on my way out the door.

Gavin is waiting impatiently for me in his pick-up truck. "Let's go, Matt!" he hollers out the window. "You don't want to be late for your own wedding."

I pull open the passenger door and settle myself into the cushy leather interior.

"That's an actual saying," he informs me.

"I do know. And one you actually got right."

His forehead creases in confusion, "What do you mean?"

I wave away the comment, "Nothin', let's go."

Gavin shrugs and throws the truck in reverse. "You know, Matt, this day almost didn't happen."

It was odd to hear him call me by my first name rather than criminal, and I was fully aware of the fact that I'd cheated death.

"If you hadn't pulled through, though, I was fully prepared to step in for you." He doesn't look at me as he says this. His attention is fully focused on the road ahead.

I'm not sure if he's trying to crack a joke about replacing me as Aiyona's husband or if he's speaking on a much more sentimental level. Even after all we've been through, I still find it difficult to read the guy.

Gavin, sensing my hesitation, turns his head my direction. With his aviator sunglasses, it's nearly impossible to read his intention. "I mean it, Matt, this is a big deal. I'll admit I'm a little jealous."

That got me, "I'm sorry, you might have to repeat that... Did you just say you're jealous... of me?"

Gavin reaches out and grips my shoulder. "I am. You were dealt a crap hand in life, and you turned it around. You made yourself an awesome little family, and now you're going to make it official. That's something, for what it's worth, anyway."

I wasn't sure what to say, "Thanks, that means a lot actually."

He nods firmly and turns his attention back to the road. "Also, you know, if things didn't work out, I'd be the one marrying Aiyona."

"Ha! That's more like the comments I've come to expect from you."

Gavin smiles, "Let's just hope your marriage goes better than mine."

"I think that's a given,"

We turn into the gravel driveway that leads to the small chapel at the top of the hill. "It's all fun and games until your beautiful bride is trying to fill you full of lead."

I shiver, "Jeez, that's dark, even for you."

He laughs as he puts the truck in park, "You got nothin' to worry about, Matt. If she hasn't tried to kill you yet, you're probably okay. Now, let's get you married!" Gavin exclaims, offering me a hearty pat on the back.

Gavin is good at deflecting with humor. Nothing is off-limits. I like that about him.

We both step out of the truck onto the limestone gravel. The impractical dress shoes Aiyona forced on me are tight; they cause my toes to cramp. We make our way across the parking area, kicking up dust as we walk. The rural white chapel gleams against the bright blue sky and lush, green landscape beyond. I close my eyes and inhale the clean Wisconsin air.

I hear Gavin crunching through the gravel beside me, "Cold feet?"

I shake my head in response. "Just the opposite."

Chapter 80
KALEY

The ceremony was beautiful. I grab a glass of champagne as I exit the church for the outdoor reception. Just beyond the building, I spot a large boulder on which to sit. It's away from the activity but with a clear view of the gathering. As I watch the attendees mingle in the sunshine, it hits me how intertwined Matt's life had become with mine. The guest list is intimate, and I know every single person in attendance. There isn't a hint of who Matt and Aiyona have been, only who they've become. To me, they've become part of my quirky, extended family. Nobody could ever replace those I've lost—my mother, Nathan, and now Henry; but I've found my people, and I believe Nathan had something to do with that.

Summer and Layla are rolling down a hill in their matching yellow tulle dresses. I can't help but smile. The dresses won't last an hour, but it's not like the girls will wear them again anyway.

The breeze picks up as the sun starts its slow descent behind the dandelion-topped hillside. I take a swig from my glass and sweep the hair from my eyes as I spot the familiar form striding across the grass toward me.

"Hiding out?" John asks.

I shake my head, "Just enjoying the view."

"May I join you?"

"Of course," I slide over, making space for John.

He sits with a sigh, looking just as content as I feel. "Ahhh, so you can see your daughter from here," he says, nodding toward the girls. They are still crawling up and then rolling down the grassy hillside not far from the entrance of the church.

I laugh, "She's having harmless fun with her best friend. If Matt and Aiyona don't care, I see no reason to stop them."

John runs his hand through his hair, "Well, that's good. I wasn't sure if I should step in or not."

"If you had, that would have been fine too. I trust your instincts, John."

"That's good because I have something to tell you. I decided to let you relax a moment before dropping a problem in your lap."

I feel my pulse rate quicken, and I straighten in response. I'd been waiting for the other shoe to drop.

John immediately notes my unease; his eyes widen in response. "Oh, no, Kaley, nothing terrible. Sorry, that was insensitive of me, given all you've been through."

I take another drink and ease back onto the boulder. "It's fine. I overact now. So, that's fun."

He smiles, "What it is—is understandable. And maybe the guy you're dating shouldn't be such a drama queen."

He winks, and I laugh aloud. "John you are many things—but a drama queen—never."

He wraps his arm around me, "In all seriousness, though, I was sent to find you."

"Okay…"

He continues, "Shane spilled ketchup all over the front of his shirt and requires your assistance before his best man speech."

I turn to look up at him, "Where the hell did Shane find ketchup? They are serving wine, cheese, and cupcakes."

John shrugs, "I'm just the messenger."

"You were right to give me another moment. See, good instincts." I raise my glass and down the last of the champagne.

He kisses the top of my head and pulls me close.

There are no guarantees in life. I know that better than most. At this moment, however, my daughter and I are surrounded by love, support, and happiness. There isn't anything in the world more important than that.

Acknowledgments

A huge thanks to all my wonderful readers. You have no idea how much your enthusiasm and support mean to me. Thank you for the gift of your time and the opportunity to tell you a story.

I'm fortunate to be part of an incredibly creative and talented group of individuals. They make me better, and I hope I do the same for them. Mary Malone, I realize how fortunate I am to have a parent with a fundamental love for language and all its irksome complications. Thank you for providing your time and skills. Francine Hanson, you have trudged through this story with me more times than I can count, thank you for your patience and feedback. Jill Kiesow, we started our writing adventure together over five years ago. Thank you for holding my hand on our DMW adventure, not to mention your superb proofreading skills. Heather Skumatz, thank you for offering your time, talents, and many observations. To the rest of the S.C. Team: Gail Pluemer, Marie Messinger, Lisa Snyder, Chris Felton, Amy Dunphy, and Priscilla Sarow, your support and encouragement are everything. Thank you for sharing your time and energy with me. I always leave our meetings with a new spark.

Nicole Aaberg (Beast), Mary Ann Grow, and Nicole Otterson – you are the inspiration for Mary Nicole. Although all of you are much more fun and friendly, you each share the same dedication and integrity.

To my family. I appreciate all the support and love. Especially, Robin, Aidan, and Griffen – thank you for putting up with my nutty creative streaks. Special thanks to Jack, Sherry, and Jason for your persistent excitement for this book; not to mention your ardent sales efforts. You're the best sales team anyone could hope for.

I am so fortunate to have people in my life that love books as much as do. A special thank you to Lana (Book Buddy) Lepinski, Nicole Aaberg, Sara Chapman, and Raven Flannery. Your recommendations always hit the mark. Also, Deana Jensen, Missy Sampson, and Kelsey Zimmerman, I truly appreciate the enthusiasm you have all shown for Forest Through the Trees. I hope you'll enjoy 30 Seconds just as much.